An American Fight
For Justice
Part 2

An American Fight For Justice Part 2

A Daughter's Duty

Linda D. Coker

iUniverse, Inc.
Bloomington

AN AMERICAN FIGHT FOR JUSTICE PART 2
A DAUGHTER'S DUTY

This is a work of fiction. All of the characters, names, incidents, organizations, and dialogue in this novel are either the products of the author's imagination or are used fictitiously.

The views and opinions presented in this and prior stories are those of the author, and do not represent the views of the Department of Defense (DoD), the military services, the military exchanges, any other government agencies, or political figures.

The actual political names used were done so in order to celebrate them for the courage and sacrifices these individuals made to protect us during this period of time, nothing more. This does not mean that they share the same views and opinions as the author.

iUniverse books may be ordered through booksellers or by contacting:

iUniverse
1663 Liberty Drive
Bloomington, IN 47403
www.iuniverse.com
1-800-Authors (1-800-288-4677)

ISBN: 978-1-4620-3660-8 (sc)
ISBN: 978-1-4620-3661-5 (ebk)

Printed in the United States of America

iUniverse rev. date: 07/26/2011

DEDICATION

Once again, I wish to dedicate this, the sequel to my first novel, to all the men and women of the United States military, past and present, for sacrificing so much for our country. This dedication is intended as well for other men and women who wear a uniform: sheriffs, deputy sheriffs, police officers, firefighters, and the National Guard.

I also dedicate this story to those who might not wear a uniform but still sacrifice so much to protect us. This includes members of the CIA, the FBI, and all other classified agencies. The identities and activities of the members of these agencies should be kept secret to protect us, but unfortunately, we have become a nation that doesn't care to keep secrets to protect its citizens.

I dedicate this to the few people left in our government who truly believe in our Constitution, who fight to uphold our constitutional rights for *all* of Americans—not just selected groups, and who believe in finding the greatness that once was instilled in all the people of this great land.

One last dedication is to my family for instilling in me, ". . . one nation under God" is "indivisible, with liberty and justice for all!"

ACKNOWLEDGMENTS

I would like to thank my little sister, Katrina J. Pavelko, Firstediting, and Jaime Polychrones for their editing.

I would like to thank all the websites for the factual historical events, as well as legal sources for gathering some factual data for my fictional stories.

I also give thanks to Army & Air Force Exchange Service (AAFES) for bringing a piece of home to our soldiers no matter where they are and for providing jobs to the soldiers' families and to civilians. I thank the AAFES family for providing great customer service to our soldiers as well. AAFES is a unique Department of Defense (DoD) agency because it is a non-appropriated funds (NAF) entity; most profits are put back into the military community. The people who work for AAFES are people who dedicate their lives to serving the troops and providing products to soldiers who normally would not have the opportunity to purchase them when they are protecting us across the globe.

I want to give thanks as well to all other NAF organizations; USO; Morale, Welfare, & Recreation (MWR); and Army Community Services (ACS).

Thanks are given to the soldiers of JAG and to Joint Personnel Service Office (JPSO). The people within these organizations have provided wonderful services to our troops and their communities. I want to give thanks to the contractors that provide transportation, supplies, and numerous other services to our troops.

One last thank you goes to our service members' spouses who volunteer their time to be a part of our Family Readiness Group (FRG) and for providing support to the families. Our service members' families are definitely heroes in their own right.

I'm sure there are other groups of people that I have forgotten to mention, and for that, I apologize, but I do want to thank all of you for being part of the biggest and greatest family of all: the American Armed Forces. Thank you for being there.

As a service member myself long ago, I have not forgotten all that you do, and I want you to know that you are truly appreciated!

PRELUDE

This story is a continuation of my story regarding the most common crime committed against service members and civilians. In my opinion, these types of crimes almost always go unpunished. The attorneys and judges in our justice system financially strip the victim when they try to fight the crime. These crimes are never taken to criminal court; instead, they are tried in the civil courts where the final ruling is never enforced.

In my experiences and in all the stories told to me by fellow service members and veterans, the judge often violates the victim's constitutional rights. The judge holds all the power; the victim has none. A statute needs to be designed so that judges and attorneys are held accountable for their actions without any cost to the victim or taxpayers.

These types of crimes are a virus spreading throughout our great country. The villains get away with their crimes because our justice system doesn't care. I have heard the following statements all my life: "Attorneys are blood suckers." "Everything is about strategy rather than about right and wrong." These are true statements. Justice only serves the rich and the rich alone. It is not for *all* the people. It seems that our justice system serves justice when the corporate community is involved, but does nothing for a private citizen. The expensive fees involved are a form of highway robbery. These are observations from my own experiences and from stories told to me.

This particular family unit is just one sad tale of the increasing meltdown of our country's core morals, values, and beliefs. Morals, values, and beliefs that this great country was founded on. As the family unit breaks down, so will our justice system, our economy, and our country. If the majority of our society is made up of family units in which greed, selfishness, stereotyping, laziness, and intolerance of other's beliefs and opinions reign, then our justice system, government, and our businesses will reflect the same values. History tells us that when this happens, we will fall just like the great societies and empires before us.

Rome was one of the first republics, and it fell for many of the same reasons that our American society is faltering today. Rome was not the only society that lost sight of what democracy really is. It happened to Athens, a Greek city-state, and to so many other great societies and empires throughout history.

Our great nation was founded on biblical principles. Our laws were derived from the Ten Commandments and many more of the six hundred or more laws that were handed down to Moses: "Thou shall not steal, Thou shall not bear false witness, Thou shall not covet . . ." When people are rewarded for these actions rather than punished, these actions spread through our society like cancer. Everything becomes acceptable because there are no consequences.

Laziness is another key player. Why work for something when you can get it for free by stealing, embezzling, or taking it through false pretenses. This includes government handouts. Our government is supposed to represent all of the people, not just the majority who voted for the individual. If one person has more than another person has, the government does not have the right to take it by taxing the individual. After all, this is the land of the free; if our government takes a piece of the American pie from one individual to give it to another, we are no longer a democracy.

Have we become a socialist or communist society? Our country was founded on the principles that you must work for your own health care, higher education, and wealth.

We are a great nation because of the sacrifices our soldiers have made. To show our appreciation, our soldiers should be provided top quality health and dental care and so much more. They should be treated as kings and queens for what they have sacrificed for our freedoms. As a great nation, we should provide for our elderly and for those who are physically or mentally unable to work, but I firmly believe that everyone else who is able to do so should work for his or her own health care, higher education, and wealth.

Democracy is a form of government in which the people vote and make the decisions of all matters of their country, but the structure of our voting process is not this case. We are nothing but a form of Democracy, not the original. We as the people should also be allowed not only to vote a Politian in, but also vote the individual out before their term has ended. The people should also be allowed to vote for punishment of a Politian's infractions against the Constitution or the will of the people. This will ensure the Politian is held accountable. This should be the case for our judges as well as our local leaders of law enforcement.

We are a nation that was formed on the belief that an individual's God given rights and freedoms will be honored at all cost.

So therefore, Democracy means that we do not covet another's wealth to the point that we pressure our government to take from those who have worked hard for what they have to give it to those who have not. This is the same as stealing because you are taking something against the will of another.

Creating laws and amendments to our Constitution to force people to think as you do violates the personal liberties and freedoms that are our God-given rights, not men's. It is a violation of our constitutional rights for one group of people to remove the freedom of choice from another individual because they consider it in that person's best interest. Remember, America, our government is for "the People."

The 18th Amendment is one great example in our history that shows us how one small group of people can take away the rights of the majority. Amendment 18 to our Constitution prohibited the rights to manufacture, sell, and transport intoxicating liquors. This amendment to our Constitution was added because one group of people caused such a stir that our government reacted. Yes, ladies, I'm referring to what the women of that time caused. One group of Americans took away the liberties of the public at large. It is time for America to wake and stop trying to take away the rights of other Americans. People are still like this today; they even resort to smearing another's reputation because they have a different opinion.

Our government (a group of our own fellow Americans) has made it legal to take from another and the one who was taken from is punished for protecting his or her property.

Because of the mentality that an individual does not have to work hard for the American dream because the government will take care of the individual that has been formed in our family units, our government has given the majority of our general labor jobs away to other countries. Our factories and farms are just two examples. We have given the backbone of our wealth to other countries because we are too lazy to work for the American dream. The majority of Americans want wealth given to them instead of working for it. Having an education without common sense and hard work means nothing. My fellow Americans, we have given so much power to our government that they are now trying to micromanage what we grow in our own backyards.

In many cities, local governments have made it illegal to collect rainwater in a bucket or drum without a well! They do not want people growing their own food because of their rules. This is not democracy! Are we going to continue to allow our government to tell us what to do? Remember, fellow Americans, democracy means that our government works *for* us, not the other way around.

Understand, my fellow Americans, that we have slowly lost our way. If we do not know our own history, both the bad and the good, how will we truly have a positive future? Do you realize that our children are learning a history different from the history that we were taught? The history books are being re-written, and God has been taken out!

Liberty and justice is for all Americans, not just the ones that have the loudest bark! Instead of putting our focus into change, let us go back to our roots and rediscover our greatness as "All the People." We need to return to our personal God-given rights. We are God's children no matter the race, religion, sexuality, or beliefs! Let us respect each other's opinions and freedoms of choice! Let us rejoice and respect each other's uniqueness! After all, fellow Americans, we are from America, the great melting pot of all races. That does not mean we all think and act the same, but that we celebrate and respect one another's uniqueness.

CHAPTER I

March 22, 2000. Once again, I found myself back on an airplane, headed for Virginia. I felt as if I had stepped back in time, back to 1999. It had actually been only a little over a year since I first headed home to clean up my mother's mess. At least this time I was not facing the challenges alone; this time, my husband was sitting in the aisle seat right next to me.

As the airplane took off from the airport in Germany, I placed my hand on top of Thomas's hand. He turned his head, looked in my eyes, and said, "Hopefully this time your daughter's duty will be finished."

I looked deep into his brown eyes, and with a half, sad smile said, "I certainly hope so."

Thomas is my true hero in every sense of the word. He is a man of principle, honor, and duty. He is a highly decorated warrior as well as my best friend and lover. He would die to protect me, and I would do the same for him. Thomas is a very handsome man with sandy brown hair, cut short in the standard military fashion. He is not only physically strong, but mentally capable as well.

Before the tears could start, I turned my head, looked out the window, and let my mind wander. I started remembering everything that had happened over the past year, since I had returned to Germany in March of 1999.

* * *

Within a week of my return to Germany, my mother called me from the jail. She could not even wait until the jail recording had finished before she started yelling at me. She was yelling and sobbing as she said, "I give you everything I own, all our family things, and you just piss it all away! You are so cowardly! You did not even have the guts to tell me that you were leaving me to rot in this jail cell! How could you do this to your only mother? They name dark alleys after people like you. I should never have counted on you to help me. Once again, you have failed me!"

I thought, *Here we go again.* I kept my demeanor in check and patiently replied, "I love you, Mom. I did the very best that I could. I told you at the very beginning that I was not going to break any laws for you or anyone else. I think I did a very good job, even if I wasn't able to finish it before I had to leave. I cannot, and will not, fight every single battle for you. I tried to fight the majority of your battles for you, but I guess my best wasn't good enough."

My mother, whom I love dearly (when I'm not disliking her), has the most beautiful white hair and is in her sixties. She is a few inches short than I am. She has the most beautiful blue eyes that capture your heart when you look into them. Those same eyes can cut you into pieces when she is not getting her way. She has endured an abusive life, but also has enjoyed a great life as well. I truly have mixed feelings regarding the crimes that she had committed against me throughout the previous decades.

Mom demanded, "What about my stuff?"

I answered her, "The only solution you have is Christina and Jay. If they are able to convince Big Pete to let them have it, then they can have it moved up to Auntie Bea's or to the Daisy house. I swear to you that Thomas and I will move it all into storage for you, but it will have to stay there until we come back to the States for your sentencing."

Mom asked, "Do you think Christina will help Jay manipulate Big Pete?"

I replied, "I'm sure she will be glad to help, as long as you make her think that she is also helping Big Pete. I know that Jay will do it for you. He considers you his mother. You know that Big Pete will do more for his own son than he will for anyone else. I know Christina will help with the dogs. She puts more value on a dog than she does a member of her family. In that way, she is just like you. So I'm sure she will help you; especially now that I'm out of the picture."

Mom said, "I can't deal with her superior attitude."

I laughed and said, "She's just like you."

Mom said, "Belinda!"

My sister Christina was a couple of years younger than I was. She was the complete opposite of me in every aspect of our personalities and our physical appearances. Christina has blond hair and blue eyes; I have ash brown hair and hazel brown eyes. I was physically stronger than she was, and we always found ourselves competing in sports against one another. I considered my little sister much more like my mother than she would ever admit, but overall, my sister was honest. From time to time, you could persuade her that her view regarding something might be incorrect.

We both suffered a small amount of mental abuse by our parents. It was because my father and his family were obsessed with the idea that I was the chosen archangel for mankind because of my special gifts that I was born with most of the attention was focused on me. My mother from time to time tried to exploit my talents for her own personal gain. I concluded that they were not perfect, and I learned not to put them on pedestals as gods to be worshipped. But my sister still did, and when one of them let her down, she would become hostile and lash out. Granted, I found myself throughout my life faltering and doing the same thing. It seems that ever since my parents divorced and it was discovered that I was destined to be the next matriarch of both my father's family and my mother's family; my sister fought me, no matter how much I was right. I never understood this, and I guess I never would.

Jay was Big Pete's son from a prior marriage and was much younger than my sister and me by at least thirteen years. Jay had grown to be about six feet tall with dark brown hair and eyes. He was extremely skinny and never excelled in sports. He had been physically and mentally abused by his father, and he loved my mother because she protected him from Big Pete's temper whenever she could.

I had heard horror stories about Jay's mother drugging him and leaving him alone so that she could go to work without paying a babysitter. This was the main reason my mother fought so hard against the legal system for sole custody of Jay. My mother may have turned into a crook, but she and my father never abused my sister and I like that. Never.

Pete King, aka "Big Pete," was the main reason my mother had found herself in trouble. He was my mother's fifth husband. He weighed at least three hundred and fifty pounds, if not more. He was about five feet and eleven inches tall with black hair, which he wore cut short, and dark brown eyes.

He had continued to fight the eighteen indictments of fraud and embezzlement brought against him. I considered him one of the most vile, evil, and pompous asses I had ever encountered. Undoubtedly, he was articulate, extremely intelligent, and very manipulative. He not only abused my mother physically, but mentally as well. I truly believe the only people in this world he feared were my husband and me. Jay and my mother had kept the dark secret of the abuse from us for a couple of decades. If I could have gotten away with killing him, I would have, but unfortunately, our society does not take kindly to vigilante justice. Thomas and I came very close to doing just that, no more than a year earlier, but Big Pete had not been worth destroying our lives.

The Daisy house where my Uncle Frank lived was a brick one story with an unfinished basement. It was a ranch style house with a quarter acre located in the middle of Bea Mills' farm. It was named the "Daisy house" because Ms. Daisy lived there at one time. Uncle Herndon, Auntie Bea's husband, had built it for his Aunt Daisy and her husband. He also had given her the quarter acre it was built on.

The Mills' farm was ninety-nine acres of land. The farmhouse where Auntie Bea lived was an old, white clapboard farmhouse built in the early 1800s by Uncle Herndon's great-great-great grandfather. I was sure that neither home had been cleaned since I left there in 1999.

Throughout the past year, I had endured my mother calling me a thief and a liar multiple times in letters. Every time she called me, collect of course, she would tell me how evil I was. Through each letter and phone call, she would continue to badger me, trying to get what she wanted. I dutifully continued to send her money for her various needs. At one point, she even told me that she needed $100 a week to survive in prison. The requests for money seemed to never end.

In one of our conversations, Mom told me that she could not get a hold of Jay. She was in tears because he would not respond to her letters. I assured her that I would take care of it. I called him and sent e-mails every day for several weeks trying to get a response. I needed him to oversee the moving of everything that was left at Mom and Big Pete's house. Thomas finally became angry with Jay for not responding to my communication, and wrote Jay the following message:

> JAY: Why haven't you answered Belinda's phone calls? You need to write Jane too! Do not run and hide just because shit hit the fan. You are still a part of the family, and you have a responsibility to help. You know that Belinda and I did most of the crap! The only issue left is moving the rest of the stuff, so that not only Belinda and Christina will

have their inheritance, but you will as well. Belinda carried you on her back numerous times. What's wrong? Does your daddy have you scared? Either you write Jane immediately or never show your face in Virginia again! Oh yeah, you never know when I might just happen to come by and see you in Chicago. Get the point? Be a man! Jane supported you when your dad did not. It is not fair to treat her this way! Grow UP!

Jay responded immediately to Thomas with the following:

Chicago has been having problems with Com Ed, our power company, and has been suffering blackouts frequently. My answering machine is constantly knocked off so I miss my messages. I am also very busy working twelve-to thirteen-hour days so I forget to check my messages a lot. I know you probably will not believe me but it is true! I am not avoiding Jane or Belinda. I have written Jane a few times, so don't yell at me; and I am not avoiding this. I could care less what my dad thinks about anything, especially me. I am not the least bit scared of him, and I doubt he would try anything on me anyway. If he did, I would hope that the two of you have my back even if I could not hack military life and never followed through. I'm not soldier material like you and Belinda, but that doesn't make me a pussy either. I am not running from this. I am trying to get my own life in line and under control. I am having my own problems, but I guess you don't care about that. I would not have been there when all this happened if I did not care, and Belinda and Mom know this. Christina has been filling my head with a lot of crap, and now I don't know what to believe, but I will do my duty since I made a promise to Belinda when I was with her in '99.

Hope this is satisfactory to your liking. I am very busy packing 'cause I got transferred and have to move again with the company I am working for. I care, but if I cannot get my own life under control, what good am I? Just tell Belinda to tell Mom to call me tomorrow and I will make arrangements to move the stuff to the Daisy house. I swear it!

3

In June of 1999, Mom called and she told me that Pete flew Jay back home using his frequent flyer miles to oversee the move of everything to Auntie Bea's and the Daisy house. Once again, I heard the name Ed Weird. Mom told me that he was going to pay for the move in exchange for the dining room table that I had left in the garage. She had bought it for me to resell in the shop. I told her that was great, and I asked her who Ed Weird was. She told me that he was a member of the church, and that he had joined a few years earlier.

CHAPTER II

I looked away from the window of the airplane because I heard Thomas asking, "Baby, are you okay?"

I looked at him and with a sad smile replied, "Yeah, I'm okay, just thinking." I turned my head back to the small window and looked out at the sky. My thoughts returned to the past year.

*   *   *

Ever since I had returned to Germany, I faithfully had called Auntie Bea or Uncle Frank every week to make sure that they were okay. I would rotate whom I called each week so that neither could claim the other had favoritism.

Auntie Bea and Uncle Frank are my grandmother's younger sister and brother. Auntie Bea was at least five years younger and Uncle Frank was about nine years younger than my grandmother was.

Auntie Bea and Uncle Frank were both walking skeletons because neither one of them ate properly. Auntie Bea had a seventh grade education, and my Uncle Frank had a third grade education.

Uncle Frank was a simpleton, an alcoholic, and he literally lied about everything. The family would cover it up with the story that he told tall tales. Whoever was taking care of him, he would follow their lead no matter the cost.

Unfortunately, I should have known not to trust Auntie Bea and I had expected her to help Uncle Frank take care of his own affairs.

When I called Auntie Bea in May of 1999, doing my duty, she told me that Ed had helped reduce her rent.

I exclaimed, "Kudos to this Ed Weird person! He is quite amazing!"

Auntie then told me that my mother had asked Ed to look after her and Uncle Frank while Thomas and I were in Germany.

When I spoke with my mother later that week she confirmed Auntie Bea's story, stating, "Belinda, I know you're doing your best, but there is only so much you can do from Germany. I feel better knowing that someone I trust can physically check up on them and give them the help they need."

I replied, "Okay, Mom, I'm a little surprised at how much you trust this man, when you never mentioned him before. You always told me about all your friends. It just seems weird to me. That's all."

Mom said, "Don't worry. Ed will take good care of your auntie and uncle."

Things remained uneventful until July that year. When I called Auntie Bea to check up on her, she screeched, "You bounced all of Frank's checks!"

I replied, "What are you talking about, Auntie Bea? I haven't touched his checkbook since I was there in March! What have you done?"

Auntie Bea said, "You stole all of Frank's money."

I replied, "Auntie Bea, are you nuts? Before I left to come back to Germany, I gave you written instructions on how to manage his finances. What have you done? Did you arrange for Uncle Frank's retirement check to be directly deposited?"

She curtly answered, "Yes, I did. I received the forms shortly after you left. Frank and I filled them out; he signed them and took them to the bank. That was taken care of awhile back."

I said, "Okay. You didn't write a check out for the utility receipts that you should have been receiving after they electronically did a transfer directly from his account, did you?"

Auntie Bea said, "Oh!"

I said, "Auntie Bea! I asked you directly if you understood me, and you assured me that you did. Now you have Uncle Frank's finances all screwed up! That's what you get for meddling in his finances to begin with. If you hadn't stolen Uncle Frank's debit card, you and Uncle Frank wouldn't be in this pickle. What I can't understand is how on earth you came to the conclusion that I have been stealing all of Uncle Frank's money when I am here in Germany. You are the one who has control of his checkbook. What in the devil is the matter with the two of you?"

After I scolded her for being so foolish, Auntie Bea immediately changed the subject. She told me, "I'm still getting credit card bills for your grandparents, and they will not stop it until I send them a death certificate. Do you have their death certificates?"

I said, "Oh crap! I forgot. Did you call the number I gave you about getting their death certificates?"

Auntie Bea said, "Yes, but they say I cannot get them. They sent me the forms for us to fill out. I'm going to send the forms to you and you can try, but the person I spoke to said he doubted that you could get it either."

A few days later, I received the form in the mail along with a note from Auntie Bea. The note said, "Belinda, enclosed are the forms for your grandparents' death certificates. They would not let me have them. They said they didn't think you could get them either. It's $8.00. Please don't call me anymore about tales your mother is telling you. I have enough problems. All I ask for is peace of mind. I'm having a real hard time. God knows I didn't ask for this. I never said you stole anything. I hope you believe that. I have enough problems with my own son. You did the best you could; best of luck to you and Thomas. Take care. Love, Auntie Bea."

I will never understand my auntie! After all the times she accused me over the telephone of stealing from her and from Uncle Frank, she now wrote that she never accused me of stealing anything and claimed that she never spread lies about me!

I filled out the forms for my grandparent's death certificates and mailed them with a money order for $16, but just as Auntie Bea predicted, I too was unable to obtain the death certificates because my grandmother had an executor.

I called Uncle Poppy, who had been the executor of my grandmother's estate. He was my mother's older brother, who had been a nasty, evil bully in our family. He had shot my mother in the back when they were teenagers.

Uncle Poppy was several years older than my mother. My uncle had beautiful white hair and blue eyes. He was about six feet tall and had lost his one leg when he was in the Navy.

I said, "Uncle Poppy, I need your help. I meant to talk with you about this before I left Virginia, but with all the other crap that was going on, I forgot. Auntie Bea is still receiving credit card bills from Gram and Pap. She called the credit card company and told them they were dead, but they said they need copies of the death certificates. She has tried to get them, as have I, but they will not release them to us. Is there any way you can help?"

Uncle Poppy said, "Give me Bea's phone number. I'll call her and straighten out this mess."

I waited twenty minutes, and then I called Auntie Bea to make sure that Uncle Poppy took care of it.

She said, "You were right. He had the death certificates, and he didn't care if your mom used them or not. He will take care of it for you."

I said, "See, Auntie Bea, you shouldn't be so judgmental. I can't believe how fast you forget the truth."

Auntie Bea said, "Just stop it, Belinda! I made a mistake."

I said, "Auntie Bea, why would you call me a thief when I am the one who bailed you and Uncle Frank out of trouble?"

Auntie Bea rudely replied, "You didn't get my land back."

Exasperated, I replied, "Auntie Bea, you know we haven't started the battle for that yet. I was with you when Miss Patson explained it to you. You are going to have to wait until I am able to return to the States. I have promised you before, and I am promising you again, Auntie Bea, I will fight the Greeds! Now stop doubting me! Tell Uncle Frank to stop lying about me, and you need to stop spreading lies about me too. You need to admit it when you make a mistake and stop blaming everyone else."

Auntie Bea said, "Okay. But stop preaching to me."

I responded, "Well, stop lying about me!"

Miss Patson was the young, intelligent, and beautiful attorney I had hired when I returned to Virginia in early 1999. I hired her to protect me from my relatives and to advise me of the laws, so that I would not break them unintentionally. I truly believe her patient demeanor had slowly disintegrated regarding dealing with my relatives.

CHAPTER III

I looked away from the airplane window because I heard Thomas asking the flight attendant for a beer. I asked for one as well. When we received them, Thomas kissed my cheek. I smiled at him, took a sip of beer, turned back to the window, and drifted back to my memories.

*   *   *

In August of 1999, I received a short note from Miss Patson asking me to call her as soon as I could. She urgently needed to speak with me. I immediately called her.

She greeted me with, "Belinda, your family has been driving me nuts! All the money that you put in escrow is gone. I had to send a check to your Auntie Bea so that she could get her car fixed or something of that nature. I sent it, and now the escrow account is in the red. I know that you established the account per your mother's request so that you could provide for your family, but they have spent it already. Another issue is your flakey sister. I'm sorry for calling her that, but I call it as I see it. She has been calling here all the time, and I have had no choice but to charge the account for my time . . . ."

She proceeded to tell me that Christina was calling frequently because of the dogs, and she was constantly pumping Miss Patson for information regarding Mom's indictments. Apparently, Mom's attorney would not tell Christina anything. Christina was also calling and talking to Miss Patson about some wine I had that Christina claimed belonged to Big Pete. Miss Patson could not tell her anything because of client/attorney privilege, and my sister didn't seem to understand that. She repeatedly told my sister to contact me because I was the only one who could explain things to her. Miss Patson told me that Christina had called her at least thirty-five times over the past several months.

Miss Patson also told me that, per my mother's instructions, Jay had picked up the pocketbook that had been kept in the law firm's safe. The pocketbook contained my mother's keys, money, and some other personal items. Miss Patson said that when Jay picked it up, he mentioned that he was going to give it to Ed Weird. Again, I wondered who he was, and why he was so involved in my family's business. Miss Patson said that Christina frequently mentioned him when she called, and he himself had called Miss Patson. From what she could tell, it seemed that Ed was creating trouble all over the place, and she felt that I would have to do something about it.

I told Miss Patson not to accept any more phone calls from any of my family members. I told her that I did not know who Ed Weird was, and that she needed to charge him directly for her time. I told her that I had not even known that he existed until just recently. The first time I had heard his name was when my mother had mentioned that he had taken her money and placed funds into an account created in Jay's name to help pay for Jay's college bills, but Jay took the money and gave it to me to help pay for the mess in 1999. I told Miss Patson that when I came back to the States, I would speak with Mr. Weird. I did not know what his motives were or why he was meddling in my family's business. I stated that I would leave it alone until after I finished helping my mother and Auntie Bea.

On October 23, 1999, I received another long letter from my mother. She had written it on October second and third.

Dear Belinda,

I just got off the telephone with Christina and she told me about the wine. It's hard to believe that it was all spoiled, but Christina said Mary lost her job because of it. I don't know how you handled the sale. Apparently, Christina and Mary expect me to pay the money back. Of course, I told Christina I cannot do anything until I get out of here. It seems to me that they should have looked at the wine before they bought it. It was stored in the back of the basement and the temperature was about 60 degrees—but if you sent that list, you missed the things that Pete had sold. He sold all of the good wine—and left the newer wines that needed to age some more. So I am very confused—you better check it out with JAG—because this crap that Mary is spreading is very fishy . . . Since it was a private sale, do I have to take it back or pay it back? Did you give a receipt? Christina said you went home because the FBI was on your tail! Ha ha. Also Jay has been talking to Mary, so that's why he won't talk to you. I just give up—I can't pay for anything. If this guy sues me, I'll just have one more judgment. So let me know what is going on. Christina said I am to blame because you did it in my name. That doesn't make sense to me at all because you and Thomas bought all that wine from Big Pete and me a long time ago, and I know you had the receipt because I gave it to you. Christina also told me that she has been talking to Big Pete and he told her that the wine was worth half a million dollars, which is not true! He told her I stole it from him when we really sold it to you. Now I don't know what to do or if we can do anything. What else can happen? DO NOT tell Christina I told you this . . . hate to drop this on you, but I have a while to go in this hole.

Take care and I love you—Mom.

The second note read:

Oct 3, 1999, I am very depressed—I don't understand Jay. I don't understand any of this. What has happened to everyone? Mary has always wanted Jay for Nancy, her daughter. So I guess he will be stupid enough to go along with it. I just don't understand any of you children anymore. Maybe this place has finally gotten to me, and I know we will never be the same. The only contact we have with Jay is his e-mail. He apparently stays in contact with Mary, and if she shot her mouth off about what she considers I have done to you and to her, then Jay will turn to her. So I don't know what to do.

After reading both letters, I was extremely upset with my sister and Mary. I decided to call the company that Mary had worked for and discover the truth for myself. I still had the papers she had given me with her company's name and telephone number on it.

Mary is my second cousin who worked for Big Pete and my mother. Mary stood about six feet tall with thin, dyed platinum blond hair and blue eyes. She had very large lips and a very large, thin, straight nose that did not quite go with her sunken, long, oval face. Like Auntie Bea and Uncle Frank, she too was a walking skeleton. She was an alcoholic and a heavy user of cocaine.

She was the manager of a branch of Pete's business that was located in Pennsylvania. I had discovered from her own admission that she was part of the scam when I was in Virginia in 1999. She convinced everyone, except for me, that she had a college degree and experience in the insurance business. Naturally, Big Pete and my mother knew the truth.

Mary had dropped out of high school and got married because she was pregnant with Nancy. She worked as a hair stylist and eventually earned her GED. She had no problem committing fraud and embezzling from Big Pete's clients, as long as she was paid very well.

For many years, my sister treated Mary as her older sister instead of me. In fact, my sister was very cruel using Mary to punish me for some unknown crime that I had committed against her. To this day, I do not know what vile crime I committed against my sister to warrant such a display of cruelty against me.

Immediately after I called the company, I called Mary. She answered the phone and we exchanged greetings as if we were best friends. She talked as if she never had said anything negative about me; she was filling me in on her children and their various activities.

I finally said, "Mary, I called because I just found out you were telling lies to my sister again regarding our wine sale. The whole transaction was done in your name, and I have the documentation to prove it. I have no clue what you sold to your boss after you left Virginia. So please explain to me what you are talking about."

Mary retorted, "I was fired because all the wine was bad, and your mother needs to give me the money back."

I calmly said, "Oh, really? Let's set the record straight, right this second, Mary. First of all, I can prove that I sold the wine to you, not my mother. I have documents showing that the transaction was done in my name and your name. As far as my mother and your boss are concerned, it had nothing to do with them. Only you and I were involved.

"Secondly, I just called your company and spoke with the manager to whom you sold the wine. He told me what he paid for it, and I told him what I sold it for. He was very upset. I also faxed him the real inventory that Little Pete and I had taken prior to you purchasing the wine—the same inventory that I had faxed to you. I also inquired as to why you were fired over the transaction, since I knew the wine I sold you was good. He informed me that you were not fired over the wine transaction. You were fired because you were drunk on the job, they discovered you never had a college degree, and you had falsified prior employment on your resume. He told me that he had filed a lawsuit regarding the wine transaction against you, not my mother or me. It was filed against you only, and it was filed not because the wine was bad but because what you sold him were cheap bottles of wine. You did not sell him the wines that were on the original list that he had.

"So tell me, Mary, what happened to the good wine that I sold to you and that you took home with you? One more thing, I also promised him if he needed me to testify on his behalf, I would be extremely happy to write an affidavit for him. It is in your best interest to pay him back for the wine that I'm sure you drank."

Mary angrily stated, "What you did was invade my privacy, and he broke the law telling you why I was fired! It's still your word against mine and there is nothing you can do about it."

I calmly replied, "Yes, I can do something about it. You try to file a lawsuit against my mother, and I swear that I will pull out the evidence I have on you regarding Big Pete's business. I will take that evidence straight to the U.S. Attorney's office. If you continue threatening my mother, through my sister, I swear the truth and evidence I have will bury you under the courtroom steps. If you ever call my sister with your crap again, I will personally get on an airplane, fly to Pennsylvania, and kick you right in your boney white ass! I mean that. It is not a threat, Big Lips, it's a promise." With those words, I slammed down the phone.

Before I even had a chance to call my sister, the phone rang. It was Mary.

She begged, "Belinda, please don't hang up. I'm sorry. I just don't have the money to pay this guy for my stupidity. Please don't tell your sister that I lied to her."

I answered her in a soft tone, "How do you expect my mother to bail you out this time, Mary?"

Mary answered, "I figured you would take care of it for her."

I said, in a disappointed tone, "I have never helped you, and I never will because I have never liked you, Mary. You remind me of a leech that sucks a person until the blood's gone! I'm tired of you. You and all the other greedy members of our family have dried up a well that never even existed. You are part of the problem, not the solution. You only care about yourself. I'm not even sure that you care about your children. You could care less about my mother, or my sister for that matter. You only care about what you can get out of them. Don't ever call me again, and I will never call you again. I will make you one promise though. I will not get involved in the lawsuit against you." I hung up the phone. I decided it was not even worth wasting my breath on my sister, so I did not call her.

On January 20, 2000, I spoke with my mother's attorney after receiving the letter from my mother. They were finally able to give me a date for my mother's sentencing. It was scheduled for April. He informed me that shortly after I left the States, my sister began started calling his office so frequently that it became intolerable. He started refusing her calls until she finally stopped. He told me that she was looking for phantom wine that did not exist. He told me that he did tell her we had already proved that Big Pete sold it all, and it had been a dead issue for quite some time. He went on and on, complaining about how weird my sister's attitude was toward my mother and especially toward me. He told me that it appeared to him that she was doing everything in her power to destroy my mother and me; he was not going to allow it. He told me she even had the nerve to call the U.S. Attorney's office and tell them it was my mother, not Big Pete, responsible for the crimes. The U.S. Attorney's office basically blew her off because of the evidence they had stating otherwise. The evil little twit either did not know, or never realized, that the U.S. Attorney's office was never really after my mother. She was the little fish in all this mess, and they wanted the big fish, Big Pete. Then, Mom's attorney apologized to me for calling my sister a little twit. I assured him that it was fine and he was not the first attorney to do so.

After hanging up the phone, I started to cry. I knew my sister would sleep with the devil before taking my side on anything, no matter how right I might be. I knew my sister truly hated me for reasons that I would never know. What had I done to her that was so vile? What had I done to her that would make her try to undo everything that I had tried to build?

I wished I had a sister that I could call my friend instead of one who chose to be my enemy.

After regaining control, I picked up the phone and called Christina. I told her the truth about Mary. I told her how and why Mary was fired, and whom I called to discover the truth. I didn't mention the wine.

After listening to everything I had to say, Christina said, "Oh really, what about the wine? Mary called me last October. She was crying and very upset. She told me that she was just fired over the wine you sold her because there were some bad bottles in it, and the wines listed on the inventory that you gave her were not there."

I said, "Please, Christina! Again you have been lied to, and you are not telling the entire truth either. Don't you think our mother's attorney has already told me what you tried to imply regarding Big Pete and the wine that he did not own anymore? What I sold to Mary, not her boss, were the cheaper bottles of wine that Thomas and I paid a small fortune for. I charged her the same amount that Thomas and I paid for it. No more, and no less. It was already proven without a doubt. It was my wine, not Big Pete's wine, so get over it." I hung up without saying goodbye. I was extremely angry and disappointed with my sister.

CHAPTER IV

I have two other sisters, Teresa and Joan. They are four and six years younger than me, respectively. Christina is two years younger than I am. In fact, there is a two-year age gap between all of us. Teresa and Joan are my father's daughters from his second wife, Annabelle, whereas Christina and I are the daughters of my father and his first wife.

I never told my other two sisters about all this mess, mainly because it involved my biological family, not theirs. I did not want them to feel like they had to clean up a mess that was caused by my mother. The other reason I did not tell them about it was because, at the time, they were both in poor health.

Teresa was still active duty in the Army. She resembles her mother with beautiful shiny, thick black hair and green eyes. She is physically and mentally strong like me. She possesses some of the traits of our bloodline, as do all my sisters.

In January of 1999, she was on a highly specialized mission and was wounded very badly. She had multiple surgeries and spent months in rehab. I thought I had lost her. There were many times when I wished she hadn't followed me into the Army because I'm not there to protect her when she needs to be protected.

When we were both in the Army, we always had each other's backs. Sometimes I felt guilty for retiring, but I did it because I was burned out and truly felt that I would not be able to keep my troopers as safe as I should. The box in my mind had begun to overflow, and basically, I felt I could not make conclusive life-or-death decisions any longer.

When I had put in my twenty-plus years and was talking with Teresa about retiring, she assured me that she would be fine. She even stated, "After all, Belinda, you basically trained me and I still have plenty of room in my box to deal with it."

I replied, "But, Teresa, you may think I don't know the conflict you have been going through all these years, but I do know."

Teresa asked with a curious tone, "What do you mean?"

I answered her with understanding in my voice, "The fight that goes through your soul because you are half lamb and half wolf."

Teresa replied peacefully, "Yes, but now I am at peace with the Mennonite world and yours. It has taken me a long time to get here, but I know that my journey through life was always meant to fight by your side. Maybe because the wolf spirit was stronger in me than the lamb spirit; maybe because I'm a mother now and it's time for me to live among the lambs again as you are. All I know is I might have changed a few things, but the one thing I will never change is being by your side. You're not just my sister you're my hero, my friend, my confidante, my protector, and everything I would like to be. I hope that out of all of our experiences I have learned there is a place to fight and there is a place to use words and reason. You have taught me to accept both worlds. I love you sister, always and forever."

I answered, "I love you too, little sis, and I'm glad you are at peace with our two worlds. I know it has been harder for you than for me. You, too, are my hero, my friend, my sister, and my confidante."

After she was released from rehab, she was stationed at the Pentagon on a desk job. She hated it, but I felt more comfortable regarding her safety. I didn't have to worry about any more bullets hitting her. She was now in a safe, secure building.

Her husband, Mark, was also in the Army; he was a chopper pilot. They met when they were both stationed in Germany. According to Mark, it was love at first sight, but Teresa took some convincing. She was a career woman and didn't want any distractions from her work. Eventually, he won her over. They had a small wedding on base, and then when they were both granted an extended leave. They had a formal vow renewal ceremony and reception in the church of her youth. It was a Mennonite church, and they were told that they could have the ceremony there as long as they did not wear their uniforms. One of the core beliefs of the Mennonite church is non-resistance. They take the Bible literally when it says that if your enemy hits you on your cheek, you are to turn your head so he can hit your other cheek instead of fighting back. I have never understood this philosophy, but I respected people who felt that way. I have heard stories of people who were tortured and killed because they refused to fight back.

For their vow renewal, Teresa wore a traditional wedding dress, and Mark wore a tux. It was a beautiful ceremony. Thomas and I were lucky enough to be at both of their wedding ceremonies. Because of her age, Teresa had joined the Army several years after I did. She joined two years after Thomas, who was six years younger than I was. I did my twenty years, and then some, before I retired. I could have stayed in longer, but it was becoming harder and harder for Thomas and I to stay stationed together because of our special ops training and the different types of missions that Uncle Sam had us performing.

Joan, the youngest of us, was an archeologist. Our father had passed his love of history on to all of us, but Joan took it one step further and made it her career. Joan was also the proud mother of four children. She almost had five, but she had experienced a very bad pregnancy and lost the child. This was around the time of my mother's incarceration. It was very difficult for her. She loved children, and she viewed being a mom as her greatest calling. Joan married her high school sweetheart, and they lived outside Philadelphia. Joan's husband was very involved with the visual arts and taught at a prominent art school.

The final reason I did not tell them was because I did not think that our father wanted them involved, even though he never actually said it. I was also afraid that they might react the same way Christina did. After all, she was their older sister as well. I was not sure which of us they would support.

I was relieved after I told them what has been happening because they both agreed without hesitation that I was acting honorably. They supported me even though Christina did not. They both offered to help me, but I assured them that I would be able to handle it. Knowing that I had the support of my other two sisters seemed to make me feel stronger. I could take on the entire world if need be. After all, I'm She Wolf and they are part of the wolf clan. We all still wear the rings that symbolize our beliefs and convictions. Christina stop wearing her ring a long time ago, but I still had hope that my sister would return to us.

CHAPTER V

I felt Thomas poke me with his elbow. I looked up at the flight attendant as she was handing me a lunch tray. While I ate, I listened to Thomas talk about how much he was looking forward to seeing his brothers and parents again. My emotions were mixed. On one hand, I was very happy for him, but on the other, I was not looking forward to seeing my own family. After we finished eating and the flight attendant took our trays, I looked back out the window and returned to my memories.

*   *   *

After I hung up on Christina, I called Auntie Bea to tell her that Mom finally had a sentencing date. I told Auntie Bea that Thomas and I would try to arrive a few days before the sentencing; we would move everything out of her house and the Daisy house and put it into storage during the last week of March. I told Auntie Bea that I would like her and Uncle Frank to be with Thomas and me during Mom's sentencing. Big Pete would be sentenced then as well, as he had finally stopped fighting the U.S. Attorney's office and had waived his right to trial just as my mother had. Big Pete's sentencing was scheduled for the day before Mom's sentencing. I wanted both Auntie Bea and Uncle Frank in attendance so that they could see firsthand what my mother did, what she did not do, and everything that Big Pete had done. I also wanted them to witness what the court was going to do.

I told Auntie Bea that I had already scheduled an appointment with Miss Patson to start the lawsuit to get Bea's land back. I said it would be done in my name and her name. Auntie Bea sounded like she was excited that we were finally going to start the fight to get her land returned.

Then to my surprise she said, "Belinda, make sure you have all your legal documents in writing stating that your mom gave you all the property."

I asked, "What do you mean, Auntie Bea?"

She responded, "Make sure you have the transfer of property in your name because Frank and I will not give it to you unless you have it in writing."

I said, "Okay. Auntie Bea. I will be sure to have it in writing."

After I hung up with her, I was puzzled, but I just assumed Auntie Bea wanted to make sure she was protected. I figured that was all it was, and I had no problem doing that. I typed up a letter with my mother's signature block transferring all of her property to me. I mailed it to the jail, and my mother mailed it back to me signed, witnessed, and there was a sealed certification on it as well.

On the last night before returning to take care of my daughter's duty, I called Auntie Bea and Uncle Frank to remind them when we were going to move our belongings. I told both of them that I would call them that night from Thomas's mom's house to give them the exact time. I told both of them that Thomas's brothers, other family members, and our friends would be there to help us move everything out. I told them that I had already arranged to rent several storage units.

Before I knew it, the plane was landing. We walked to the luggage carousel. I was intently watching for our suitcases when I sensed someone behind me. I quickly turned around and saw Thomas's mom. She motioned for me to remain silent and then quickly poked Thomas in the shoulder. He quickly spun around and yelled "MOM!" He impulsively hugged her. His mom was crying because she was so happy. They hadn't seen each other in over a year.

Thomas asked, "Mom, what are you doing here? You didn't have to drive three hours to pick us up. Belinda has already reserved a rental car for us so we could drive right home."

Thomas' mother replied, "I know, baby, but I couldn't stand the wait anymore. I had to come meet you!"

Thomas said, "Just one more suitcase and we will be ready." He grabbed the last one and said, "Let's get out of here!"

Once we settled in at Thomas's mom's house, I called Auntie Bea and Uncle Frank as promised. I told each of them we would see them the next morning at 8:30, and that I couldn't wait to see them. I also told Auntie

Bea that I had the papers that she requested. She said that was good, and they both said they would see me in the morning.

Before we left Germany, Thomas had contacted his brothers and his friends in the Snobville area. They all agreed to meet us at the Mills' farm around 11:30 to help us start moving. Everyone agreed it would take us at least two days to do it. Thomas had his specialized orders, so we could be reimbursed for the storage units and for the large rental truck.

CHAPTER VI

We arrived at the Daisy house after renting the largest rental truck available. At 8:45, we drove up and parked in the driveway in front of the Daisy house. I went to the sliding glass door and knocked because apparently the doorbell had broken after I had left the last time.

As we were standing there, Thomas said, "I'll fix that for Frank while we are here."

I responded, "That's a great idea. I guess Uncle Frank hasn't gotten up."

A few minutes later, Uncle Frank appeared and walked from the kitchen to the Florida room door. He stood in front of the door but would not open it. I said to him through the glass door, "Uncle Frank, did you sleep late? Let us in. We are here to start moving everything."

Uncle Frank just looked at the two of us, shaking his head. He walked back to his favorite chair and hit the speed dial button, which I knew was Auntie Bea's.

I asked Thomas, "What is going on?"

Thomas said, "Frank, what the hell is the matter with you? Belinda just spoke with you last night. Stop playing games, and let us in so we can start moving this stuff out of here."

Uncle Frank just looked at the two of us and shook his head, answering, "No."

Thomas and I walked back to the rental truck. I lit a cigarette, and I said, "As soon as I finish this, we will walk over to Auntie Bea's. I want to find out if Uncle Frank has Alzheimer's or something."

Thomas responded, "I agree. I'm getting very angry!"

As soon as I put my cigarette out, and we were about to walk over to Auntie Bea's, Thomas and I both looked up because we heard sirens. We then saw a county sheriff's car speeding around the turn in the road. It pulled up into the Daisy house's driveway.

Two deputy sheriffs quickly got out of the vehicle and ran toward us. As they were running toward us, they started to slow down. They both had puzzled expressions on their faces.

I said, "We did not call you yet because we were going over to my auntie's house to find out what is the matter with my great-uncle, so who called you and for what?"

Both of the deputy sheriffs looked at each other, and the one said, "We just received a call from an elderly lady who said you two were beating up an old man."

Thomas became angry and said, "What? We came to move our stuff out from where we had it stored with Belinda's godparents. Frank here will not let us in to retrieve our belongings. We think he may be senile. We were just about to go over to Bea's house to see what the problem is. Now we see she is involved in this as well."

The one deputy sheriff asked to see our IDs. We both gave them our military IDs. Both deputy sheriffs looked at our IDs and then looked up at us. One of them walked back to the car to check us out. The other became flushed in the face and angrily said, "Well, Sergeants, you guys didn't plan this very well. Where are you coming from?"

Thomas answered, "Germany, what more is there to plan? Belinda has been calling her godparents every week for the last year. They have known that we were planning to move this out of here since January. In fact, Belinda just called them again last night and let them know exactly what time we would be here this morning. Explain to me, sir, what more needs to be planned. To set the record straight as well, we are also planning to file a lawsuit to get this farm and the two houses back for Belinda's great-aunt, the lady who called you."

The deputy sheriff then became much friendlier. The other deputy sheriff approached us and whispered something in his partner's ear. Suddenly they became very, very friendly and apologetic. In fact, both of their cheeks became beet red. One of the deputy sheriffs said, "Let's see if we can get this old fart to give your things back." He went to the sliding glass door and said, "Mr. Gibbs, open this door this second!"

Uncle Frank just cracked the sliding glass door.

The deputy sheriff said, "You know that stuff isn't yours. Why won't you let the Stars move it? You knew they were coming today."

Uncle Frank answered, through the crack of the sliding glass door, "I know it's theirs. I don't know why I can't let them have it. I just can't."

Thomas and I stared at Uncle Frank because we couldn't believe what he was doing.

As the deputy sheriff continued trying to persuade Uncle Frank to do the right thing, a voice came over the handheld radio the other deputy sheriff was holding as he stood in front of us.

The voice said, "What's going on? Are they beating that poor old man?"

As he looked at Thomas and me, the deputy sheriff responded, "No, sir, it was a false report. It isn't what it appeared to be."

The other deputy sheriff, who had been speaking with Uncle Frank, walked over to us and said, "What the hell is the matter with that stupid, nasty, old man? Is he really senile?"

I answered, "I don't know, but we are about to walk over there," as I pointed to Auntie Bea's house, "and find out what the two of them are up to."

One of the deputy sheriffs replied, "No, you better not. I'm just trying to protect the two of you. I'll go over there and find out what these two are up to. I don't know if you realize this, but I believe the two of them are planning on stealing everything you had stored here. They are not going to give it back. Look at what that old lady tried to pull already."

I explained to the deputy sheriffs, as I handed them a certified copy of the letter that Auntie Bea requested from me months ago, that if he gave her the letter, maybe they would let us move our things. The deputy sheriff said he would give it to her. He recommended that Thomas and I go ahead and return the moving truck back and call our family and friends to cancel the move.

Thomas and I drove the moving truck back to the rental place, and both of us were totally in shock. Thomas was so angry and made sure that anyone within hearing distance knew exactly how angry he was! I was in a state of shock. I felt some anger, but it just didn't make sense that Auntie Bea would rather steal my things than get her land back. It just did not add up. Then I remembered one of my mother's latest phone calls.

She said, "Belinda, I have a bad feeling about this."

We filled the truck's gas tank back up to replace the small amount of gas we used. We had just parked it and were about to go inside to settle up with the company when the deputy sheriffs pulled up in the parking lot. We stood there as they walked toward us. They greeted us, and the older one who had spoken with Uncle Frank said, "Well, Sergeants, we suggest that you guys get yourselves an attorney."

He handed the papers back to me and said, "Ma'am, your great-aunt read them but refused to accept them. She babbled on and on that your mother stole her land. I tried to explain to her that you and she were supposed to take legal action against the people that bought her land, but she refused to accept it. All I can tell you is that there is no justification in stealing from veterans, especially when they had nothing to do with whatever happened to her. I told her that I could ticket her for lying to the law, and she retorted that she had no other choices. She claimed that this was the only way she could get her money back. Get yourselves an attorney and get a warrant in detinue, and we will be more than happy to get your stuff back. I'm a veteran myself. I was a Marine, and I served two tours in Vietnam. I have seen a lot of my buddies come back, and all their money and property were stolen from them by their own families. So I would love to see justice served on this one."

Thomas said, "We have an attorney here, but we are stationed in Germany. Belinda has hired an attorney to take the Greeds to court. She was going to file a lawsuit in her name and her great-aunt's name to force them to sell her great-aunt's land back to Belinda and me. So I guess Belinda and I will be meeting with this attorney to sue Bea and Frank instead."

We stood there and talked about what had happened, and Thomas and I told them quite a bit of what had happened when I was there a year before.

We then drove up the road to a store that had a pay phone. Thomas called everyone and canceled the move. I still had Mom's address book, and I found Ed Weird's number in it. I called it and began speaking with him for the first time in my life.

When he answered the phone, I greeted him with, "Mr. Weird, my name is Belinda Star. What have you done to my godparents? My husband and I just tried to recover our property that we had stored with them, and they refused to return it."

Mr. Weird answered, "Belinda, you don't want that junk."

I became very angry as I responded, "Excuse me? My family property is not junk! It may be to you, but it's not to me. What was the name of the moving company that you and Jay used?"

He gave me the name.

I then asked, "I'm going to call my attorney now. Do you have the telephone number of the moving company?"

Ed Weird answered, "No. I don't."

I said, "Well, you may have to give permission for us to retrieve a copy of the moving papers because I already tried to reach Jay and could not get a hold of him."

He replied, "Oh, Belinda, you don't need to get your brother involved in this."

I didn't understand why he said that, but I simply stated, "That's none of your business. I don't know the extent of your involvement in all this, but you better pray to God I don't find out." I simply hung up the phone.

Thomas had been standing beside me during the conversation, and he had become angry at what he overheard. He said, "There's something wrong with that creep! I have a sneaking feeling he is behind this whole thing." I nodded my head in total agreement with my husband.

I called Miss Patson next, hoping she was in her office. As soon as we greeted each other, I said, "Miss Patson, you are not going to believe this!"

Miss Patson asked, "Oh no, how bad is it?"

I told her most of the story, and she stopped me and said, "Belinda, you and Thomas get to my office right now. I'm clearing my schedule for today. I just can't believe how ignorant your godparents are! They are foolish and so gullible! After all that you and your mother—as much as I hate to admit anything good about her—have done for them, they now pull this? Just get to my office now. We will discuss this further and make plans as to how we can best deal with it. I want those two characters held accountable this time!"

CHAPTER VII

Thomas and I drove straight to Miss Patson's office. As we were sitting in the same chairs that I had sat in numerous times a year ago, Miss Patson said, "We are going to file a warrant in detinue. I will mail you the court date when I get it. Then as soon as you get a copy of it, I want you to call me. Now we have a problem! You claim your property is worth a million dollars or so, but you can't prove it because Frank and Bea have all your receipts, appraisals, and pictures. The judge in the higher court doesn't like these types of cases. I have repeatedly seen him victimize the victims all over again in the courtroom. He has even let murderers get away! We can only put $15,000 maximum on the value because that is the highest value you can get in the lower court."

I said, "Miss Patson, I'm not going to lie. I know that our property combined with what my mother gave me, and my ancestor's property, is worth over a million dollars."

Miss Patson responded, "I don't expect you to lie. I'm hoping that the judge will hear our case anyway because you will be flying from Germany. We will have a fair judge in the lower court, but we will not have a fair judge in the higher court."

I said, "The detailed inventory I have is thousands of pages."

Miss Patson responded, "I don't want to clog the court up with all that. We will do a schedule that summarizes it. The more general it is, the easier it is to prove it. We are not worried about the dollars or detail; we are just worried about recovering the property itself, correct?"

Thomas and I both answered at the same time, "Correct."

Miss Patson said, "Good, don't worry anymore about the details; that's what you pay me for. I haven't let you down yet, Belinda."

I responded, "I know you work hard for your salary."

Miss Patson said, "After you leave here, go get me a copy of the moving papers. If for some reason they don't give it to you, then I will subpoena them."

I responded, "Okay."

As we were leaving her office, I thought, *I am very fortunate that I have one of the few attorneys who is honest, and is in the field to uphold the law, not just to line her pockets.*

After leaving Miss Patson's office, Thomas and I went to the moving company. I spoke with the manager, Bob Shinski, and I filled him in on what was going on. I gave him Jay's phone number. Then Mr. Shinski called Jay right away, but no one answered.

I then asked, "Mr. Shinski, may I use your phone for a minute?"

He nodded his head granting me permission. I called Ed. When he answered, I told him that I was at the moving company's office, and I wanted him to speak with the manager. I passed the phone over to Mr. Shinski. He spoke briefly with Ed.

After he hung up he said, "I'm sorry, ma'am, but Ed said not to give them to you."

Thomas and I exchanged glances. We knew that our suspicions were correct. From that moment forward, we knew why Ed was so willing to help my family members. He was doing it for his own personal gain. He had conned and stolen a lot of property from my godparents. Now we knew. Why would he be doing this if he wasn't trying to cover up the truth, and what was the truth that he was concealing from everyone?

I called Miss Patson next, once again using Mr. Shinski's phone. I told her about Mr. Shinski's conversation with Ed.

She responded, "Who the hell is this Ed Weird character? Put Mr. Shinski on the phone."

After Miss Patson was done speaking with Mr. Shinski, he passed the phone back to me. Miss Patson said, "Belinda, you and Thomas come back to my office, ASAP."

As we were leaving, Mr. Shinski said, "Ma'am, I have no trouble giving the documents to your attorney with a subpoena."

Thomas and I didn't say another word in response. We just left.

We still did not understand the betrayal committed against us by my godparents, but we did know for a fact that Ed was behind it. We were even more determined now to take down Bea and Frank. They both knew better than to steal, especially from family. There was absolutely no justification for stealing from family, especially one who has given blood, sweat, and tears to protect their freedoms. Ed had simply used them and preyed off their greed, just as Pete King had done.

We arrived at Miss Patson's office, and as soon as we settled in our chairs, she called Auntie Bea. "Mrs. Mills, this is Miss Patson, Mrs. Star's attorney. What in the devil is the matter with you? I was going to also be your attorney, per Mrs. Star's request, but I am not going to represent you at all now. I have taken on Mrs. Star's case against you. She has spent enormous amounts of her personal time and money, and now you and Mr. Gibbs are stealing from her. I am telling you right now, Ed is just another Big Pete." She was silent for a few moments and then said, "What are you talking about?" Another few moments went by, "Well then I guess there is nothing more to say. My advice to you is you better get yourself an attorney, a real one." She hung up the phone.

She looked at Thomas and me, shook her head sadly, and said, "Ed is representing her. She has instructed me to call him. She claims that Ed has told her that you were nothing but a liar and crook like your mother. She said that she is grateful that you cleared the debt in her name and the crimes that she committed against Christina. She said she is grateful that you did not tell on her to other family members, but there was nothing we could do to prove it now. She told me that she is getting her money back for the land that you mother stole. She claims that she was told by Ed that he would help her get her land back in exchange for your personal belongings. She told me that Mr. Weird told her to pass along a message to you that you need to prove that the items are yours."

After that statement, Miss Patson picked up the phone and called Ed. I had handed her his number when we walked in. She said to him, "Mr. Weird, this is Miss Patson, Mrs. Star's attorney. My simple advice to you, after speaking with Mrs. Mills, is that you had better get her a real attorney or I will have charges filed against you for trying to practice law without a license."

There was silence and she said, "We will just see about that, Mr. Weird," and she hung up the phone.

She looked over at Thomas and me and said, "What an arrogant, stupid idiot! Would you please wait a moment? I need to go speak with one of the senior partners."

When she returned, she said, "Belinda, there is nothing I can really do about Ed, but we are going to have to deal with him in some way."

We stayed in Miss Patson's office for about another hour, and we planned our lawsuit against Bea and Frank. We all agreed that it would be better to do it in my name since Thomas was still active duty and would not be able to get back to the states as easily as I would. We decided to take the case to the lower court. If I was asked to tell the truth of the value of what I thought it was worth, then I would tell the truth. Miss Patson would have the subpoena for the moving company issued, and she planned on having the subpoena served by the following week. We agreed to let the Greeds keep the land. Bea deserved her fate in that regard. We were not going to sue them for the return of it.

Miss Patson pulled out the file that contained the paper trail that I had sent her as evidence to use against Bea and my mother in the event I would have to prove what really happened. We reviewed the file and discussed the contents. Once again, my heart was breaking. My mother did not deserve this. It was not anyone's place to judge her outside of our country's justice system. We all agreed that Bea, Frank, and Ed had not only committed defamation of character against Thomas and me, but also against my mother. We did not know the extent of Christina's involvement, so Miss Patson decided she would call my sister. She did so while we were there but did not let her know that we were listening.

Miss Patson said to my sister, "Hello, Ms. Bishop, this is Miss Patson. I am calling to find out what you know, or what your involvement is, regarding the property that Mrs. Mills and Mr. Gibbs are storing for Mr. and Mrs. Star."

There was silence for at least ten minutes. Then Miss Patson said, "Thank you for your honesty, Ms. Bishop, but to set the record straight, your sister did not lie about suing the Greeds to sell the land back. The suit has been planned since she spoke with Mrs. Greed in 1999. It's sad that you put such low regards on your own flesh and blood. Goodbye."

Miss Patson said, "Well, your sister has known about the planning of this crime by Ed and Bea for several months now. She has no problem with it because she agrees that you lied to Auntie Bea regarding your attempts to recover Mrs. Mills' land. Christina said she wasn't aware of your property, just her mother's, and she didn't see any problem with Mrs. Mills and Mr. Gibbs taking it because she didn't want it. She doesn't care about it. She thought it was justice being served and she still feels that way. There was nothing I could do to change her mind about it."

I broke down crying because of how little my own sister thought of my husband and me. My own sister didn't care about my feelings at all! I realized this was the nastiest and most evil thing my sister had ever done to me, and believe me, she had done many evil things throughout our lives.

Thomas became angry and asked, "Is there any way we can sue that snobby little tramp?"

Miss Patson sadly replied, "Mr. Star, it's not worth the amount of money. I can see the property is worth it, but not defamation of character."

Thomas stated, "What gets me is how Belinda's entire family worked together to make sure we didn't see this coming. We would never have left our things here, nor done anything for Frank or Bea, if we knew they were planning this all along."

Miss Patson responded, "I agree with you. Bea is like an old spider. She is patient, and she waits until the fly is trapped in her web before striking; then it's too late. This is an old lady who is very sly and very experienced at preying off other people. I never saw an elderly person so evil and so good at it. God only knows how many victims there have been throughout that woman's life, and I'm sorry to have to say this to you, Belinda, but I feel the same way about your mother. I can see the evil behind all her lies, but unfortunately you love her."

I simply responded, "I don't think she is evil. There is also a good side, and I see it sometimes. I don't think my mother is pure evil; she's greedy and selfish. Now I know, and I can clearly see, that my great-aunt is something entirely different. I know she is pure evil. I already know my great-uncle is a pathological liar, but he always has been. I just didn't think they would do this. It never was about the land for Auntie Bea; it's just money. Uncle Frank just loves getting the attention, and he enjoys pretending to be a victim. He will lie and do just about anything to be the center of attention."

CHAPTER VIII

The day flew by because most of it was spent with Miss Patson. After meeting with her, we went to Thomas's mother's house where we had dinner with his brothers and their families. They, of course, were very upset by what Auntie Bea had done. The following morning, we headed to the courthouse. We arrived later than we wanted, but Thomas and I found a seat in the overcrowded courtroom waiting for Big Pete's sentencing. There must have been close to a hundred people there waiting for his sentencing. Thomas and I squeezed in the middle of a row.

There were two young women sitting beside me, and they were talking softly. I heard the one woman ask the other, "Are you testifying?"

The other woman said, "Yes, and even though it's not true, I'm going to say the same thing during his wife's sentencing tomorrow. In fact," she giggled, "I don't even know his wife, nor did I ever speak with her."

I was livid! Thomas must have heard the woman's comment as well because he grabbed my wrist and whispered in my ear, "We will call your mom's attorney when we get out of here. Don't say anything."

I just looked at my husband and nodded my head.

The courtroom was filled with the sounds of whispering and soft conversations until everyone saw Big Pete walking through one of the doors in the front of the courtroom. He was accompanied by a very pregnant woman. She was his court-appointed attorney. I could not believe that they did not handcuff Big Pete like they had my mother! In fact, there was not even a marshal around. I could feel my blood beginning to boil. Now the courtroom was completely silent. In fact, it was so silent that I could hear the lady next to me breathing.

The bailiff said, "All rise."

The judge entered the courtroom. After he entered, we were instructed to be seated.

There must have been at least thirty victims testifying against Big Pete. Each one told their painful story of how Big Pete had tricked them out of their hard-earned money. After listening to the testimonies, the judge left the courtroom to deliberate. He returned after only about ten minutes and sentenced Big Pete to four years in prison and four years of probation. Even after he was sentenced, he was allowed to walk around unshackled. The judge even gave him a month to settle his affairs before beginning his incarceration. After we left the courtroom, I immediately called my mother's attorney regarding the conversation that Thomas and I had overheard. He told me he would take care of it.

When we returned to my mother-in-law's house, she had supper waiting for us. Neither of us was hungry, but we managed to eat a little because we wanted to make her happy. After supper, she gave me a prayer cloth that her church congregation prayed over. She said that they had prayed for the court to have mercy on my mother. I had asked months ago for her congregation to remember my mother in their prayers. I kissed her and thanked her before Thomas and I went to bed.

CHAPTER IX

Once again, we started our day at the courthouse. This time it was for my mother's sentencing. We assumed it would be held in the same courtroom, but we found out that it was in a different room. Because of that, we were a few minutes late, but we still made it before the judge entered. This courtroom was three times the size of the one we had been in the previous day, and it was completely empty. A few people wandered in after us, which included Miss Weasel, our pastor, a man, and an older couple. The older couple, I would soon find out, was Ed and Tammy Weird. That was it.

When my mother entered, she was still handcuffed. I tried to give her the prayer cloth, but the U.S. marshal would not allow me to do so. Instead, I handed it to her attorney. He just stuck it in his pocket. The sentencing had not even started, and I was already livid.

I approached the marshal and said, "You didn't even handcuff the creep Big Pete yesterday, but you have my mother handcuffed. Please remove her handcuffs."

The marshal just glared at me, but he did take the handcuffs off my mother's wrists. Then he allowed me to hug her.

Mom was wearing the clothes I had purchased for her while I was still in Germany. I had shipped them to her for the sentencing. She looked good, and she was healthy. I was thankful for that.

Again, we were called to stand as the judge entered into the courtroom. It was the same judge that had presided over Big Pete's sentencing. The U.S. Attorney only had one witness, and my mother's attorney easily proved that there was no crime committed against him because his own employer did not pay for his insurance.

The judge allowed my mother to give a verbal plea before making his final discussion. I patted Mom's attorney on the back and asked, "Please let the judge know about the beatings she suffered from Big Pete."

Mom's attorney said, "Also, Your Honor, we request that you take into consideration the physical and mental abuse committed against Mrs. King by her husband."

The judge answered, "Yes, I will take that under consideration before making my final decision on her sentencing."

Everyone stood as the judge left to deliberate. It must have been thirty to forty minutes before the judge re-entered the courtroom. His next words will forever ring in my ears. This judge was truly a man of character, and I would respect him for the rest of my life because the words he spoke were so true and were full of common sense. My mother and her attorney stood as the judge passed sentencing.

The judge said in a loud, strong voice, "Mrs. King, you have proven to this court that your intentions were noble, and that you mainly committed your actions for your aunt. However, there is no room in this society for a modern-day Robin Hood. There is no—and I mean no—justification for stealing. None! Whether it is stealing from a bank, company, or even a private identity people are hurt. Do you understand, Mrs. King? This court is going to consider your abuse, but Mrs. King, you had a choice. You could have walked away, but you chose not to do so."

He sentenced my mother to two years, with the first year counted as time already served. Then he stated that time was reduced already for the abuse and gave her a supervised release for one-two years. I broke down crying for my mother. He pretty much threw the book at her, but he was right.

The marshal allowed me to hug my mother, and I kissed her on the cheek once more. Thomas and I were walking toward the exit of the courtroom when Mrs. Weasel had the nerve to stand right in front of us. She tried to block us from leaving. She asked with a smile on her face, "Belinda, we finally meet again. Can I ask you a few questions?"

Before I had a chance to reply, Thomas said angrily, "No comment, we have to fly back to Europe. We don't have time to answer your questions so you can misconstrue our answers to put in your gossip column in your rag newspaper."

He put his arm around my waist, and we quickly walked out of the courtroom.

We turned in the keys to the rental car at the airport and checked in our luggage. As we waited to board the airplane, Thomas hugged me, kissed me on the cheek, and said, "I thought my family was bad, but Belinda, yours takes the cake!"

I responded sadly, "I did warn you years ago, but you married me anyway."

Thomas said, "I know. I hope our justice system is going to protect us now."

I stated, "It better, since we fought for it."

CHAPTER X

August 2000, and once again I was flying back to the United States. This time I was alone. I looked out the window and started thinking about everything that had occurred over the last five months while I had been in Germany. I was returning to the States once again to battle the evil in my family, primarily Uncle Frank and Auntie Bea. They had finally crossed the line. Once again, I was their victim, and this time, I was going to fight back. I had no one else to take up my battle for me; my beloved husband was engaged in a life-and-death battle to protect our freedom.

My decision to fight my family was not an easy one. I agonized over it for months, but with my husband's support, I came to the conclusion that I had to fight for what was mine. My mother's family had taken from me my entire life. The time had come to sever the strings linking me to my beloved godparents. I had finally acknowledged that the love was only one-sided. They did not really care for me; they only cared about what they could get from me.

There was only one rule of engagement for this battle. I must fight them in my country. I really wished that I could have simply taken both of them across my knee and given them the spanking that they deserved. They were acting like greedy, undisciplined children, and they should be treated as such. However, children act that way because they do not know any better. My godparents had reached the age of accountability many years ago. They knew the difference between right and wrong. There was no excuse for the way they had treated me. Their actions had shown that their hearts were pure evil.

I guess they had believed that I would not do anything about it. After all, I had forgiven them before and even helped them make things right again. They honestly believed the lies that they had created and had been spreading for over a year. Auntie Bea was an expert at using her age to manipulate people.

Throughout my military career, it had been drilled into my head never to underestimate my enemies. I now knew that love was blind, and I realized that I had grossly underestimated my godparents. I guess I was like many Americans. I stereotyped them because of their age and lack of education, and they were family and I loved them. Who would have thought it would be my godparents that ended up taking us down? Who would have thought that we could be brought down by two old people? Maybe this was one reason Auntie Bea was so good at stealing from the younger generations. Uncle Frank simply followed Auntie Bea's lead, wanting all the attention that would once again come his way.

CHAPTER XI

After her sentencing, my mother was moved from the county jail to a minimum-security state prison to serve out the remainder of her sentence. Even though the prison was just a few hours away from the county jail, the transfer took two weeks. I wasn't sure how many county jails she stayed in during the transfer, but she called me from at least three different county jails during that period. She managed to cause a stir every place she stayed regarding her medication. Even though my mother was in prison, she still had to rock the boat and bring some kind of attention to herself. My mother was truly like my Auntie Bea in that respect. She used anything at her disposal to cause people to feel sorry for her. There was one major difference between the two of them though. Auntie Bea did it out of pure evilness, but my mother wasn't evil.

While she was at the county jail, she had been diagnosed with bipolar disorder. Once she told me that, I read everything I could get my hands on regarding the disorder. Knowing this new information, her behavior began to make sense, especially her rapid mood swings. I felt better knowing that she could not help it; it was part of her genetic makeup. I would always love her, and I would continue protecting her—my daughter's duty was for God, country, and family. I would try to fight for justice no matter the cost to her and to myself.

I released a huge sigh because I knew that once my mother was released, I would be her jailer. I would have to keep an eye on her for the rest of her life to prevent her from hurting anyone else. I knew she would hurt me again, but if I could prevent her from hurting others, at least that would be worth something.

The burden of my future responsibility slowly sunk in, and I could feel the heaviness settle on my shoulders. I was sacrificing the right to live my life the way I wanted. My life would revolve around my mother as long as she lived, and a long life was written in her genes.

Shortly after Thomas and I returned to Germany in May of 2000, I had received a letter from my mother. It read:

Dear Belinda,

This is the biggest mess I've ever seen. Pete has given his part of the property to Auntie Bea. Yet he's filed for divorce saying that everything is settled between us. He looks like the golden goose. Oh well, I can't help it now. I told Ed that I never wanted to see Auntie again. She can get her help from Pete or her son.

I called Auntie Bea and told her that she could have everything. She just had to get it through you, Belinda. She thinks you filed the suit against her with your power of attorney, so I didn't tell her any differently. I told her that Pete had all of his stuff in Snobville. She kept asking me why I signed the transfer of property to you, so I told her to ask Pete. He was still sitting there, waiting to go to jail. I told her I just couldn't fight over it anymore. Miss Patson thinks we can settle it for something, but God knows what that is. Auntie Bea said I gave you that transfer letter out of spite, and she wouldn't take it even though Pete and I gave you everything verbally in 1999. She said Thomas is just as bad as you, but that Christina understood. I told her Christina had told me what she had said.

So Belinda, leave Christina alone. Now they have it all. They gave my dogs away, and no one gives a shit. Then Auntie Bea said, "You sound like you don't love me anymore." That's when I told her that I would never have issued a no trespassing order against her. Then she said that was the landlord, and I told her that the landlord didn't do it or even tell her to do it. Then Auntie Bea said I had "one" of my friends call you. And I told her to leave Judy and JR out of it. Auntie Bea said I didn't say who it was, and they didn't pass along any info about her. I think I really shook her up. I told her I hoped her son would come home and live with her. She kept trying to put you down. Auntie said you were trying to control her and Frank. I cut her short and said I didn't know of anything that you had done to hurt either of them. In fact, I told Auntie that you had bailed her out of trouble along with Frank and that the two of them owed you a lot. I told her that she stole from my daughter, not me.

If we settle, Belinda, I don't want her to get one thing of mine. We'll do it with money. I just called Pete and asked if he really wanted me to give Auntie Bea his watch. And of course, he said that he gave that watch to his son and Bea better give it back. Ha, ha. I told a big fat lie, but we'll see what he does now. I just called and said, "I lied to you." He's recording everything I say.

The Weirds called and talked to Christina for an hour Saturday. Let's see what she has to say to me about it. Ed also told me that all the wine had turned to vinegar. So Mary must have called Pete. I guess I don't understand what's going on.

Belinda, I don't know who to trust anymore. Christina said she called you about the dogs and everything is going around in circles. Everyone is running my life but me. Everybody wants my stuff. I don't understand. Ms. Weird said the basement is full of mice. I hope I have some clothes left. I can't take any more of this. It's hurting me.

Belinda, please do something about your sister and the rest of these nasty people, but leave don't bully Christina. I know what you do to her. You just will not realize that your sister has mental issues like me, and she isn't as tough as you are. So mess with everyone else, but be gentle with your sister.

I hurt so deeply for my mother as I remembered this letter. Her one soldier was fighting a huge nasty battle for her because she was unable to do so. The betrayal that I felt was nothing compared to her feelings of betrayal because she loved these people even more than I did. She had given so much help and support to these people, including my sister, and they had turned around like the snakes they were and continuously spewed their venomous lies to her and poisoned her soul against me. I was the only soldier she had left to fight for right and against wrong. I was the only one who had the insight to see the black and white between the gray. I was the only one who had the strength to carry the wounded on my back.

After reading that letter, I picked up the phone and called Big Pete. I thought Mary was leaving my mother and me alone and going after Big Pete, but I wasn't sure so I had to find out. Of course he did not pick up the phone, the answering machine did. I hadn't spoken to him in over a year at that point. I left a message. "Hi, Big Pete, it's Belinda. I know you want nothing to do with me, but I need to speak to you regarding Mary and her silly crap. If you decide that you need my help, my advice is that we need to put our differences aside, and you need to tell me what she's up to." I hung up the phone.

As soon as I hung up the phone, it rang, and I answered it. Much to my surprise, it was Big Pete.

He said, "Hello, Belinda, you're right. I have a problem with Mary. I know she is full of crap, but she's trying to blame me for what you or your mother did. I honestly don't have the money to fight her."

He proceeded to tell me everything she had said to him and what she was going to do about it. He said that she had an attorney and was going to file a suit against him.

I said, "Big Pete, I know you are my enemy, but you did not do this, nor did my mother or me. She did this to herself by lying and trying to cheat someone out of something. Now she's trying to pin the blame on everyone else. I may be your enemy, but I know you had nothing to do with this, and I will take care of it so don't worry about it anymore. She is my blood, and my problem, so I will deal with this."

Big Pete asked, "After all that I have done to hurt you, you are still going to help me?"

I said, "No, Big Pete, I'm doing this because my blood relative is wrong and needs to be put in her place once again. I know what you are, Big Pete. I said this to my mother, and I will say the same thing to you. You are responsible for your own actions, not anyone else's. I know you had nothing to do with this. Mary is a liar, and I will take care of it."

Big Pete said, "I will believe it when I see it."

I said, "Okay."

We said our goodbyes and I hung up the phone.

I then called my cousin Mary. After we exchanged greetings, I stated very calmly and dangerously, "Mary, you fuck with Big Pete one more time, and I swear I will take you down."

Mary became very angry and said, "I'm not after you or your mother, Belinda. I thought Big Pete was the enemy of the family, so I'm going after him."

I said, "No you're not! Give me the name of your attorney so I can fax the evidence to him. You did this to yourself, and I'm preventing you from making another mistake. Big Pete doesn't have the money to pay you anyway, so leave him alone. You will call him as soon as I hang up and apologize to him. You will never get another dime out of my family, or Big Pete, again. Have I made myself clear? Sell the diamond bracelet I gave you, and be happy."

Mary said, "I don't understand you, Belinda. Why would you get in the way of me taking down Big Pete?"

I said, "Because, Mary, I believe in truth, and all you are doing is causing my family misery. This battle isn't worth it. It's over! Leave us all alone so we can fight more important battles."

With that statement, I simply hung up the phone.

About an hour later, my phone rang again, and I answered it. It was Big Pete. He said, "Thank you, Belinda. Mary just called me and said she was sorry. She didn't know you were on my side on this one."

I thanked him for calling and made sure he knew that the only reason I intervened was because I stood for what was right, and what Mary was doing was wrong. I made sure he understood that it had nothing to do with the way I felt about him. That was the last time I ever spoke with Big Pete. I knew this kindness on my part would be short lived with him, but I knew in my heart I had done the right thing.

CHAPTER XII

My mind then drifted to Ed and how he was sticking his nose in my family's business and trying to practice law. To my knowledge, he did not have a law degree. I thought of all the letters that had been faxed back and forth between my attorney and Ed for the last five months as Miss Patson tried to settle matters. He was trying to keep all of our property. He would only agree to return one or two things out of thousands and thousands of items. He had involved himself in my mother's business and was trying to use her crimes—the ones that she was currently being punished for—against me.

He was demanding thousands of dollars from Thomas and me for the return of our property. He claimed it was for storage fees for my great-aunt and great-uncle. We knew that our property was not even worth a million dollars. To me, however, it was because much of it was priceless. In reality, it was only worth several hundred thousand dollars, if that, or at least that was my best estimate.

The reason I did not have dollar amounts for our property was because the joint personnel services office (JPSO) had not wanted dollar values. They only wanted dollar values after the military had already moved you and your family's things, and that was just for the items that were lost, stolen, or broken. Of course, my one old computer was stored in the Daisy house basement with the spreadsheets that had purchase prices listed. I only had printed the detailed descriptions and year of purchase because that was all I had needed for the split move.

I thought back to a letter of response that I had written and then faxed to Miss Patson on April 26, 2000. At that time, I did not know the extent of the involvement of Ed Weird. I wrote:

Dear Miss Patson,

I am writing this letter in response to your letter dated April 10, 2000. Regarding a time frame for me to be available for trial, any Thursday, Friday, or Monday during the first half of June will be fine. Our cheap flight only flies on Wednesdays. If you cannot arrange for the trial to be held in June then it will have to be August. Again only the above-mentioned days of the week during the first half of the month will be acceptable because of our flight.

In response to your question in paragraph four of your letter, Jack Jones, Attorney-at-Law, has copies of all documents I spoke of. He handled all the matters regarding Bea Mills. I spoke of all these documents because, at the time, my mother was legally able to do so. Now, my great-aunt and great-uncle are trying to claim this property by saying she was not legally in the right, and this is why my great-aunt and great-uncle are not allowing me to take my property. My understanding is they have no legal claim, and I wanted to make you are aware of this because I do not know what my great-aunt and great-uncle are going to do or say next. This may not have anything to do with it, but I do not know. Jack Jones is listed in the phone book if you need copies or need to know about the existence of these documents. I do not have his number here in Germany.

As far as the mortgages are concerned, that is all I know. How much, when, who the attorney is, I do not know. I do know that my mother can answer all these questions. This, also, has nothing to do with the criminal charges against my mother and Big Pete. This was all legal and given free of will by Bea. It does not have anything to do with this, at least not that I know of. Again, I will state I do not know how far Bea will try to take this. I wanted to prepare you for the worst. I wanted my attorney to be aware of anything that might jump out of Pandora's box. Also, my mother can answer all questions pertaining to Bea's bankruptcy.

No, the Daisy house is not relevant to this case, but when I do try to retrieve my personal effects at a later date, it will be relevant. The bankruptcy papers state that all my belongings were there before Frank moved in. I will be able to retrieve these copies once I am allowed access to the basement room where I stored most of my mother's and my papers. I do not want Frank or Bea to know they are there. It will save me money by getting the copies instead of going through Mr. Packerson. He did not give you everything.

As I stated in my previous letter, it was by word of mouth only that the property was given to Thomas and me in 1999. Nothing was done formally at that time. The property transfer officially took place in 2000 when Bea requested to have the information in writing. I state this because that was the reason my husband and I were storing our property there. I want you to know this for future reference.

Regarding phone bills and other expenses accrued during my stay with Frank, I paid in cash to my great-aunt and great-uncle. I have very little proof that I paid for it, but I do have some cancelled checks. I do not know if my great-uncle and great-aunt will lie about that also. I wanted you to know that I did pay for all my expenses and much more while I stayed with them. As far as I am concerned, I owe them nothing. They have told many lies and half-truths to other family members, and I do not know how far they will go. If I do have to pay for my expenses again, I will. This experience has taught me a valuable lesson. I will never again pay for something without getting a receipt, but I guess 20/20 vision regarding relatives makes you even blinder.

Also, there was never any mention of storage fees or any other fees regarding the storage of our property. If there had been, we would not have stored our possessions there. We had no idea that my great-aunt and great-uncle would do this. They both repeatedly told me that they would help to support my mother throughout this bad time. The entire year of 1999, my great-aunt told me everything was okay each time we spoke. She also told me, during each conversation that year, that she forgave my mother. She acted as if she knew nothing nor had anything to do with the loss of her land, but she did know. I have already proven that to you, and she told me herself of her involvement in 1999. As you can see, they lied to you and everyone else. I have no issues with using Bea Mill's paper trail to show the truth. As I stated to you previously, I will not help her recover her land now, not after this.

If Auntie Bea and Uncle Frank do not show up for this trial, or if they decide not to fight us, I would like to ensure that we have a court order telling the police they may use any means to protect us against them in retrieving our property. In other words, I want it documented that I may collect my property myself. I will oversee the movers, and I want have free access to all rooms, buildings, and any area on both properties to ensure I retrieve everything belonging to me. They may not put a no-trespassing warrant or anything against us, or call the sheriff on us like they did the last time we were there, or serve us with a no-trespassing order like they did to my mother. This will ensure that I retrieve everything needed without any resistance. All of this, of course, with both of them present. What do we do if we find missing items or a refusal on their part to release any, or all, of the property? Does she or Frank have a claim for storage fees after the fact? If so, is this against my mother or against Thomas and me?

Regarding the bankruptcy schedules and the list of property that Kelly Hanks has requested, I do not have power of attorney regarding my mother's affairs any longer so my answer is no. You may not give copies of these papers to this person without written or verbal permission from my mother.

Respectfully,
Belinda Star

Blackmail is just a word until you experience it firsthand. It is just a word in the dictionary until there are people who try to use something against you, even if you have done nothing wrong. In my case, my family was using my property and items that I valued to blackmail me. They were using my personal property, most of which was very important to me. First, it was Big Pete using my mother's beloved dogs and family heirlooms; then, other people joined in. They were trying to use my mother's crimes against me. Now Ed and my godparents jumped on the blackmail wagon. What a sad world we live in. It seemed to me there were more greedy, nasty people in the world than there were decent, honest ones. Just look at my family!

I truly realized how a person in a communist country must have felt. My great-aunt and all the rest stole my wealth and gave it out to everyone. Now there seemed to be nothing left for anyone. The more I thought about it, the angrier I became.

CHAPTER XIII

I looked away from the airplane window because the flight attendant was offering me a drink. I asked for two vodkas and a can of tomato juice. I just wanted the pain of my breaking heart to go away.

I still could not get over my auntie and my great-uncle letting Ed con them again, but of course, it was my mother who had brought him into our lives. It appeared that if Auntie Bea and Uncle Frank hadn't stolen from me, Auntie Bea would have had her land back. In my opinion, that seemed far more valuable than our household goods.

I remembered a statement that my maternal grandmother once said to me. I had come home from school one day upset over the decision our government had made to no longer back our dollar with gold. My views of our government were not very favorable at the time.

She said, "Belinda, when you own land you are wealthy because you can be born on it, live off it, shit on it, and die on it. You will never need money because of this! Freedom is not a given by many men's rules. You, as an individual, must always fight for it. You must also fight for liberty. Freedom and liberty are your God-given rights. Our forefathers knew this, and that is why we have the right to bear arms. We can protect our land; defend it from people that want to take it because they covet it. God has created this entire planet for us, and given it to us. It belongs to all the people. Of course, our government is now taxing it, and they do not have the right to do so.

"Even our government is greedy and selfish because our government represents *all* the people, or I should say *the majority*, so you have the majority of our people that believe in one thing: greed. And they have our government take away our God-given rights because they believe differently. This is not what liberty is all about. It's not about taking from one group of people, and giving it to others instead of just taxing us for our military, infrastructure, and our public servants' salaries.

"I watched as other women fought for my liberties. They fought to have the right to vote. I have also watched these women fight for our equality. Now all I do is watch and do nothing as my freedom, liberty, and the pursuit of happiness are being chiseled away by my own government and by my own fellow Americans.

"I know, my child, this doesn't make sense to you, but I pray that your liberties are not completely taken from your generation. I pray that I will be dead and buried before I have to witness my grandchildren's freedoms striped from them. For I fear the majority of our people are going to steal it from you, by taxing you severely so that they can spread the wealth around to everyone. Then, we will all have nothing. I have worked hard all my life, as have your ancestors, and it is my God-given choice if I choose to give to others or not. It is the right of each and every one of us as an individual to choose to give or not to give."

My grandmother was right. I did not truly understand what she was trying to tell me that day. I was too upset because our dollar was no longer worth anything except for the paper that it was written on. I believe a country as wealthy as ours should have gold or some type of precious metal to back up the monetary system. We needed to keep our dollar forever strong. At that point, I didn't believe that our country was turning into a population of lazy, greedy, and self-centered people, but I do understand now. I also fear it is too late for people to change because that's the way they believe.

"Nothing else matters except for the almighty dollar; and how you can get it without working for it."

I then felt sick to my stomach as I thought of everything Ed had tried to pull over the past five months. I thought that people trying to extort money from others only existed on the television and in movies, until all of this happened to me. I was just a middle-class, average, hardworking, unknown person. I wasn't rich or famous. Why was my family doing this to me all over again? I started crying as I asked myself, *Am I so stupid, naive, and evil to deserve this all over again?*

Maybe I was foolish to think we lived in a perfect country, but I still could not help myself but to hope for it. Just like I hoped my sister would love, respect, and support me. I was truly all alone, and I guess I always had been. I only had my husband, and I was so grateful to have found him. He was my best friend, my protector, and my lover. Even though I had him, it still felt as if I had no blood family I could call my own. I had no one that I could be proud of, no one that supported me even though they disagreed with me, no one that had unconditional approval and respect for my beliefs and values from my mother's side of the family.

CHAPTER XIV

I finished my drink, opened the other bottle of Vodka, and chugged it down. I saw the flight attendant and put my hand up. She nodded her head acknowledging that she saw me. Within a few moments, she was standing beside me, and I asked her if she had any cognac. She did, so I asked for three bottles and paid her for them. I opened the first one and poured it into my empty plastic cup. I start sipping on the cognac as I turned my head, looked back out the window, and started remembering more of what happened.

My mother had called me, of course, to complain about Miss Patson. Apparently after she read my letter, Miss Patson ended up visiting my mother and yelled at her for her whining and for her derogatory attitude toward me. I asked Miss Patson not to do that again because of the backlash from my mother. I did not know how much more emotional stress I could take from her. The bottom line was that my mother had brought another crook into our lives. Another crook and con just like Big Pete! I wished I could understand why she was attracted to men like that. Was it their power, or was she just gullible?

I also discovered that Big Pete had conned Auntie Bea into forgiving him. Auntie Bea even sat beside Big Pete at church after I left for Germany. Why should I have expected anything less from the two of them?

In April of 2000, two weeks after Thomas and I returned to Germany, I called May. I asked her what was the matter with her father. I told her that he would not return my possessions to me. May told me that she went to visit her father and Auntie Bea in the middle of April in 1999. She had no idea what was going on, but she knew they were up to something.

She said, "Remember Belinda, there is a good reason that none of us wants to help our father. He is not trustworthy. I admire everything you have done for him, but look where it got you. That's not a risk I am willing to take."

Now it made sense why Auntie Bea and Uncle Frank had been hurrying me back to Germany. After speaking with May, I realized that Auntie Bea and Uncle Frank had planned from the beginning to steal from us. My heart broke again.

May told me that the last time she had visited them that Auntie Bea had given her my great-grandmother's wedding ring. May told me that she would never take it off her finger again. I told May that it had not been Auntie Bea's ring to give to her. I told her that the ring belonged to me, and I had loaned it to Auntie Bea. I informed May that she would have to return that ring to me. May stated that I would have to pry it off her dead finger! I told May that I hoped it would not come to that. I was not sure, but at that point, I began to wonder if May was involved in this mess more than I had thought.

CHAPTER XV

My mind then drifted back to one of my conversations with Christina. I had called her during the week Thomas and I discovered that we were being robbed again.

"Christina, what is with Auntie Bea and Uncle Frank? Why are they stealing Thomas and my things?"

Christina replied angrily, "It wasn't your stuff! It was Mom's and Big Pete's and that's the only way Auntie Bea is going to get some of her money back after Mom and Big Pete stole her land."

I laughed and said, "Bull, Christina; you're lying! I was sitting in Miss Patson's office when she spoke with you last. You knew for a fact that I was going to fight the Greeds to get Auntie Bea her land back! You know else, dear sister? I know about the nasty lies that you have told both Miss Patson and Mom's attorney about me. I just can't get over how cruel you are toward me, and how much you must truly hate me. Please, Christina; tell me what I have done to you that was so vile to warrant this betrayal."

Christina simply responded, "You have done nothing. This is how I feel. I believe everything Ed has said, and he has proven it to me. I believe Auntie Bea, Uncle Frank, and Mary—not you."

I replied, "Oh, Christina. How do you even know Ed?"

Christina answered, "He called me back in June of 1999 because Big Pete gave him my number."

I said, "Oh, I see, so you put this stranger's word over mine? Did you think for one moment that maybe he was out to profit off our misfortune and to prey on us as bottom feeders do?"

Christina said, "Please, Belinda, he is a member of our church, and he has known Mom and Big Pete for a long time."

I said, "So that excuses him for meddling in our family business, preying off them, and taking from us? You do not even know him yourself, but you still will take his word over mine. Did you know that he was fired from a position of trust for embezzling, just like Big Pete? Did you know this he tried to pull this same scam with an elderly couple and our church pastor? He did not get away with it because the elderly couple had common sense."

Christina said, "Bull; you are lying."

I said, "See, Christina, I tell you the truth, and you still will not believe me about anything. When you lie with dogs, you get fleas. So remember my words."

Christina said, "Well, I do know Mary is telling the truth."

I said, "Did you know, Christina, that Mary did not even graduate high school? Remember how she got herself knocked up, dropped out of high school, and married the guy that got her pregnant? She worked as a hairdresser all her life, and all of a sudden, she became a manager of an insurance office within Big Pete's company. Think about it, Christina. Her former manager told me that she was fired because she lied on her application. All you have to do is call her old employer, and I am sure he will tell you the same thing. He sued her, not us."

Christina retorted, "Mary does too have a college degree!"

I said, "Oh really, and how do you know that?"

Christina said, "Because she told me."

I said, "Christina, again you have been lied to. Maybe the next time you speak to her you should ask her to send you a transcript, or maybe a copy of her degree. You could even just ask her what degree she earned. All I know is that she is a liar like the rest of our family, and that, my dear sister, includes you."

Of course, Christina got angry and hung up the phone. As smart as my sister was, she was just as blind as I was when it came to our family. I guess she would learn the hard way just like I had learned. I could do nothing to save her heart from being broken all over again.

CHAPTER XVI

Miss Patson suggested that I try to talk with my auntie and great-uncle again. I called both of them in May of 2000.

I called Auntie Bea first, and asked her, "Why are you doing this to me again?"

Auntie Bea simply answered, "Because I can." Then she continued, "Oh, by the way, Belinda, you owe Frank money for a phone bill that you never paid."

I said, "What phone bill?"

She answered, "The one that I received after you left."

I said, "That's bull! Send me a copy of it. I paid Frank in cash for it. He better stop lying and tell the truth."

Auntie Bea said, "Frank says you did not pay for it."

I responded, "Yes, I did, plus I paid for phone calls that he made as well. I paid the total of the last bill in full."

She said, "I will send you a copy, and I expect you to pay it if you want to see your stuff back. In fact, that will be added to what Ed is asking for from you."

Then she just hung up the phone on me.

I immediately called Uncle Frank and as he answered the phone, I began, "Uncle Frank, you know damn well I gave you cash to pay for that last phone bill! You are lying to Auntie Bea. Now she is trying to extort more money out of me for that as well."

Uncle Frank said, "Calm down, baby girl! Calm down! You're right, I forgot. You did give me cash for it. I cannot deny that."

I said, "Are you going to continue to lie about me, Uncle Frank? Why are you stealing my stuff?"

Uncle Frank said, "I'm not stealing your stuff. This is what Sister Bea wants. I have no other choice but to do what she says. You left me, and so did your mother. I will never trust anyone again."

I said, "Uncle Frank, what the devil is the matter with you? You are the one that practically begged me to leave, and yes I know why, because of May. Has May been part of the conspiracy to steal from Thomas and me as well?"

Uncle Frank answered me, "Yes, she is helping us keep the stuff. Ed has already taken a lot of stuff from the basement that you and Thomas had packed down in there. I don't like that guy! There is something fishy about him, but Sister Bea trusts him . . . I can't talk to you anymore, Belinda. I do love you and your momma, but I have to do what I have to do."

I said, "Uncle Frank, you are going to die a lonely miserable death, and your gravestone will read for all eternity, 'Here lies a liar and thief!' I hope you burn in hell forever for this."

Uncle Frank just simply hung up the phone on me. I could not believe the madness of my family. I didn't deserve this kind of treatment!

A few days later, I received the telephone bill that Uncle Frank lied about. I simply typed a letter stating that the phone bill was paid in full over a year ago. I mailed the letter along with the phone bill to Auntie Bea. I never heard another word about it.

About a week later, I received a certified letter through the Army post office (APO) mail system. I did not sign the return receipt request. I opened the letter, which I knew Ed had typed and then convinced my great-uncle to sign. It stated that my name was removed from his will.

I thought, "How convenient! I did not want to be part of his will to begin with." I knew this letter was written simply to hurt me, but Uncle Frank knew it would not. I was just glad that he did not take his children out of the will again, even if it was more than the lying thieves deserved. I thought back to 1999 and how I helped my great-uncle repair his relationship with most of his children. How sad I felt! All the good I had done to rebuild our family and this was my payment.

The plane landed at JFK. I made my two connections and arrived at the Snobville Airport. It was around 11:00 p.m. when I arrived because of all the layovers. I got my keys for the rental car and looked for a hotel close to Greenville. I finally checked in and requested a 5:00 wake-up call. I was so exhausted that I was asleep before my head even touched the pillow.

CHAPTER XVII

I received the wake-up call as requested. Once awake, I quickly showered and got ready for the day. I put on my navy blue business suit with a white silk blouse. I decided to keep my jewelry simple. In addition to my wedding ring, I wore the pearl ring and pearl necklace that my husband had given me when we were stationed in Hawaii after returning from our tour in Iraq.

I arrived at the courthouse several hours before I had to be there because I was too nervous to wait at the hotel. The wait felt like an eternity. I had brought a book along as a diversion, but it was not very effective. I checked my watch every few minutes, and the time seemed to drag on.

Finally, I saw Miss Patson get out of her car, and I got out of my car quickly to meet her. I met her at the steps to the courthouse.

We greeted each other and she asked, "Did you bring everything I asked you to bring?"

I answered, "Yes, ma'am, it's all here in my briefcase," and I patted my black briefcase.

Miss Patson said, "Good, we will go inside and go through it."

I responded, "Okay."

There was still a case ahead of us, so we sat in the back rows. After we sat down, I opened my briefcase and showed her the bounced checks with Bea's signature on them, along with the deposits slips. The checks had a fake business name with my sister's name and Auntie Bea's name on them. They had a post office box for the address. These were the bounced checks I had picked up on behalf of my great-aunt. I pulled out the documents that showed that Auntie Bea was the one who originally bought the Daisy house, and then I retrieved the documents that Mom, Big Pete, and Auntie Bea had signed for the mortgage. I showed Miss Patson the new CD account that was set up for Auntie Bea after Auntie Bea received the borrowed money. I showed her where the bank had combined the parcels of land, and I also showed the letter where my mother tried to have it corrected. Then I pulled out the credit card statements with my canceled checks attached; these showed that I paid off the debt except for the two accounts that Uncle Frank requested to keep. I even had the statement for the one account where I had paid half of it.

The only thing I had to prove that I paid Uncle Frank for the phone bill was a withdrawal slip for cash the day that I flew back to Germany with my airline ticket. I kept the canceled check that Auntie Bea wrote to pay Little Pete's wages (instead of paying me for picking up the bounced check on her property taxes), along with the check that I made out to her because she wanted her money back. Miss Patson was very pleased that I had made copies and kept so much documentation. Uncle Frank and Auntie Bea told Ed and the attorney that I had stolen all of Frank's money. They also claimed that I had stolen jewelry and forced Auntie Bea to give me money. I guess Auntie Bea didn't expect me to be able to have such an extensive paper trail.

Miss Patson left to use the bathroom, and I walked up to another bench that was closer to the front of the courtroom so I could hear the case taking place prior to mine.

They had just adjourned the case, and the judge was still seated. He looked directly at me and asked, "Are you a new attorney here in town?"

I turned beet red and answered, "Oh, no, sir, I just flew in from Europe. I am here because I filed a suit against my relatives."

He grinned, looked down at his papers, and said, "Oh, you must be Star vs. Mills and Gibbs?"

I stated, "Yes, sir," as Miss Patson walked up behind me.

The judge looked at Miss Patson and asked, "Then you must be the attorney."

Miss Patson smiled at him and replied, "Yes."

The judge asked, "Are all the parties present so we can begin?"

Miss Patson answered, "I believe so. I will go out and bring in the defendants' attorney."

The judge said, "That will be fine. I will clear my calendar for the rest of this afternoon for this case because I just learned the plaintiff has come from Europe."

Miss Patson said, "Thank you, Your Honor."

I turned around and saw Auntie Bea walk through the door. Uncle Frank was right behind her. I watched as they were scanned for weapons, and then I saw Ed. I recognized him from my mother's sentencing. I immediately became angry. Then I saw a young man walk through the security device. I assumed that he was their attorney. Ed had a stupid smile on his face as he looked directly at me. I imagined running toward him and snapping his neck like a twig. He was about my height, and it would have been very easy to overtake him. Instead, I gave him the deadliest stare I could possibly muster. I guess Miss Patson saw me, and she whispered, "Belinda, stop that."

I innocently looked up at her.

She said, "I know what you were doing! Now follow me."

We walked toward the front of the courtroom and sat down at the two tables with chairs that faced the judge's bench and the witness stand. After we sat, Miss Patson whispered in my ear as I looked at the judge, "You cannot allow the judge to see you acting in a threatening manner toward Ed. You know I feel the same way about that man, but we cannot conduct ourselves in this courtroom like that. Do you understand?"

I then looked over and watched Ed as he pretended to be very concerned as he helped my great-aunt to her seat at the other table beside ours. I nodded my head as if I understood her. I truly believed I had another Big Pete on my hands, and this one seemed to be even more evil, if that was possible.

I asked Miss Patson, "Why is he here?"

Miss Patson whispered in my ear again, "He is on the witness list for your godparents."

I whispered, "For what? He did not witness anything."

Miss Patson whispered her response, "I don't know yet."

I whispered back, "Can you get him out of this courtroom?"

Miss Patson responded in a whisper, "I will not have any problem doing that. I will do just about anything to keep you from attacking the creep before our case even begins."

I whispered, "Thank you."

The judge said, "Are both parties ready to begin now?"

Miss Patson and Mr. Dickerson, Auntie Bea's and Uncle Frank's attorney, stood up. Miss Patson answered first, "Yes, sir."

Then Mr. Dickerson answered, "Yes, sir."

I realized this judge was not as formal as the judge who had presided over my mother's and Big Pete's sentencing. I liked him, but I was still scared to death of him. My fate, after all, was in his hands.

Miss Patson remained standing and asked, "Your Honor, may we request that all witnesses be excused from the courtroom until they are called?"

The judge answered, "Yes, I will grant that."

Mr. Dickerson said, "I have no objections."

The judge explained to Ed why he was being excluded, but he instructed him to stay close by in preparation to testify. I loved watching Ed leave the courtroom; he did not have that smirk on his face this time.

Miss Patson gave an opening statement, and she summarized everything that happened in 1999 regarding the incidences between my godparents and me.

Then, Mr. Dickerson gave his opening statement and stated all the lies that were told to him by Ed, Auntie Bea, and Uncle Frank.

The next thing I knew Miss Patson was calling me to the witness stand.

The bailiff approached me. He was holding a black Bible in his hand, and said, "Ma'am, please raise your right hand." I automatically put my other hand on top of the Bible, and he continued, saying, "Do you swear to tell the truth, the whole truth, and nothing but the truth, so help you God?"

I answered with one hand on the Bible, and my other hand raised, "Yes, I swear to tell the truth, the whole truth, and nothing but the truth, so help me God."

Then he removed the Bible from under my hand, and I walked to the witness stand. I opened the little door, walked up one step, and sat down with the microphone in front of me. I was very nervous because I felt like I was in a soap opera or a television drama. I still could not believe this was happening to me in my real life!

Miss Patson walked toward the witness stand and said, "Could you please state your name, your address of residency, and your occupation."

I answered, "My name is Belinda D. Star, I reside in Hanau, Germany, and I am a veteran of the United States Army."

Miss Patson then asked, "Mrs. Star, could you explain to the judge why you are here?"

I answered, "Yes. My godparents, Bea Mills and Frank Gibbs, begged my husband and me to store our furniture, artwork, and family heirlooms with them until we were stationed stateside. Bea stated that it would be much safer leaving our belongings with them, rather than putting them into military storage. When my husband and I returned from Europe about a year later, Frank and Bea refused to return our property to us. Bea Mills called the sheriff, and lied to them stating we were beating my godfather. From my understanding—"

Mr. Dickerson interrupted me and said, "Objection, Your Honor."

Miss Patson asked, "Your Honor, may I approach the bench?"

The judge answered, "Yes, what's this all about?"

Mr. Dickerson and Miss Patson both approached the bench. She started whispering, and I could not hear what they were saying as they whispered among themselves with the judge. The only thing I did pick up, and only because Miss Patson had raised her voice a little bit, was ". . . Before Mr. Dickerson makes a fool out of himself . . ."

When they stopped whispering, the judge, who had been leaning forward to hear what was being said, leaned back in his chair. The attorneys resumed their conversation at a normal volume, so everyone could hear them.

The judge said, "We will take a twenty-minute recess." Then he asked the attorneys, "Would you like to use my chambers?"

Miss Patson said, "Yes, thank you."

I stepped out of the witness stand and walked toward our table. Miss Patson said, "Belinda, give me your briefcase."

As I handed her my briefcase, I asked her, "What's going on? We just started."

Miss Patson said, "I am going to prove to their attorney that he has been lied to. Mr. Dickerson is one of the few, like me, who will drop them as clients if he discovers that they have lied to him. Keep your fingers crossed and hope we have enough solid evidence to prove to him what they are."

I answered, 'Yes, ma'am."

The judge had already left the courtroom. As Mr. Dickerson and Miss Patson were leaving the courtroom, I looked over at Auntie Bea. I noticed she was having a hard time walking. She was heading toward the door, and I assumed she was going outside so she could smoke a cigarette. As I watched her, she started looking all around the courtroom. Once she saw I was the only person left, she stood up straight. Without using her cane, she walked normally toward the door that went outside. She turned her head and looked directly at me and just started laughing. Uncle Frank followed her, and he was smiling as well.

I knew that I had already been conned, but never did I realize the extent of the deceit that involved my auntie Bea, my mother before me, and now my sister. She wasn't even trying to play on my sympathies anymore. I guess it was so easy for society to be deceived by such trickery. I guess we jump to conclusions too often. Even the elderly may not be what they appear to be, and I had to learn it the hard way. I knew now it was going to be even a harder fight with this evil than it was with Big Pete. The thing that broke my heart was this was my own flesh and blood.

Mr. Dickerson followed closely behind Miss Patson as they returned to the courtroom through the same door they had exited earlier. Miss Patson was carrying my briefcase. Mr. Dickerson's face was as white as a sheet. He looked at me, and red rapidly replaced the white of his face. He smiled briefly at me as he walked past me. He walked straight out the main door of the courtroom. I know that he was headed outside to where Auntie Bea and Uncle Frank were smoking.

Miss Patson walked over to me, leaned down, and said quietly, "Belinda, I can't go out there to hear what's going on. Please go out there, smoke a cigarette, then come back in here, and tell me what Mr. Dickerson and your godparents are talking about. I proved they were lying. Your briefcase contained enough evidence to convince him."

I quickly walked outside with my cigarette pack and lighter in my right hand. Everyone was standing a few feet from the entrance. As soon as they saw me, there was instant silence. I acted like they were not there, and I walked around the corner as if I were leaving the area. Quietly, I snuck back around and stood by the corner where they could not see me. I could hear them very clearly because they resumed their conversation in normal voices. Ed was in the thick of it all.

I heard Ed angrily demand, "Why can't I testify?"

Mr. Dickerson replied, "Because there is nothing for you to testify about. Mrs. Star's mother has nothing to do with this. It is already proven it is her property, not her mother's property. I recommend, Mrs. Mills and Mr. Gibbs, that you settle with your great-niece right this minute, or you will get nothing but heartache. She is going to fight you to the bitter end, and she can prove that all of you are lying."

They continued arguing. I finished my cigarette, and I calmly walked back inside.

I told Miss Patson what I had overheard. She softly giggled and said, "They are going to settle, or at least Mr. Dickerson is going to try to convince them to settle."

I smiled and stated, "Good."

Miss Patson said, "Well, we will see in a minute."

Miss Patson and I walked back to our table and sat down. We heard the door open. We both turned around and watched as Mr. Dickerson, Auntie Bea, and Uncle Frank walked inside and sat at their table. A few moments later, the judge returned to the bench, and we all stood.

He sat down and said, "Please be seated." He looked at Miss Patson and Mr. Dickerson and asked, "Well?"

Mr. Dickerson asked, "I would like to cross-examine Mrs. Star, if that is all right with you, Miss Patson?"

Miss Patson smiled and looked at me. I nodded my head in agreement and answered, "Okay."

Miss Patson looked at Mr. Dickerson and answered, "Okay."

The judge reminded me that I was still under oath.

Mr. Dickerson approached the witness stand and asked, "Mrs. Star, how much is your property worth?"

I answered, "I think it's worth several hundred thousand dollars, but I am not certain."

He looked over at the judge and said, "Your Honor, I ask for a dismissal. By the plaintiff's own testimony, she has stated the value of the property is much more than what was declared on the warrant in detinue."

Miss Patson stood up from her chair and said, "Objection, Your Honor."

Before Mr. Dickerson or Miss Patson could utter another word, the judge, who was looking at the Schedule A, put his hand in the air, as if he were telling them to stop. He looked up from the schedule, and he asked, "Mrs. Star, I know this camera is worth more than twenty dollars. Please tell me how you came up with this dollar amount."

I looked him straight in the eye and answered, "I didn't. Miss Patson and I just guessed because we were not experts. I was here to recover my property, not the value of the property."

The judge said, "Now that does make sense."

Mr. Dickerson said, "But, Your Honor, Mrs. Star has admitted that the property she seeks to be returned is greater than this court is allowed."

The judge became very angry and said, "Mr. Dickerson, this is my courtroom. I will make that decision, not you. Mrs. Star has flown from Germany just for today, and I will hear this case. If we have to stay here all night to satisfy my judgment, we will. Have I made myself clear?"

Mr. Dickerson meekly answered the judge, "Yes, Your Honor."

Then Mr. Dickerson asked the judge, "Sir, may we have a recess so I can speak with my clients regarding a settlement with Mrs. Star?"

The judge replied, "Yes, how long do you need?"

Mr. Dickerson looked at Uncle Frank and Auntie Bea, let out a sigh, and said, "I do not know, Your Honor."

The judge stated, "I'll give you an hour. Then we will resume. We will continue until this matter is resolved."

Mr. Dickerson and Miss Patson went to one corner of the courtroom and were whispering with each other. Then, they came back to where Uncle Frank, Auntie Bea, and I were seated in the courtroom.

Mr. Dickerson asked me what I was willing to part with to settle, and how much I would be willing to pay to the defendants.

I looked at Miss Patson and she nodded her head, giving me the okay for me to answer him directly. I stated, in front of Auntie Bea and Uncle Frank, "I will give them $3,000 because that is all I can afford. They receive nothing else, and they return all my property immediately."

Auntie Bea said, "I have to think about that."

Mr. Dickerson said, "No! You either accept this, or we continue with the lawsuit."

Auntie Bea said, "Well, let me go outside and smoke a cigarette."

Mr. Dickerson looked at Miss Patson and me.

I said, "I need one too."

The attorneys, Uncle Frank, Auntie Bea, and I walked outside. Ed rushed over as soon as he saw us. I looked directly at him, and firmly ordered, "Get out of here! This is none of your business."

Before he had a chance to say anything, Mr. Dickerson said, "Mr. Weird, please remove yourself from the premises. This does not concern you." He went back to his car, clearly annoyed and frustrated.

After thirty minutes of struggling to convince Auntie Bea to make a decision, we came to the following agreement.

I would not be able to set foot on the farm or the few acres that the Daisy house sits on during the move. My husband and our friends would be able to move the property, and I would sign over the title to my mother's car. I would pay them $1,500 each. I would let them keep a bed, the wood chipper, and the grandfather clock. I would give them at least three days' notice prior to the move. The date of the move would be left open because Thomas had orders to return to the States, but we did not have an exact date. Ed would not be present or interfere with this move whatsoever.

Finally, everything was settled. I agreed with Miss Patson that even though it was extortion, it was much cheaper than paying attorney fees. So I truly had won the first round of this war. Mr. Dickerson went to the judge's chambers to let him know we had reached a settlement.

I assume the judge released the bailiff because we were his only case for the day. I had not seen the bailiff for a long time. The judge re-entered the courtroom, sat down at his bench, and said, "Please be seated."

We all sat down, and the judge said, "Well?"

Miss Patson answered, "Your Honor, both parties have settled." Miss Patson read from her notes the settlement agreement that had been reached.

The judge was very pleased. He said, "I'm glad this matter has been resolved. Are you satisfied with the agreement, Mrs. Star?"

I answered, "No, Your Honor, but I can live with it."

The judge laughed and said, "Good. Miss Patson, after the transfer of property is returned in whole to Mrs. Star, I want Mrs. Star to report to the court confirming the move."

Miss Patson answered his orders, "Yes, Your Honor."

The judge then asked me directly, "Mrs. Star, will the middle of December of this year be alright?"

I answered, "I'm not sure, but I will do my best because we do not have an exact date for the military move yet."

The judge replied, "We will put December for the date, but we can always reschedule. Well, let's call this a day, shall we? Court adjourned." Then, the judge quickly left the courtroom.

I looked over at Miss Patson, and we shook hands. As Mr. Dickerson was putting his papers into his briefcase, I extended my hand to him. He took it and said, "You're damn lucky that both Miss Patson and I are honorable attorneys. If it were anyone else, Mrs. Star, this would have had a different outcome."

I gratefully stated, "Thank you, sir."

He replied, "Don't thank me, Mrs. Star. I did my job."

That was the first and last time I ever saw Mr. Dickerson.

I told Miss Patson that I had to go because I had a flight to catch back to Germany. She said she would fax the draft of the settlement agreement to me when she received it from Mr. Dickerson.

I looked at Auntie Bea and said in a calm tone, "You can fool some of the people some of the time, but you can't fool all the people all the time." Then I left before she had a chance to respond.

Before I knew it, I had made my connections and was on the long flight headed back to Germany.

After settling into my seat, I noticed that I had the same flight attendants I had the day before. One flight attendant recognized me. As she was closing one of the overhead compartments, she asked me, "Were you on this flight coming to the States yesterday?"

I giggled and answered her, "Yes, ma'am. I'm surprised you recognized me with all the different people you see every day."

She smiled at me and said, "You looked so sad yesterday, and you were deep in thought. I just realized it was you again, but this time you look happier."

I simply stated, "I guess I am happier today."

I looked out the window and felt pride that I had stood up for myself this time against my family. I felt I was much wiser than I had been a year before. I now knew who my family was, and I had come to the realization that I truly did not need them. It felt good to know that there were good and decent attorneys and judges in the justice system. This time, I felt their outrageous fees and salaries were actually worth it. I had respect for this judge, just as I had for the one who had sentenced my mother and Big Pete. I truly hoped it would be that easy to just move our property and be done with it.

CHAPTER XVIII

November 26, 2000 found me, once again, on an airplane headed for the States. This time I was on a military commercial flight with my husband. This would be my final flight from Germany. My husband was PCSing to Colorado (permanent change of station). My husband had already completed a one-year extension in Germany, and he had been denied a second extension. Colorado was one of the states that we had put on Thomas's dream sheet. The other two locations were Alaska, and of course, Virginia. We knew wherever Uncle Sam deposited us, we would live there for the rest of our lives. We were done with moving around. I had lived that way for over 26 years, and I was ready to settle down.

On this flight, we were seated in first class. Thomas and I had only flown once in commercial first class. The seats were a little larger and more comfortable than in coach. In addition, you did not have to pay for your drinks, and they served them in glasses instead of plastic cups. Your dinner was even served with silverware and china. The only reason that we had flown first class before was because they had overbooked the flight. That was when I was still in the Army, and we both were stationed in Hawaii. Unfortunately, on a military commercial flight, everyone from the front of the plane to the back of the plane is considered coach, and you were treated as such. The only benefit was that the seats were larger and provided more legroom.

I looked over at Thomas as we were taking off and asked, "Did I tell you Christina is getting married today? This is her second husband; I think his name is Bob. Isn't it funny that she gets married in my birth month? It's too bad she didn't send us an invitation."

Thomas responded, "We wouldn't be able to go anyway."

I stated, "I know, but it would have been nice if she had called me, or at least sent me an invitation. I had to find out about it from one of Mom's letters. I think she truly deserves Mary. She invited her, and Mary is not going to her wedding."

Thomas just leaned over and kissed me on my cheek.

I smiled at him and then looked out the window. I thought back to the past three months, remembering why I wasn't able to finish my duty regarding my mother and my family.

*   *   *

My mind went back to August of 2000, the week after the warrant in detinue. I was back in Germany when I received a fax from Miss Patson. She was very upset because Mr. Dickerson did not type the agreement according to what we discussed and the conclusion reached outside the courthouse. I read over the agreement, and they had already breeched it. I couldn't believe it!

Miss Patson had included a letter in the fax. She stated in the letter that she had spoken with Mr. Dickerson, inquiring as to why he made the changes. According to Mr. Dickerson, after I flew back to Germany, Ed had contacted Mr. Dickerson. He convinced him to make changes to the agreement. Miss Patson also stated in her letter that she received my car and pickup truck title from Ed, and she sent it to the jail for my mother to sign it so that we could transfer over the one car into Auntie Bea's name.

I wasted no time faxing my reply. I stated that we would not give them anything until they removed Ed Weird's name from our agreement, and they must leave the date of the actual move blank, as previously agreed. Thomas must comply with Uncle Sam's directions, not theirs. Thomas still did not have an exact date yet, and I said that we would give them three days' notice, as previously agreed.

A week later, I received another fax from Miss Patson. She stated that she received the car and pickup titles back from the jail, unsigned. She asked me to please speak with my mother regarding this.

I called Miss Patson as soon as I could and she said, "Belinda, this is becoming ridiculous! Your godparents instructed Mr. Dickerson to deal with Ed and not them. Ed is playing nasty games, and Mr. Dickerson cannot get him to comply with the agreement. The jail has sent back the titles unsigned again, so I am going to send them to you to deal with it. I spoke with your mother, and she says they will not allow her to sign it."

I said, "But they allowed her to sign a transfer of property."

Miss Patson said, "I'm sorry, Belinda, but I yelled at your mother because I know she is lying."

I thought, *Here we go again with greed.* I said, "If she refuses to sign them, then I'll do it. Don't forget that I have that new power of attorney that you prepared. So, problem solved."

Miss Patson said, "Oh yes, I had forgotten about that, but my problem is the following: If you have to sign them, your mother could turn around and try and pull something with you. I do want to try once more to force your mother to sign them herself."

I said, "Okay, but I will sign them if it comes down to that."

Miss Patson said, "I will send an e-mail to Mr. Dickerson and let him know that you may have to sign them because of the circumstances with your mother. I will also tell him to tell his clients to correct the agreement because they will not receive anything until that is done."

Of course, my mother refused to sign the car title over, and she stuck by the lie that the jail would not allow her to sign it.

I received a phone call in the first week of September. When I answered it, the person on the other end said, "Hello, Belinda, this is Ed Weird."

I immediately became very upset and said, "How did you get this number? How dare you contact me directly."

Ed replied, "I'm sorry, Belinda, but all I'm trying to do is help your aunt, uncle, and your family."

I said, "First of all, Mr. Weird, you will address me as Mrs. Star, not Belinda! My family dealings are none of your business. I know you have stolen something, and all you are doing is covering it up by using my godparents. To set the record straight, they are also my great-aunt and great-uncle. They are not my mother's brother and sister. They are my grandmother's brother and sister."

He angrily replied, almost shouted, "I was just informed that your mother refuses to sign the car title over. You are going to have to pay an additional $1,800 for it, or I will take you back to court!"

I retorted, "Again, Ed, you do not know what you are talking about. You, Auntie Bea, and Uncle Frank have already breeched the agreement! If they weren't my godparents, I would ask the judge to have them held in contempt of court. Your meddling is only digging them deeper into trouble."

Ed shouted into the phone, "I don't care who I hurt! I am helping Bea and Frank! I'm the one who hired the attorney, and if I decide to allow you to move the stuff, I will be the one telling your husband what to do!"

There was no need for me to continue this nasty argument, so I simply said, "Don't you ever call me again. If any calling needs to be done, I will contact you." I hung up the phone.

My godparents and my mother continued to play games until the first part of November. At that point, I had to call Miss Patson and tell her we would have to drop the lawsuit because Thomas and I were PCSing. I did not want to deal with this until I was settled back in the States because the judge ordered to have all property and settlement done by the first of. Since they had breached the contract, I couldn't continue until the next year. "Can I even do this?"

Miss Patson answered, "Yes, you can. You have a two-year statute of limitations."

I said, "Great! Go ahead and make it so. I will contact you next year to start all over again."

Miss Patson said, "I will mail you copies of all the documentation that I will file to the court."

I said, "Okay."

CHAPTER XIX

We arranged our flight so that we would fly into Baltimore, Maryland, where I had lived as a toddler. We had our car shipped there a few months earlier, from Germany, so we could visit with an old Army buddy of mine, Almez, whom I had not seen in a decade or so. She was at the airport waiting for us. It was so good to see her again. We hugged like old friends, and we kissed each other on the cheeks. She and I had been through hell and back during several of our tours together. She was truly a "She Wolf." She was one of the few people with whom I had shared the tale of the She Wolf. After sharing family tales, we discovered that my ancestors and hers were from the same tale. At one point, we felt like we could have been reincarnated but laughed the silly thought away. It was still bizarre to think that our ancestors fought alongside each other, but one thing I discovered was parts of the legend my great-grandmother and her mother told were positively true. Of course, her legend was dramatically different, but at the same time, it was very, very similar. Her ancestor still owed my ancestor, She Wolf, several lives for saving her ancestor, and the debt was never paid in full. Almez had saved my life on more than one occasion. When we fought side by side, after learning the legend, I could tell she was truly a descent of the Amazon warriors. It was very uncanny how we were born on opposite sides of the earth, yet our destinies brought us together.

She treated us to dinner at a popular seafood restaurant, and we spent the rest of the weekend with her.

After I told her the story of my thieving relatives, Almez said, "If you need my help, Belinda, I will be there for you."

We continued to catch up on what was going on in her life and why had she separated from her husband. It was because of Post-Traumatic Stress Disorder (PTSD), but it manifested itself in the weirdest of forms. He would constantly be accusing her of being an alien from another planet and tell everyone that she was poisoning his food. He even told her that he was afraid she and I would kill him. Apparently, we would come to him in visions trying to seduce him and then we would turn into monsters and bite his head off. Of course, Thomas and I were very familiar with soldiers losing it, but we had never heard of anyone having hallucinations like this. Most of the time, the hallucinations dealt with combat and the soldier was reliving the past.

Almez had been born in violence because her mother and father lived in a war-torn country in Africa. Her father promised her mother that he would get her mother, herself, and her six other siblings out of the country, which he did, and he deposited them in England because he could not move them to America. Several days later, he abandoned them there. Her mother died a few days after Almez turned ten years old. She took care of her younger siblings until the local authorities found out and removed them from the home. She and her siblings were put into foster care where she was abused by her foster parents. They placed her into servitude and treated her as badly as a slave would have been treated in our own country's dark history. She learned that she could obtain U.S. citizenship if she joined one of our military branches, and she did.

She told me her sad story when we were on a secret mission in a land far away. It was almost a distant nightmare to me now, but both of us had been shot and we barely made it out of there with our team. I had practically carried her on my back since all six of us had been wounded. Of course, we took out our intended targets, but it was just another mission that didn't go according to plan. None of us wanted to be left for dead because our country could not even acknowledge that we were there. Something, I guess, I would do all over again.

Almez had loved this country and had fought for it and spilled blood for it. Now she was having a similar experience with our justice system as well. But her troubles involved strangers; she considered me her only family. She fought according to our justice system's rules of engagement and had won the battle, but she had lost the war because she was never refunded the money that was stolen from her. She was truly the spirit of "She Wolf."

CHAPTER XX

On Monday morning, Almez dropped us off where our car was being stored. After we retrieved our car, we traveled around Virginia visiting Thomas's family. Before driving cross-country, we went to visit my mother who was now in a federal prison in West Virginia.

It was actually more like a camp than a prison. There were mountains surrounding it and the view was spectacular. There was a metal mesh fence surrounding the prison grounds, and a small building instead of an entrance gate. There were no guards to be found.

We walked through the small building from the parking lot. Once inside, we saw signs instructing us to fill out a form. After filling out the form, we walked through the door that went into the prison grounds. The buildings looked like Army barracks, and I never saw a single bar or cell. We followed the signs to the visitors building and walked inside.

There was a prison guard in uniform sitting at the entrance desk. I handed her the form, and we showed her our IDs. She asked us to have a seat in a huge room with tables and chairs. She told us it would be a few minutes.

Thomas and I waited about five minutes. I looked out through the glass doors that we had walked through earlier, and I saw my mother walking down the cement path from one of the barrack buildings. I ran out of the building, up the hill, and hugged her. She had on khaki pants, a white T-shirt, and a nice thick cotton coat. She looked healthy and seemed to be the person I remembered from before her marriage to Big Pete. She was so happy to see me, and of course, she said, "You are my first family visitor!"

We walked back into the building where Thomas was sitting at one of the tables. He got up and greeted her with a hug. We sat down at one of the tables. They had a small room with vending machines on one side of the room, and Thomas asked, "Jane would you like something from the vending machines?"

As she got up from the bench, she answered him, "Of course. I have not been in this building before because you two are my first family visitors." After we bought about five dollars worth of junk food and soda for my mother, we sat back down at the table. My mother ate the candy and chips like she never had eaten them before. Thomas and I just watched her eat and told her about our adventures in Europe.

As we visited, my mother kept looking at my 14K gold loop earrings. She finally said, "These earrings I have on are a set that my friend made for me in here. We can't have the nice earrings you have in your ears, Belinda, unless you already came here with them on. Trade earrings with me?"

I answered, "Okay, but I don't want you to get into any trouble."

Mom stated, "I shouldn't if we are quiet about it. The guards shouldn't even notice."

I removed one earring and passed it to my mother under the table. She set the earring in her lap and removed one from her ear and passed it to me. I put that one in my ear as she was putting on the gold one. Then I removed the other gold earring from my ear and passed that to her as well. She was so happy and said, "Oh, I will be the envy in here now!"

I stated, "I hope you don't get robbed or hurt over them since they are gold and a bit pricey."

Mom laughed and said, "I'll take my chances!"

We walked outside. The countryside was beautiful. It reminded me of our family hollow, and I said so. Of course, my mother agreed with me wholeheartedly.

My mother seemed to be at peace with everything now, and it seemed like a large weight had been lifted from her shoulders. I wondered if going to prison would ever bring her back to what truly was important in life, and not money. It was having the love and respect from those whom you hold dear and keeping your loved ones safe from harm. Life is about choosing the right path, which is not necessarily the easy path. I had discovered in my lifetime that the correct path to take was almost always the hardest one to take. I wondered if my mother would ever see life as I did again. I was just thankful to have this one good moment in time with her. I was very thankful for this moment. I really loved my mother, for all her good and all her bad. It was time for me to let go of all the bad choices in life that she had made and hope that I had saved my mother. I just had to accept that my mother was bipolar and she couldn't control her actions sometimes. Perhaps that would change now that she was on medication for her illness. I would have to deal with it by keeping her close to me so I could protect her from herself. I needed to do my daughter's duty.

My mother told me that our pastor from the church had visited her a few times, and he always gave her communion before he left.

The U.S. Attorney also had been there to see her. He told her that they had no interest in our family property. He had inspected it, and from what he could determine, it was not worth the time or effort to fight her daughter over it since they did not know what belonged to whom. The U.S. Attorney also felt that it would be too cruel to do that to her children and would cost more money than it was worth to liquidate the property. He told her that he knew her daughter would fight the U.S. Attorney's office so hard that it would ruin their reputation in the community. He repeated numerous times that he would put this into writing. Mom said her interpretation of the meeting with the U.S. Attorney was that he did not want his office tangled up in this domestic battle because he felt that her daughter was justified after helping them. She said he also promised that if we needed their help in any way that they would testify for me regarding the family property.

"Wow!" I exclaimed. "It was the U.S. Attorney himself, not his ambitious assistant?"

Mom replied, "I don't know about her. She's not the boss; he is, so if he says that is what is going to happen, then that's what it is."

I stated, "He may have put his foot in his mouth because we may need his assistance now that Auntie Bea and Uncle Frank are playing nasty games."

Thomas went back inside for a while; he then returned to the table where Mom and I were sitting. He sat back down and gave me a puzzled look. I ignored his look and kept talking with Mom about her life in prison. Before I knew it, it was time for us to leave.

As Thomas and I were leaving, Mom's eyes welled up with tears. I ran back toward her from the door and hugged her tightly. I pressed my lips hard against her cheek and kissed her. Tears started forming in my eyes as I sadly stated, "Momma, I love you, and I'm very proud of you."

Thomas already left the building, and Mom said, "Belinda, I forgot to ask. Can I come and live with you and Thomas when they release me?

Please tell Thomas that I'm not a mooch. I will clean your house and work hard for a roof over my head and food in my belly."

I let go of my mother because we were still hugging each other. I looked into her tear-filled blue eyes and said with a smile on my face, "Oh, Momma, you know better than that! Of course, you can come live with us! Nobody else will put up with your shenanigans anyway. You don't have to clean, unless you want to. You know I will provide for you and protect you for the rest of your life. Now, woman, stop being so mushy."

She grabbed me and hugged me again, kissed me on the cheek, and said, "Be good. Go on now, get up the road, and find us a nice place to live."

As I ran to the small building that I came through when we first entered the prison, I thought, *Only my momma!*

CHAPTER XXI

After Thomas and I were settled into our new home and were feeling comfortable with our new community, I called Miss Patson. It was March of 2001. She told me her plate was very full, and she didn't really want to deal with my nasty family again. If she did take me as a client again, it would be for only me, not my mother.

I stated to her, "I really don't have much time, and I need to get this started again."

Miss Patson responded, "Belinda, I really wish I could help you. The only thing I can do right now is pass your case on to one of my associates."

I replied, "Thank you, but I think I'll just search for someone on my own. That way we can start off on my terms."

She said, "I know how important this is to you and wish you luck; may justice prevail."

I replied, "Thank you. I do appreciate everything you have done for me. You are truly one of the few honorable attorneys that I have encountered."

She answered, "Thank you. I do my best. Good luck."

With that, we said our goodbyes and hung up.

I immediately started to research attorneys in Snobville, Virginia. I must have called at least half a dozen law firms, and each one of them said that they had a conflict of interest because they had represented my mother, Big Pete, or both of them. Some of the law firms even said that Big Pete still owed them money! Finally, I reached a law firm that had not worked with either of them, and my call was transferred to Attorney Simms.

I filled him in on my situation as briefly as possible and told him all about my mother. When I was finally finished, he said, "Even your mother deserves representation. Unfortunately, our society sees her only as a convicted felon, and nobody wants to touch her. Since you started the warrant in detinue in your name, we will follow through with that. We still have plenty of time before the statute of limitations runs out. I will contact your mother as well, since you would like me to take care of some legal matters for her. I will obtain the records from Miss Patson and contact you as soon as I'm abreast of the case."

I gratefully responded, "Thank you, sir, for your willingness to take our case. I was about ready to give up. I look forward to working with you."

When my mother called again, I was able to tell her that I finally found an attorney who had no connections with our family.

She replied, "Belinda, I think that is the law firm that represented your Uncle Poppy when I tried to break your grandma's will."

I replied, "You have got to be kidding, Mom. Do you have any idea how many phone calls I had to make before I found someone who was not involved with you or Big Pete? I finally find one firm, and now you tell me they have been involved with one of your cases! I have to call Mr. Simms. Bye, Mom."

I promptly called Mr. Simms and told him what my mother had said. He paused for a moment and then said that he didn't think it would be a conflict of interest, but he would do some research, speak with the partners, and call me back.

He called back a few hours later. He told me that one of the senior partners called my mother's brother to verify that he had no part in this property dispute, and he had no issues with me retaining their services. The message given to him from my Uncle Poppy was, "Go get 'um." I felt relieved that my Uncle Poppy was on my side. No matter what he was, it was nice to have at least one member of the family on my side. It was even more encouraging that he stated it to the attorney and helped me retain his services.

As soon as I hung up with Mr. Simms, I called my Uncle Poppy and said, "Thanks, Uncle Poppy."

Uncle Poppy chuckled and said, "What did I do to deserve your thanks?"

I laughed and said, "You know, for helping me retain Mr. Simms."

Uncle Poppy chuckled again and said, "Oh, that. You're welcome, but I'm not getting any further involved, and I don't want the rest of the family to know because then I won't be able to pass you good gossip about what Bea and Frank are up to—if they know I'm actually for your mother instead of against her."

I giggled and asked, "Why are you taking her side this time?"

Uncle Poppy answered, "Because this time, I think she's right, and I think she has been punished enough. After all, Belinda, she is my sister, and I feel no one else has the right to fight with her except me. Plus, she is all I have left after your grandma passed away."

I laughed and responded, "I should have known better than to ask."

I talked with my uncle for at least thirty minutes, catching up on what was going on in his life.

After hanging up, I realized my mother's brother had really changed over the years. I liked him now, and for the first time in my life, I believed that he truly loved my mother.

I decided that I would try to call Great-Uncle Frank again and see if he would speak to me. He picked up the phone, and he started chatting with me and telling his lies of adventures in his youth that never happened.

Then he finally said, "Baby girl, I'm sorry, I will tell you what Sister Bea and that Ed are up to, but I'm still not giving you and your momma's stuff back because of them." He continued, "They did a 'no trespassing' on you and Thomas. That nasty Ed even tried to get a court order of some kind that keeps you a distance away from Bea and me. I think it has something to do with you and Thomas hurting us or something. Apparently, it was denied because they could not prove any misdoing. Bea has already had Ed sell some of your momma's jewelry and Ed keeps coming over here and taking stuff from the basement. I lied about my life insurance so Ed took more stuff and sold it to pay off that loan I took out on the life insurance for your momma. Now I'm stuck in this mess, baby girl, and there is nothing I can do to help you but tell you what's going on behind their backs. I told May a bunch of crap and I wish I didn't, and May and that Hank, her husband, have been planning stuff with Sister Bea and Ed."

I was very angry after hearing this. "Uncle Frank, how can you be sorry when you plan to go along with the dirty crap they are doing? I'm angry with you! I will call you back later."

Before I had a chance to hang up the phone, Uncle Frank asked, "Belinda, please tell your momma I do love her, and I'm so sorry."

I replied, "I'll tell her, but you don't deserve it."

I decided to call Samantha to see if she was involved in this as well. We talked for a while. I told her how I felt about my family stealing from me, and she said, "Belinda, nobody can steal your memories. Let it go."

I then knew that Samantha was part of this, but I just wasn't sure how yet. I didn't know how far her involvement went. I simply chatted with her more about it and told her I would try and call her back soon.

A week later, I decided to call Uncle Frank again. This time, there was no answer. I tried to call Auntie Bea. There was no answer. I was worried, so I then called Ed. When he answered, I asked in a calm voice, "What have you done with my godparents?"

Ed started stuttering and carrying on as he spoke, "Your uncle had a stroke, and your great-aunt fell and broke her hip. They are both doing fine and they are both in the same room in a nursing home because their insurance wouldn't pay for them to recuperate in a hospital, only a nursing home. Because they could not get private rooms your auntie requested that they be both in the same room."

I demanded, "Give me the room number and phone number. Don't even think about denying me because if you do, you better start sleeping with one eye open."

He immediately gave me both numbers. I think I scared him. After getting the phone number and room number, I hung the phone up without saying another word. I thought, *What better punishment could God give than to stick Uncle Frank in the same room with his evil sister, to have to listen to her cackling all day long?* I did not have one ounce of sympathy for my great-uncle. For that matter, I didn't have any for my great-aunt either.

I called the number, and Auntie Bea answered the phone. I did not identify myself. I simply said, "May I please speak with Frank?"

Auntie Bea asked, "Who is this? Belinda?"

I heard Uncle Frank fussing in the background, and I asked again, "Is Frank there?"

She finally passed the phone to Uncle Frank. He greeted me, "Hello."

I replied, "Well, old man, I guess God is truly punishing you to be stuck in the same room with Auntie Bea."

Uncle Frank said, "Oh, shut up."

I laughed, and I heard him chuckle too. I could hear Auntie Bea in the background pestering Uncle Frank to find out who was on the telephone. Finally, Uncle Frank said to Auntie Bea, "Bea, mind your own business. It's one of my girlfriends." I could even hear Auntie Bea make a huffing sound. Uncle Frank then said, "Girl, I better hang up now before you get me into more trouble with Sister Bea."

I stated, "I really miss you, Uncle Frank.

Uncle Frank said, "I miss you and your momma. Call me at home at the end of next week, baby girl, and I will talk with you then."

I replied, "Okay, Uncle Frank, I will."

The following Thursday I called Frank, but there was no answer. I kept calling and called for two days, but no one answered the phone at the Daisy house. I decided to call Samantha. She answered the phone, and we exchanged greetings. It sounded like she had been crying, so I asked what was wrong. She started sobbing, and she told me that her father died. They thought he was dead for at least three days before someone discovered it. Auntie Bea, who was still in the nursing home recovering from her broken hip, had been calling him. After not getting an answer for several days, she finally sent John to go check on him. John found his body on the floor in the kitchen. Samantha asked me if I would call May and tell May to call her. She requested that I not tell May anything because she wanted to tell her.

I agreed with her and stated, "It's not my place, but I will call her for you." Apparently Samantha did not have long distance service on her phone because her teenage children had used her phone to make numerous long distance calls.

After hanging up the telephone, I regretted telling my godfather that he would die a lonely, miserable death because that is exactly what had happened to him. I sat there for a few minutes trying to absorb it all. I felt sorrow and regret for what had been a wasted life. I dreaded telling my mother because of how close they had been. I knew that the news would hurt her.

I picked up the phone again and called May. I told her she needed to call her sister as soon as she hung up with me. It was very important. I told her that I loved her. She tried to get me to tell her what was going on, but I simply stated, "Just call your sister, now."

I then called Sam and told him to call his sister Samantha because I knew that he and John did not speak to each other. I was once again doing my daughter's duty, despite the fact that my godfather had stolen from me.

When my mother called from prison, I told her that Uncle Frank had passed away. As I expected, my mother was very upset and hurt. She sobbed throughout the rest of our conversation. She wanted to go to his funeral. I told her that I would talk with the prison warden to see if something could be worked out. She told me that he was gone for the day. I told her that I would try to speak with her first thing in the morning. After I hung up with my mother, I called the prison nurse. I told her that my mother had just been informed that her favorite uncle died. I said my mother was very upset, and I asked if they could give her something to help her calm down. The nurse said she would consult the doctor but thought they could do something for her.

Over the next several weeks, I was in frequent communication with all four of Uncle Frank's children, my cousins. I also worked on making arrangements so my mother could attend the funeral.

When speaking with Samantha at one point, she said, "Belinda, you are more than welcome to come to Daddy's funeral since you are, after all, his one and only goddaughter. We feel you did good things for all of us, and especially for encouraging me to make amends with him when you were here in '99. I'm thankful, but your mother is not welcome and she may not be here."

Because Samantha had opened Pandora's box, I replied in a hurtful tone, "How can you say that? Especially after all the good things my mother has done for all of you?"

I could hear anger in Samantha's voice as she retorted, "I'm just not going to get into it with you, Belinda, because I know you will bully me into changing my mind, and then I will have to deal with my brothers and sister."

I sadly responded, "Okay, Samantha. What about my family property that is stored in the Daisy house? Can I come and get it?"

Samantha replied sharply, "I'm not part of that! You will have to talk with May! She has moved into the house. I swear, Belinda, I'm not getting involved in all of that."

I asked in shock, "What? When did she move in? Oh, never mind, I'll call her to find out what is going on. Goodbye, Samantha."

I took a deep breath and then called May at the Daisy house. I really hoped that what Samantha had told me was not true. I didn't want to believe that my baby cousin, even though she was a bottom feeder like the rest, would do that to me. Much to my dismay, May answered the phone. We gave our greetings, and I ask if I could come and get my things out of the house the following week. She told me that she wasn't going to give me anything back and that I could kiss her ass! Then she hung up the phone on me.

Well, now I knew what I was dealing with. Instead of it being just my godparents, now it was my great-aunt and Uncle Frank's four kids, along with Ed. Could things get any worse? I should never have asked that because of course they could always get worse.

I had to tell my mother that she was not welcome at Uncle Frank's funeral. Of course, she cried, and I tried to console her. "Mom, you know that Uncle Frank would want you there! I'm not sure what his kids are up to, but it seems like the nasty bug has bitten them too. I think they are in cahoots with Auntie Bea and Ed. You know that you were Uncle Frank's favorite."

Mom calmed down and with a soft sob said, "I know, Belinda, but it breaks my heart that I can't be there to give him one last kiss and to say my final goodbye."

My mother and I made no attempt to attend Uncle Frank's funeral. My mother told my sister Christina about Uncle Frank. She did not attend either.

CHAPTER XXII

Mom was scheduled to be released later in the year, and I had to get things prepared for her. I spoke with the prison parole representative and was told that she would have to be accepted in the community prior to relocating because she still had to serve out her supervised release. At the time, Thomas and I were renting a small two-story house because we had not been stateside very long. We decided we would purchase a larger home before my mother was released.

After the arrangements were made, two local probation officers had to inspect the house that we were renting to ensure it was a good environment for a newly released prisoner. At first, the two gentlemen were cold and not very pleasant. I started talking about the human side, telling them about my family and why my mother had committed her crimes. One probation officer stated that they very rarely hear the emotional side of the story and the reasons as to why a criminal committed their acts. After hearing our story, he had empathy toward my husband and me—and even toward my mother. Before they left, the probation officers told me that they were accepting my mother in the community after meeting with me.

Thomas and I purchased our first home! We hired a contractor to paint the inside. We hired other contractors to remodel the inside of the house. The remodeling was in full swing when Mom called and excitedly said that she would be released soon! I purchased an airline ticket for her and had it mailed to the prison so she did not have to ride a bus from West Virginia to Colorado. Mom mailed a catalog to me. She had marked clothing and jewelry that she liked. I ordered her the business suit and shoes along with some inexpensive jewelry to wear with the suit from the catalog. She also sent me the address of the halfway house where she would have to stay for three months. She said she had two hours after her airplane landed before she had to report there. I told her we would get her there in time.

CHAPTER XXIII

Before I knew it, it was August 5, 2001, and the beginning of my mother's freedom from the prison. Thomas and I were excitedly driving to the airport to pick up my mother. We were running a little late because we had a nosey neighbor checking out all the inside construction going on in our new home. I gave her the tour and tried to subtly ask her to leave, but she just wasn't taking the bait. Finally, I told her that I had to go pick my mother up from the airport, and we had to leave.

As we pulled up to the curb of the local airport, I spotted my mother! She was wearing the new outfit that I had purchased for her. She was standing on the curb outside the arrival terminal looking up and down the road impatiently waiting for us. Thomas did not even have a chance to come to a complete stop before I opened the door and jumped out of our car. It was a bad habit of mine from my Army years.

I ran up to my mother, and before she even realized who it was, I yelled, "Momma! I'm here."

Mom quickly dropped the purse, which I had also bought for her, and ran to me. We hugged, and she started kissing me all over my face. By then, Thomas was beside us, and she hugged and kissed him as well, but she only kissed him once on his cheek.

I expected her to be upset with us for being late, but she did not say anything as we loaded her one small bag and her purse in the trunk. I apologetically said, "I'm sorry we're late, but I had a nosey neighbor who I had to get rid of."

Mom looked at the ground as she spoke to me, and I realized when Thomas and I visited her that one time, she did the same thing. I did not like seeing this broken woman in front of me. She said in a happy but timid voice, "Oh, I had just gotten my luggage. It wasn't very long at all."

Before we got into the car, I hugged my mother again and whispered in her ear, "It's just about over, Momma. You will not have to bend down and lick another person's boots again. I promise. Come back to me when you are ready. You just have to put this bad experience in the box that's in your mind and close the door. I promise you, before long, this brief moment of your life will be a distant nightmare. It will just take some time. I love you, and don't you ever feel you are beneath your own flesh and blood." I let go from my hug, and my mother was crying. I looked deep in her blue eyes and said with conviction, "I love you."

Thomas knew exactly what I was talking about because he and I had been on the battlefield too many times, and we were some of the few soldiers that knew how to deal with battle stress. It's very hard to do, but it can be done. I would know because I had successfully done it. Thomas took my mother in his arms, hugged her, and said to her, "You will be safe soon, just a few more months to endure. Toughen up, little soldier, and find yourself again."

I knew my mother's experience was nothing compared to our experiences, but I recognized the similarity. I knew how my mother felt because of what she had to endure; for her it was the same thing as being tortured. I knew my mother, and her feelings were just as strong as if she were on a battlefield fighting for her life to survive.

My mother reached for me while Thomas was still hugging her and I joined the hug as well. Thomas and I hugged her, giving her our strength to get through the emotional anxiety that came with battle fatigue.

Thomas and I let go of my mother, and I said with a smile on my face, "Why don't you sit up in the front seat with Thomas, Momma? That way you can see more of the prairie. I want to take you to our new home so you can see it before we take you to the halfway house."

Mom wiped the tears from her cheeks, smiled, and answered, "Yes, I would love that very much. I want to see our new home."

Mom chatted the whole way to our house about her airplane trip and about an old codger who was trying to pick her up on the airplane. We laughed, and it seemed she was coming back to us. I knew it would just take a little bit at a time. I knew I was going to have to help her get through the aftermath of what she had endured and of what she had yet to endure.

We pulled up into our little driveway, and my mother's eyes became large, and she exclaimed, "Wow! Your house is almost as big as mine was." Then she started to cry.

I said to her, "Momma, this is your home too, so stop crying."

Thomas said, "Yeah, Jane, stop crying. This is your home too."

Momma quickly jumped out of the car and almost ran straight to the front door. She waited impatiently for Thomas to unlock the door. She barely restrained herself from running inside as she said, "Oh my goodness, Belinda, you guys have all kinds of construction going on in here!"

Thomas said, "That's one reason we got it so cheap. The house isn't that old, but the owners before us did some crazy things to the inside of it."

We gave her a grand tour of all three floors and showed her the backyard. Before we knew it, it was time to take her to the halfway house, which was on the other side of town.

I had Thomas go through my mother's favorite fast-food drive up window. I wanted her to have a dinner that she had not had in a while. She wolfed it down as we were driving her to the halfway house. Before any of us were ready, we arrived at my mother's temporary home.

Thomas and I were very disappointed because the halfway house was an old rundown motel. The outside was dingy and looked as if it had not been cleaned in years. The whole building seemed sad and neglected. My mother turned her head to face me in the back seat, and she gave me a disappointed look.

I simply stated, "Just a few more months, Momma, and then this will all be over. You can do this; just reach down deep inside yourself. Remember, you have our love and our strength to pull from too."

Thomas parked the car, and we went inside. We stood in line with my mother and talked as we waited for her turn to be checked in. Finally, after about thirty minutes, it was my mother's turn. They gave her forms that stated what they were going to do to her. I read them. They were going to check my mother's rectum and vagina for any drugs and strip-search her! I became very angry and stated it to the woman, "Hasn't my mother been through enough while she was in your prison system? For God's sake, she didn't go to jail for drugs. Why must you people constantly have to violate her in this manner? She is a little old lady, and I can attest that she doesn't do drugs."

Before I knew it, a female officer came toward me and in a stern voice said, "We don't want any trouble. Your mother's ass still belongs to us, and it is in your best interest to let us follow our procedures."

Mom looked at me and said, "It's alright, honey. I'm used to it now."

I let go of my temper. Thomas hugged me, and we sat down at one of the filthy tables they had in the large room.

I simply said to Thomas, "She didn't do drugs! She stole! There is no reason why they have to constantly stick their nasty fingers where they don't belong and rape her over and over again."

Thomas said, "I agree with you. I don't understand our nasty justice system at all. I could see if she went to jail for drugs, but she didn't, so in my opinion it is wrong for them to degrade her in such a manner. No wonder your mother has been broken. To me, it seems that in your mother's case they are violating her constitutional rights. Unfortunately, there's nothing we can do, honey. Once she is out of this hell, we can begin to fix her mentally."

I softly replied, "I hope we can." Then, I boldly stated in a louder voice for them to hear me, "In fact, it's a waste of taxpayer's money to begin with regarding drugs, and a violation of our constitutional rights as well as our God-given rights to put whatever we choose into our own bodies. What gives one American any right to dictate to another what they can or cannot consume, and then punish them for it because they believe differently?"

Thomas leaned forward and whispered in my ear, "You are right, honey, but there is nothing we can do. We understand what liberty is, but most of our fellow countrymen have forgotten why our ancestors came to this country to begin with. They forget why our servicemen and servicewomen continue to bleed for it, and why we as individuals must join together to take our country back. Unfortunately, there are only a few of us. When you fear making your own choices, right or wrong, then this shows we have lost our way as a nation."

I simply nodded in agreement with my husband.

CHAPTER XXIV

After we PCSed, the first thing I had done was find a job that I knew I would enjoy without too much stress. I was hired by a company located on Fort Carson, which was only a few minutes from our house. Every day after work, I faithfully visited my mother. On the way, I either went home to pick up some leftovers from the previous night's dinner or stopped to get some fast food for her. I did not want her to have to eat any more of the food produced there than she had to.

By the third week after her release, my mother had a job working at a catalog company. Of course, the probation personnel would embarrass her by showing up every few days and speaking with her supervisor. They made sure the company knew about her crimes as soon as they hired her.

Now I know why people who go in our prisons always seem to go back to a life of crime. I thought our society was supposed to give the individual a second chance in life after they paid for their crimes, but I now know this is so untrue. During the entire time my mother was incarcerated, I made sure she had money for her basic needs and some luxuries also. Everyone knew that my mother had family support, even if it was only my husband and me. I do have to give Christina credit for writing to my mother; at least she did that.

My mother even told me a lot of the friends she made in prison would tell her how envious they were of her because she had a family member who provided for her, emotionally and financially—someone who cared about her well-being. They would always tell her they wished they had someone that loved them as unconditionally as her daughter did. My mother said she would tell each and every one of them, "The one good thing I did in life was giving birth to my daughter. I'm truly blessed that God gave me a guardian angel. He also gave her to all of you. My daughter was a soldier, and she gave her life for all of us so that we may enjoy the basic freedoms that this country was founded on. Even if it's not perfect, we have her and men and women like her who are willing to die so that we may have these freedoms."

I would just giggle each time she told me that and say, "Don't you think you were being a bit overdramatic about me?"

She would say, "No. I may be a crook, Belinda, but I have always been proud of you, your sacrifices, and your accomplishments; even if I never told you so."

By the fourth week, I was allowed to take my mother on Saturdays and Sundays from 10:00 to 6:00 p.m. The first place I took her was shopping to buy undergarments and some clothing for work. She couldn't buy them herself because she had not received a paycheck yet. I had already set up a checking account with direct deposit for her. Then we went to a brewery for a late lunch. She ate that hamburger slowly as if she were savoring each bite of it and sipped a glass of wine in the same manner.

After she finished eating, she said, "Oh, it's amazing what you miss when it's taken from you. I did the same thing with the fast food burgers as well."

I asked the waitress to prepare the same meal as a "to go" order. Mom put her hand on top of mine on the table and said with tears in her eyes and a smile, "Thank you, baby."

I said, "Oh, Momma, you haven't called me that since I was a child."

Momma grinned and said, "No matter how old you get or how tough you get, Belinda, you're still my baby. No matter what your sister thinks of me, she is still my baby too."

I just giggled at my mother. We spent the rest of the day driving all over town.

Our day flew by, and before I knew it, I had dropped her off at 5:55 p.m. at the halfway house. She started to cry as she watched me back out of the parking lot. I threw the car into park, took off my seatbelt, jumped out of the car, and ran back to my mother. I hugged her and kissed her, and then I said, "Just two more months, Momma! Just two more months, and you will be free again."

She kissed me on both of my cheeks and said, "I know, but the more freedom they give me, the harder it is."

I said, "You're tough, you will get through this." I got back into the car and went home.

On Sunday morning, Thomas and I went to go pick up Momma. We decided to take her on post because every time she had visited me around the world she always asked me to take her on the military post. I knew she would enjoy it, so that's what we did for the morning. Then, we drove her up in the mountains and took her out to a nice restaurant.

CHAPTER XXV

September 11, 2001 was a typical morning for me. I always went to work early and prepared for my business day while it was quiet. I guess it was about 7:25 a.m. when I sat down in my cubicle and began preparing to do the daily bookkeeping as part of my workload.

My fellow co-workers were slowly drifting into our large office area. They greeted me as they entered. My telephone rang, and I was a little surprised because we were not yet officially open for the day. The caller ID showed that it was my sister, Teresa. She and her husband, Mark, had been stationed at the Pentagon for a while. They, like Thomas, were still active duty.

I was surprised and happy to hear from her. Due to our busy lives, we had not spoken in a couple of months. Before I had a chance to say anything, she shouted in my ear, "Belinda, it's me, Teresa! We have just been attacked! The Twin Towers were just hit and are in total flames!"

I fearfully asked, "What? Where are you, little sis?"

She answered, "I'm on the west side of the Pentagon, outside."

I asked, "Who did this?"

Teresa answered, "Guess, and it's three words."

I stated, "Oh my God! Osama bin Laden!"

Teresa said, "Yes! It looks like he did it this time. You already know that all of our intelligence agencies have been warning the previous administration and this administration that this was going to happen. They were saying that even when you were still in the Army. Not to mention that he has already tried this before."

I replied, "I know, that bastard has been a thorn in our country's ass for a long time. Even before I was in! He was even at it when we were just children. I wish we had taken him and his evil followers out a long time ago. My God, there must be thousands of people in those buildings!"

She sadly replied, "I know they have murdered thousands of our people."

I ordered to her, "Get away from the Pentagon. I have a bad feeling."

Teresa said, "I have already started walking away to the outer parking lots, but I can't get a hold of Mark because he is in some classified meeting this morning."

I exclaimed, "Oh, my God!" The gravity of the horrible news started sinking into my brain. "Why do our leaders think we are so invincible? Why aren't leaders trained to realize the simple truth is that we must never underestimate our enemies! No matter how small they are."

Teresa simply answered, "Because we have become a country filled with arrogant, selfish people that think peace is just a given, and protection is unnecessary. You know this, big sis. I called because I'm worried about you and Thomas. You know the mountain ain't no secret anymore, and I'm afraid they may also attack you guys there."

I responded, "I know it isn't a secret anymore, and that's why I know they wouldn't be that stupid to bring our commander-in-chief here. I'm sure they have other good hiding places for him." Then I continued, "I will call Thomas as soon as I hang up with you. Just get your ass away from that building because I'm afraid they will hit you next before us."

Teresa yelled in the phone, "Oh my God, there's an aircraft flying straight into—"

I heard a loud explosion, and it sounded like my sister fell to the ground. I started yelling, "Little sis! Little sis! Answer me. Are you hurt?"

Within a second or two, my sister picked up the phone. "I'm hurt, Star. I'm hurt real bad. I can't move my arm. I wasn't far enough away from the building. My husband—"

I heard the phone drop again, and I knew my sister was seriously injured. I hung up the phone and looked up from the desk. All twenty of my co-workers, my manager, and my supervisor huddled about me. They all had fear in their eyes. I ignored them and called an old, well-known phone number that exists only in the memories of a select few. It is the number to a top-secret division called, "Ghost." There are several organizations like it in our country. It is one of a few top-secret, highly classified organizations that are buried so deep in our military that I don't think our commander-in-chief even knows they exist. When you are handpicked by one of these organizations, it is considered an honor. It means that you are superior at what you do. My husband and I had carried out many ghost missions for our government.

I gave my old, classified identity code, hoping that it was still active. Thank God an old buddy of mine, who owed me several favors, answered the phone. Tanner angrily said, "How the hell do you still have your clearance number for this line?"

I answered in a firm, direct tone, "Never mind that. The Pentagon has just been hit. My sister is hurt badly. She's outside on the west side of the building. Get some emergency help there immediately."

Tanner said in a firm tone, "Star, the towers were just hit, but I will do what I can. Are you sure? I don't even know about the Pentagon being hit yet."

I angrily stated, "Damnit, Tanner! I was on the phone with Lighterman when an unidentified aircraft flew straight into the building. Get your ass up and do something! You owe me, damnit!"

I was yelling at him, and I didn't give a shit if anything was classified or not. Tanner said, "Okay, I'll take care of it. Call me back in a couple of hours—better yet, give me a number to reach you."

I answered, "Damnit, Tanner, you got my number on the damn ID. Stop playing games, you know it's me! Just hang up and help my sister, her husband, and everyone else over there." I hung up the phone. I knew he would do something, and I knew I would not hear from him.

I'm sure that my codes would be disconnected once they realized after all these years they never had deactivated them. Thomas and I hadn't been under their command for a very long time at this point.

I turned around, and the entire department was still huddled around my desk. I knew they did not understand anything that was happening because they had not been in the military. Most of them were civilian spouses or civilians, and I knew they never heard of the crap I was talking about on the telephone. I didn't really care at this point. I had no intentions of explaining anything, at least not right now. I had more important things to take care of.

I picked up the telephone again and called my husband. He was in a meeting with his commander and others. I barked at the specialist who answered the phone, "I don't give a shit if he is in a meeting or who else is in that meeting! This is a national emergency! Get his commander as well!"

Within a few minutes, Thomas answered the phone and angrily said, "Belinda, what the hell is the matter with you? You know better than this. I'm in a meeting—"

I cut him off and stated in a loud voice, "We have just been attacked! The Twin Towers in New York City were hit and the Pentagon! Lighterman was on the phone telling me about the Twin Towers when another unidentified aircraft flew straight into the Pentagon. She is concerned that we may be next. Find a computer with internet access, and see if it's on the news yet. Do it now! We need to get this post on red alert! ASAP!"

Thomas, in a confused and disbelieving tone, said, "What? I didn't hear you correctly."

I responded, "Yes, you did. Are you by a computer? Talk with your commanders, and alert the post commander now."

After I hung up the telephone, my manager finally spoke. She said, "We have one computer at one of the empty desks that we can get straight to the news."

I said, "Okay."

Miss Pent said, "I don't know how to use the internet."

I said, "That's okay. I do."

The entire office personnel followed my manager and me to the computer. I turned it on. She typed in her user ID and password. It took me two seconds to pull up the video that was playing over and over again footage of the attack on the Twin Towers. We all gasped with horror. My supervisor, Mrs. Lane, said, "This can't be real. This must be some kind of hoax."

I replied, "Tragically, it has happened, and I hope our commander-in-chief goes for the jugular. I pray to God that he picks a place for the battlefield to keep those terrorists off our soil so this never happens again."

All the ladies in the office were agreeing with me wholeheartedly. One of my younger co-workers asked, "Belinda, what does this mean regarding our husbands who are active duty?"

I answered passionately, "War! Pray to God that our commander-in-chief takes the fight to their lands and away from ours."

We then heard the sirens going off, and I could hear a muffled voice over the intercoms that were placed throughout the large military post. I rose from my chair and ran outside. All the women in the office followed me. Once outside, I could hear the announcement better. "This is a red alert! All non-essential personnel must evacuate immediately! This is not a drill!" The male voice repeated the statement continuously.

From where we were standing, we could hear several telephones ringing in our office area. I walked back inside the building, and all the ladies followed me. I walked to my cubicle to see if one of the phones was mine. Sure enough it was.

I picked up the telephone. It was Thomas. He stated, "You were right, baby. The commander-in-chief just put the entire country on full red alert. You need to go home. You know this is going to be a mess. Don't expect me home tonight."

I responded, "I expected that. I love you, and I'm going to go to Mom's work now after I call my father."

Thomas replied, "Call your father when you get home. Just get off the post! Now!"

I rebutted, "But Lighterman is hurt."

Thomas said, "I know, but it will not do you any good to call your dad from work. Go home, baby, just go home. I need to know that you're safe."

At that point, I wished I was still wearing a uniform. I felt totally worthless, and there wasn't a damn thing I could do about it.

My manager was standing beside me with a questioning expression. She asked, "What do I do?"

I answered, "You must comply with the post commander's orders. We are non-essential personnel. We must evacuate now."

She asked, "I need to call my boss to get authorization, don't I?"

I picked up my phone and passed it to her as I told her, "Call and cover your ass."

She obediently did as I told her and dialed the number of her boss. She spoke with him for several minutes. After she hung up the phone, she said to everyone within hearing range, "Everyone, leave now; even those of you that live on post. You all will be paid regular time."

Everyone collected their purses and lunch bags and left. As everyone was leaving the building, my manager turned toward me and asked, "What will happen tomorrow?"

I stated, "It will be a new, fresh day. We Americans have an uncanny way of rebuilding. We wipe our tears away, lick our wounds, bury our dead, put all our differences aside, pull ourselves up out of the ashes, and seek justice against those that murdered our own. That much, I know. With all the problems and imperfections we have had since the beginnings of our country, we always have an uncanny way of righting a wrong—at least a big chunk of us do, and that's good enough for me."

My manager hugged me as she started crying and said, "Our world has changed, hasn't it?"

I answered as I hugged her back, "Yes, ma'am. It will never be the same, but our soldiers will seek justice on behalf of our people. That much I can definitely promise you. I know our commander-in-chief will do whatever is necessary to take this fight to their soil and keep them off ours. The next blood that spills will be theirs, and all others like them. Someone will pay, and the price will be high. I pray our commander-in-chief unleashes our great military forces to strike this evil virus down with a fury from hell that has never been seen before. If our blood is what they want, then they shall have it because we will drown them in it."

I guess what I said scared her because she let go of her hug and looked in my eyes like a scared cat that had been trapped in a corner. She said, "I'm scared."

I responded, "I'm sorry, I spoke too much because I'm very angry."

I left the post and went to pick my mother up from work to drive her back to the halfway house in case they released her from work. As I suspected, her management released their personnel early as well. Mom was sitting on a bench outside reading a book.

Before I had a chance to put the car in park, my mother was trying to get into the car. I hit the unlock button, she got into the car, reached over, hugged me, and asked, "Did you hear?"

I answered, "Yes, ma'am, Teresa called me. The Pentagon was hit when she was talking to me, and I think she has been hurt badly."

Mom said, "You need to call your father."

I stated, "I know, and I'm thinking of driving to find her. With all the chaos that is occurring there, I have no other choice but to do the drive. It will probably take me a couple of days. I have a couple of old contacts that I'm sure will help me find her quickly, if she's not already at a military hospital. I have no idea if her husband, Mark, is okay or not. If I don't receive a call from him tonight, I'm going to plan to leave first thing tomorrow."

Mom ordered, "Just call your father so he can tell your sister's mother. Drop me off and take care of this."

I answered, "Yes, ma'am."

We were silent for the rest of the trip to the halfway house. Each of us was deep in thought, contemplating the events of the morning.

As I was walking into the door of my home, the telephone was ringing. I ran to the phone in the kitchen and quickly picked it up. It was Mark, Teresa's husband. Before I even had a chance to speak, he said, "Belinda, Teresa is okay. She has a slight concussion, a broken arm, and a few minor cuts and bruises. Apparently she was pretty close to the building when it was struck."

I asked, "Thank God, where is she?"

He gave me the information and asked me to call our father to let him know that they were okay.

Mark then said, "Belinda, please tell him not to come. There is total confusion and chaos in this area. Tell him that Teresa or I will call him as soon as we can. You know how your father is. He is worse than the two of you put together."

I laughed and said, "Nobody could be as bad as Teresa and I put together."

Mark chuckled and said, "Yeah, I believe your father is worse."

Then Mark said, "Oh, by the way, I have a message to give you from a person by the name of Tanner. I found him and this brigadier general helping Teresa. I found it odd because they were not helping anyone except for her. After he interrogated me as to whom I was, he simply gave me a message to pass to you and Thomas. Tanner's message is, 'Well, Stars, you can take my name out of your black book now. The affair between us is over now, but Tanner's back door will be left unlocked just in case the two of you want to come out of the rain again.'"

I just laughed and stated, "That guy is a stinker."

Of course, I knew exactly what the message implied. Mark of course did not and asked, "What the hell did that mean? Was he the one setting up the operations that we did? I never knew who the boss was since we all were taking direct orders from you."

I laughed and simply stated, "If I answered you, I'd have to kill you."

Of course, Mark laughed because he thought I was joking, but I was sure he suspected that Tanner was the one giving the orders during that time in our lives.

After hanging up the phone, I thought, *I'm truly glad that part of my life is over.* The crazy things that Teresa and I did, in the name of our country, were frightful, but of course, I would do them all over again. I knew that Mark, Thomas, Teresa, and I lived and breathed: "God, country, family, duty, honor, and loyalty." Believe me, we fought for it. But our time was done, and a new generation had risen to take our places to protect our freedoms and the interests of our great country. I could only speak for the four of us as I thought, *We are true-blooded patriots of our great country.*

I picked up the telephone again and called my father. Of course, he already knew we had been attacked. The entire country knew by then. He was worried because he could not get through to Mark and Teresa, or Thomas and me. He said he left a message on my answering machine. I looked down at my answering machine and realized the message light was blinking.

He said, "All the telephone lines must be jammed."

It occurred to me that he thought that was the reason he couldn't get through to Teresa.

"Daddy, I just got off the phone with Mark. Teresa was outside the Pentagon when it was hit. She's okay. She has a slight concussion, a broken arm, and a few minor cuts and bruises. She's at Walter Reed now. Mark has asked that you not visit right now. He said the area is crazy, and it is safer if you stay where you are."

Daddy replied, "Thank God! Did you hear that, honey?"

Teresa's mother, who had picked up the phone when she heard it was me, started crying.

She asked me, "Belinda, are you sure Teresa is going to be okay? I think a broken arm is serious, even though you consider it minor."

I told my stepmother, Teresa's mom, "I'm sorry, ma'am. I didn't mean to make light of the injuries of your daughter, please forgive me. Mark and Teresa just don't want you guys to worry and don't want you driving to her at this time."

Daddy then asked, "Who did this to us?"

I answered, "I think Osama bin Laden, the terrorist, organized this because he has tried such an attack before. I would truly be surprised if it was someone other than this evil, vile individual."

Daddy then asked, "What kind of name is that? That's not a Christian name. It's Muslim. Why would a Muslim attack us?"

I answered, "Daddy, just follow the news, and you will know why. Basically, in my opinion, he is a male chauvinistic pig who hates women, hates America, Jews, and any other religion or government that doesn't believe the way he does. He hates us because we flaunt our wealth, we drink, we smoke, we live, we have fun, we are free, we treat our women with respect and equality, and we worship our God as we choose. We have the freedom to argue among ourselves without violence, the freedom to talk, talk, and talk some more, to give our opinions without the threat of violence, and he is basically a jealous antichrist that thinks his god put us on this earth to worship and cater to individuals like Osama bin Laden.

"But the God we worship, from my understanding, says, 'It's a sin in itself to try and force your beliefs and religion upon another.' Yet this character states otherwise. He tries to force his beliefs and religion on the world. Our God doesn't dictate his followers to murder people in his name, but this character murders in his god's name. It is murder when you kill innocent people and then call for a war. You call war first, and you must have a country to declare war, and he has no country. He claims a war against us and the world in God's name. Is that not a type of antichrist? Our God, from my understanding, says if you commit suicide it is still murder and a sin, but this Osama character dictates that his god says killing oneself in his god's name is an act of bravery. So the bottom line is that this is one more battle of good versus evil, a never-ending battle among mankind."

Daddy responded, "I can't argue with you. I have raised you and your sisters to believe exactly that; to have open minds and acceptance of other cultures and beliefs. You are correct, we do have these freedoms, and it makes logical sense that individuals like this cretin are jealous of our beliefs. You are right, Belinda, our country is up against pure evil."

My father and I talked further regarding the attacks that had happened against our country. He was an educated man with a deep knowledge of history and warfare, and talking to him made me feel strong and empowered.

After hanging up the phone with my father, I called my attorney, Mr. Simms. He was already aware of what had happened. I requested that we postpone our trial date until the latter part of the next year. He agreed and hoped that my great-aunt would agree so that we could put our battle to the side as our country prepared to go to war against the bloodthirsty terrorists who had attacked us. I told Mr. Simms that I would call my great-aunt after speaking with him and try to convince her that we needed to put our differences aside for the time being.

After speaking with Mr. Simms, I called my great-aunt. No matter her other faults, I knew she loved our country as much as I did. Of course, she agreed to put our fight to rest until the end of the next year. We agreed that we would resume it at that time.

Mr. Simms called within the hour and said he had received a phone call from my great-aunt. She agreed that we should put our personal fighting to the side until the end of the next year. A few minutes later, he received a phone call from Ed, who was trying to resume our court date for September 17, 2001. Mr. Simms told Ed that our country had just been attacked. The nation was on full alert, and he had nothing to do with this family matter. He advised Mr. Weird to speak with my godmother. Then he received a phone call from her new attorney, who agreed to put the trial on hold for the time being. I called the airlines and canceled my flight to Virginia. That fight could wait.

In the following days, months, and years after this tragic, bloody day, the newspapers and news were filled with basically the following information: *America under attack! Thousands dead! On Tuesday September 11, 2001, terrorists flew passenger planes into the World Trade Center's Towers One and Two. Both towers collapsed. Another plane flew into the Pentagon causing the building to partially collapse. On a fourth plane, the passengers fought back, and the plane crashed into a field near Shanksville, Pennsylvania.*

Throughout the next several months, our commander-in-chief made speeches to our great nation, vowing that we would use any force necessary to contain this vile evil, to unleash our military forces, and demand justice for our people.

Before our country knew it, we had taken the fight to Afghanistan and Iraq, their soil. Little did the country know that we would be there for a very long time, keeping the battle contained on the other side of the world. Even though we won the battle in just a few short weeks, we would be destined to police the area and spill more blood to keep the evil contained. "An American soldier never surrenders."

Our enemies may have tortured us, killed us, bombed us, but our soldiers would keep coming wave, after wave, after wave . . . . We would wear down our enemies until they drowned in our blood. Through the ashes and destruction, great leaders would rise in the years that followed: Colin Powell, General Petraeus, Condoleezza Rice, Senator John McCain, and so many more. Our great military forces would be tested to the brink, but we would "never surrender" our American way of life. No one would take our God, our freedom, or our flag from us.

"I pledge allegiance to the flag of the United States of America, and to the republic for which it stands, one nation under God, indivisible, with liberty and justice for all."

CHAPTER XXVI

In September 2002, I was once again on an airplane heading for Virginia. This time I was flying from Colorado instead of Germany. Once again, I was returning because of my daughter's duty, and I hoped that this time I could complete it. My mother was accompanying me this time because she was now a free woman.

After we settled into our seats, my mother patted me on the hand and said, "I hope Auntie Bea and Frank's kids return our property to us this time."

I looked at my mother and sadly said, "I hope so."

I looked out the window as we were taking off and thought of all the events that had happened in my life and in the lives of the citizens of my beloved United States of America.

In January 2002, I was employed by a government contractor as a supply technician/material expeditor/administrative coordinator. I was the right-hand for my manager who supervised over 300 personnel. Although I did not officially have the responsibility of supervising anyone, I was the one who everything was filtered through. The majority of my co-workers were veterans. Each branch of our great military was represented in our company. My manager, whom I greatly respected and admired, was a retired CW5 (Chief Warrant Officer).

The company I worked for on September 11 had been closed because all the bookkeeping offices were consolidated. There was now only one location in another state. They did offer me a job, but I would have been bored and miserable working for just a two-man contract. God had blessed me! About a year before, I had submitted my resume to my current employer. One week prior to the office closing, they called and offered me a job. I took two weeks' vacation and started the new job.

As I mentioned earlier, my mother had completed her time at the halfway house. She moved in with Thomas and me two days before

Thanksgiving in November 2001. We had established our continued lawsuit in my mother's name, hoping that my great-aunt would be more inclined to return our property to her than to me.

My mother seemed to have recovered from the humility of prison life and was becoming increasingly more self-assured. Unfortunately, despite her medication, the bipolar disorder showed its ugly fangs from time to time. This had been a strain on my relationship with her and also on my marriage. I loved my mother dearly, but there were days I just couldn't handle her mood swings. She had episodes of mania where she went shopping and spent her entire paycheck. She had opened numerous credit accounts and was very close to reaching their credit limits. On the other side of the spectrum were her depressed days. There were days she hated herself and everyone around her. During her episodes of depression, she tended to read more into a conversation than was really there.

If I told her that I'd clean up a mess later and for her not to worry about it, she'd reply, "What? Don't you think I'm good enough to clean up after you? I know that's the only reason you want me to live here—so I can clean up after your lazy ass."

A few minutes later, she would be in tears begging me to forgive her and not to make her leave. She would begin saying that everyone would be better off if she were dead. I had to hide her pills so that she didn't overdose, which was something she had threatened several times.

Living with someone suffering from bipolar disorder was like a never-ending roller-coaster ride. Love is the only thing that can get a person through it, and sometimes that doesn't even seem like it's enough. I had learned over the years to give my mother space when she was at either of her extremes because when she was like that, she could not be reasoned with. When she returned to the middle, where she was stable, then we could talk. I prayed that someday there was a medication that could keep her level.

CHAPTER XXVII

Since her release from prison, my mother had put a great amount of time and effort into trying to build a positive relationship with my sister Christina. She had finally come to the conclusion that she could only have a relationship with her if she followed Christina's rules. From my vantage point, it appeared as if my mother had to do all the giving, and Christina simply did all the taking. Neither my mother nor I trusted my sister, and we did not tell her anything regarding the lawsuit. Unfortunately, my mother felt obligated to try to create a positive relationship with her youngest daughter. I was all for trying to work things out as a family, but there came a time when the line had to be drawn. It hurt me to see how my sister was hurting our mother.

Mother tried to tell Christina over the telephone how she and I felt about the situation with Auntie Bea and Uncle Frank, but Christina replied, "I will not give up my family for you."

I would never forget those words. Christina did not know my mother had my speakerphone on at the time. I heard every word, and I also witnessed the devastation exposed on my mother's face. I guess Christina did not realize that her nuclear family unit was our father, our mother, our father's second wife, and our two other sisters. Christina continued to believe that Auntie Bea and Uncle Frank were her godparents even though she had been told otherwise.

As Christina kept spouting her stupid, ignorant rhetoric, I watched as tears cascaded down my mother's cheeks. I could not take it any longer. I spoke up and said angrily, "You have just given up part of your family now, Christina—Mom and I! To set the record straight, you stupid girl, Grandma and Uncle Poppy were chosen as your godparents; and Auntie Bea and Uncle Frank are mine! Even I know that! You don't even know your own history, stupid girl! You're so self-absorbed—"

My mother cut me off and said, "Christina, you're my daughter. You came from me, and no matter how much you hate and loathe me, I still love you. I always will be here for you. I'm sorry for what I did; I'm sorry I hurt and embarrassed you. I'm sorry for every wrong thing that has happened in your life, but I will never stop loving you. You are my daughter."

Christina said, "This is not about any of the mistakes you made, Mother, it's about you stealing from Auntie Bea."

Before my mother had a chance to say anything, I angrily replied, "You stupid, stupid girl! This is about Auntie Bea stealing from you and me, not Mom stealing from her! Auntie Bea is stealing my history, my life, my present, my future, and everything in between! I swear, I will never forget your deceit, your betrayal, and your apathy for our feelings! I'm tired, Christina! Tired of walking on eggshells around you! You're not worth it anymore! Maybe it is because you are an atheist by your own admission. Maybe it's because you don't believe in God, and you think there are no consequences for your actions, but there are consequences. There are always consequences."

Mom said, "Enough, Belinda. I love you, Christina, and that's all that matters to me. I will call you soon."

Christina said, "I love both of you, but I'm not giving up my family for the two of you."

I sadly replied, "Christina, we are your family; not these other people. They are extended family, not part of your nuclear family, but I guess you do not understand that."

I thought back to a phone conversation I had with Christina in March of 2001. At the time, I was preparing to continue my lawsuit. I had previously talked with her regarding what my godparents had done.

A few days later, she called me and said, "You stole all the jewelry! You're a jewelry thief!"

I told her, "How can I steal something that belongs to me?"

I knew then that my mother had been up to old tricks again: divide and conquer.

I didn't quite understand why, but it seemed like my mother had been pitting my sister and I against each other our entire lives. Maybe it was just her mental illness. I didn't know.

CHAPTER XXVIII

I looked over at my mother and wondered if she now regretted dividing my sister and I for most of our lives. She needed us united now.

I looked back out the window of the airplane. I thought and prayed that justice would be served against my great-aunt for her deceit and thievery. Miss Patson was correct when she said that because I had protected Bea, she would not be punished for her crimes. Because she never had to suffer negative consequences for her actions, she would continue them. Now I was on this airplane, preparing to fight for justice against the very woman I had protected. I put everything I had into protecting her, and now I had to fight her.

Big Pete was communicating and fighting with my mother through their mutual friend and attorney, Bill Bank. He was trying to coerce my mother to sign forms giving up her half of his retirement from the insurance company where he had worked. He was also trying to divorce her even though he was in prison serving out his sentence.

I was very proud of how my mother was handling his harassment. She did the right thing and promptly contacted the U.S. Attorney's office. She reported all the hidden income. After Big Pete died, they would put a garnishment on his benefits and took the entire monthly payments, which of course hurt her in the end.

All of a sudden, Big Pete changed his mind. He had Bill Bank contact my mother to tell her Big Pete didn't want to divorce her. He realized that he still loved her, and he pleaded with her to forgive him.

On December 29, 2001, Bill Bank called my mother. He told her that Big Pete had died the night before in the prison. Bill told Mom that before Big Pete died, he had asked to speak with my mother. He was unable to call her because they did not have my telephone number at the prison. My mother was shocked.

She said, "He had cancer? He's dead?" She then handed the phone to me and I turned on the speakerphone.

She had not known that he was dying. Bill Bank said he was very surprised that my mother did not know Big Pete was ill. He said the prison had Christina's phone number on file as the only contact. Since that was the only number they had, that is who they had called. Big Pete spoke to his stepdaughter during the last few moments of his life instead of his wife.

Bill asked, "Doesn't Christina have Belinda's phone number?"

I replied that she most certainly did. Bill said he could not understand why she didn't give the prison my number so that Pete could speak with my mother, especially since that had been his dying request. I simply replied that I could not believe the depths to which my sister had sunk. I thanked him for calling and hung up the phone.

After this conversation, my mother was emotionally distraught. I don't think I had ever seen her cry so hard before. We were both in shock and confused as to why Christina was communicating with my mother's husband. It was not her place at all to do so! How could Christina even consider Big Pete family since Big Pete and my mother hadn't even married until after the two of us had reached adulthood? I was very glad Big Pete was finally out of our lives forever. If he had lived, I knew that my mother would have gone back to him, and the nightmare would have started all over again. No matter what my mother said, I could not believe he would continue to be a changed man after he was released. Some people are just too vile to change. I believe there is a point that, once crossed, there is no returning from it.

As I reflected on the conversation and my sister's betrayal, I could feel my anger rising. The more I thought about it, the more the anger mounted in me for this act of my sister. My mother never did anything to Christina like this and she didn't deserve such treatment!

My mother contained her emotions, to some degree, turned the speakerphone on, and called Christina. The moment Christina answered the phone, my mother asked her, "Christina, why didn't you tell me Big Pete was sick? What did he say to you before he died?"

Christina answered in a triumphant tone, as if she had won some battle, "Oh, Big Pete told me he was sorry, and that he loved me, that he lied to me because he needed to survive. He was sorry for trying to lay the entire blame on me because he didn't want to go to prison, and he said he was sorry for what he did to Belinda. He just wanted his family back."

My mother and I both looked at each other. We both knew Big Pete thought he was talking with my mother, trying to make peace and give closure to my mother before he died. Nothing he said was about Christina at all, yet she acted as if he were saying it to her personally. She acted as if she were the wife and not my mother. I could not believe this vile individual came from the same womb that I did! I honestly believed, at that point, that Christina was mentally ill. If by some slim chance she was not, then she was positively the most vile, evil individual I had ever encountered in my life. That was pretty sad to say because I had encountered the lowest of the low during my time in the Army.

Then my mother asked, "How long have you been in touch with Big Pete, Christina?"

Christina replied, "Since Belinda was in Snobville in '99 and went back to Germany. He has been writing me and calling me since he has been in prison."

At this point, my mother's tears were gone, and anger was written all over her face. I was amazed at her self-control as she kept it contained. Then my mother asked, "Christina, what have I done to you that would cause you to take away the closure that I needed from my husband?"

Christina's voice had an edge of anger as she replied, "You are divorced! He didn't call you, he called me to give me closure, and to remind me that he is the good guy and you hurt him."

I thought that didn't make a bit of sense at all.

Mom then said, "Christina, Pete begged me not to divorce him. So what are you talking about? We were still married."

Christina said, "What? That's a lie!"

Mom said, "No, Christina, it's the truth! Christina, does Bob know what you have done? Isn't Bob your new husband? Why are you doing this to me? There is no reason for this at all. Are you mentally imbalanced?"

I could not stay silent any longer. I said, "Christina, Big Pete was our mother's husband, not yours. You have done something that can never be taken back. This is the last straw with you. I promise you, nasty little people like you always get their comeuppance."

With that, Christina hung up the phone.

I started to vent my anger toward Christina, and the next thing I knew, Mom was defending her. She said, "She is still my daughter too, and I love her."

I said, "Mom, how can you forgive this?"

Mom said, "I don't forgive her, but I love her."

We must have argued about this for several minutes, and my last comment was, "That is your choice, Mom, but I'm not going to have anything else to do with her. I know she is your daughter and my sister, but this in unforgivable! To intentionally interfere in a marriage when one spouse is dying is beyond my comprehension. She should put her energy into her own marriage. I bet she wouldn't like it if someone did to her what she just did to you."

I must have gotten an evil gleam in my eye because my mother said, "Stop that thought right now. I will not tolerate you meddling in your sister's affairs!"

I replied, "Oh, Momma! You know I would not stoop to her level, but it is fun thinking about it."

Mom chuckled and rolled her eyes. At least I got that out of her. She then looked sad again and said, "I guess I have to make the arrangements."

I left the room to give her some privacy. I went to the next room so I could hear her if she needed me.

CHAPTER XXIX

My mother called the prison number that Bill Bank gave to her. She was in the process of making arrangements to have Big Pete's body cremated at the prison when she was informed that Ed had already made arrangements to have the body flown back to Snobville. The body had already been transferred.

My mother and I could not believe this. Her husband's body was already at a funeral home located in Snobville. My mother called Bill, and he was totally baffled about the situation as well.

Bill called the funeral home immediately and then told us that Ed had made arrangements, purchased a casket, and given the funeral home additional instructions. The funeral home thought that he was a relative of the deceased and did not question anything. He had scheduled a viewing, and from Bill's understanding, it was scheduled for that evening and the services would take place the following day at our church. Bill said he was going to call Ed next. He instructed my mother to call the funeral home and take charge of this mess.

After speaking with Bill, my mother picked up the phone and called the funeral home. She stopped all the arrangements Ed had made and informed them that she would make all the arrangements. She informed them that she was the widow, not Ed. The funeral home gave her a list of prices for everything. She told them that she would have to talk with her daughter because her daughter would be paying for everything.

After everything was stopped regarding Ed's plans, my mother and I sat down and discussed what her wishes were. We decided to have Big Pete's body cremated because that was all I could afford to do for my mother, and it was what she originally had wanted. We would then have his ashes mailed to my house for my mother.

My mother called the funeral home and told them her decision regarding Big Pete's remains. She then put me on the phone. I gave them my credit card information to pay the bill in full. Then, I passed the phone back to my mother, and she turned on the speakerphone again.

The funeral home owner said, "Ma'am, I'm so sorry for this entire mess. I have never encountered someone trying to steal a body before in my life. I have already spoken to Mr. Weird, telling him that he had no right involving this funeral home in some kind of twisted scam. He claimed that Big Pete had a will and he was the executor of his estate, but he could not produce any documentation. He stated it was a written letter, which he could not produce either. Mr. Weird stated that you were divorced from Big Pete and you had no legal right. I spoke again with your attorney, Bill Bank, and he stated that Big Pete did not have an estate, nor did he have a will, and he was still legally married to you; a divorce never took place. Again, ma'am, please forgive me during this time of mourning for you."

My mother said, "There is no need for an apology. I completely understand your confusion. I never thought in my wildest dreams someone would stoop this low."

My mother then called Bill again. He had spoken with Ed, Rick Cart, and our pastor at the church. Bill said that Ed claimed that Big Pete left all of his possessions for Ed to sell to pay for his burial, and that whoever paid for his burial could keep everything he owned. He claimed that he wanted to be buried with his glasses on. Bill even stated that anyone who truly knew Big Pete also knew he hated to wear glasses. He always wore contacts. Big Pete had always complained about glasses. Of course, my mother and Bill laughed because they knew Ed did not know Big Pete on a personal level. Bill stated that Big Pete did not have a will, but Ed claimed Big Pete told him that Bill had the original will, which was not true. Ed claimed that Big Pete told him that he was divorced from my mother, and that was not true. Bill informed Ed that he begged my mother to drop the divorce and forgive him. No divorce ever took place. Bill told him if he continued interfering in Jane's family business, he would take legal action against Ed without charging Jane's family a dime.

Bill said he also told Ed that he knew, for a fact, from the letters that Big Pete sent to my mother in prison, copies of which went to Bill, that Pete only had a few things left. He wanted those few things to go to his wife, my mother. Ed told Bill that he was going to fight us and keep us from taking the body. Bill said he threatened him again that if he tried he would be very, very sorry. Ed became scared. He told Bill that they were going to hold a memorial service at my church, and there was nothing we could about it. Bill stated that he first had to get permission from my mother.

As soon as we hung up the telephone, it rang. It was the new pastor from our church in Virginia. She said she believed everything Ed had told her about what my mother did to Big Pete. My mother said if she continued down this path, she would report her to the bishop. It is not her place to take sides in situations such as this. She had been lied to by Ed, and she should speak with the old pastor before jumping to conclusions. He would tell her what Ed tried to do to him by meddling, and he could inform her about how Ed appeared to profit off families in crisis. He mainly tried to prey off the elderly. Ed was terminated from a position of trust for embezzling, just as Big Pete had been. My mother also told her if she was going to take sides, she should at least do her homework first.

My mother did give the pastor her permission to allow Ed to have the memorial service, but he wasn't going to get the body. She told the pastor she wanted all her property returned from these people.

We found out later from Bill Bank that only Ed Weird, the Cart brothers, and Ed Gibbs showed up for Big Pete's memorial service. These were all people who had mooched off my mother and Big Pete for years, and now they were all part of the conspiracy to steal everything that was left of my family property.

Two weeks later, we received the box of Big Pete's ashes. Thomas and I were concerned because we did not want his remains in our house. My mother started crying and complaining because she didn't want us to put him in the shed located on our small parcel of property. So we finally agreed to allow my mother to store the ashes in the closet of her bedroom.

Thomas and I felt strongly that if Big Pete had lived, my mother would have gone back to him eventually.

CHAPTER XXX

The airplane landed, and we had to transfer flights. After we were in flight again, the flight attendant was serving drinks. I asked for a vodka and tomato juice. I pulled out my notepad and started taking notes of my thoughts to remind me why I was here and what I was fighting for as well as prepare myself for trial.

As I was jotting down random thoughts, my mother asked, "What are you doing?"

I answered, "A small timeline and reminders of what has happened over the years."

Mom asked, "Can I help?"

I answered, "Sure."

After reading my list, I realized that my country and I were now on parallel paths. We were both seeking justice for crimes committed against us. Even though the crimes that were committed against me were nothing compared with the tragedy of September 11th. This was just coincidence, but I still felt that I had to fight harder. Thinking about what my country was going through made me want justice even more.

After several layovers and flights, we landed at the Snobville Airport. We picked up our luggage, and I got the keys to the rental car. I checked us in at the cheapest hotel I could find. My mother fussed and complained the entire time because the room was dirty and they needed new mattresses. Neither one of us slept very well the entire time we were there. I had us in town two days before the trial so that we could prepare.

The following morning, we met with Mr. Simms in his office. We went over the details of the trial that would take place the next day. This was just another bloodsucker that charged ridiculous prices for his services. Even though I felt he was a nice person, I just didn't think he was as sincere as Miss Patson had been. This appeared to be just another case to him.

CHAPTER XXXI

Before I knew it, my mother and I were at the Greenville courthouse. It was about 12:30 p.m. and the lawsuit did not begin until 1:40 p.m. I had stopped by a fast food place on the way, getting a cup of coffee for myself and some lunch for my mother. I was too nervous to eat.

As we sat on one of the courthouse benches waiting for our case to be heard, we saw John Gibbs and May Harp, Uncle Frank's oldest son and youngest daughter, Auntie Bea, Ed, and Mr. Pricket, their new attorney. There was also an older woman who followed close behind them. My mother whispered to me, "That is Nancy Greed." I had only spoken with her on the telephone in 1999, when I was trying to convince her to honor her husband's word. He had agreed to sell the Mills farm back to Thomas and me for the amount he paid.

Why is she here? I wondered. Then I remembered the loan sharking that her husband was involved in with Big Pete and everything made sense.

Now I had a face to accompany the voice of Nancy Greed. All the diamonds, jewels, and expensive clothing could not take away the white trash that stained her demeanor. She had beady dark brown eyes, a long straight nose, thin lips, and a long slim face. She tried to hide her large ears with the style of her short black and gray, teased hairdo. She was not only an ugly person inside, but her physical appearance was evil and shady. No wonder her husband had cheated on her; she deserved it.

John was just a lazy piece of shit and now in his older years he looked it. I considered him a coward simply because he was gay and did not have the courage to come out of the closet. Even though my mother's family were backward hillbillies, they would have naturally accepted him for what he truly was. They loved him and I did too, which is why I kept his secret all these years. It had not been my place to tell, and I never would. He maintained the lifestyle of a heterosexual man and married a dysfunctional, ugly, obese woman. He had been cheating on her with other men for years and they even have a child.

I considered him a simpleton like his father and he allowed his wife to rule him. His wife was an only child who had been spoiled all her life. When opportunity presented itself she would take, and if need be, steal without any remorse for whom she may hurt.

I still can't believe May was one of the ringleaders in all this. Even though she was slightly mentally retarded, she had graduated from high school. She was still a pothead and from what I had learned, she was addicted to cocaine and heroin.

Her physical appearance proved the addiction to these deadly drugs. She was much younger than I was, but looked older than my mother. She was missing several teeth, and the ones she still had were black and rotten throughout the front of her mouth. She was shorter than I was and my mother's clothing hung off her. I thought to myself, *You can dress up a turd, but it's still a turd when you look at it or smell it.*

May had married another pathological liar and a pedophile as the gossip had been told to me. It had been rumored that May and her husband poisoned his adopted mother but they were never arrested or prosecuted. They sold the farmland under her husband's brother's nose. I researched this myself and discovered that they did sell the land. It did not surprise me that these rednecks could have committed murder it. What was really sad was that May's young daughters were also addicted to drugs.

Ed was nothing but a conniving piece of shit like many of the other thieves. I believed him to be the ringleader because none of my relatives possessed enough knowledge of the law to get this far. He portrayed himself as a cocky little bastard. He was dressed down with blue jeans, and strutted around with his boots on displaying his bowed legs. His short legs were so bowlegged that they formed an oval when he tried to stand straight. He was half-bald with beady brown eyes, and he stood no more than five feet two inches tall, if that. He looked to be about fifty-six years old.

The bailiff ordered everyone into the courtroom, "All rise." The Honorable Judge Colburn entered the courtroom. "Please be seated," he said as he motioned to us.

He then addressed the attorney that was representing my mother. "Mr. Simms, if we could address the status of your case. Is the matter ready to go to trial?"

"Yes sir," he answered.

Judge Colburn acknowledged, "All right. This case appears first on the court's docket. This is also a date on which the court will be able to stay for the balance of the afternoon but will not be able to extend its session late into the evening. So the second case on the court's docket is going to have to be adjusted. I'll let the two of you stand aside and I'll address that case."

The judge spoke with the attorneys regarding the case after my mother's and instructed them that their case would be heard the following day.

He then addressed the courtroom again. "The case of Jane King vs. Bea Mills, et al. shall now commence. Let the record reflect that Mr. Simms, counsel for the Plaintiff, and Mr. Pricket, counsel for the defense, are both present. Counselors, shall we—"

Mr. Simms broke in, "Your Honor, I believe that there are some individuals who may be present in the courtroom who will be testifying today."

The judge replied, "We're going to address that. Don't worry. The court will organize the case for you. I'm going to let the two of you get situated; then we'll call the case and I'll proceed according to my usual custom. Let's give Mr. Pricket's client a chance to be seated. Take as much time as you need, ma'am."

Auntie Bea was doing her "old lady" routine. She was walking to her seat with her back hunched and leaning heavily on her cane. On second thought, maybe she wasn't pretending anymore. Who knew since she had broken her hip? Maybe she couldn't walk normally anymore.

Once she was finally seated, the judge continued. "Before we proceed, let me address the counsel. I think both attorneys heard my remarks earlier. This is one of those unusual days where my options in terms of extending the session are somewhat limited; having said that, I do expect to be able to remain until about 5:30 or 6:00. I would certainly hope that we can finish the case by that time. If for some reason we can't, we may have to make an adjustment, but I do expect to stay at least through that period of time. Normally I can continue later, but this happens to be a day in which I don't have that—I don't have that option. All right, so we are addressing then the case of Jane King vs. Bea Mills. Mr. Simms, you represent the plaintiff?"

Mr. Simms answered, "Yes sir."

The judge then asked, "Mr. Pricket, you represent the defendant?"

Mr. Pricket answered, "Yes, sir, Your Honor, there are two defendants. Mrs. Bea Mills is one defendant and then the estate of Frank Gibbs is the other one. And there are two executors for that estate present for today's case. May Harp is the co-executor of Mr. Frank Gibb's estate."

The judge asked, "All right. I take it both parties are ready to proceed?"

Both attorneys confirmed that they were ready.

The judge asked, "All right. Is there a motion to exclude witnesses?"

Mr. Pricket motioned to do so, and Mr. Simms agreed.

The judge then looked out into the courtroom and said as he pointed to the small gateway leading into the two tables for the defendant and plaintiff, "All persons who are present in the courtroom who expect to testify, if you'll come forward at this time please. Come through the rails right here and remain in this open area to where I'm directing you."

Ed and I walked through the gate and stood beside the attorneys in front of the judge's bench. When I walked by Mrs. Greed, who continued to sit in her seat, I saw that she was laughing at me. The judge continued speaking, "Anybody present who expects to be called as a witness, come forward at this time unless you're a party." May started to rise. The judge looks at her and said, "Ma'am, you can stay where you are. The parties can remain where they are. All right, I'll ask counsel to check the identity of the witnesses and make sure they're satisfied. Check the courtroom and make sure there isn't anybody present who should be designated as a witness." He then asked both attorneys if they were satisfied, and they answered that they were.

The judge then addressed Ed and me. "There has been a motion to exclude witnesses. What that means is that the two of you are going to have to remain outside the courtroom until you're called in to testify. Now, during this period of time, there are a couple of instructions that you have to follow. First, you are not to discuss the case with one another, nor should you discuss it with any other individuals. The exception to that rule is if you wish to do so, you may speak with either of the attorneys who are involved in the litigation. They are aware of the court's practice of limiting those conversations to a one-on-one discussion. That is, the attorney and the witness speak without any other persons present.

"The other instruction that you must follow is that you must remain in close proximity so that we can call you in for your testimony as soon as possible. We certainly recognize and appreciate that there is an inconvenience to witnesses in cases such as this. On the other hand, I'm sure both of you can understand that the only way that we can try a case such as this is to have the witnesses available and ready to testify.

"Now, on that note, we have a witness room down the hallway that can be used. It's a reasonably nice day now, although it might become a little bit rainy later on, but if you wish to sit right outside the courtroom, the court will give you permission to do that. The key point, however, is that you don't have permission to leave the court's premises. We'll request your testimony as soon as we possibly can. On that note, I'll ask that the witnesses be excluded and thank you for your attendance.

"All right, the witnesses have been excluded. Mr. Simms, do you wish to make an opening statement?"

This was the last I heard because I went outside with my coffee and smoked a cigarette.

CHAPTER XXXII

While I was excluded from the courtroom, my mother's case continued. Mr. Simms started with his opening statement.

"Your Honor, the evidence will show that the defendants in this case are the aunt and the estate of the deceased uncle of the plaintiff and that approximately three years ago the plaintiff was charged with and awaiting trial on charges that potentially could have incarcerated her for a substantially long period of time. Under those circumstances, the plaintiff made arrangements with her aunt and then-living uncle to store her personal belongings at their properties here in Greenville.

"The evidence will also show that this was done as a favor by family members and at that time, there were no animosities or conflicts between the parties.

"The evidence will also show that there were no discussions at that time regarding storage fees or terms for the storage of these items. The agreement between the parties was essentially a favor among family members.

"Subsequently, the relationships between the parties changed when the plaintiff was incarcerated, and it became clear that she was not going to be able to repay her aunt, Bea Mills, the approximately $200,000 that her husband had borrowed from her. This debt was discharged in her personal bankruptcy.

"The plaintiff even stole from her own children trying to make things right with her aunt even though it was the plaintiff's husband who borrowed the money and not her. The plaintiff considered it borrowed money even though her aunt legally gave her and her husband the thirty-three acres as a gift for the $100,000 borrowed, and money paid over a decade to maintain the land.

"The plaintiff even sent her own daughter, a veteran of the U.S. Army, to her aunt's rescue to bail her aunt out of trouble with the law because

Bea Mills was a party to fraudulent check scams. As you can see sitting in this courtroom, Mrs. Greed can testify that the plaintiff's daughter requested that Mrs. Greed sell the land back to her daughter, but Mrs. Greed refused to honor her husband's verbal contract.

"The evidence will show that the plaintiff's aunt became angry and upset with her, as is reasonable and understandable. As a result, she has refused to allow the plaintiff to recover her personal belongings.

"The evidence will show that the defendants have acknowledged that this property is the plaintiff's and, in fact, have offered to return it to her in the past. No dispute exists as to the ownership of this property, and while it's understandable that the defendant is upset with the plaintiff, she has no legal right to retain the plaintiff's personal property."

Mr. Pricket then made his opening statement. "To please the court, Judge, the motion for judgment was couched in terms of an action for detinue. Under the common law, which governs this case, in order to prevail, Mrs. King is going to have to prove that she has a property interest in the items that she seeks to recover. She's going to have to prove that she has the right to immediate possession of the items she seeks to recover. The items must be capable of identification. They must be of some value, no matter how small. And finally, the defendants must have possession of the items sought.

"In the case you will hear today, Judge, the primary issues will focus on ownership. The evidence, we believe, will show that prior to May of 1999, Pete King and Jane King owned a residence in Snobville, Virginia. The result of their arrest was an indictment for a large number of federal crimes involving fraud, banking schemes, and other acts of financial impropriety. Mr. and Mrs. King plead guilty to charges in federal court. In the course of this, their personal residence in Snobville entered into foreclosure. In order to prevent a loss of their jointly owned possessions, a gentleman by the name of Ed Weird, who will be a witness today, moved these belongings from Snobville to Greenville to be stored in the homes of Mr. Gibbs and Mrs. Mills. Mrs. Mills is the aunt of Mrs. King, and Mr. Gibbs was the uncle of Mrs. King.

"The evidence will show that although Mrs. King made the arrangements for the move, she did not consult in advance with either Mr. Gibbs or Mrs. Mills. When Mr. Weird and the moving trucks arrived in Greenville with these items, Mrs. Mills and Mr. Gibbs were totally surprised. Nonetheless, because they were Mrs. King's possessions, the items were stored in their respective homes.

"In April of 2000, almost a year later, Mr. King conveyed in writing to Mrs. Mills his interest in these possessions. That transfer is evidence by a written document, a copy of which will be offered to you in evidence today. At that point, Mrs. Mills, we contend, became an owner of a one-half undivided interest in whatever possessions had been delivered.

"Now, I might point out to the court that when these goods were delivered, there was no inventory and no contracts were signed. The items were contained in various boxes and parcels, many of which remain unopened.

"Subsequent to this transfer, there was an action instituted in the general district court in this county by Mrs. King's daughter. In that action, she claimed ownership through a warrant in detinue of many of the items that Mrs. King is now claiming are hers. That case was disposed of in general district court by agreement between the parties. Pursuant to the agreement, several motor vehicles were transferred to the daughter, Mrs. Star. And one of the exhibits that you will see today, Judge, is a document signed by Mrs. Mills to Mrs. Star's attorney regarding the detinue case.

"Unfortunately, Judge, the detinue papers or the exhibits were destroyed and the original property transfer signed by Mr. King was included among those documents, but we have a copy and a witness who is going to be able to identify his signature.

"That's basically what the evidence is going to show as far as the status of these goods. Significantly, Judge, as part of her plea agreement with the government, Mrs. King executed a pleas agreement. The pleas agreement is dated June 21, 1999. And in this agreement—and I think this goes to the heart of the case and it also supports the demurrer we filed in this case. In this agreement —Mrs. King states the following at page nine, paragraph L. 'I agree to immediately forfeit all rights, title, and interest in any property owned by me and in my possession or the possession of relatives at my direction to the United States as partial restitution in my case.' We take the position, Judge, that this document alone deprives her of ownership and any interest in the property, which she seeks to recover today. And on the basis of this document, we will ask you to dismiss her claim.

"If the court is not disposed to dismiss her claim and is inclined to think she has some interest in the property, we have filed a counterclaim.

In our counterclaim we are saying, if this is your property, we stored your property since May of 1999 and we ask for some storage fees because Mrs. Mills leases her property and home from Dr. Greed. Mr. Gibbs also leased his house and land from Dr. Greed. Upon his death, it was transferred to Mrs. Harp. Approximately twenty percent of Mrs. Mill's house is taken up with this, for lack of a better word, stuff. Approximately seventy-five to eighty percent of Mrs. Harp's house is taken up with this stuff.

"We will offer evidence as to how much rent they paid and what percentage of the unit these possessions consumed so that if, indeed, the court finds that Mrs. King has some interest, then she should be required to pay Mrs. Harp and Mrs. Mills a storage fee for having the items stored there. We are asking for $100,000 for storage.

"Because we felt strongly, Judge, about Mrs. King's lack of ownership in this property, we've also asked for an award of attorney's fees. Even though—even though there's no underlying agreement, we feel that, based on this pre-agreement, which she signed, giving up her interest to all property she may own, she does not have the right to even be here forcing these individuals to come here, expend considerable sums of money to defend this action. That's our opening, Judge."

The judge replied, "All right, all right. Mr. Simms, you may proceed with your evidence. You may call your first witness if wish to proceed with ore tenus testimony."

Mr. Simms replied, "Yes, Your Honor, we call Bea Mills please."

The judge looked at the court's secretary and said, "All right. Ms. Solomon, you can assist her if you wish. Mrs. Mills, take as much time as you need. I'm going to let her seat herself before she worries about the oath. I'm going to let her remain seated while the oath is administered. Take your time, ma'am. Ma'am, if you could turn around this way. The clerk's going to come over here. I'm going to let you remain seated because of your condition. Ma'am, do your best to try to speak up as well as you can. It's very important that we all be able to hear and understand you. I know you're not used to this, but do your best to project your voice; all right? You may proceed, Mr. Simms."

Auntie Bea placed one hand on the Bible, raised her other hand as the bailiff said, "Bea Mills, do you swear to tell the truth, the whole truth, and nothing but the truth, so help you God?"

Auntie Bea answered softly, "I do."

Mr. Simms started his examination of Auntie Bea. "Mrs. Mills, my name is Mr. Simms and I'm Jane King's attorney. Could you let me know during my questioning of you today if can't hear me?"

Auntie Bea looked up and said, "I can't hear you very well." This was her first lie under oath. There was nothing wrong with her hearing. In fact, her hearing was better than mine was. I groaned when I was told that the judge fell into her ploy and instructed Mr. Simms to move closer so that "poor" Auntie Bea could hear him. It seemed to me that from the beginning, the judge believed that Auntie Bea was the victim, not the perpetrator.

Mr. Simms continued his questioning. "Would you state your name and address for the judge please?

Auntie Bea responded. "Yes. I live at Burnwood, Greenville, Virginia."

Mr. Simms replied, "Okay, and your name?"

Auntie Bea answered, "Bea Mills."

Mr. Simms asked, "You are the aunt of my client, the plaintiff, Jane King?"

Auntie Bea answered, "That's correct."

Mr. Simms asked, "And are you the great-aunt of her daughter, Belinda Star?"

Auntie Bea replied, "Yes."

Mr. Simms asked, "And is it true, ma'am, that you feel that Jane caused you to lose your property?"

Auntie Bea replied, "Yes."

Mr. Simms asked, "Is it true that you feel Jane King and her husband, Big Pete, owe you about $200,000, which was never repaid to you?"

Auntie Bea responded, "Yes. I believe the figure was what—"

At that point, Mr. Pricket jumped up and stated, "You can't guess!"

The judge replied, "Just answer the question to the best of your ability, Ms. Mills."

Auntie Bea replied, "Okay. Yes. That's about right."

Mr. Simms asked, "That debt was discharged in bankruptcy, is that right?"

Auntie Bea answered, "That's right."

Mr. Simms asked, "So would it be fair to say that you're angry with Jane because she caused you to lose your property and she failed to pay you back what you believe she owed you?"

Auntie Bea retorted, "You bet your fancy blue suit I am!"

Mr. Simms asked, "And as a result of that, you're not willing to return her property, is that right?"

Mr. Pricket objected, "Judge, there's no evidence at this point that it's her property."

The judge sustained the objection.

Mr. Simms continued, "Ma'am, somewhere around May of 1999, you received certain items of personal property that belonged to my client, Jane King, is that right?"

Auntie Bea answered, "Yes."

Mr. Simms asked, "And that included furniture, clothing, two vehicles, and some antiques?"

Auntie Bea coyly replied, "Yes. I really don't know what was there because I wasn't able to go down and inspect it."

Mr. Simms grinned and asked, "Do you remember if it included two vehicles?"

Auntie Bea answered, "Oh, yes, they are there. They've been there ever since Belinda stayed with Frank."

Mr. Simms asked, "Do you remember whether the property included various pieces of furniture?"

Auntie Bea answered, "Yes."

Mr. Simms asked, "Do you remember if the property included clothing that belonged to Jane?"

Auntie Bea responded, "I didn't see no clothing."

Mr. Simms said, "Okay. Was it a number of boxes that were delivered?"

Auntie Bea's answer was too soft to be heard.

Mr. Simms replied, "I'm sorry. You have to answer—"

Auntie Bea almost yelled, "Yes!"

The judge looked at Auntie Bea, smiled, and said, "Do your best to speak up, Mrs. Mills. We all understand you're not used to this process, but do your best to speak up."

Auntie Bea smiled at him and said, "Okay."

Mr. Simms continued, "At the time the property was delivered to your house, Jane had not filed for bankruptcy yet, is that right?"

Auntie Bea responded, "I believe she had."

Mr. Simms corrected himself, "She had. I'm sorry. You're correct. She had actually filed for bankruptcy back in 1997."

Auntie Bea replied, "I don't remember the date, sir."

Mr. Simms said, "Okay. But your recollection was that it was before the property was delivered to your house?"

Auntie Bea answered, "Yes."

Mr. Simms said, "At the time the property was delivered to your house, Jane had been charged with committing certain crimes, correct?"

Auntie Bea responded, "Yes she had."

Mr. Simms asked, "And do you remember whether or not she was in jail at the time the property was delivered to your house?"

Auntie Bea grinned wickedly and answered, "Yes. She was sitting in jail. Served her right too."

Mr. Simms asked, "Is it true that you were aware your niece was likely to go to prison and you were trying to help her out by storing property?"

Auntie Bea shouted, "No!"

Mr. Simms addressed the judge, "Your Honor, I'm not sure what the court's protocol is with respect to exhibits, whether you want them marked first—"

The judge replied, "Well, you need to show them to Mr. Pricket first. And then if you're going to introduce it into evidence, why, I'll mark it for you. Do you wish it marked at this point?"

Mr. Simms responded, "Yes, Your Honor."

The judge said, "All right. I've marked what appears to be a copy of a letter as well as an attached envelope as Plaintiff's Exhibit Number 1."

Mr. Pricket said, "I have no objection, Your Honor; I only request that you show it to the witness, and ask her to identify it."

Mr. Simms handed the letter and attached envelope to Auntie Bea. She slowly reached out her hand for the papers, as if it took her great effort.

Mr. Simms spoke, "Mrs. Mills, I'm handing you what's been marked as Plaintiff's Exhibit 1 for identification. I ask that you take a moment to examine the document please. Mrs. Mills, I don't like to interrupt your reading, but let me ask you, do you know what that document is?"

Auntie Bea replied, "Yes. It's a letter that I wrote to her when she was, I assumed, in jail."

Mr. Simms asked, "Is that a true and correct copy of the letter that you wrote to my client?"

Auntie Bea responded, "Yes. It is my writing."

Mr. Simms asked, "And that letter is dated May 9, 1999?"

Auntie Bea answered, "Yes."

Mr. Simms said, "Your Honor, we move to have Plaintiff's Exhibit 1 be received into evidence."

Judge Colburn asked the defense, "Is there any objection?"

Mr. Pricket replied, "None."

The judge then asked Auntie Bea to hand him the letter, which she did, but only with exaggerated effort. The letter was then admitted as Plaintiff's Exhibit Number 1. The judge then asked Mr. Simms if he would like it handed back to the witness for further questioning. Mr. Simms replied that he did have a few more questions.

Mr. Simms asked, "Mrs. Mills, in your letter to Jane, do you see the first page?"

Auntie Bea answered, "Yes."

Mr. Simms continued, "That's a name you call my client, is that right?"

Auntie Bea responded, "Yes."

Mr. Simms continued, "And on page two of your letter, I'd like to direct your attention to the sentence near the top where you write, and I quote, 'What do you plan to do with all that furniture?' Do you see that question?"

Auntie Bea answered, "Yes."

Mr. Simms said, "The 'you' in that sentence, I take it that refers to my client, Jane King, is that right?"

Auntie Bea answered, "That's correct."

Mr. Simms asked, "The furniture that you're referring to in this sentence is the furniture that was delivered to your house that was hers, is that right?"

Auntie Bea responded, "That's right."

Mr. Simms said, "The next sentence you write again, I quote, 'I don't know what Mrs. Greed and doctor will say when they come out and inspect the house.' Do you see that sentence?"

Auntie Bea answered, "Yes."

Mr. Simms asked, "'Mrs. Greed and doctor' refer to your landlords, the Greeds, is that right?"

Auntie Bea answered, "That's right."

Mr. Simms directed, "Now, on page three I'd like to direct your attention near the bottom of the page, you write, 'I don't want your money, what little you have.' Do you see that?"

Auntie Bea answered, "Yes."

Mr. Simms stated, "Nowhere in this letter did you make any mention of charging Jane for the storage of any of her property, is that right?"

Auntie Bea responded, "That's right. It was never discussed."

Mr. Simms asked, "In fact, you said you didn't want any of her money, is that right?"

Auntie Bea replied, "But I didn't have anything. I didn't have any money. At the time I wrote that, I didn't realize I did not have anything at all. I had no money. She took it all; all but my social security." With that statement, Auntie Bea wiped away a tear.

Mr. Simms reached in his briefcase and pulled out another form. "Your Honor, if I could—"

Judge Colburn responded, "All right. You have another document you'd like marked?"

Mr. Simms replied, "Yes, Your Honor."

Judge Colburn said, "So this copy of this document, which appears to be a letter, as well as the envelope will be marked Plaintiff's Exhibit Number 2." He then handed it to Mr. Simms.

Mr. Simms said, "Thank you, Your Honor. Mrs. Mills, I hand you what's been marked as Plaintiff's Exhibit 2 and ask you again to review that document and tell me whether you're familiar with it." With those words, he handed them to Auntie Bea who looked confused.

The judge said, "Just tell us if you know what it is, Mrs. Mills, once you've had a chance to figure that out."

Auntie Bea responded, "Well, evidently she asked me about keeping the dogs and I can't have pets."

Judge Colburn asked, "Well, is that a letter?"

Auntie Bea answered, "Yes."

Judge Colburn said, "All right. Is that a letter you wrote?"

Auntie Bea answered, "Yes."

Judge Colburn directed, "All right. You can go ahead, Mr. Simms."

Mr. Simms said, "Thank you, Your Honor, and the letter that's been marked as Exhibit 2, Mrs. Mills, I note that there's a postmark on the envelope with a date of June 21, 1999. Is that consistent with your recollection as to when you wrote this letter?"

Auntie Bea responded, "I don't know. I can't see the postmark. 1999, I believe that is."

Mr. Simms asked, "Do you remember if you wrote this letter back in about June of 1999?"

Auntie Bea answered, "It's possible. At that time, I was so upset. I really don't know."

Mr. Simms asked, "Okay. And this is a letter that you wrote to my client who was then still incarcerated—she was still in jail?"

Auntie Bea replied, "Yes."

Mr. Simms asked, "And is this a true and accurate copy of the letter that you wrote to my client?"

Auntie Bea responded, "Well, I haven't read it all."

Mr. Simms stated, "If you complete your review and let me know if you believe that's a true and accurate copy, I would appreciate it."

Auntie Bea answered, "Yes."

Mr. Simms addressed the court, "Your Honor, we'd move the—"

Auntie Bea interrupted, "I wrote the letter."

Mr. Simms continued, "All right. Your Honor, we'd move that Plaintiff's Exhibit 2 be received into evidence."

The judge asked Mr. Pricket if he had any objections. Because he did not, the letter was entered as Plaintiff's Exhibit Number 2. Mr. Simms continued his questioning.

Mr. Simms carried on, "Mrs. Mills, you write in the first part of your letter, 'I can only do so much. We cannot have any dogs here.' Do you see that sentence?"

Auntie Bea responded, "Yes. Well, that is true."

Mr. Simms asked, "Is that because Jane had asked you to keep her dogs?"

Auntie Bea answered, "I assume so. Well, I wouldn't have written that if she hadn't."

Mr. Simms said, "Okay."

Auntie Bea continued, "I couldn't keep dogs. I can't keep any pets."

Mr. Simms said, "You also write, 'I think we have been pretty good to you piled up to the ceiling.' Do you see that sentence?"

Auntie Bea answered, "No."

Mr. Simms said, "Let me see if I can read—I—I might be reading your handwriting incorrectly, but starting from the beginning of your letter, 'Jane, what makes you feel like you do? I can only do so much. We cannot have any dogs here. The Greeds said so. What should it be, the dogs or us? I think we have been pretty good to you piled up to the ceiling.' Do you see that?"

Auntie Bea answered, "Yes."

Mr. Simms asked, "Are you referring to her belongings that were delivered to your place that were 'piled up to the ceiling'?"

Auntie Bea answered, "Yes."

Mr. Simms asked, "Does the 'we' that you write in this sentence refer to you and Frank Gibbs?"

Auntie Bea questioned, "The what?"

Mr. Simms restated, "The 'we' that you used in your letters, are you referring to you and Frank Gibbs?"

Auntie Bea responded, "Yes."

Mr. Simms said, "Now, when you state that 'We have been pretty good to you', did you mean pretty good—did pretty good mean that you were doing her a favor?"

Mr. Pricket interjected, "Objection, Judge. The letter speaks for itself."

Auntie Bea responded, "No, no."

Judge Colburn directed, "Well, I'll let her answer the question. She's answered it. She said no. All right; next question."

Mr. Simms returned to his line of questioning. "Now, is it true that you refused to allow Jane's daughter, Belinda Star, to retrieve the personal belongings in early 2000?"

Mr. Pricket objected to the form of the question. "Judge, to the extent there's no basis for the statement that the possessions belong to Mrs. King?"

The judge allowed Mr. Simms to rephrase the question. "You may give reference to the items that are the subject of dispute as opposed to the ownership, which the court will determine."

Mr. Simms restated, "Mrs. Mills, is it true that you refused to allow Belinda Star to retrieve the belongings that had delivered to your house back in early 2000?"

Auntie Bea answered, "Yes. I was told by Ed Weird that we did not have to let anyone in our homes that we did not want in there. Therefore, we refused and called the sheriff's department; they came out and escorted them away. They came without permission. They didn't ask."

Mr. Simms continued, "In fact, you had a no trespassing notice issued against—"

Auntie Bea asked, "Pardon?"

Mr. Simms said, "You had a no trespassing notice issued against my client in—"

Auntie Bea interrupted, "That is correct, and it's still in effect."

Mr. Simms addressed the court, "Your Honor, if I could have this marked for identification please."

Mr. Simms handed something to the judge and asked for it to be entered as evidence. The judge accepted it, and then passed it to Auntie Bea.

Mr. Simms asked, "Mrs. Mills, I show you what's been marked as Plaintiff's Exhibit 3 and ask you if you can identify that document?"

Auntie Bea answered, "Yes."

Mr. Simms asked, "Is that a copy of the notice that you had issued against my client?"

Auntie Bea answered, "Yes."

Mr. Simms continued, "Mrs. Mills, the notice that you've had issued is dated February 29, 2000, is that right?"

Auntie Bea responded, "Yes."

Mr. Simms asked, "And it—it concerns two properties, is that right?"

Auntie Bea answered, "That's right."

Mr. Simms asked, "Which property was your residence?"

Auntie Bea answered, "Mine was the lower numbered one on Burnwood. I can't think of the number at this time."

Mr. Simms said, "And—"

Auntie Bea interrupted, "I—I don't remember the—my brother's was right next door. I don't remember—I don't remember the number of his house."

Mr. Simms said, "So you don't know whether your brother's was the residence or the property listed as—"

Auntie Bea responded, "Frank."

Mr. Simms continued, ". . . So this number . . ." He showed the address to Auntie Bea. "Is this the correct address for Burnwood?"

Auntie Bea asked, "Is that right?"

Mr. Pricket said, "You can't ask her."

Auntie Bea answered, "I believe that is correct, sir."

Mr. Simms responded, "Okay. Was it your intent when you took out this no trespassing notice to prevent my client from retrieving any of the property that had been stored?"

Auntie Bea answered, "That I'm not sure of."

Mr. Simms asked, "What was your intent when you had this trespass notice issued?"

Auntie Bea answered, "I did not want her there or her daughter."

Mr. Simms asked, "Did you understand that the trespass notice would prevent her from retrieving her property?"

Mr. Pricket interrupted, "Objection, Judge. There's no evidence at this juncture that it's her property."

Mr. Simms responded, "I'll—I'll withdraw that."

Judge Colburn directed, "All right. That's fine."

Mr. Simms asked, "Was it your understanding that this trespass notice would prevent my client from retrieving any of the property that was stored?"

Auntie Bea responded, "No."

Mr. Simms asked, "I'm sorry?"

Auntie Bea shouted, "No!"

Mr. Simms asked, "How would my client be able to retrieve her property if she was not allowed on your property?"

Auntie Bea answered, "I don't know. I—I didn't want them on my property period."

Mr. Simms asked to have another piece of evidence entered. It was a letter and was marked as Plaintiff's Exhibit Number 4.

Mr. Simms stated, "Mrs. Mills, I hand you what's been marked as Plaintiff's Exhibit 4 for identification and ask you if you're familiar with that document?"

Auntie Bea responded, "Yes. I am."

Mr. Simms asked, "And that is a letter dated February 29, 2000, that you sent to my client, is that right?"

Auntie Bea answered, "That's right."

Mr. Simms asked, "And is that your signature that appears on the letter?"

Auntie Bea answered, "Yes. It is."

Mr. Simms said, "Mrs. Mills, I would like to direct your attention to the second sentence in this letter where you wrote, 'In addition you owe me the sum of $1,500,000.' Do you see that?"

Auntie Bea answered, "Yes."

Mr. Simms said, "Was it your understanding that my client owed you a million and a half dollars at the time—"

Auntie Bea interrupted, "Yes."

"—you wrote this letter?"

Auntie Bea again answered, "Yes."

Mr. Simms asked, "How did you come up with that sum?"

Auntie Bea answered, "Well, it was my farm, my home, and all the money I had, CDs, all the money that I had. She cashed them."

Mr. Simms continued, "And is it your testimony that your farm, your money, and your CDs were—"

Auntie Bea raised her voice as she interrupted, "My house, my home, everything!"

"—And all that—"

Auntie Bea screeched, "I had nothing left! Absolutely nothing!"

"Mr. Simms asked, "Is it your testimony that the value of the possessions that you lost—your farm, your CDs, and your cash—was $1,500,000?"

Auntie Bea responded, "Yes."

Mr. Simms said, "Now, you also go on to state, 'And I fully intent to proceed against you and your tangible and intangible property, i.e. cars, furniture, property, et cetera, in an effort to attempt recovery of my losses.' Do you see that?"

Auntie Bea answered, "Yes."

Mr. Simms asked, "I take it you meant that when you wrote it?"

Auntie Bea replied, "I did."

Mr. Simms asked, "And referring to 'you and your' that you're using in your letter refers to my client, is that right, Jane King?"

Auntie Bea answered, "Yes."

Mr. Simms asked, "So the cars, furniture, property, et cetera, that you specifically mentioned in this sentence would be her cars, her furniture, and her property, is that right?"

Mr. Pricket interrupted, "Judge, the letter speaks for itself."

Judge Colburn interjected, "All right. What about that, Mr. Simms? The letter is fairly concise. It does speak for itself."

Mr. Simms assented, "That's fine. I'll withdraw."

Judge Colburn said, "All right. I sustain the objection."

Mr. Simms continued, "Is it true, ma'am, that from about February of 2000, you've done everything in your power to prevent my client from recovering what you've described as her property?"

Auntie Bea asked, "That I did what?"

Mr. Simms rephrased, "That you've done everything you can to prevent my client from recovering what you've described as her property?"

Auntie Bea answered, "Well, I wouldn't say it was her property."

Mr. Simms said, "Now, after the trespass notice and the letter that was—we've just been discussing in February of 2000—you were sued in general district court by my client's daughter, Belinda Star, is that right?"

Auntie Bea replied, "That's right."

Mr. Simms asked, "And she's your great-niece, is that right?"

Auntie Bea replied, "That's right."

Mr. Simms addressed the court, "Your Honor, could I have this marked as Exhibit Number 5?"

Judge Colburn accepted the evidence, looked it over, and stated, "So the copy of the warrant in detinue has been marked for identification purposes as Plaintiff's Exhibit Number 5."

Mr. Simms said, "Thank you. Mrs. Mills, I hand you what's been marked as Plaintiff's Exhibit 5 and is that a true and correct copy of the warrant in detinue and the attached Schedule A that was part of that?"

Auntie Bea answered, "Yes."

Mr. Simms said, "Ma'am, the warrant in detinue is dated April 14 of the year 2000. Do you recall if you were served with it sometime after that date?"

Auntie Bea responded, "I don't remember the date, but I do remember when the deputy brought it there."

Mr. Simms said, "The warrant in detinue indicates that Belinda Star was represented by an attorney named Miss Patson. Does that name ring a bell with you?"

Auntie Bea answered, "Yes. She was the lawyer that Belinda Star hired to try and recover my land, which never took place."

Mr. Simms asked, "You had communications with Miss Patson concerning the detinue claim as well, is that right?"

Auntie Bea answered, "Yes."

Mr. Simms asked, "You had communications with Miss Patson concerning the location and the return of items that were listed on Exhibit A, is that right?"

Auntie Bea replied, "She wanted me to settle for just the Cadillac. She refused to represent me with Belinda regarding my land from prior telephone calls."

Mr. Simms said, "Okay. What do you mean by prior telephone calls?"

Auntie Bea answered, "When Belinda was here in 1999, the Greeds refused to honor their contract with me and Jane. The agreement was Mr. Greed would sell my farm and the Daisy house back to me for the amount they picked up the notes for, to Belinda, but Mrs. Greed refused to honor her husband's agreement. Even though I had spoken with Miss Patson, I believed Belinda was lying to me because it was almost a year and nothing was ever done about it."

Mr. Simms continued, "Didn't Miss Patson have a telephone conversation with you regarding why you and Belinda needed to wait before taking action?"

Auntie Bea replied, "I don't remember."

Mr. Simms asked, "You don't remember?"

Auntie Bea shouted, "I don't remember!"

Mr. Pricket interrupted, "Objection, Your Honor, she said she didn't remember."

Judge Colburn directed, "She already answered you, Mr. Simms. Move along."

Mr. Simms said, "Okay, Your Honor. Mrs. Mills, why don't you take a moment—"

Auntie Bea asserted, "I said no."

Mr. Simms said, "You said you didn't know what was on Exhibit A. It's in front of you as part of Exhibit 5 here. If you'd just take a moment and look at is so you're familiar with what it is."

Auntie Bea asked, "What's this—you mean all these?"

Mr. Simms asked, "You've—you've seen that list before haven't you, ma'am?"

Auntie Bea answered, "Yes."

Mr. Simms continued, "And my question was that you—you had communications with Miss Patson concerning the location and return of items that are listed on the Exhibit A; isn't that right?"

Auntie Bea responded "I believe there was a list that was—that was circled with some—if I remember correctly, I believe that Belinda Star circled certain things."

Mr. Simms asked the court, "Okay, if we could have this marked as Exhibit 6 please."

Judge Colburn responded, "All right. So Plaintiff's Exhibit Number 6, which will be marked for identification as such, consisting of a Schedule A, summary of items, some of which have been marked, others of which have been circled, but the court will mark it for identification purposes as Plaintiff's Exhibit Number 6."

Mr. Simms said to Bea, "I'm handing you what's been marked as Plaintiff's Exhibit 6, ma'am, and ask you if you're familiar with that document? Please take a moment to review it. It's an eight—or nine-page document."

Auntie Bea answered, "Some of these things I did not circle because I did not know what was in that one room in the basement. It was locked."

Mr. Simms asked, "Are you familiar with this document?"

Auntie Bea answered, "Yes. Her daughter locked that room and no one could get into it."

Mr. Simms said, "Okay. Isn't it a fact, Mrs. Mills, that the U.S. Attorney already came and inspected the property that you claimed was locked and you removed the lock yourself because the daughter gave you the key? Wasn't it to keep as many people, other than you and Mr. Gibbs, from going into the one small room in the unfinished basement?"

Auntie Bea replied, "Oh, I had forgotten."

Mr. Simms continued, "Okay. If you could try to just answer my question. Your attorney will have an opportunity to ask you questions."

Auntie Bea answered, "All right."

Mr. Simms asked, "And is that—on the last page, is that your signature that appears with a date of June 25, 2000?"

Auntie Bea responded, "Yes. It is."

Mr. Simms asked, "And is the handwriting, which appears on this document, your handwriting?"

Auntie Bea answered, "Yes."

Mr. Simms asked the court, "Your Honor, we'd move that Plaintiff's Exhibit 6 be received into evidence."

Judge Colburn asked the defense, "Any objection?"

Mr. Pricket stated, "Yes, sir, that's an offer of settlement. It's not admissible evidence."

Judge Colburn asked, "What's your response to that, Mr. Simms?"

Mr. Pricket responded, "I realize the court's going to have to read it to make a ruling on it."

Judge Colburn directed, "Let me hear his response. I will take a look at it if I need to."

Mr. Pricket said, "Okay."

Judge Colburn continued, "She's already said she's written on it. She's already described it. It came in connection with the settlement, but—"

Mr. Pricket agreed, "All right."

Judge Colburn finished, "If I feel the need to look into it further, I will. Go ahead, Mr. Simms."

Mr. Simms said, "Your Honor, because in this document Mrs. Mills admits and makes statements of—or admits to material facts in the case, it would be admissible even though it is in the context of a compromise."

Judge Colburn said, "Let me take a look at it. Hand it up, Mr. Pricket. What facts does she admit to?"

Mr. Simms stated, "She admits to the location of these items as well as to the return of them. This is a specific summary list of items and the location and existence of these items as well—which we believe is also an issue in this case, and it's our understanding that the defendants are claiming that a number of these items are no longer in existence. Your Honor, also, I do have a case that I believe is on point here."

Judge Colburn replied, "Well, tell me what it is and what it says."

Mr. Simms said, "I'm sorry, Your Honor, if you'd just give me a moment, I—"

Auntie Bea interjected, "I think he's lost."

Judge Colburn directed, "Ma'am, don't make any comments. Mr. Simms, if you can't retrieve it, you'll just have to argue it generally. What's—what's the thrust of your argument? I mean—"

Mr. Simms stated, "The argument, Your Honor, is that when a party admits to certain facts or liability in a case, those admissions are admissible into evidence, even though the admissions are now taking place in the context of a settlement action. I did bring a copy of the case because I anticipated that it would come up today and if I could just have a moment to try to locate it here, I believe I can."

Judge Colburn asked, "What admissions do you allege she made that pertain to this litigation?"

Mr. Simms replied "She made admissions as to the location of this property being at her residence. She crossed out certain items, which aren't very many, that she indicated no longer were in existence. She also circled items—"

Judge Colburn interrupted, "She's never—how is it an admission that they were at her residence when that appears to not even be in dispute?"

Mr. Simms stated, "Well, I believe it will be disputed, Your Honor, but these—we received in discovery documents, which indicated that many, many of these items are no longer in existence or located at her residence. So . . ."

Judge Colburn determined, "I'm going to sustain the objection at this point to the admission of the document. All right, you can continue with your exam."

Auntie Bea asked, "May I say something?"

Judge Colburn replied, "No, ma'am, you may not. Do not say anything except for answering the questions."

Auntie Bea consented, "Okay."

Judge Colburn turned to Mr. Simms, "All right. What's your next question?"

Mr. Simms said, "Your Honor, I'm sorry. I did just locate the case and I would like to cite it for the record."

Judge Colburn stated, "I've just ruled. You can move on and if it comes up again, we'll address it."

Mr. Simms said, "Your Honor's indicating you're not inclined to reconsider based upon the case authority that I was overly applied of pressure a moment ago and I found it within seconds."

Judge Colburn replied, "Hand it up and tell me what it says."

Mr. Simms said, "The case is City of Ricker—"

Judge Colburn interrupted, "Tell me what it says."

Mr. Simms stated, "It says, Your Honor, that an expressed admission of liability made during negotiations for a compromise is admissible and the specific language of the court overruling is that the recognition of the existence of a binding contract in that case was in the nature of admission of an independent fact pertinent to the correctness of the claims. That's our point in this case, Your Honor. And she's admitted the location and existence of these items at her property and those are pertinent independent facts that bear correctness of the claims in this case."

Judge Colburn decided, "All right. Mr. Pricket, I'll let you respond."

Mr. Pricket pressed, "Well, Judge, in that case it says, at page 879, the recognition of the existence of a binding contract was the nature of an admission of an independent fact pertinent to the issue of the correctness of the claims. But in this case, Judge, if you read that document that he tries to submit into evidence at this juncture, it says at the very end, this offer is good until 7/14/2000. So everything that precedes this—this offer is good until 2000—is in the nature of an offer. And I don't see anything in there that at this time would be construed as admission. If his purpose in offering this is to rebut a defense that some of these items no longer exist, that defense has not been presented, Judge. It's not before the court. So it's actually objectionable for two reasons. One, it's an offer of compromise. Secondly, there's nothing to rebut."

Judge Colburn stated, "All right. The court will sustain the objection. All right. You can continue with your examination, Mr. Simms."

Mr. Simms returned to his line of questioning, "Well, Mrs. Mills, in this case you were represented—in the detinue action in general district court you were represented by an attorney by the name of Mr. Dickerson, is that right?"

Auntie Bea answered softly, "Yes."

Mr. Simms asked, "I'm sorry?"

Auntie Bea responded, "Yes."

Mr. Simms said, "Mr. Pricket mentioned an agreement that was reached in the general district court detinue action, do you remember that?"

Auntie Bea responded, "No."

Mr. Simms asked the court, "Could we have this marked as Exhibit . . ."

Judge Colburn responded, "This will be Number 7."

Mr. Simms continued, "Ma'am, I hand you what's been marked as Plaintiff's Exhibit 7 for identification. And the first page of this document is a letter dated August 14, 2000, from Mr. Dickerson to Miss Patson. It indicates that you received a copy of this. Do you recall receiving a copy of this document?"

Auntie Bea answered, "No."

Judge Colburn responded, "All right. She's answered; next question."

Mr. Simms asked, "Do you recall reaching an agreement in the general district court case that called for Belinda Star to pay you $3,000 as part of the settlement of that case?"

Mr. Pricket interjected, "Judge, evidence of a settlement should be either a court order or a signed agreement, neither of which he's offered into evidence. If there was a settlement of the case, it's between Mrs. Mills and Mrs. Star, not Mrs. Mills and Mrs. King."

Judge Colburn responded, "I understand that."

Mr. Pricket continued, "We're going to object."

Judge Colburn responded, "Well, I'll overrule it at this point. I'll see if she can answer the question. The question is whether she recalls.

I agree that perhaps the best evidence of whether it actually took place or is in existence is the agreement itself, but I'll allow the question as to whether she recalls. All right, why don't you just briefly repeat your question again?"

Mr. Simms restated, "Ma'am, do you recall whether you agreed, as part of your settlement with Belinda Star, that she would pay you $3,000?"

Auntie Bea answered, "No."

Judge Colburn directed, "All right; next question."

Mr. Simms asked, "You mentioned earlier discussions about transferring the title to a car to you, would that have been the 1987 Cadillac automobile?"

Auntie Bea answered, "Yes."

Mr. Simms said, "And do you recall whether you had agreed to settle if the—"

Auntie Bea interrupted, "I said—"

Mr. Simms: ". . ."—a part of that vehicle was transferred to you?"

Auntie Bea restated, "I said no."

Mr. Simms said, "Okay. Do you recall any agreement to settle the property claim brought by Belinda Star that called for you to receive a rug and antique dressers, a grandfather clock, a Craftsman chipper, and a Kenmore upright freezer?"

Auntie Bea responded, "Yes."

Judge Colburn interjected, "All right; next question."

Mr. Simms asked, "And do you recall that, as part of that agreement, Frank Gibbs was to receive two beds?"

Auntie Bea asked, "Pardon?"

Mr. Simms rephrased, "Was Frank Gibbs to receive two beds as part of that settlement?"

Auntie Bea responded, "I don't think so. I think there was some agreement or something for him. I don't remember that."

Mr. Simms said, "Okay. You remember that you were supposed to receive the automobile, the rug, the dresser, the grandfather clock, the chipper, and the freezer, is that right?"

Auntie Bea answered, "Yes."

Mr. Simms asked, "And everything else that was on that list of Exhibit A that you've seen a couple of times today was supposed to be turned over to Belinda Star; is that right?"

Auntie Bea answered, "I suppose so. I—I don't—I don't remember that."

Mr. Simms said, "Okay. Do you remember a concern that you didn't want Belinda Star on your property?"

Auntie Bea agreed, "That's right."

Mr. Simms asked, "And so the person who was supposed to come get the property was going to be her husband and Ed Weird was going to make sure that everything was proper—is that what you remember?"

Auntie Bea replied, "Yes."

Mr. Simms asked, "Isn't it a fact, Mrs. Mills, that Belinda Star specifically stated that Ed Weird was not going to be party to this?"

Auntie Bea replied, "Well, yes, but she also made it with no dates, only three days' notice, and Ed decided that we did not have to comply. Since it was our attorney drafting it, we could modify it to our liking."

Mr. Simms stated, "Now, is it your testimony that prior to the property being delivered to your house and Frank Gibbs' house, you weren't aware that it was coming to be stored at your home and his?"

Auntie Bea answered, "No."

Mr. Pricket interrupted, "Judge, if—if he's done with that other line of questioning, I'm going to move to strike the previous group of questions about Mrs. Star. If, in fact, there was some agreement that he is claiming that Mrs. Mills breached and that action was properly filed by Mrs. Star against Mrs. Mills for breach of a settle agreement of some sort, then that would not seem to be relevant to an action by Mrs. King against Mrs. Mills to recover possession of the same property."

Judge Colburn directed, "I'm going to overrule the objection. I understand your point. It's in evidence. I think that would go to the weight and that argument may be revisited."

Mr. Pricket assented, "All right."

Judge Colburn stated, "When we get to that stage in the proceedings. All right, Mr. Simms, if you could move this along and get to the heart of the issues."

Mr. Simms replied, "I'm almost there, Your Honor. Ma'am, I'm sorry, I don't remember if you answered my question, but prior to these items being delivered to your house and Frank Gibbs' house, you weren't aware that they were coming, is that right?"

Auntie Bea answered, "No, I didn't know."

Mr. Simms asked, "And prior to these items being delivered to your house and Frank Gibbs' house, you had no personal knowledge of who acquired the items, is that right?"

Auntie Bea asked, "That who acquired what?"

Mr. Simms asked, "Who acquired these items that were subsequently delivered to your house and Frank Gibbs' house?"

Auntie Bea responded, "I don't understand."

Mr. Simms asked, "Who bought them? Who paid for them?"

Auntie Bea said, "No."

Mr. Simms asked, "No? You don't know who paid for them, is that right?"

Auntie Bea said, "No."

Mr. Simms again asked, "You don't know how they were acquired or how they were purchased, is that right?"

Auntie Bea responded, "No. I don't know who purchased them, no."

Mr. Simms asked, "You don't know how long they were in the possession of my client before they were delivered?"

Mr. Pricket interrupted, "There's no evidence, Judge, that they were ever in the possession of his client."

Judge Colburn sustained the objection.

Mr. Simms continued, "You don't know how long they were in the possession of my client or her husband prior to them being delivered?"

Auntie Bea responded, "No."

Judge Colburn asked, "What's your next question?"

Mr. Simms replied, "I have no other questions at this time, Your Honor."

Judge Colburn responded, "All right. Mr. Pricket, any examination of—"

Mr. Pricket answered, "I only have two questions for right now. I'm going to reserve the rest of them for later."

Judge Colburn agreed, "That's fine."

Mr. Pricket walked from the defendant's table, stood in front of the witness box, and began his cross-examination of Bea.

Mr. Pricket said, "Mrs. Mills, before the furniture was delivered to your house, did you have a trust that was set up for you by your late husband?"

Auntie Bea answered, "Yes."

Mr. Pricket asked, "And who was the trustee of that trust?"

Auntie Bea responded, "Jane King."

Mr. Pricket asked, "The plaintiff?"

Auntie Bea answered, "Right."

Mr. Pricket asked, "Was everything that you owned, except for your clothing and your—your personal effect, in that trust?"

Auntie Bea replied, "No, I had a will also."

Mr. Pricket said, "Okay. But was the—was the farm and the house in the trust?"

Auntie Bea answered, "No, that was—"

Mr. Pricket said, "Okay. Let me ask you this, did Mrs. King also have power of attorney over you?"

Auntie Bea answered, "That's correct. She did."

Mr. Pricket said, "Okay. Now, either as trustee of your trust or using her power of attorney for you, did Mrs. King spend all your money and take all your assets away?"

Auntie Bea stated, "That is correct."

Mr. Pricket asked, "When did that happen—what year?"

Auntie Bea answered, "I'm not sure of the year."

Mr. Pricket asked, "Was it before the furniture was delivered?"

Auntie Bea answered, "Oh—yes."

Mr. Pricket asked, "And after she took everything that you owned, did she then file bankruptcy?"

Auntie Bea said, "On my—"

Mr. Pricket interrupted, "Yes, ma'am."

Auntie Bea answered, "Yes."

Of course, Bea lied about all the facts. She had begged my mother, Jane King, to help her establish a trust long after her husband had passed away. She had all her clothing, assets, and land in the trust. Her reasoning for doing this was because she didn't want the state to acquire any of her possessions when she passed away.

Mr. Pricket continued, "Okay. Now, at the time you were in general district court with Mrs. Star, were you aware of the plea agreement that Mrs. King signed with the federal government? Had you become aware of that yet?"

Auntie Bea replied, "No, no, not at that time, no, I found—"

Mr. Pricket interrupted, "Okay. When did you first become aware of a plea agreement, which Mrs. King signed with the federal government?"

Auntie Bea answered, "Sometime after that."

Mr. Pricket asked, "After you were in general district court up here with Mrs. Star?"

Auntie Bea answered, "Yes. Yes."

Mr. Pricket addressed the court, "Okay. Judge, that's all I have at this time. I'd like to reserve the right to recall this witness."

Judge Colburn responded, "Case in chief. That's fine. All right. Mrs. Mills, thank you very much for that testimony. I want you to take your time. You can resume your seat with Mr. Pricket, but take your time doing so. Be careful."

Auntie Bea said, "All right. Thank you very much."

Judge Colburn cautioned, "Watch that step down. All right, Mr. Simms, you can call your next witness."

Mr. Simms stated, "Jane King; Your Honor."

Judge Colburn directed, "All right. Mrs. King, if you'll come forward, ma'am. Just come to the witness box, stand, and face the clerk. She'll administer the oath to you. Mrs. King, as you heard me do with Mrs. Mills, do your best please to speak up so we can all hear you and understand you. You can hand those up to me. Thank you. All right, you may proceed, Mr. Simms."

After about an hour, the judge took a recess and I caught May, Nancy, and John talking about the case to Ed.

I walked up to them and angrily said, "John, May! If you keep running your mouths to Ed, I am going to report the two of you to the judge." Both of them practically ran away from Ed and Nancy in fear that I would keep my threat.

I looked over at Mrs. Greed and I said, "I am here because of you not honoring your husband's word. You have completely destroyed my family! You should be ashamed of yourself! Nasty little people like you always get their comeuppance. I know why you are here. You are only here to make sure my mother doesn't testify about your husband and his illegal activities. I hope you burn in hell, you rich, redneck piece of crap!"

Before she even had a chance to respond, I turned toward Ed and said in an even angrier tone, "You, Mr. Weird, are a scumbag, thief, liar, and Big Pete's whore. Here I am still fighting the monster after he is dead and gone! I know you are using my godmother and godfather's children to steal from us. You're lower than a bottom feeder by playing off their greed. Society will catch up to you someday! I pray for it every day!"

I then walked away from Ed and Mrs. Greed. I knew what I said was true because they looked at me in total shock. I was the first person who had the balls to say it to their faces.

CHAPTER XXXIII

My mother was sworn in and Mr. Simms focused his line of questioning on where the property came from and on her plea agreement.

Mr. Simms questioned my mother as to Bea's involvement and her awareness of everything my mother had done for her. He asked her about Bea's involvement in the check scam. He asked about the crimes that Bea committed against my mother's children. Evidence was provided showing that my mother was telling the truth and proving that Bea was party to her own demise. Mr. Simms put forth evidence proving that Bea was the one who spent the money left to her by her deceased husband to purchase the Daisy house. It proved that Bea technically owed the money to the Kings, instead of them owing her money. In addition, evidence was put forth showing that I had rectified the crimes regarding the check scam that Bea committed to the best of my ability.

After my mother finished her testimony, the judge ordered a recess and stated that Mr. Pricket's cross-examination would take place after the hour recess.

Of course, I was outside the courtroom the entire time. While I was standing on the side of the courthouse smoking, I caught May, Nancy, and John talking about the case to Ed again. I walked over to them and said, "John! May! If you keep running your mouths to Ed, I am going to report the two of you to the judge this time." They practically ran away from Ed and Mrs. Greed.

Mrs. Greed was getting ready to say something to me, but I cut her off. "Go fuck yourself! Don't you dare speak to me!" I turned around and walk to the other side of the courthouse.

After the hour recess, I went back inside and waited by the courtroom entrance. I watched as everyone filed back inside. During his cross-examination, Mr. Pricket tried to discredit my mother by speaking of the crimes she had committed. He tried to paint her as a lying, conniving thief, but Mr. Simms prevailed with the physical evidence that he put forth.

Time passed quickly, and before I knew it, the bailiff came outside and said, "Ma'am, they are ready for your testimony."

I nodded my head in acknowledgement and followed him into the courtroom.

CHAPTER XXXIV

I was sworn in, called on behalf of the plaintiff, my mother, and testified as I sat in the witness stand. Mr. Simms positioned himself in front of me and started his direct line of questioning.

Before we started, Judge Colburn instructed, "Ma'am, in answering the questions, do your best to speak up so that we can all hear you and understand you."

I replied, "Yes, sir."

Judge Colburn said, "All right. Mr. Simms, you may proceed."

Mr. Simms started by asking me to state my name and address for the court record, which I did. He then asked me what my relationship was to the other parties in the case.

I replied, "The plaintiff, Jane King, is my mother and the defendant, Bea Mills is my great-aunt and my godmother. Frank Gibbs was my great-uncle and godfather."

Once the groundwork was laid, Mr. Simms proceeded with the exam.

Mr. Simms asked, "Did you ever have any communications with Mrs. Mills concerning the property that was placed in her house?"

I answered, "Yes, sir. It started on January 8, 1999, when I came home to Virginia from Germany. After my mother was arrested, I asked Auntie Bea if I could store my mother's vehicles and her safes at her house. We discussed it again in February when my husband was home on leave."

Mr. Simms asked, "What was your Auntie Bea's response when you made that request?"

I answered, "Yes. She said that I could go ahead and store it there as long as I needed to. That everything would be safe there. She said that I could put the safes and the dog ashes in her house."

Mr. Simms asked, "Why did you make that request of her?"

I replied, "Because I had no other place to store the safes and dog ashes at that time."

Mr. Simms asked, "Why did it need to be stored?"

I answered, "Because my mother had turned herself in; she was charged on January 8, 1999. After the charges, she was sent directly to the county jail. My mother and her attorney instructed me to remove her property from the house as quickly as possible."

Mr. Pricket interrupted, "Objection, Judge, as to what she was instructed to do."

Judge Colburn responded, "Sustained; next question."

Mr. Simms said, "Okay. You indicated there was another conversation in February. At that time, was there any discussion regarding any charges or the extra expense that your aunt would have for storing the belongings?"

I answered, "No, sir. There was never any mention of money for storing my mother's belongings."

Mr. Simms asked, "Did you personally have anything to do with the transportation of those items to your aunt's property?"

I answered, "Yes, sir. I personally moved my mother's property from her house. The day she was incarcerated, I moved her vehicles, the dog ashes, and safes, which I promptly stored at Auntie Bea's house. I spent the rest of January and a large portion of February moving her clothing, books, and personal items. I did have some assistance from my stepbrother and my mother's hired hand."

Mr. Simms asked, "Who else was present when you did that?"

I answered, "My Auntie Bea and my Uncle Frank."

Mr. Simms said, "Okay. Subsequent to the initial conversation you had with your aunt, did you have any other communications with her concerning the storage of your mother's property at the house?"

I replied, "Yes. I did. At the end of February or the beginning of March of 1999, before I flew back to Germany, my husband and I planned to remove all the property and put it into military storage along with the rest of the property that we had not moved yet from my mother's house. Auntie Bea insisted that we keep it there with her and Uncle Frank. She said it would be safer with her and Uncle Frank than in military storage. My great-uncle also said that my mother and I could store whatever we needed to at his home."

Mr. Pricket interrupted, "Objection, Judge, to the great-uncle."

Judge Colburn directed, "All right. That will be hearsay."

Mr. Simms said, "Unless there's some independent corroboration to be brought by—"

Judge Colburn firmly said, "I'll sustain that objection; next question."

Mr. Simms asked, "Your conversations that you had with your aunt at that time, what was her response?"

I answered, "She had no problem with us storing things there. She said I could keep my possessions there as long as we needed to do so."

Mr. Simms said, "Okay. And I take it that during the time you had these conversations with your aunt, your mother was incarcerated?"

"Yes, sir," I replied.

"When was the next conversation that you had with your aunt?" Mr. Simms asked.

I responded, "Before I left for Germany, I told her that I would call either her or Uncle Frank each week to check on them and make sure that everything was okay. I called her from the airport in Germany right after I got off the plane. I wanted to let her know that I had arrived safely because she tends to worry. After that, I called her every two weeks. On the weeks that I didn't call her, I called Uncle Frank. The rest of my mother's property was moved to Auntie Bea's and Uncle Frank's houses around the middle of May. In June, Auntie Bea started asking, 'When are you and Thomas coming to get the property because, you know, Frank's living in a warehouse over there? The stuff is packed to the ceiling and the stuff needs to be gotten out of there.' At that time, I told Auntie Bea that I would remove the property when my mother was sentenced. I told her that I wanted to wait and take care of everything in one trip. She continued to scold me each time I spoke with her until January or February of 2000. That was when my mother told me that her sentencing had been scheduled for April. Of course, I passed that information on to Auntie Bea. Once she had a general idea of when I would move everything, she calmed down."

Mr. Simms asked, "When was the next time you had any contact with your aunt concerning the retrieval of the property?"

"The beginning of February of 2000. I called Auntie Bea once my husband and I had decided when we were coming to Virginia. At that time, I told her that we would be there around the end of March to move everything. I said that we would have it all moved before my mother was sentenced in April. That's when Auntie Bea told me that would be fine, and she also told me to make sure I had my legal documents in order. I asked her what she meant by that, and she replied, 'Just make sure you have your legal documents in order and that will be fine.' After that conversation, I was puzzled and had a feeling that something was not right. I called the attorney that I had hired to take care of personal matters for us previously. My attorney told me to go ahead and do—"

Mr. Pricket interrupted, "Objection, Judge, as to what her attorney told her."

Judge Colburn directed, "Overruled."

"What did you do?" Mr. Simms asked.

I answered, "I went ahead and typed up a letter of transfer. The letter stated that my mother was giving me all the property that she had stored at Auntie Bea's and Uncle Frank's houses. I already had power of attorney over my mother. I wrote the letter in February, but it was the middle of March before everyone signed it. We had to send it to the prison, then my mother had to have it notarized, then she mailed it back to me, and then I had to go through the same process."

Mr. Simms responded, "Okay. So when did you attempt to retrieve the property?"

I said, "It was the latter part of March. Once I made the flight arrangements, I called Auntie Bea to let her know exactly when we would be at her house. I told her that we were staying at my mother-in-law's house in Virginia. I called her again the night before to remind her that we were going to pick up everything the next day. During that conversation, I told Auntie Bea that I had my legal documents in order, and that my husband and I would be there to retrieve the property in the morning. I specifically told her that we would be there around eight or nine the following morning. She told me that would be fine as long as I had my legal documents in order. I said we were going to start with Uncle Frank's house and then come over to her house. When we arrived at Uncle Frank's the next morning, he wouldn't let us in the house. He just kept shaking his head and saying that he was sorry. The next thing I knew, two deputy sheriffs drove up."

Judge Colburn interrupted, "So you couldn't get your stuff; the stuff that you flew all the way from Germany to get?"

I responded, "No, sir. The deputy sheriffs took the legal documents that I had brought with me, looked them over, and asked Uncle Frank if he would let me take it."

Judge Colburn directed, "Next question."

Mr. Simms said, "Okay. You were unable to retrieve the belongings. What did you do next?"

I answered, "We went to Auntie Bea's house. She refused to accept the letter of transfer. She refused to let me take my property. Then the deputy sheriff followed us back to where we rented the rental truck. He told us to get a warrant in detinue so that they could help us retrieve my family property."

Mr. Simms asked, "What did you do next?"

"I called my attorney and issued a warrant in detinue so I would be able to retrieve my mother's belongings," I answered.

Mr. Simms asked, "Okay. Did you file a warrant in detinue against your aunt?"

"Yes. I did," I responded.

Mr. Simms asked, "What happened in that case?"

I answered, "We settled."

Mr. Pricket said, "Objection, Judge. I object to uh, the uh, the court papers!"

Judge Colburn ruled, "Sustained."

Mr. Simms asked, "Were you able to reach an agreement with your aunt?"

I answered, "Yes. We reached an agreement. I was going to pay her $3,000 for storage fees. I also gave her some other items that my mother had purchased over the years. There was a grandfather clock, an antique dresser, and a wood chipper. Uncle Frank was going to buy the pickup truck from me and then I was going to give the Cadillac to my great-aunt."

Mr. Simms asked, "Your Honor, could I have Exhibit Number 7?"

Judge Colburn answered, "The one you never offered into evidence? All right."

Mr. Simms said, "Belinda, you've been handed what's been marked as Exhibit 7, which appears to be a letter to Miss Patson from Mr. Dickerson. Mr. Dickerson, who was he representing?"

I answered, "He was representing my great-uncle and my great-aunt."

Mr. Simms said, "Okay. This is referencing Belinda Star vs. Bea Mills. Is that the detinue action that you filed against her?"

I responded, "Yes, sir, it is."

Mr. Simms asked, "Have you seen this document before?"

"Yes, sir," I answered.

Mr. Simms asked, "Did you receive this from your attorney?"

I answered, "Yes, sir."

Mr. Simms asked, "And attached to this document is a copy of an order that was signed by Mr. Dickerson, but was not signed by your attorney, correct?"

I answered, "Correct. The government was involved then."

Mr. Simms said, "Okay. Now, does this order that was attached to the letter from Mr. Dickerson, does that reflect the agreement that you reached with your aunt concerning the settlement of their action?"

Mr. Pricket interrupted, "Wait a minute, Judge."

I answered, "Yes."

Mr. Pricket objected, "I object to—no. This is a case today by Mrs. King against these folks for a recovery of this property and now he's introducing evidence of an agreement between Mrs. Star and my folks regarding the same property."

Judge Colburn asked, "What about that?" As Mr. Simms was trying to respond to the judge's question, the judge interrupted. "Hold on. I'll let you address it, but my inquiry is if your action in detinue seeks relief on behalf of Mrs. King, why are you seeking to introduce evidence of an agreement regarding the same property made by another party?"

Mr. Simms didn't seem to understand. "Your Honor?"

Judge Colburn asked, "Would that not undercut your theory of recovery?"

Mr. Simms answered, "Well, let me respond to that first."

Judge Colburn assented, "All right."

Mr. Simms replied, "We haven't gotten to the reason why this became run aground, so to speak, that has to do with the federal government's lien."

"Well, you said that, but I mean we're dealing with the evidence in the case at this point," said Judge Colburn.

Mr. Pricket stated, "Judge, I'm going to withdraw my objection."

Judge Colburn agreed, "All right. That's fine. You can continue."

Mr. Simms said, "We request that the document be received into evidence, Your Honor."

Judge Colburn asked, "Is there any objection?"

Mr. Pricket replied, "I'm going to object to the document. I'm going to not object to the agreement that she reached with Mrs. Mills and the estate—what is now Mr. Gibbs, I guess, regarding disposition, Judge, of the property that's the subject of this action."

Mr. Simms asserted, "Well, the reason we're offering this document as evidence is that it indicates that we have this discrepancy. We have this list and we've tried a number of times to bring evidence as to what items were actually in the possession of the defendants. This document shows that the items on that list were in her possession because it states that certain items will go to the defendant and certain items will go to Mr. Gibbs, who is deceased. The remaining items on the Exhibit A, which the court has that list attached to the warrant in detinue, were all being transferred to Belinda Star. There's no indication of items that are not on the list and therefore aren't going to either of the parties."

Judge Colburn stated, "Mrs. Star, hand it up to me and let me take a look at it so I can consider that argument."

Mr. Pricket stated, "Judge, the agreement speaks for itself."

Mr. Simms said, "It does and in paragraph 5 it states, plaintiff, Belinda Star, is hereby declared to be the owner of the remaining items of personal property listed on Schedule A."

Mr. Pricket responded, "We don't object, Judge."

Judge Colburn said, "All right. I'm going to overrule the objection to the document itself. Your argument is well taken, Mr. Pricket. It might be corroborative."

Mr. Pricket stated, "We're withdrawing our objection."

Judge Colburn agreed, "That's fine. All right. It will be admitted then. All right. This has already been marked for identification as Plaintiff's Exhibit Number 7. I take that it is offered as proof that another party made an agreement regarding this property?"

Mr. Simms said, "Mrs. Star, this agreement that you had in settlement of the detinue action called for certain items of your mother's property to be conveyed to your aunt—for example, the 1987 Cadillac—is that right?"

"Yes, sir," I answered.

Mr. Simms asked, "Was there any reason why that could not be done?"

Mr. Pricket interrupted, "Objection, Your Honor. I don't think what happened pursuant to this agreement is relevant in this case."

Judge Colburn responded, "I'll sustain the objection to that."

Mr. Simms asked, "Was this agreement completed, Mrs. Star?"

Mr. Pricket interrupted, "Object to that, Judge."

"No, sir," I answered.

Mr. Pricket continued, "The parties had an agreement. If the agreement's been breached, it's an agreement between Mrs. Star and my clients and not between Mrs. King and my clients."

Judge Colburn assented, "I'll sustain the objection."

Mr. Simms asked, "Was there any reason that you were unable to perform any of your obligations under this agreement?"

Mr. Pricket again interrupted, "Object to that, Your Honor."

I answered, "Yes, sir."

Mr. Pricket said, "This is not an action between Mrs. Star and my client."

Judge Colburn responded, "I'll sustain the objection."

Mr. Simms asked, "Did you ever have occasion to have any communications with Mrs. Mills during the time your detinue action was pending?"

I answered, "Yes, sir, I did. What happened—"

As I was trying to explain exactly what happened, Mr. Pricket objected again. This time, he was objecting to the communications. He claimed that the dispute was already resolved. Mr. Simms rebutted that it was not resolved, and stated that was the reason we were all in court that day. He said that any statements Auntie Bea made to me regarding the transfer of title or any property were very relevant to this case. Mr. Pricket continued to argue, but the judge overruled his objection. He wanted to hear what I had to say.

"I explained to Auntie Bea that I could not get the titles signed for the vehicles because of the government. Every time we sent a title to the jail, they were returned. My attorney called the U.S. Attorney to find out what was going on. Then the U.S. Attorney changed his mind and said they were not going to fight me regarding the property any longer. He had forgotten that he had made a promise to my mother, and he stated that even though it had slipped his mind, he was going to honor it. He said that the property was mine and I could do with it as I chose—"

At that point, the judge raised his hand for me to stop speaking. I kept talking because once I started, I had a hard time stopping. The judge then told me to hold on for a minute. Mr. Pricket jumped in and claimed that what I was about to say was hearsay, and he was arguing about the format. He and the judge started arguing about it.

Judge Colburn replied, "It's not responsive. The question was regarding statements as I understood it."

Mr. Simms agreed, "Right."

Judge Colburn asked, "Did Mrs. Mills say anything?"

Mr. Simms asked, "Well, was that something you said to Ms. Mills?"

Judge Colburn asked, "Was there a solicited admission, not something else that was said?"

Mr. Simms asked, "Was that something that you said to Mrs. Mills in the form of a question?"

"I was telling Auntie Bea that we couldn't get it signed at that time because the government told us there was a lien on both properties and both—"

Mr. Pricket interrupted, "I'm going to object to the hearsay."

Judge Colburn responded, "That's hearsay. The court will sustain the objection her repeating what the government told her. That's clearly hearsay."

I agreed, "Okay."

Judge Colburn said, "If somehow that is the foundation for some alleged admission, why let's see what develops."

Mr. Simms asked, "What, if anything, did Mrs. Mills say to you concerning this?"

"I talked to Auntie Bea and asked her if she would just take the money and if we could just drop the rest of the transfer of the grandfather clock and the other. And she said she would have to think about it, but more than likely she would take the money at that time," I replied.

Mr. Pricket objected again, "I'm going to object to that, Judge, because it's not relevant to the action between Mrs. King and Mrs. Mills and the Gibbs estate."

Judge Colburn seemed unconvinced, "Well . . ."

Mr. Pricket continued, "It's only relevant to this issue between Mrs. Star and Mrs. Mills on their agreement."

Judge Colburn decided, "I'm going to overrule the objection. I understand your argument. That would be revisited."

Mr. Pricket assented, "All right."

Judge Colburn said, "The court is accepting the evidence, but also recognizes that it has to do with some unresolved dispute between this witness and your client; all right."

Mr. Simms continued, "Now, I take it you were not able to recover your mother's property in the detinue action?"

I responded, "I was not able to recover it."

Mr. Simms finished, "No further questions, Your Honor."

Judge Colburn asked, "Cross examination, Mr. Pricket?"

Mr. Pricket agreed, "Yes, sir."

As Mr. Pricket approached the witness stand, I thought, *Oh no, he's going to rip me a new one during his cross-examination.* I was very nervous.

Mr. Pricket asked, "Mrs. Star, when the safes were delivered to Aunt Bea's property, were they opened and inventoried?"

"Yes, sir," I answered.

Mr. Pricket asked, "By whom?"

I responded, "My stepbrother and I."

Mr. Pricket said, "Okay. Did you prepare a written inventory?"

I answered, "Yes, sir."

Mr. Pricket asked, "Did Mrs. Mills sign anything acknowledging receipt of any of the contents of the safes?"

I answered, "Not that I'm aware of."

Mr. Pricket asked, "Did Mr. Gibbs sign any receipt or document acknowledging the receipt of the contents of the safes?"

I answered, "No because he didn't go through them."

Mr. Pricket asked, "Who went through them?"

I repeated, "Me and my stepbrother."

Mr. Pricket asked, "Did you do that before or after their delivery to Mrs. Mills?"

I answered, "We did it when we were at Auntie Bea's. Auntie Bea was standing there with us watching as we went through them."

Mr. Pricket asked, "Did she sign anything while she was standing there with you?"

I answered, "No, she just asked to see my great-grandmother's ring."

Mr. Pricket said, "Okay."

I continued, "She then asked if she could wear it until I asked for it back and because she didn't want it to get lost."

Mr. Pricket asked, "Did Auntie Bea have a combination to the safe?"

I answered, "When I left in March of 1999, I gave the two vehicle keys to my great-aunt. I gave her the combinations to the safes and to my mother's briefcase. I gave some other small items her. She took them out and put them in a small cedar box that she had on her fireplace mantle."

Mr. Pricket asked, "During any of your subsequent conversations with her, did she tell you that she'd opened up the safes?"

I answered, "She told me when I gave her the combinations that she wouldn't open up the safes because she didn't know how. While I was staying with her, she asked me to open her personal safe anytime she needed in it."

Mr. Pricket said, "Okay. So she needed assistance. So even though you left her the keys and the combination, she didn't know how to do it?"

"Not that I'm aware of, sir," I responded.

Mr. Pricket asked, "Now, after you left for Germany on August—excuse me—on March of 1999, when did you come back?"

I answered, "I came back in March of 2000 to retrieve my mother's and my property."

Mr. Pricket said, "All right. And it was at that point where your mother signed over her property to you, is that correct?"

I answered, "Yes. Because Auntie Bea said she wanted my legal documents in order."

Mr. Pricket asked, "And then you went to try to get your property and couldn't get it, is that correct?"

"That's correct, sir," I answered.

Mr. Pricket asked, "And you filed a warrant in detinue in the general district court?"

I answered, "Yes. I did."

Mr. Pricket held up a document. "And is this a copy of the warrant in detinue?"

I responded, "I think it is. I think that's the original, but I'm not going to swear to it."

Mr. Pricket said, "Well, let me show you what is before the court. I'm sorry. I was just trying to—this is the one the judge has."

"Okay," I agreed.

Mr. Pricket asked, "Just make sure they're the same thing, okay?"

I said, "I think it's the original list, but I'm not positive."

Mr. Pricket asked, "Who prepared the list?"

"I did," I answered.

Mr. Pricket asked, "You prepared the list?"

I answered, "Yes. I prepared the schedule. It is not a list, but a summary of thousands of pages of inventory."

Mr. Pricket asked, "So you prepared the summary that was filed, is that correct?"

I answered, "Yes, sir, with the help of my attorney, Miss Patson."

Mr. Pricket said, "Okay. And on this detinue warrant, which is in evidence, you were listed as the plaintiff, is that correct?"

I answered, "Yes. That is what my attorney instructed me to do."

Mr. Pricket asked, "And Mrs. Mills and Mr. Gibbs are listed as the defendants, is that correct?"

"Yes. The address, I think, is incorrect, though," I answered.

Mr. Pricket said, "Okay. Well, and this is an action by you seeking recovery of the property, which your mother had transferred to you by her letter, is that correct?"

I replied, "Yes."

Mr. Pricket said, "Okay. And when this action was settled, and the judge has—has—Judge, I'm not sure which exhibit this is."

Judge Colburn affirmed, "Seven. That's number seven."

Mr. Pricket said, "I'm sorry. The judge has received into evidence Plaintiff's Exhibit Number 7, which is the letter from Mr. Dickerson and he refers to the agreement?"

I replied, "Yes."

Mr. Pricket said, "Okay. And it says on page two, paragraph five, that plaintiff, Belinda Star, is hereby declared to be the owner of the remaining items of property listed on Schedule A, right?"

I said, "At that time we thought we were doing it legally."

Mr. Pricket said, "Right."

I continued, "But apparently it wasn't."

Mr. Pricket answered, "Now, the Schedule A referred to here, the same Schedule A that's attached to the detinue warrant, are we talking about the same Schedule A?"

I answered, "I'm pretty sure this is it. There were so many revisions and everything else that was done to it."

Mr. Pricket said, "Okay. That's all I have, Judge."

Judge Colburn asked Mr. Simms, "Any redirect?"

Mr. Simms responded, "No, sir."

Judge Colburn stated, "All right. May we excuse this witness or would you like her to remain?"

Mr. Simms said, "If she could remain in the courtroom, that would be fine, Your Honor, at this point."

Judge Colburn said, "Well, the reason I make the inquiry is if you anticipate calling her again."

Mr. Simms stated, "I'm not going to recall her."

Judge Colburn responded, "All right. Mr. Pricket, is there any objection to this witness being excused?"

Mr. Pricket answered, "No, sir."

Judge Colburn said, "All right. Mrs. Star, thank you very much for your testimony. You've been excused. That means if you'd like to remain in the courtroom now you can do that. On the other hand, you're also free to depart. It's up to you."

"Okay," I replied, thankful to have completed my testimony.

Judge Colburn stated "Thank you again for your attendance."

Mr. Simms said, "Your Honor, we have no other witnesses."

Judge Colburn said, "All right. So the plaintiff rests; all right."

Mr. Pricket interjected, "Judge, we'd move to strike. I think there's two items of evidence before you in this case that warrant your concluding, without any doubt, that Mrs. King does not have a property interest in the items she seeks to recover.

"I first direct the court's attention to the plea agreement. The plea agreement contains a clear forfeiture of—of all of her property period, whether it's in her possession or somebody else's possession. She claims that there's an exception, and that being the property is sufficient for her to pay her attorney's fees. However, she has not produced into evidence today any agreement with the government, any document, any schedule showing what property is or is not accepted from the forfeiture. And since she's the one that made the forfeiture, it would be her burden to come forward with what was accepted from the forfeiture. That's grounds Number One.

"Grounds Number Two, Judge, if you accept that she did not, in fact, forfeit her property interest in the items on the Schedule A, and then she certainly can't get beyond the testimony of her own witness, Mrs. Star. The evidence is clear and contradicted that in March of 2000 Mrs. King transferred her interest in this property to Mrs. Star. Mrs. Star then, because she was not able to retrieve the property, filed a warrant in general district court naming herself as the plaintiff. She didn't say she was suing as agent for Mrs. King, on behalf of Mrs. King, or any such capacity whatsoever. Mrs. Star settled her case. One of the terms of the settlement was an acknowledgement by my clients, Mrs. Mills and the late Mr. Gibbs, that all of the items on Schedule A, except for the ones that were specifically enumerated prior to that, were the property of Mrs. Star.

"So Mrs. King can't rise above her own evidence in this case. Mrs. Star was her witness. The evidence before you is that this is the property of Mrs. Star and not Mrs. King. There's been no evidence, Judge, that the transfer of ownership was ever revoked or rescinded. So—and even if it were—even if they come back and argue well, she couldn't do it to start with to the extent that she claims now that the items on Schedule A were covered by the exception in the forfeiture agreement, she certainly had a right to transfer her interest in those items.

"So, Judge, I don't see how there's any way that she can stand before you and tell you, taking the evidence in the light most favorable to her, that she has an ownership interest in any of these items."

Judge Colburn nodded. "All right. Mr. Simms, I'll hear you."

Mr. Simms stated, "Your Honor, the plea agreement is the basis for much of this argument, and Mr. Pricket started out with his opening statement reading only a part of that plea agreement. And he's come to acknowledge that there is another sentence in that plea agreement. I think that the second sentence prevents this case from being decided at this point, Your Honor."

Judge Colburn said, "Well, what about his argument that he acknowledges that, but his argument in response is that it's the burden of your client to go forward with evidence to justify any exemption or exception to the forfeiture? How do you respond to that?"

Mr. Simms replied, "We would state, Your Honor, on that, the document speaks for itself. It does not require that there be an additional agreement documenting specific pieces of property with the U.S. Government. It states right there in this document that it automatically accepts such property or assets, which are necessary to fully and fairly reimburse the attorney. That's the—"

Judge Colburn interrupted, "Well, how can the court make a finding that any such funds or assets are necessary to fully and fairly reimburse the attorney for fees without any evidence or information to satisfy that clause of the agreement, assuming that your argument is—"

Mr. Simms continued, "The evidence that's been presented, Your Honor, particularly in the light most favorable to my client, is that my client incurred and owes attorney's fees as a result of that case. These are the only assets, the only property, that she has left in the world. And that evidence, we think, is sufficient to allow this action to proceed. The assets—the proof of the value of the assets—is less than the value of the property based upon the testimony of my client."

Judge Colburn said, "Well, what about the second argument? The one that—if you should not get around the agreement itself—by the evidence the plaintiff establishes that she transferred all of her right, title, and interest in the property to Mrs. Star, who then instituted some sort of litigation with Mrs. Mills and Mr. Gibbs. She then resolved that litigation with the findings that Mr. Pricket has made reference to, specifically taking into account that the property that your client claims she has some sort of remedy for in this action is listed on Schedule A and is the same property that Mrs. Star said she owned and pursued. How do you respond to that?"

Mr. Simms said, "The argument is that she doesn't own the property anymore. Therefore, she can't bring this action because she conveyed it to her daughter. The argument that he's making is that she can't bring this action because she's already conveyed the property to her daughter. Is that right?"

Judge Colburn said, "Well, I think if he's making the argument, but I think you've proved that. I think that's what he's really arguing."

Mr. Simms said, "For one thing, the—I think what we—we've proven is that that agreement was never—the agreement to settle between Mrs. Star and Mrs. Mills was never finalized, was never performed. And the reason for this is within the evidence that's before the court in terms of this plea agreement in which my client relinquished her authority to convey property. It's also before the court with respect to the judgment that the federal government has recorded as a judgment lien in this circuit. That's a matter of public record that it's attached to all of this property."

Judge Colburn asked, "Well, what's your authority for the proposition that it's been introduced into evidence in this particular proceeding?"

Mr. Simms responded, "Well, we would ask that the court take judicial notice of the—the recorded documents within this circuit."

Judge Colburn asked, "Well, the evidence has been completed, has it not?"

Mr. Simms said, "Well, Your Honor, with respect to the evidence that the court heard on this particular matter. What the court heard was that there was an attempt to transfer title of this personal property to my client's daughter as an effort to recover it from her aunt and uncle who were, at that point, refusing to return it. The court saw evidence on an agreement that those parties reached that was never performed and the testimony and the evidence is that it wasn't performed because this plea agreement came to light in which my client had relinquished her authority to convey the property in the settlement of her detinue action."

Judge Colburn asked, "But how does the evidence—what evidence is there that supports that conclusion?"

Mr. Simms answered, "The evidence is the language in the plea agreement, which states that my client relinquishes her possession, title, and interest in the property subject to the one exception that allows her to retain such properties necessary to pay her attorney's fees. The language in that plea agreement makes a conveyance to her daughter without consideration, as apparently was done in this case void, because it's in violation of the plea agreement, Your Honor. That's the evidence that's before this court. Because that conveyance was void, the settlement agreement between the parties in the district court case—the general district court case—was not performed. That's why we're here today. If that had been enforceable before we wouldn't be here today."

Judge Colburn said, "But the agreement was between another party, Mrs. Star and Mrs. Mills. You said it wasn't performed, but that's the key to the analysis that—that—and I'm trying to understand your—your argument here because I want to give you a full and fair shake on the—on the evidence and on the law, but the—the agreement was not between Mrs. King and Mrs. Mills. The agreement was between Mrs. Star and Mrs. King. So, you're saying that—that the proof that you brought forth proving that your client transferred her interest in the property to Mrs. Star should simply be rejected? In other words, you've proved that, but it should have no legal effect, and it all gets back to the plea agreement—is that the gist of your argument?"

Mr. Simms replied, "Well—yes. What we've proven is that the attempt was void because of the plea agreement in which she relinquished her authority to do that. She didn't know that. The evidence was that she didn't know that at the time. She hadn't read her plea agreement, and her daughter did not know that then. Their attorney did not know that either. That's what the evidence that was submitted to the court was and, further, they found that out in the context of the settlement of the general district court detinue action. Then they were fully apprised of the nature of the plea agreement and that the attempt of conveyance—"

Judge Colburn interrupted, "What evidence is there in the case of that?"

Mr. Simms questioned, "I'm sorry, Your Honor?"

Judge Colburn restated, "What evidence is there in the case that they were apprised of the plea agreement with legal implications? What proof is there in the case of that?"

Mr. Simms responded, "I believe there was testimony to that effect, Your Honor. That they found out that they were unable to pursue it because of the plea agreement and conversations with the U.S. Attorney."

Judge Colburn replied, "I thought a hearsay objection was sustained to that testimony. I—maybe—I'm—I'm just going on my memory."

Mr. Pricket interjected, "It was, Your Honor."

"I'm not looking at my notes," said Judge Colburn.

Mr. Simms asserted, "Well, Your Honor, we believe that the court has sufficient facts before it in the form of this plea agreement to draw reasonable inferences that the attempt at conveyance from my client to her daughter was in violation of the plea agreement void and, therefore, there was no conveyance as a matter of law. And, therefore, the argument that my client conveyed the property to her daughter is not a real party in interest fault and that the court has the plea agreement in front of it. The reasonable inferences that can be drawn from that plea agreement are that my client did not have the authority to convey the property to her daughter without any consideration."

Judge Colburn nodded, "All right. All right; Mr. Pricket, you may rebut."

Mr. Pricket stated, "Judge, very briefly. If there was a problem with the transfer between the mother and the daughter because of the plea agreement, then that's a dispute between the mother and the daughter. It's not a dispute between the mother and my clients. So, therefore, if Mrs. King can't recover her property from these folks because of some problem with that plea agreement, then she and her daughter are going to have to resolve that. That's number one. Number two, let's assume, Judge, that the exception to the forfeiture allies—that second sentence—their argument is that the second sentence gives Mrs. King some property interest in the property that would be necessary to pay her lawyer. If that's the case, then she had the authority to transfer that property interest, and if, in fact, she did—if the items on Schedule A are what the items accepted, as she contends—then she had the authority to transfer that to her daughter.

This is exactly what we contend she did, and her daughter then pursued a claim against my clients for the recovery of that property. We still go back to base one. It's a claim by Mrs. Star against my clients, not a claim by Mrs. King. Judge, there's no evidence before you whatsoever that supports ownership at the time this action was instituted by Mrs. King."

Judge Colburn assented, "All right. All right; the court has considered the arguments of counsel. What I'm going to do is take just a brief recess. I want to reflect on these arguments and I'll rule on the motion to strike. I would anticipate ten to fifteen minutes. The court simply wants to organize its thinking before I rule."

Mr. Pricket asked, "Can we go outside, Judge?"

Judge Colburn answered, "Yes. Counsel can stand aside for fifteen minutes. I'll give you ample time; all right."

I went outside because I was going through serious nicotine withdraw. And my nerves were shot. My mother and Mr. Simms stayed inside the courtroom. I stood and listened as Mr. Pricket tried to explain to my adversaries what he was trying to accomplish. I had to admit that I did not understand anything that was happening. I just knew that the attorneys and the judge had taken the truth and twisted it to serve their purpose. It didn't matter if my mother had forfeited her rights to the U.S. Attorney or not because that was between the U.S. Attorney and my mother. My mother did not forfeit her rights to Bea and Frank. The recess flew by, and once again, we were seated in the courtroom once.

Judge Colburn began, "All right. I thank counsel and the parties for their patience during that recess. The court took a bit longer than it had anticipated. I wanted to think through the issue carefully before ruling on the question. All right; this is a motion to strike. So, of course, the court will view the evidence in the light most favorable to the plaintiff, and, of course, taking into account the evidence and all the reasonable inferences there from, we rule accordingly.

"Of course, we start out with the fact that this is an action sounding in detinue. It seeks the recovery of certain property by the plaintiff alleged to be in the possession of the defendants. So, as Mr. Pricket argues, the heart of the issue comes down to whether taking in the light most favorable to the plaintiff, there is sufficient evidence to establish an ownership interest in the property in question. That obviously is a threshold element for a detinue action. It has to be established before the matter can go forward.

And here, there are two principal arguments made by the defendants and I'll analyze them separately.

"The first argument, and Mr. Pricket alluded to this in his opening statement, has to do with the direct unequivocal language of this plea agreement, which has been introduced into evidence. And, of course, I'm quoting from the agreement where the plaintiff in this case, with reference to property owned by her, which she in her own testimony conceded included this property, agreed as follows: 'I agree to immediately forfeit all rights, title, and interest in any property owned by me and in my possession or the possession of relatives at my direction to the United States as partial restitution in my case.' So that language makes it very clear that, if that language is the end of the matter, why the plaintiff would have no ownership interest in this property that would entitle her to any relief under a detinue theory. Of course, as both counsels have pointed out, we need to address the next clause of this agreement to the extent that it has any impact on this case because there's an exception to that. That language says 'I understand that the United States accepts from this agreement only such funds or assets as are necessary to fully and fairly reimburse my attorney for fees related to these proceedings.'

"Well, in the court's judgment, why if, in fact, there is any exception to the forfeiture element of the agreement, the court has to analyze the evidence here to see even if taken in the light most favorable to the evidence—most favorable to the plaintiff such evidence exists. Now, here the—the principal evidence that's been cited is the testimony of the plaintiff that she owes her attorney fees and her testimony regarding the assets themselves. This testimony indicates the approximate values that she places on these items, given based on her opinion. But in the court's judgment, even taking that evidence in the light most favorable to the plaintiff, why that's certainly not sufficient for the court to make a finding that those funds or assets are necessary to fully and fairly reimburse the attorney for fees related to these proceedings. There's been no evidence on those points whether the fees were fair, whether they were full, and whether they were necessary. There has been nothing for the court to reach any conclusions on that matter. So even in the light most favorable to the plaintiff, the court finds that the evidence is not sufficient.

"However, the court will also address the second argument raised by Mr. Pricket and that is that if the court is incorrect and these assets, in fact, are funds or assets that are necessary to fully and fairly reimburse the attorney for fees related to the federal proceedings, if the court has incorrectly ruled on the other issue, why the court will next address the second argument. And the second argument is a bit more difficult to analyze in the sense that it—it really points out the contradiction in the plaintiff's case.

"If, in fact, the assets in question—the items that are the subject of this litigation—are accepted under the terms of this agreement, why then it follows that the items in question are the plaintiff's. They belong to the plaintiff under the instruction of the agreement, and as Mr. Pricket perceptively argues, if that's the case—in other words, if the court's wrong in its interpretation of the evidence in connection with agreement, why if the exception applies that means she owned the items in question. And as a result, she had the legal authority to transfer them to her daughter. Now, it may well be that by doing that, she could get into trouble with the federal authorities. And it might lead to some trouble or some problems under this plea agreement, but if the items in question are an exception to this forfeiture clause, there's no evidence before the court that would legally prohibit her from making the transfer to her daughter the way it was described in great detail by both her and the daughter. And the plaintiff herself testified that she did this; the daughter said it was done. The daughter admitted that all these items were transferred to her, and then after that, she proceeded to institute the prior litigation. Plaintiff's Exhibit Number 5 and Plaintiff's Exhibit Number 7 make it clear that the prior litigation was between Belinda Star exclusively and the defendants in this case. And the evidence before the court is that the settlement that arose from that litigation could not be completed or was breached. But there's no evidence before the court, other than the argument made by the plaintiff's counsel, there's no evidence before the court whereby the court could find that any such transfer or attempt at settlement was legally void.

"To rule otherwise, at least in the court's judgment, would be first to find that the forfeiture clause of the plea agreement doesn't apply. But then, the court would have to find that even though the exception applies, with her own proof, it shows that she did know that the exception was illegal and void and that part of her own evidence, in effect, should be ignored. And the court, even as I said, taking the evidence, is sufficient to allow the case to go forward. So, the court is going to strike the evidence in the case based on both of the arguments made by Mr. Pricket.

"Mr. Simms, your exceptions to that ruling are noted and preserved in the record. Mr. Pricket, you've, in effect, prevailed. I'm going to ask you to draw an order reflecting the ruling of the court. Mr. Simms, you can endorse the order in any manner that you deem appropriate; all right. That is the ruling of the court. Mr. Simms, is there anything else that you'd like addressed in connection with the case?"

Mr. Simms asked, "Well, Your Honor, I assume that takes care of Mr. Pricket's counterclaim because the court's ruling that my client didn't have an ownership interest in the property; therefore, would it be appropriate to charge her storage fees for that?"

Judge Colburn said, "Well, we certainly—"

Mr. Pricket interrupted, "Logically there follows, Judge—"

Judge Colburn said, "That hasn't been argued. I haven't ruled on that. Is that an issue?"

Mr. Pricket continued, "You haven't ruled on that, but I guess if it's not her—"

Judge Colburn asked, "Is there any argument that if—"

Mr. Pricket stated, "If it's not her property, Judge, I don't guess we can claim storage. We would like to withdraw our counterclaim for storage fees, at this time."

Judge Colburn agreed, "Well, it would seem to me that would be the logical conclusion of the court's decision, but if you have an argument otherwise, I'll let you address it."

Mr. Pricket said, "No, I think it follows from your ruling. If, based on your ruling, if she has no property interest, our claim is withdrawn."

Judge Colburn agreed again, "Well, of course—well, let's—I believe that's correct based on the evidence that's been introduced in this proceeding."

Mr. Pricket nodded, "Yes, sir."

Judge Colburn stated, "But in any event, that's the ruling of the court. It's based on the evidence that's been introduced here; all right. Mr. Pricket, is there anything else you'd like addressed?"

"No, sir. I'll put in the order based upon the court's ruling," said Mr. Pricket.

Judge Colburn nodded, "That's fine. All right; is there anything else then from the defendants?"

Mr. Pricket stated, "No, sir."

"All right. I believe that concludes this matter then for today. I believe this is the last case on the court's docket. So on that note then, court will stand adjourned," said Judge Colburn.

"Thank you, Judge," said Mr. Pricket.

I looked down at my watch on my wrist, and I was shocked to see that it was 5:06 p.m. This must have been the judge Miss Patson had talked about. I still could not make sense of his ruling. He did not look my mother, Mr. Simms, or me in the eye, as he babbled his ruling that did not make a bit of sense.

As Mr. Simms was packing up his papers in his briefcase, he turned his head toward me and immediately knew my mother and I were just as stunned as he was.

Mr. Simms said, "Belinda, don't worry, that silly judge unwittingly left us a back door. I have never lost and won at the same time before."

My mother said, "Belinda, you are going to have to finish this battle."

All three of us walked outside together. May, John, and Ed were laughing as they looked at us.

I was so angry I said, "Why are you laughing, you stupid little people? You didn't win anything. The judge just left it up in the air. I'll be back."

The three of us just walked to the parking lot and Mr. Simms said, "Call me before you leave town, and we will plan our next move."

CHAPTER XXXV

A year or so had passed and my mother and I were again flying back to Virginia. Mr. Pricket had filed a plea in bar trying to prevent me from going any further with my lawsuit against my great-aunt and my great-uncle's estate. We still hadn't recovered my family's property, and I had spent most of our savings on attorney's fees.

I looked over at my mother and she patted my hand. I was once again sitting in the window seat. My mother looked into my eyes, smiled sadly, and said, "You will get justice this time, Belinda. I just know God will give us justice. I just know he will. After all he gave me you, my only soldier, my 'She Wolf.'"

I looked deep into her beautiful blue eyes. They were so blue that I could almost see the sea in them. I moved my other hand to pat her hand that was rested on top of mine and said, "I don't know if the spirit of She Wolf still prevails in my blood. I'm tired, I'm older, and I have spilled a lot of blood for this country, my God, and for you. I just don't know, Momma, if my back is still strong for you. I don't know if I have enough to fight this one."

My mother looked at me and her gaze left my eyes for a moment before she spoke in an almost whisper, "She Wolf will always be in your blood, as she is in mine and your sister's blood, but you have the strongest part of her. You always did have the strongest part. You're a fighter, a female warrior, as She Wolf was. You carry her blood thicker in your veins than any of us do. You do what is right, as you have always done. I know you will prevail this time. Your name still means honor; mine doesn't. Your name alone will prevail, Belinda. We will win this battle this time, because I know you."

I smiled sadly at my mother, leaned over, and gave her a kiss on her cheek. I knew she had too much faith in me sometimes. I turned my head from her without saying another word and looked out the window.

I started drifting into my memories of the war and my own battle that I was fighting with my own flesh and blood.

Our commander-in-chief had sent our great military forces into Iraq again. Within a few months of the invasion, my husband's unit was called to fight.

Part of me was glad our commander-in-chief had taken the battle to the Middle East. A battlefield had to be created to keep the terrorists off our own soil. Militarily speaking, the best plan was to contain the situation and take the fight to another location. Saddam Hussein had to be taken out anyway, but he should have been the icing on the cake, not the cake itself.

My husband left with his regiment for Iraq, and I was left in charge of the support group for the family members of the soldiers. Of course, this group was called something else originally, but unbelievably, people filed complaints because they took offense to the word "support." The tradition of each company was that the first sergeant's wife would coordinate this type of support for the troopers in his command along with the commander's spouse. The reasoning behind this was that if the troopers' families were taken care of while the troopers were on the battlefield, then the troopers would have their minds on the battlefield instead of worrying about their families at home. This helped all of us—both at home and abroad—to unite as one family unit "taking care of your own."

Sadly, this tradition was slowly fading away from our military communities. I really hoped that someday it would be returned in full strength. Now that I was "just a spouse," I had a different perspective on the hardships that the family members endure while supporting their loved one in uniform.

Once I really thought about it and finally admitted the truth to myself, I wanted to be with my husband because I knew I would have his back and he would have mine. They always say two TOPs are better than one. The reverse of that was that you had double the lives to worry about, not just your own. Nonetheless, they didn't call us the "Star team" for nothing. I guess the worry of not knowing for the first time in my life was more than I could bear.

I had a newfound compassion for the spouses and family members of our soldiers. It truly was a hardship when one is left at home; this was especially true for me because I knew from first-hand experience what the soldiers were up against. I knew the horrors of warfare all too well, but I would do my best to keep it in the box with all the other bad memories of what I had experienced and endured. I would gladly go through it all again if my body and mind were willing.

Since Thomas had been deployed, I had bent the rules on behalf of him and his entire regiment numerous times. At the time of his deployment, I was a transportation and supply specialist. Whenever Thomas called me for something they could not obtain through normal channels, I made it happen, with the blessing of my boss. I even communicated back and forth with rear detachment and Thomas; there was such a time difference and communications had not been established yet.

Once Thomas' regiment settled in their new temporary home, I wasn't needed as much. In other words, they had more of the luxuries of home, and they were able to communicate much easier with rear detachment.

I remembered reading or hearing somewhere of a female senior (NCO) reservist, who had served her tour and then returned to her normal life as a homemaker and mother of two. She killed herself because she felt like she was obsolete and unneeded. When she wore a uniform, she was needed and received great respect. Now that I was just a civilian and there was a war going on, I could truly relate to that young woman. There were days when I felt like I was not making a difference and my work didn't matter, but nothing was worth killing myself. Every suicide was just as tragic as a combat death, but there was no respect and glory in suicide. I wasn't from the school of thought that suicide meant your soul would go straight to hell, but I did believe that God shed a tear each time one of his beloved children decided that what he created was worthless.

I heard my mother's voice and looked up. The flight attendant was asking if we would like something to drink. I asked for my usual, a vodka and tomato juice. My mother ordered a glass of burgundy. After I paid for my mother's wine and my drink, I looked back out the window returning to my thoughts.

I decided that I was not going to think of my husband and the dangers that he could be facing. Instead, I focused my thoughts on all the legal crap that was going on. Focusing on my concerns regarding my family's possessions and this fight was much easier than thinking of the precious blood being spilled to protect our freedoms. Our freedoms allow us walk without fear of being killed, to worship as we choose, to sleep at night without fear of a nuclear attack; these same freedoms had been taken from many throughout our world and they are slowly being taken from us as well.

I had spent so much money over the past several years trying to recover our belongings, and I started to wonder if it was even worth it anymore. I could not understand why things were going this way. Why did our justice system have to be so complicated, with no common sense? After all, our country's laws, which are based on God's laws, are so simple. Why couldn't everything be black and white instead of including numerous shades of gray? Stealing was stealing no matter how it was done. Here I was spending another small fortune just to defend my right and my mother's right to sue Auntie Bea and the estate of Uncle Frank to have my family property returned. It was not their property; it never was. I spent thousands of dollars from my personal bank account, not to mention my time, sweat, and tears, to bail them out of trouble, and this was how they thanked me. In my heart, I knew this was not what Uncle Frank would have wanted, but he did not have the guts to stand up to his sister.

I already knew I was going to have the same incompetent, stereotyping judge that my mother had when she tried to sue for the return of our property. He was a judge that ruled from the bench and not by our laws. I truly hoped that my financial sacrifice would not be in vain.

When it came to our court system, you were lucky to have your case heard within a year's time. My case had been delayed repeatedly because their nasty slick attorney was trying to stop me from going any further. This plea in bar, which I still did not understand, had stopped Mr. Simms dead in his tracks from preparing to fight. It was not Mr. Pricket, and not my relatives, but the nasty judge we had. As Mr. Simms had said to me numerous times, "This judge shoots from the hip, and not by the law. Belinda, he is truly against us, and I honestly don't know how I'm going to fight him."

Throughout all this, Mr. Simms had kept defending the law, stating, "Belinda, our justice system is made up of checks and balances, and that is why I want us to have a jury. You are entitled to this."

Once again Mr. Simms' opponent, Mr. Pricket, had pulled something out of Pandora's box, a plea in bar, because Mr. Pricket could not blow smoke in the air as easily with a jury as he could with the judge. We tried to take my case back to the lower court, but Mr. Pricket fought to keep it in the higher court because he knew Judge Colburn would do everything and anything to prevent me from seeing that the law was upheld.

Before I knew it, we were at our last layover in Pennsylvania. There was a nice little shop that sold costume jewelry. My mother walked over and stared at the items. Her eyes welled up with tears as she started remembering aloud the times she bought some nice pieces in that store. I had a few extra dollars in my pocket so I told her, "Well, since we have a two-hour wait, let's go inside and see what we can find."

My mother's eyes lit up and a smile spread over her face as we walked into the small shop. She walked to the various counters and looked at each piece. She pointed to several of them, and we discussed them. I even found some nice pieces. I walked back to the main counter and Mom followed me. I asked the young lady behind the counter to let my mother see the pretty baubles that were displayed in the glass counter cases. I bought several pieces for my mother and for myself. She immediately put several of them on and giggled like a schoolgirl.

Our two hours flew and before I knew it, we were on the small plane for the short flight to Virginia. My mother became sad again as she spoke out loud regarding the pieces of jewelry that once belonged to my great-great grandmother; jewelry that had been stolen from her. I knew not to say anything.

After we arrived in the Snobville airport, I got our luggage, our rental car, and I drove us to a nice hotel. I learned my lesson about renting a cheap motel room the last time we had been in Snobville. That time Mom and I didn't get a wink of sleep because of the horrible room we had.

I used my military ID and received the standard discount for the room. After we settled in, I took my mother down to the restaurant in the hotel, and we ordered a nice dinner. Over dinner, we talked and my mother prepared me to answer the questions that would be asked of me during the plea in bar the next morning.

CHAPTER XXXVI

Mr. Simms instructed me to park behind the courthouse and wait outside in the back parking lot.

Mr. Simms said, "Belinda, I have a strong suspicion that the judge does not like you or your mother. I have no idea why, but I'm hoping that if he doesn't see you, he will do the right thing. Also, if you stay out of sight, you will not have to testify."

I replied, "Okay, Mr. Simms. You're the expert here. We will do what you think is best. Good luck in there!"

He smiled and disappeared around the building.

I was sitting in the driver's seat with the window rolled down, smoking a cigarette, and my mother was working on her needle point when Mr. Simms walked up to the driver's side. Only twenty minutes had passed.

Mr. Simms exclaimed, "You're not going to believe it, but the judge from your mother's trial isn't presiding today! He was unable to make it today and Judge Roser is filling in for him. Mr. Pricket wants us to delay—shocking I know—but the judge is willing to hear the plea in bar because you have come from Colorado. This is great news! From my experience, and what I have heard, Judge Roser is a fair and noble judge. He instructed me to locate you and see what you want to do."

I didn't even need to think about it. I excitedly replied, "Let's do this now!"

Mom and I got out of the car and locked it as quickly as we could. My hands were shaking with excitement! As we briskly walked to the courthouse entrance, we discussed our plan of action. Mr. Pricket was waiting for us at the entrance. As we approached him, he stopped us and pleaded, "Mrs. Star, this is a different judge. Would you mind rescheduling? Don't you have family members you need to see instead of this? Can't you put this off until our original judge is able to preside?"

Before I had a chance to say a word, Mr. Simms gently pushed me to the side and placed himself between Mr. Pricket and me. He said in a low, but stern voice, "How dare you. You know better than that, Mr. Pricket. If you have an issue, you will address the attorney of record. You will not address and attempt to badger my client outside this courtroom. You are begging only because Judge Roser is not a crooked, arrogant, pompous jerk that rules by his whim and not by the law. You're attempts at blowing smoke up everyone's asses will not work this time!"

Mr. Simms picked up his briefcase and grabbed my hand. I grabbed my mother's hand and the three of us walked into the courthouse with our heads held high. I had to admit I was completely bewildered with this tough attitude Mr. Simms was exhibiting. He was a tall and handsome man, and he was normally gentle and soft-spoken. This was the first time I had really seen him lose his composure and act with aggression.

At that moment, I realized that Mr. Simms had taken this case to heart. He seemed every bit as disgusted with the immoral judge and attorney as I was. He was doing his absolute best to try to uphold the laws of our great country. He was truly a fellow warrior, but he fought a different type of battle on a different front. He was truly a son of the Unites States of America. "Truth, justice, and the American way!"

We approached the security guard who was stationed outside the courtroom. The doors were opened, and as I handed my briefcase to the guard and walked through the scanner, I looked to the front of the courtroom. The courtroom was completely empty! Auntie Bea wasn't even there. The only person in the large courtroom was their attorney, Mr. Pricket. He was standing by the defense table. Mr. Simms motioned for me to have a seat at the plaintiff's table. As I was sitting down, I glanced over at Mr. Pricket. He glared at me in response. When Mr. Simms saw the way he was looking at me, he said, "Stop trying to intimidate my client. You should know by now, Mr. Pricket, she is not intimidated very easily."

Mom sat in the bench behind Mr. Simms and me. Before we knew it, the bailiff called the court to session and the judge walked in. The judge ordered everyone seated and called our case. This time, the proceedings were not as formal as the other trials we had been in, and I started to relax. In retrospect, I guess it was because this was not a trial; it was a plea in bar.

From my understanding of the numerous conversations with Mr. Simms, a plea in bar was simply a hearing orchestrated by the defense stating that this was a frivolous suit. In this case, Mr. Pricket was stating that because we were mother and daughter this case was basically the same as my mother's previous case.

The lawyers started their verbal debate. I could barely hear what they were saying, and what I could hear did not make any sense to me.

Suddenly, Judge Roser said, "Mrs. Star, would you please come to the witness stand?"

Both attorneys stared at me in surprise. I smiled at Mr. Pricket and approached the bailiff who swore me in. I then stepped up into the witness box and sat down in the chair.

The judge looked at me and gently said, "Mrs. Star, I want you to start at the beginning and give me the short version to what has happened and why we are here."

I did my very best, but it took me thirty minutes to give a short version of how and why we were there. I told him what had happened to my mother, and I told him what my great-aunt and my great-uncle had done. I told him how long our property had been stored at their residences. I told him about the agreement made during the warrant in detinue; I told him why my mother filed her lawsuit. I pretty much told everything that had occurred since 1991. I was very happy that I had taken the time during the flight here to make the list. My story would have gone much more quickly, but Mr. Pricket repeatedly interrupted me. In my opinion, he only succeeded in making Judge Roser angry with him because the judge kept telling him to stop interrupting.

When I finally finished, the judge told me that I could return to my seat. Before I even had a chance to sit in my chair beside Mr. Simms, both attorneys were back in front of the judge arguing again. From what I could make out, Mr. Pricket was claiming that we were mother and daughter claiming the same property and it was just another means to continue suing his clients repeatedly and arbitrarily. He was spewing out cases as examples. He asserted his peremptory plea to prevent me from going any further with my lawsuit.

Mr. Simms was arguing that I filed a warrant in detinue, and Mr. Pricket's clients breached it. He also claimed that during my mother's case, I claimed that my mother had given the property to me. He claimed it was a mother and daughter transfer and the property either belonged to me or my mother. The other judge ruled that the only thing that Mr. Simms proved during my mother's lawsuit was that the property was legally mine.

Then I heard the judge ask, "How can this be a plea in bar when it's mother and daughter fighting against your clients for the return of the property? It's not the mother and daughter fighting against each other for the same property against your client or acting as one entity."

The two attorneys continued arguing, and before I knew it, the judge said, "I rule that this case can go forward. There is no evidence showing a plea in bar."

I looked over at Mr. Simms as we stood up because the judge was leaving. He was smiling from ear to ear. I leaned forward to look at Mr. Pricket, but he was already gone.

With a huge smile on his face, Mr. Simms said, "See, Belinda, our laws do work when you have people that follow them, like this judge."

"But we don't have this judge, we have the other," I said with an air of defeat.

Mr. Simms said, "I will fight him the best I can, Belinda. I promise."

I called Thomas' mother and asked her if she was able to meet Mom and I for a celebration dinner. We met at a local seafood restaurant, and over our shrimp and crab legs, Mom and I told her about our day. This was the second battle that I had won against my great-aunt, and once again, I had a different type of warrior who fought against the strange and sometimes obscure rules of engagement that our justice system dictated.

CHAPTER XXXVII

Mom and I caught a flight home to Colorado the next morning. Once we returned home, we spent the rest of the day celebrating our victory. Early the next morning, my darling husband called. He was very upset because he had a "Betty Crocker" for a commander. He stated she was too busy writing about herself to the local newspaper back home and running around taking pictures of everyone and everything instead of effectively commanding her own unit. She was constantly making him and his troopers pose for pictures so she could send them back home to show her community what a hero she was.

Thomas stated, "Belinda, she is constantly coming into my room, uninvited of course, with some pitiful excuse that she had to see me right away. She's always hugging and touching me in front of my troopers and other officers. She tells me all the time how happy she is that I'm her first sergeant. I think she only says that because she knows I'll keep her and her command safe and allow her all the glory. Belinda, I don't know what to do about her! I'm losing the respect of my troopers and other officers. I'm always getting into arguments with her because she doesn't like the way you are running the support group.

"In addition to our verbal arguments, we have an ongoing argument regarding your emails because she wants you to raise money; and you and I keep telling her that the support group is not about raising money. She is running away from the reality that she has a responsibility to lead. She is one of the few females in the Army who definitely should not be in command, and probably shouldn't even be allowed to wear the uniform. She is using it for her own benefit instead of honoring it as she serves and fights for our country.

"Belinda, she is a disgrace to the uniform, and I am ashamed to have to serve under her. Baby, I really wish you were here to keep her in check. She doesn't share information with me or anyone else. We're supposed to share a laptop, but she keeps everything a secret and has the laptop password protected. I have no access to it, and I have to rely on you and the other commanders of the brigade to know what is going on. I have to oversee the daily operations and missions because she does absolutely nothing!

"I have been running the company primarily by myself. I do have two lieutenants, but they're still very raw. I think she is doing everything in her power not to take responsibility for making decisions. She knows that each decision could be a life-or-death situation for the troopers in her command. She's terrified of making the wrong decision, so she's running from it. I'm doing everything in my power to prevent any type of routine mission for Al-Qaeda to detect. I'm changing the mission's route every single day with no pattern. I'm physically leading each mission myself and it is weakening me as a leader. I have already lost my first trooper because of her lack of leadership. Baby, I have to be there for every mission so that I can do everything in my power from losing another. She is useless!"

He told me he was constantly worrying about losing one of his troopers again. He was very upset that he had lost one already, and he was constantly fighting with her because he wanted to make sure every one of his troopers that was wounded received a purple heart, even if it was considered minor. He told me about the one female trooper in his unit who had been shot in the ass. His commander refused to sign the paperwork for her to receive a purple heart simply because she had been shot in the ass. She even laughed every time she said the word "ass." To him, it was not funny, and I totally agreed with him. A wound at war is sacred, regardless of where the injury happens to be.

Thomas then told me about another female trooper that was PCSing to another command; she was back in Colorado. She and her two baby daughters had been killed by a drunk driver.

I replied with shock and sadness, "Oh, my God! I read that in the local newspaper, but it didn't click that she was directly in your command. I'm so sorry, baby."

I then proceeded to give my thoughts regarding the other issues he was facing. "Thomas, you are going to have to get your two lieutenants to speak with the brigade commander. If the brigade commander takes the word of the lieutenants and comes to you about it, you should tell the truth and let the brigade commander deal with it. If the brigade commander thinks it is unnecessary to remove her from command, then,

Bear, you will have to tell her to stop hugging and touching you and entering your room. You're going to have to tell her that she made you feel uncomfortable. If that doesn't work, tell her that you are going to file sexual harassment charges.

"Bear, what she is doing is sexual harassment. If you were doing that to a female under your command, you would have charges thrown at you, and you'd be facing a court-martial. You need to tell her that you have enough to deal with over there and that you should not have to put up with her crap on top of the responsibility of keeping your troopers alive. If she keeps up with her behavior and doesn't take the responsibility of helping you make decisions on the missions, you should request a transfer into another company within the brigade. If for some reason that doesn't work and she becomes hostile toward you, just tell her that I will reenlist as an officer, come over there, and kick her boney white ass back into reality!"

Thomas laughed and said, "Come on, Belinda, you know damn well I'm not going to allow you to do that."

I laughed and said, "I guess that is an extreme, but you know if I put my mind to it I will do it. I know it's hard, TOP, but you have overcome a lot worse than this silly female. I don't think she is deliberately making sexual advances toward you. I think she is very insecure and scared to death of making the wrong decision. I don't think she wants the consequences of the wrong decision on her conscience."

Thomas responded, "Yeah, I guess if I can survive you after all these years and all the missions that you and I have been on, I guess I can survive this female as well. But, Belinda, it's a big difference on our off time pretending to be supply sergeants and transportations sergeants—you know what we really are."

"I know, but that's what you really are now, and I guess the job is much tougher than we thought," I said.

Thomas sighed. "It is, Belinda, because it was just us and your sister, Mark, and a few others. I never had this type of responsibility of worrying about hundreds of lives before. You know this job's missions are deadlier than what we did, in my opinion. You got out, and we were at peace when you were the TOP in Supply and Transportation."

I said, "I know, but dealing with all these spouses is mentally exhausting. They don't understand what it's like being in the military. All they know is the pain and fear, and they're constantly worrying about the unknown. I truly have a new respect for the spouses, children, and other family members. They're heroes in their own right."

Thomas finally let out another sigh. "I love you. I'll deal with it, and I'll think about what's the best course of action. I support my commander because I don't know any better, but I just don't want to get her into trouble. After all, I'm trained to respect my chain of command and deal with it without complaining. I think this is the first time I actually whined about something so petty. I guess this is a sign that I'm getting old and weakening."

I replied sadly, "I know I'm burned out, too! I know I have too many demons in my box, so I think I know you may have too many now as well. Do your job, soldier, and come back home to me safe and sound."

Thomas sighed and said, "I'm glad you're my She Wolf. I'm proud and honored to call you my wife. I love you, don't forget that, and don't forget us, and who we were. I'll do my duty no matter what the challenges, but I don't want you to fight my demons for me. I just need you to listen to me and help me through this bad patch, no matter what my decision is."

"I'm your wife, Bear, and I'm honored and proud to call you husband, friend, and lover. No matter the distance between us and no matter what obstacles you must face, I'll always have your back. I love you and I swear to God if anything happens to you because of this silly female, I will seek vengeance, no matter the cost," I replied with conviction.

Thomas became slightly angry and sternly responded, "No, you won't. I will not allow that. You will not carry that on your shoulders. It is, and always will be, my choice to be here. It is not your burden, and I will not allow you to take that honor from me. Do you understand? I guess I'm used to being around 'She Wolfs' throughout my military career. Granted, many of them didn't have the spirit of the She Wolf as strong in them as you and your sister did."

"Yes. I understand, but, Thomas, not all women have the Spartan blood running through their veins like Teresa and I have. We have even encountered many of the male gender that cannot deal with the reality of the battlefield. You know this," I said.

Thomas agreed.

We talked for a few minutes longer before he had to get off the phone. We told each other how much we loved each other, and I hung up the phone.

I stood there staring at the telephone and thought, *I have a bad feeling this time—a bad feeling indeed.*

As I stood there in my kitchen staring at the telephone, I knew he would do nothing regarding his female commander. I just knew it, and I had a feeling something bad was going to happen because of it.

I decided to take a hot bath and hoped it would be enough to make the hairs stand down on the back of my neck. Then I thought, *I can't take a hot bath when my husband and his entire brigade have no running water at all.* I simply took a shower and gathered my clothing and things together for the next day.

I reported to work early and decided to talk to my boss about the situation. After all, he was a retired chief warrant officer (CW5) and I knew his opinion on this matter would be reliable. I asked if I could speak to him privately. He and I always came in an hour or two early, only the two of us. Old habits never die. I was very loyal to my boss, more so than others before him.

He told me to close his office door and sit down. I closed the door to his office and walked to the large chair in front of his big desk.

He said, "Well, what's on your mind, Belinda?"

I just spilled it out. I told him everything that Thomas had said and what my thoughts were.

After I had finished, he let out a sigh and said calmly and firmly, "I still have friends that are active duty. In fact, Thomas's brigade commander is an old buddy of mine. I'll take care of this, Belinda, because I know that if I don't, I will lose you. I have a sneaking feeling you're getting ready to reenlist just to go over there to try to protect your husband, and I will not allow that. You already have a fight going on with your relatives here in the States. Don't you think this time that just maybe your plate is too full? Just let me take care of this matter. I can't promise you anything, but I will give it my best shot to put this fire out if you allow me."

I stood up from the chair. I looked him straight in his weather-beaten eyes and I started to salute him, but remembered we were civilians, so I extended my hand to shake his. He stood up and, with a firm grip, shook my hand.

I then said, "Thank you, sir."

As I was walking toward his office door, he said, "Belinda." I stopped, turned, and looked at him. He continued, "Belinda, just don't do anything foolish until I get back with you regarding this matter. Promise me you will not make any decisions regarding this without talking to me first. That's all I ask."

I simply answered him, "Yes, sir. I promise I will not do anything foolish until you get back to me."

He let out a sigh as he stood behind his desk. He was looking straight at me as he was studying my facial expression and he said, "Good, then. Don't worry about this matter today, we will worry about it another day. Go and perform your duties."

I replied, "Yes, sir."

I walked out of his office and closed the door behind me per his request.

A few days later as I was walking through the large warehouse, from the side door, I spotted my boss as he was talking to a few lower-ranked managers that he supervised. He looked toward me and said, "Mrs. Star, I need to talk to you in private. Please go to my office after you have settled in for the day, and I will be there in a few minutes."

I looked over at him and said, "Yes, sir."

After unlocking my office and putting my things down on my desk, I went straight to his office. He was already sitting at his desk. When I knocked on his open door, he said, "Please, Belinda, come in and close the door behind you."

"Yes, sir," I said.

After I sat down in the chair in front of his desk, he said, "Belinda, I received a return phone call from Thomas's brigade commander. He recorded the conversation with Thomas's company commander and asked me to record the tape with this old answering machine of mine, so I hooked it up to the phone because he wanted to be sure there was no doubt from either one of us of his actions regarding this issue. He said that this is unprecedented but felt very strongly about it, so that is why he did it this way. I'm going to play this recording for you to hear. He said that neither one of us can ever speak of this matter again. We must never discuss this or ever tell Thomas about it. As you will hear, he informed Thomas's commander that he was recording their conversation."

Then my boss turned on his old answering machine and we both sat in our chairs looking at the answering machine as it started to play the conversation.

Sure enough, the conversation started out with Thomas's brigade commander informing Thomas's company commander that he was recording their conversation and asked if she had any objections, to which she responded that she had none.

The brigade commander started out verbally reprimanding Thomas's company commander by ordering her to start performing her trained duties. He ordered her to straighten out her priorities, and he informed her that if she was unable to handle the pressures of a command, then he would relieve her. He told her that if he heard of her hugging and touching anyone under her command again, he would relieve her of command and send her back to the States to undergo a physical and mental examination. He also gave her the opportunity to have a transfer back to the States for a desk job; there would be no blemishes on her record. He told her it was her choice in this matter and he had not given choices to his soldiers before, but he was willing to give her one more chance because his sources felt she just needed to be reprimanded and reminded of her duties and priorities. He stated to her that it was the only reason he was giving her this chance.

He proceeded to remind her of the essentials of weeding out the weak links, and she was the weak link. He told her if her behavior continued under his command, he would have no other choice but to take appropriate actions to be rid of the weak link. He reminded her that our first sergeant and sergeant majors were our demigods and the backbone of our military forces. Officers can be made or broken by their right-hand man, and weak officers can break their right-hand man as well. He also reminded her that our senior NCOs cannot and should not have to carry the weight of all decisions made and that she can work her right-hand man into the ground and ultimately weaken the entire command. He then went on and said a weak officer breaks down the morale of all who are under his or her command and this can result in unnecessary death.

After he had blasted her out, she thanked him for this last chance and stated that it would never happen again. Then she asked who had complained against her. He answered her by stating it was outside sources that came and made the complaint because she was weakening their commands. He restated that he was not going to tolerate her crap any longer and he meant it. He stated he would be keeping a close eye on her.

After my boss turned off the machine, he said, "So, Belinda, I think she will get her act together now for fear she will pay severely for her actions. So you don't need to take any drastic measures. I have handled it.

Everything should be running smoothly again for your husband and the brigade over there."

I couldn't help myself. I stood up from my chair as my boss stood up from his. I walked over and met him beside his desk, and I gave him an old-fashioned bear hug and gratefully said, "Thank you, sir, and God bless you."

As my boss let go of my bear hug, his cheeks turned red and he laughed and said, "Good God, woman, you don't need to be so mushy about it. I hope you weren't like this when you were in. Now get out of here and go to work."

With a smile on my face, I said confidently, "Yes, sir."

As I was walking toward his office door, my boss ordered, "Now leave my door open."

I responded again as I was opening the door, still with a smile on my face, looking back at him, "Yes, sir."

A few weeks later, Thomas called again. I could tell by the sound of his voice that he was himself again. He said, "Belinda, I don't understand it, but my company commander has done a 180-degree turn around. She is acting like a commander again just like she did when we were stateside. She has taken charge of our daily mission planning and is now working with me instead of against me. She has even put the laptop out in our office so both of us can access it. Unbelievable!"

I replied with relief in my voice, "I'm so glad everything is working like it should for you. Now just come home safe and sound. I love you, Mr. Star."

He laughed and said, "I love you too, baby."

We chatted for a while, and we talked about our home and the things he missed. Before I knew it, his time was up because there was a line and he didn't want to make his soldiers wait so long because of him. Phone time was valuable and cherished.

CHAPTER XXXVIII

The years had flown by and my mother and I were once again flying back to Virginia to continue my lawsuit against Bea Mills and Frank Gibbs' estate for the recovery of my family property. It was now June of 2006.

As we are taking off, my mother and I looked at each other, and I silently prayed that this fight for justice would soon be over one way or the other.

It seemed like I always spent most of my time in the air reminiscing. Once again, I let my mind drift back in time. Since my last trip to Virginia, Thomas had retired from the Army and was now working for a government contractor. He almost did not get out because the military ordered a stop-loss, but thank God, he had submitted his paperwork within the small window of opportunity he had. He had reached his limit, just as I had several years ago when I retired. He was even more burned out than I had been. It was time to claim a piece of the American dream for which we had sacrificed so much of our lives. We had spent the majority of our adult years fighting so others could have an opportunity of freedom and a chance to make their dreams come true. It was time to let the new generation of soldiers fight and protect our borders from those that would cause us harm.

Teresa and Mark were still in the Army. Teresa had been stationed at Ft. Dix, training new recruits. Mark was still part of an elite group that primarily carried out ghost operations. My recent conversation with Teresa was still fresh in my mind. I had just finished my lunch when she called me at home.

Her voice was a bit shaky. "Hey, sis, are you sitting down? You'll never guess what just happened!" Before I had a chance to respond she blurted out, "I've just received my orders to deploy to Iraq. I leave in two weeks."

I took a deep breath. This was not news I wanted to hear. I wanted my little sister to stay safe on American soil, but she was a warrior so I just asked, "How do you feel about it?"

"I'm excited that I'll be able to use my training again. Part of me misses the excitement of combat, but it's different this time. I'm also a little scared, not for myself of course, but what if something happens to me? Who will take care of Maria and Taylor?"

I could tell she was fighting tears as she talked about the fear for her children's well-being.

Teresa had been told by military doctors many years ago when she and I returned from what the military thought was going to be a victorious special ops mission, that she could not have any children. During the attack, Teresa had been severely wounded in more ways than I would like to think about. Almez, Teresa, and I were the only survivors on a ghost mission of six. I really regretted what I told her that day, but at that moment, it was either survive or die. I remembered telling her, "Swallow it, soldier, and put it in the box. Did you really think putting on a man's britches that this wouldn't happen? Put it in the box if you want to be a She Wolf."

I don't know if suppressing memories was the right way to go or not. They say it's better to talk about it, but I've found it's not. I truly hope that my sister was okay from that and so many other things that I have made her swallow over the years.

When she was stationed in Bosnia, there was an orphanage on the outskirts of the base. Teresa fell in love with a little girl named Maria. She easily convinced Mark that they had to adopt her. It wasn't even a month after the adoption was finalized that Teresa found out she was pregnant! She and Mark were elated, and Maria was excited about being a big sister. A few days after Maria's fifth birthday, baby Taylor was born. She was the most beautiful baby I had ever seen. She looked just like Teresa.

Teresa continued, "You're the first one I've told. Mark has been out of contact for about a month now. Of course, I have no idea where he is, but I would have heard if he wasn't okay. I've been trying to figure out whom to ask to watch the girls. My first thought was Joan, but she has her hands full with her kids. I know Brandon's autism keeps her busy, and James is still in diapers. I'm not even considering you because I know you and Thomas don't have the patience for kids. Maybe I'll ask Mom. Do you think she and Daddy could handle two active girls?"

I said, "I'm sure they would consider it an honor. You know how your girls have Daddy wrapped around their little fingers. They bring out a side of him that I never saw before. He would do anything for his grandkids!"

Teresa sighed and said, "Thanks, She Wolf. I can always count on your advice."

I finally broke down and I told Teresa directly, "Don't worry about it, little sis. I'll take care of it. You will not be going to Iraq or anywhere else for that matter for a long, long time. Do you want to get out? I know you have done over twenty."

Teresa answered, "Belinda, the stop-loss is in place. I couldn't get out if I tried."

I responded, "Teresa, don't worry about it. As soon as I hang up, I'll make some calls. You know I have your back."

Teresa said, "I know you do, but I don't want to be seen as a slacker or a coward."

"Teresa, you and I both know you're far from a coward. Let it go this time. Let the new generation take on the burden, you've served your time," I said.

Teresa finally agreed. "I've given so much for our country, Belinda, and I'm tired and burned out. I want a piece of the pie now. I fought hard for it, and I have almost died for others to have it."

I said, "I know, little sis, I know. You have done your twenty and don't worry about it. Things will work out in your favor this time. I promise."

Teresa talked more about her children and her life and I talked a little bit about mine before we hung up.

After hanging up the telephone, I called Tanner because I knew he knew exactly where Mark was, and I knew that sorry ass son of a bitch was behind Teresa's orders as well. I just knew it. It shouldn't take a month to complete the missions that Tanner and his organization issued to a squad of commandos. The longest mission Teresa and I were on, had lasted three weeks because things did not go as planned for us. Instead of four to five days, it took us three weeks to get out because Tanner left us for dead. That was one reason Teresa and I had learned how to fly so many different types of aircrafts. We were never going to be left in a position like that again. I guess I never trusted Tanner after that. I knew in the back of my mind that he was just trying to do his job to the best of his abilities. I knew he had orders to follow as well, but that was still no excuse for what had happened to my sister and me.

I picked up the telephone and called the number that I thought for sure was deactivated by now, but to my surprise Tanner never changed my codes. Of course, this time an unknown voice answered and I gave the information required. I asked Tanner to call me when he had a chance; within minutes after hanging up, the telephone rang.

I answered and after Tanner gave his normal cowboy greetings, he asked, "Well, I guess your sister debriefed you a little bit."

I said, "No, you know better than that. She would never leak out a mission, not even to me now. You know damn well I'm a civvy now, but I know how to read between the lines. I may be retired, but my mind is still there."

Tanner then said, "I don't know anyone as well qualified for this mission as your sister."

I said, "Bullshit, Tanner. You're playing games again. I know something has happened to Mark and his team. Of course, you haven't told my sister anything and I know the place ain't Iraq. Why all of a sudden does she come down for orders when you yourself told me when I got out, oh, what were the words, 'Who needs you anymore anyway? You're all obsolete.' It's always 'just one more mission, just one more mission' with you. You have hundreds of new recruits that are braver, smarter, younger, and tougher than we ever were. You were right, Tanner, we are the 'obsolete' and it's time for us to turn over the reins to your new and younger generation. I swear to God, Tanner, if something has happened to my little sister's husband, I will personally see that your career is over under dishonorable conditions. I swear it. You know I have the proof to do it. I want you to see to it that Teresa is honorably discharged as a retired veteran along with Mark. I'm surprised you didn't go after Thomas!"

Tanner, of course, had become angry because of my threats and retorts. "Oh, get off your all mighty high horse, She Wolf. You know damn well if I recruited Thomas again that you would have come after me with full vengeance. You know damn well during that mission that you and your sister were on all those years ago, or should I say, the Bishops, since neither one of you were married at the time . . . . Damn it, I made a mistake! I was new in the job. You have never let me live that down. Don't you think it's been hard on me too, She Wolf? Shit, you know damn well you have to sign documentation for every one of the missions that if you are killed or left behind we don't take responsibility. I made a fucking mistake, okay? I underestimated you, your sister, and Almez's strength and will to survive. I had no clue the three of you had survived and practically humped it back through that entire God-forsaken country. I'm still amazed that the three of you survived that. I'm sorry, Belinda, all I can do is say, I'm sorry. This is one reason I'm sending another team to get Lighterman and his team out of there if they are still alive.

"After what happened to the three of you, I have never left another man behind. I've never recruited a woman either. The three of you, I don't know how to explain it, but there will never be a group like that again. The spirit, the bravery, the intelligence,—it was amazing; I always knew I could count on you to accomplish a deadly mission, always. I guess I underestimated women, so I guess our enemies did as well. You have an uncanny way of using that to your advantage. I just can't explain the spirit or the mind behind you."

I then asked, "Tanner, are you crying?"

Tanner answered angrily, "Damn it, woman, I have feelings too. I'm not the monster you seem to think I am. When you called when the Pentagon was hit, didn't I immediately run to your sister's aid? I care about you. Believe it or not, you were the best damn soldier I ever had the privilege to command."

I guess I let my anger go after holding it against him for so long and I said, "I'm sorry, too, for failing you and my country. You're right, I held you responsible for that particular mission, but it is time to let go of my sister and her husband."

Tanner simply said, "I wanted you back, and I guess I was using everyone closest to you. You're right, Star, I'll send another team in to get Lighterman and his team out. I swear it. Just tell your sister to submit her paperwork through normal channels and not to worry about the stop-loss. I'll personally see to it."

I simply said, "Thank you."

We said our goodbyes and I knew it was completely over now.

I called Teresa back and told her the good news and she promised she'd go ahead and submit her paperwork. After hanging up the telephone, I let out a sigh. She Wolf's spirit was at rest once again.

CHAPTER XXXIX

I looked up from the window of the airplane and my mother was talking with the flight attendant. I tuned into the conversation and asked for a beer this time. After Mom and I chatted a little bit about the upcoming events, I turned my head back to the window, stared out, and let my mind drift back in time again.

Like Thomas, I had been working for an Army contractor, but a few months ago, my contractor lost the contract. My boss offered me a job in Kuwait with him for our company since they had won the contract for over there, but Thomas and I decided it was not in the cards. I had to be available to go to court and finish this battle with my family. Besides, Thomas and I had been separated too many times during our careers. I was now unofficially retired. We had lost most of our savings, and we were now in the red from all the costly attorney fees and traveling expenses of this long fight for justice. I prayed the villains were held accountable and I was reimbursed from this long financial burden they had put upon my husband and me. I also considered my mother partly responsible for this because this should have been her battle, but she had preyed on my honor, duty, and loyalty for all these years regarding this vile act that had been committed against her as well as my husband and me.

About a year ago, Mr. Simms went to federal court to have a judge determine the legal interpretation of my mother's plea agreement with the U.S. Attorney. My mother and I did not have to attend the hearing. I was glad because Mr. Simms reported that it was a three-ring circus. Mr. Simms had become frustrated and angry with my relatives, Ed, and their attorney regarding this entire mess. He had tried, along with my mother and me, to convince them to return our property.

According to Mr. Simms, Auntie Bea, Uncle Frank's kids, and Ed showed up along with Mr. Pricket. Mr. Pricket and the rest of the herd had no business being there, but Mr. Simms was required to inform Mr.

Pricket that he was going to a federal judge. I had to admit that it made no sense to me why he did that. Why do you have to let the enemy know your battle plans? I now firmly believed that all attorneys were friends outside of the courtroom, and they scratched each other's backs from time to time, even if it didn't benefit the people who hired them.

Mr. Simms called me as soon as it was over. I put him on speakerphone so that my mother could be part of the conversation. He informed us that the assistant U.S. Attorney was there. The assistant U.S. Attorney spouted off at the mouth along with Mr. Pricket, but we prevailed because the judge ruled.

"It says what it says and means what it means. Mrs. King forfeited her rights to the government, not these other parties. She had the right to give the property to her daughter because the U.S. Attorney, not you, the assistant attorney, had no interest in it. Mrs. King did not, and I mean did not, forfeit anything to these other parties, and to me this is a total waste of time. What kind of judge do you have, Mr. Simms? Never mind, Mr. Simms, I see the name on the suit!" the judge had said.

I was in shock! I said, "Mr. Simms, you mean to tell me that the federal judge clearly saw what kind of judge we have, and he did nothing about it? Where is the justice in that?"

He replied sadly, "I don't know, Belinda, I don't know."

I retorted, "I strongly believe that judges and attorneys need to be held accountable for their actions, and we the people should not have to pay out of our life savings and go into massive debt because we seek justice. Our country was founded on that justice. We're supposed to have a system of checks and balances! I believe our entire judicial system is a profit-making machine that preys off the victims and the villains, no matter how good or how bad they appear to be. Throughout this entire ordeal, I have paid and paid and paid and paid and nothing has been paid back to me! In fact, justice has not been served in any form thus far. Thomas has told me many times over the past several years that this is becoming ridiculous, and, Mr. Simms, I have to agree with him."

Mr. Simms let out a sign. "I know, Belinda; somewhere throughout the years we've lost our sense of justice. There are a few of us who are still fighting for justice and believe in our country and what our founding fathers believed in."

Mom jumped in and said, "Mr. Simms, you just keep doing your best. I know that you are one of the few honest attorneys, and I believe you are trying your best."

I glared at my mother because she was just blowing sunshine up his butt. She frequently said all kinds of nasty things about him to me.

Mr. Simms replied, "Thank you, Jane. I really appreciate those words. I have to go now, ladies. There is lots of work to be done."

*   *   *

I looked up and the flight attendant was asking if we wanted more beverages. We both ordered our usual. I paid for it and looked out the window again. I was starting to fidget because I was becoming angry and wanted to be off this flight soon, but I knew we had a long way to go before arriving at the Snobville Airport.

I guess my mother sensed this and said, "Let's go over the facts again so you are prepared to answer the questions. You need to be ready for the attack their attorney will be throwing at you. We don't know exactly what he'll ask, but we do know his style. Let's review the past few years."

I answered, "Okay, Mom, but I don't see the point. We don't know what questions he will ask. I don't even think our attorney even knows what he is going to do or say."

Mom said, "Oh, Belinda, let's just do it and time will fly by faster."

I said, "Okay."

Mom pulled out what I had dubbed our "timeline," and we went over it again and again to make sure I had the dates correct and my memory was in check. My mother's diversion trick worked because the rest of the flights, including the layovers, went by quickly. Before we knew it, we were already landing at the Snobville Airport. I was to the point where I hated flying. For the past several years, the only time I'd been on a plane was because of a court date. There had never been a pleasant ending to my recent flights.

We retrieved our luggage, got the rental car, and headed to the hotel we had stayed at the last time. I had reserved a room, and we checked in. I didn't have much of an appetite, but Mom insisted I would feel better if I ate something. We went down to the bar because bar food sounded mildly appetizing. I did feel better after my burger and fries, chased by a good beer. My last thought before falling asleep was that this would never end, and I would never see justice served against my own flesh and blood.

CHAPTER XL

I slept soundly until we received the wake-up call at 6:00 a.m. My mother and I dressed. I wore the same business suit that I had worn to every proceeding. My mother put on casual clothes because Mr. Simms wasn't planning to put her on the stand. Once again, "out of sight, out of mind" was his intent. This judge had already stereotyped her because she was a former felon.

As we were getting ready, I said, "Mom, it is so sad that we have judges who rule by whim instead of the law. This judge makes me so angry because he has already judged you because of your felony. He's also using that to judge my character instead of viewing me as a victim. I always thought our society believed in second chances and a fresh new start. I also always believed in this day and age the children of the condemned were not held accountable because of the deeds of their parents, but in the real world, I have discovered this isn't the case at all regarding most of the people within our judicial system."

Mom stopped what she was doing and looked down sadly. "I'm so sorry, baby. I'm sorry I got you into this mess. This whole thing is my fault."

I threw my arms around her and said, "Oh, Momma, I wasn't saying that to place blame on you. Please don't cry! I'm mad at the judge because he is not upholding our laws."

Mom looked at me, smiled, and said, "I guess we better get going."

I did have some hope for the day. This time I had put my fate in the hands of my fellow Americans. I had requested and been given a seven-man jury. This time, the final decision had been taken from the wicked, incompetent judge we had; no matter what their decision, I truly trusted these strangers more so than I trusted the judge. My mother, however, still believed that the judge would do the right thing.

I felt sad because I would have to leave my mother sitting in the car behind the courthouse, and I knew she would be waiting there for hours because it had taken us years to get to this point. After I parked the car, I walked to the passenger side of the car, bent down, and put my head through the open window and gave my mother a kiss on her cheek, as she was doing her needlepoint. I said, "Sorry I have to leave you here alone, Momma."

She looked up at me with a sad smile and tears in her eyes and said, "She Wolf, fight for me, your ancestors, and yourself as hard as you have for your country and our God."

As I heard the words, a bit of pride toward my mother seeped into my heart, and I bent down and kissed her again on the cheek. "I will fight with every ounce of my wit, integrity, and honesty. I will carry the shield of truth in my one hand to shield me from their lies, and the sword of justice in the other to strike them down with the jury's decision. I will bury them under the courthouse and destroy them with the truth to the best of my ability."

My mother looked up at me with pride and said, "I know you will. Get in there and win our family treasures back."

I smiled at my mother and said, "Yes, ma'am."

CHAPTER XLI

As I was walking toward the front of the courthouse, I looked down at my watch and it read 8:30 a.m. As I approached the front door, I saw Mr. Simms with his briefcase and papers in his hands. He saw me.

"Good morning," he said. "Did you have a good flight?"

I answered, "It would have been good if my final destination wasn't here."

Mr. Simms said, "I completely understand. Are you ready?"

I answered, "I'm as ready as can be expected." I let out a sigh and stated, "Let's win this battle."

Mr. Simms said, "I'll do my best, but I can't promise anything."

As Mr. Simms and I were talking, I saw Miss Patson walking toward us and then I saw Mr. Jones, one of the assistant U.S. Attorneys, walking toward us as well. Miss Patson hugged me immediately, and Mr. Jones shook my hand as he introduced himself. The four of us chatted amongst ourselves for a few minutes.

As we were preparing to go inside, I asked, "Do I have time to feed my nasty habit?"

Mr. Simms answered, "Yes, but make it quick, Belinda."

I replied, "Okay."

I stood beside the ashtray near the front door and took out my cigarette pack and lighter from my purse. I had just lit it when I saw a car pull up in the front parking lot. I watched as Ed got out of Auntie Bea's car from the driver's side, walked over to the passenger door, opened it, and helped Auntie Bea out of the car. As he was helping Auntie Bea, May got out of the back passenger door to help Auntie Bea as well. A young girl, which I assumed was one of her older daughters, got out of the opposite back side door. I saw Sam's truck pull up, and he parked it and walked over to Auntie Bea's car. Then, John and his wife pulled up in their car.

Before I knew it, they were all huddled together close to where I was standing and talking amongst themselves. I was approached by a deputy sheriff who asked if I was Belinda Star. After I acknowledged that was, he handed me a no trespassing notice for Auntie Bea's house and the Daisy house and property. He asked if Thomas Star was present, and I answered no. Then, he walked away from me.

I looked over to my thieving relatives. Ed, May, and her daughter looked straight at me and started laughing.

I simply stated, "Nasty little people like you always, and I mean always, get their comeuppance." I put my cigarette out and walked into the courthouse.

I joined Mr. Simms at the plaintiff's table. He was bent over the table, shuffling through his papers. He looked up at me as I approached him, and I passed him the no trespassing notice. He looked over at Auntie Bea, May, and Sam, who were already sitting at the defendant's table.

He looked back at me and began telling me more of the procedures for jury selection. I looked toward the back of the courtroom where the front doors were and saw numerous people scattered throughout the rows. I saw a few male veterans. I could tell they were veterans by their posture and the style of their haircuts. I turned my attention back to Mr. Simms and said in a soft, almost whisper, "Mr. Simms, please get as many veterans as possible for our jury. I prefer to put my fight in their hands."

Mr. Simms nodded his head in agreement with me.

As Mr. Simms was pulling out more papers and notes from his briefcase and arranging them for the proceedings, I looked straight at Auntie Bea, May, and Sam. I still couldn't believe Sam was here. Even though he was co-executor of his father's estate, he had stayed away from this fight, and it had appeared to me that he wasn't involved. Then I remembered Mr. Simms telling me that Sam was on the witness list. He had a tape recording of Sam and me, stating that I sold all of my family jewelry. This, of course, was a lie because there never was such a conversation, and I knew there was never any tape with anything of that nature, unless he had created one. Who knew?

I looked over at the defendant's table and every one of them looked straight back at me, so I simply said to Sam with a fake smile, "Hello, Sam."

With a shocked expression, Sam simply said, "Hello, Belinda."

I sat there staring at them. None of them could look me in the eye for more than a fraction of a second.

Before I knew it, court was called to order and Judge Colburn entered the courtroom. Mr. Pricket still had not arrived. I watched as Mr. Simms looked behind us, searching for their attorney. The judge then asked if all parties and counsel were present. Mr. Simms stood up and answered, "Your Honor, it appears that the defendant's counsel is not here at this time."

The judge looked irritated as he said, "Well then, we will proceed without him. Are you ready to select the jury, Mr. Simms?"

Mr. Simms answered, "Yes, sir."

The judge then looked out to the numerous people scattered through the courtroom. He asked everyone who was there for jury duty to stand. He started weeding out the ones who were not eligible to serve by asking questions from a list. It didn't take long until he had it narrowed down to around 20 potential jurors.

Mr. Simms picked out the remaining three who appeared to be veterans. The judge and Mr. Simms asked each one of them questions to rule out any conflicts of interest. I guess I was lucky because none of the three veterans were dismissed. Instead, they were all asked to take a seat in the jury box. Before I knew it, the judge and Mr. Simms had narrowed it down to twelve jurors sitting in the jury box. Then the judge dismissed the remainder. Mr. Pricket still had not arrived yet and the judge asked again where the defendant's counsel was.

Because no one knew, Judge Colburn and Mr. Simms continued to weed out more jurors trying to have the best selection of seven jurors. They continued to ask each one questions.

Suddenly, Mr. Pricket appeared at the defendant's table out of breath. He immediately apologized to the court. The judge was still irritated with Mr. Pricket and told him so without mincing words. He then told Mr. Pricket how far they had gotten with the jury selection. Much to my surprise, Mr. Pricket was content with the progress.

The judge then told him what questions had been asked and informed him that he could not ask those again. The jury selection seemed to drag on now that Mr. Pricket was also questioning each potential juror.

Finally, they were down to seven. I looked at my watch. It had taken two hours to select the jury. Judge Colburn then instructed the remaining jurors on their duties and what would be involved. Then he gave orders to recess for twenty minutes before starting the trial.

During our twenty-minute recess, all of my relatives and Ed went outside leaving Mr. Pricket at the table as he was going through his papers. Mr. Simms and I remained at the table and whispered back and forth between each other regarding his plans of attack and defense.

CHAPTER XLII

Everyone was back in their seats and settled in after recess before the twenty minutes was up. A few moments later, the bailiff ordered everyone to rise, and he announced Judge Colburn again. The judge requested that everyone be seated. Then the judge ordered the jury to come in, and they all settled in their seats in the jury box. The judge explained the jury's duties and the court's procedures. The fight for justice had begun.

Of course, Mr. Simms requested that all the witnesses be excused from the courtroom, and Mr. Pricket had no objections. I loved it as I once again watched John, his wife, his in-laws, and Ed walking out of the courtroom. I silently chuckled as I watched them leave.

The judge then focused his attention on Mr. Simms and asked him if he was ready for opening statements. Mr. Simms answered, "Yes, Your Honor, I am."

Mr. Simms stood up, approached the jury, and started to give his opening statement. As he was talking, he was also walking from one end of the jury box to the other, notes in hand. He looked each juror in the eye as he said, "My name is Chris Simms and I am the counsel for the plaintiff, Mrs. Belinda Star.

"This case that has been brought before you is about very personal property. The most personal kind of property one can own—such as personal papers, birth certificates, ancestral marriage licenses, life insurance documents, family photo albums, ancestral journals and mementos, traditional holiday decorations, clothes, personal furniture and ancestral furniture, decorations, dog ashes, dog photos, jewelry and ancestral jewelry. Most of this property was passed from one generation to another until it was passed to the plaintiff, Belinda Star. Not the kind of things where there is any real question about ownership. These items hold special meaning and great value to the true owner.

"All of these things were placed in storage with the defendants, between 1991 to the middle of 1999, by Belinda and her mother, Jane King. The defendants are relatives and they agreed to store the personal property. This was not a commercial transaction where there was any charge for storing the items. Belinda Star is a highly decorated veteran of the United States Army. She has served our country for several decades and is now retired.

"In January of 1999, Jane transferred possession of this property to her daughter, Belinda. Per the request of Belinda's great-aunt, one of the defendants, Jane put this in writing in 2000. In March of 2000, Belinda tried to retrieve her personal property from her great-aunt and great-uncle, Ms. Mills and Mr. Gibbs. They refused to give it to Belinda. Belinda had to make a choice. Either she could forget about her family property, or she could take her great-aunt and great-uncle to court. She decided that it would be wrong to let her aunt and uncle keep what was not theirs. She made the difficult decision to take them to court. Belinda filed suit in the county general district court in April of 2000.

"The case she filed was called a warrant in detinue. Someone files that kind of case to recover possession of personal property. Attached to the warrant Belinda filed was a Schedule A, a summary of the personal property. She wrote a summary because her detailed inventory consisted of thousands of pages. Per the advice of her attorney at that time, it would be more reasonable to work off a summary rather than a large inventory. It was agreed by both parties to work off this schedule as opposed to the voluminous spreadsheets.

"The case was not scheduled to go to trial until August of 2000. Belinda was living in Germany with her husband who was still active duty. Like most cases there were efforts made to compromise and settle. That's what this case is about because, ultimately, the parties were able to reach an agreement.

"The negotiations that resulted in the parties reaching an agreement started with a letter from Belinda's lawyer, Miss Patson. That letter had attached to it the summary, Schedule A. Belinda offered to give certain items to the defendants, which were circled, and she agreed to pay some money. The defendants were supposed to respond within a specified time if they accepted the offer.

"Although defendants responded by the time frame, they did not accept Belinda's offer, but instead made a counter offer. Belinda's lawyer received it back with circled items that they would let Belinda have; crossed out items that were missing; out of a summary they offered Belinda 16 titles of grouped property to be returned to her. Twenty-one of these titles were listed as missing. This means hundreds of items 'walked away.' As to ownership—Ms. Mills wrote 'I've stored these items for over one year.'

"Aunt Bea's counter offer was not accepted. They went to trial in August of 2000. In the middle of the trial, the parties reached a settlement; six things made up their agreement: (1) the title to Belinda's mother's car signed over to Mrs. Mills; (2) Belinda agreed to pay $3,000 jointly to Ms. Mills and Mr. Gibbs; (3) the personal property listed on Schedule A would be moved out by Belinda's husband and friends, but not Belinda; (4) Ms. Mills would be allowed to keep certain items from the Schedule A summary, i.e., a dresser, rug, freezer, grandfather clock, wood chipper, and a bed; (5) there would be a three-day notice given before the move would take place; and (6) the defendants' Ms. Mills and Mr. Gibbs lawyer, Mr. Dickerson, would draft an order that stated these agreed terms.

"We know that this was not the end of things because we are here today. What happened? Before Belinda had the chance to do anything, the defendants violated the agreement. Not only did they breach the agreement, but instead of just keeping six of the thousands of items, they have kept them all.

"How did that happen? The very first thing that was to be done was that defendants were to prepare a court order that reflected the agreement that was reached. That was something the defendants agreed to do. That did not happen. Right away, instead of preparing the order that reflected the agreement reached, they prepared an order reflecting a very different agreement, and from that point on, they refused to honor the agreement they had made. The new agreement that the defendants insisted on was different in two critically important ways.

"Number one: Ed. The agreement actually reached did not provide for Ed to be involved. His presence was added by the defendants, and not just in some small-bit part. He was added to act as referee—to supervise the move and report to the court. This was unacceptable to Belinda. Belinda felt strongly that Mr. Weird had played an important role in the division of the family. Belinda believed that he had placed himself in between the family and instigated a great deal of the trouble. She felt that he had stolen her things and that he was using her great-aunt and great-uncle, who were her godparents. Belinda simply did not trust Mr. Weird and there was no way that she would ever agree to allow him to be involved in the move.

"Number two. The other reason the order did not reflect the agreement was that the defendants had put in a specific requirement on when the property was to be picked up. Instead of the agreed-upon three-day notice, the defendants changed the term to require Belinda's husband to pick up the property on a specific weekend. Since Belinda's husband, Thomas, was serving overseas, he could not simply go whenever the defendants insisted. That's why the actual agreement allowed flexibility—it did not stipulate a specific date.

"Those two conditions the defendants threw into the order were not part of the agreement. These were major changes and by putting those conditions in, the defendants violated their agreement. They did not do as they promised. Those two provisions in the order violated the part of the settlement agreement by which the defendants were supposed to prepare an order that reflected the agreement of the parties. Not only that, but they actually said to Belinda, 'We are not going to do what we promised.'

"The evidence will show that the defendants committed the first breach of the agreement by not preparing an order that reflected the agreement reached and this was a major breach of the contract. Although Belinda and her attorney continued to make the effort in good faith to work out the matter, none of those efforts really mattered because the agreement had been violated already.

"Anticipate that the defendants will try to look past their initial violation of the agreement to try to say that it doesn't really matter. There will be no evidence that the defendants couldn't get what they were entitled to. What were they entitled to? Possession and use of six items or the value of those items. Evidence will show not only have they had the possession of the six items, but they have had the possession of *all* the items. They have had more than the benefit of their bargain, even though they refused to honor their agreement.

"The defendants may attempt to justify keeping property that is not theirs and their violation of their agreement by saying that the federal government has some interest in the property. There will not be any witnesses from the federal government testifying that the U.S. government has any interest in the clothing, family photos, jewelry, old furniture, and cars involved in this case. All the property has been there not only in the year of 1999, but Belinda's and her husband's property as well since 1991.

"There is no evidence that the federal government has made any effort to take possession of the property over these past seven years. There was some confusion, for a time, as to what the federal government's interest in the property might be, but that was after the defendants had already breached the agreement. The plaintiff has a witness today from the U.S. Attorney's office who will testify they have no interest in the property regarding this case.

"Since the defendants violated the agreement in 2000, obviously a great deal of time has passed. Mr. Gibbs has passed away and he is not here today. Instead, we have the executors of his estate. Since 2000, Ms. Mills has crossed off more items indicating that they were not located; recently she has reported that the missing number has grown to include several thousand items. The evidence will be clear that Ms. Mills recognizes that this personal property belongs to Belinda. How?

"Evidence of conduct on Ms. Mills' part that is inconsistent with her position that Belinda is not entitled to the property. Ms. Mills herself has asserted a claim in this case that she should be paid $100,000 by Belinda for storing the items that she refuses to let Belinda take.

"We will prove: That the parties reached an agreement. What the agreement was. That the defendants committed the first breach of the agreement by refusing to prepare a proper order. The identity and value of the property that was part of the agreement.

"What we will be asking you to do is to uphold the agreement made and bring the end to this matter that was already agreed to by the parties. Do this by enforcing the agreement that the parties already made and find that Belinda is entitled to the benefit of her bargain. Find that Belinda is entitled to the items of personal property summarized on the Schedule A, and where those items no longer exist that she be entitled to monetary damages in the amount of the true value of each of the items. Those values have been used by the parties from the outset, but are not true values. The schedule used those values as the basis for the parties' agreement, but it does not represent true values because the items are worth much, much more.

"We are also asking that you award Belinda interest on the true value, once it has been established by an expert, of the property that the defendants have retained since the date of the agreement—August of

2000. In conclusion, we are asking that you enforce the agreement that was made by the parties and which was first breached by defendants."

With his right hand, he held up the no trespassing notice that I just received, and he continued speaking with more conviction in his words. "Here in my hand is a no trespassing notice that the plaintiff, Belinda Star, was just issued outside this very courthouse today by the defendants. This just shows that they will do anything to prevent the plaintiff, Belinda Star, from recovering her family property."

During this intense opening statement, I watched as my attorney continued walking in front of the juror's box and continued to look directly into the eyes of each of the jurors. In several instances, Mr. Simms would put his hands with his notepad in one hand on the rail of the jury box and bend his upper body toward them looking at them. I even noticed during several sentences that the three male veterans would move forward in their chairs along with several of the women looking directly at me. I had no clue what that meant. It was so quiet in the courtroom, you could properly have heard a pin drop.

I was extremely proud of Mr. Simms and his opening statements. He was very prepared this time, and I was thankful to have him representing me.

CHAPTER XLIII

Then, Mr. Pricket was in front of the jury with his opening statements. It appeared to me that he was not prepared and that he planned on blowing smoke up everyone's asses again.

Mr. Pricket did not talk in a firm and loud voice; instead, Mr. Pricket was almost yelling at the jury when he spoke. He looked over at Mr. Simms before he started to speak and he said, "Well, what an almost perfect sermon from the plaintiff's counsel. I almost wept during part of it, but I will first address the last statement that Mr. Simms made regarding the no trespassing notice.

"He stated Mrs. Star is a veteran, which we all know means that she has probably been on the battlefield numerous times. This is the reason the defendants in this case served her with the notice. They fear for their lives because they know what she is capable of doing."

As he spoke, I was watching the facial reactions of the jury. One of the jurors, a large, black, male veteran, moved forward in his seat, and he looked very angry after Mr. Pricket's statement. Within a fraction of a second, the white male veteran and the veteran of Asian descent had the same expressions on their faces. The one black elderly woman looked directly at me with fear in her eyes as did the young blond girl, but the one woman who was around my age had the same expression of anger toward Mr. Pricket. I could not tell what the white elderly woman was thinking because she had no expression on her face, and she did not look my way at all. She continued looking at Mr. Pricket.

Mr. Pricket stood there in front of the jury box with one hand in the side pocket of his trousers and continued his opening statement. "What Mr. Simms left out was that Jane King stole everything that Ms. Mills owned, and Ms. Mills is now a pauper.

"Jane King and her husband Pete King were indicted on numerous counts of embezzlement and fraud, which was millions of dollars. Mr.

Simms has pointed out Jane King's plea agreement, when he was referring to United States Government's interest in this." Then he pulled the plea agreement from the notepad and waved it in the air just as Mr. Simms had waved the trespassing notice. Mr. Pricket continued, "Evidence will show that Jane King did not have the right to give anything to her daughter. In fact, Jane King herself filed a lawsuit against the defendants regarding the same property. So who owns this? Evidence will clearly show that the plaintiff has no claim to anything. The evidence will also show that if any agreement was made in 2000, Belinda Star was the one who breached it.

"Belinda Star has sued and sued the defendants to death. Evidence will prove this is just another frivolous lawsuit that wiggled its way into our court system. If by some chance you feel the plaintiff is entitled to this property, then evidence will show that she is only entitled to half of said property because Pete King gave his portion to the defendants. Also evidence will show that in 1999 Belinda Star and Jane King sold all of the property that is in question today and that the defendants never had possession of the said property to begin with.

"Once all the evidence is shown it will be clear to you, the jury, that the plaintiff is not entitled to anything, and we request that the defendants be awarded all attorney fees expended regarding this matter."

Then Mr. Pricket walked back to the defendant's table. I could not believe this pompous ass. I imaged going over there and smacking him in his mouth for such slanderous statements.

CHAPTER XLIV

Then the judge asked Mr. Simms if he was ready to call his first witness and he called Miss Patson.

Miss Patson was sworn in. After she was settled in the witness chair, I smiled at her and she winked back at me. Mr. Simms asked her to state her name, her occupation, whom she worked for, and what her relationship was to me.

Miss Patson answered all the questions and stated she was the attorney who represented me regarding the warrant in detinue.

Mr. Simms asked, "Was there an agreement reached during this civil action?"

Miss Patson answered, "Yes, there was an agreement reached."

Mr. Simms asked the judge to admit Miss Patson's notes of the agreement into evidence. After the judge filed it into evidence, he passed it to Mr. Simms.

Mr. Simms asked, "Are these your notes of the agreement that was made by the plaintiff and the defendants during this action?"

Miss Patson looked at her notes and answered, "Yes, they are."

Mr. Simms then read aloud the agreement that was written as notes by Miss Patson. Then, he asked, "Is this the exact agreement?"

Miss Patson responded, "Yes, it is."

Mr. Simms then handed her another document and asked, "Is this an incorrect agreement prepared by the defendants' first attorney, Mr. Dickerson?"

"Yes, it is," she answered.

Mr. Simms then asked the judge to admit it into evidence as he passed it to the judge. The judge read it and admitted it into evidence. Mr. Pricket provided no response regarding either piece of evidence.

"Why didn't you sign the agreement that Mr. Dickerson had prepared?" Mr. Simms asked.

Miss Patson responded, "Because it was incorrect. Mr. Dickerson added the clause regarding Ed Weird to supervise and report to the court. The agreement had been that Belinda Star would report to the court per the presiding judge. The other key clause that was added into the agreement was a specific date included and not the three-day notice with an open date."

Mr. Simms asked, "Why were these clauses added by Mr. Dickerson unacceptable to you?"

"I agreed with my client, Mrs. Star, that Ed Weird appeared to be the primary cause of this entire mess. The second reason was because my client's husband was still active duty and he could not move the property whenever the defendants chose; that was the whole point of having a three-day notice with an open date," said Miss Patson.

Mr. Simms continued, "So in your opinion, did they breach the contractual agreement?"

Miss Patson agreed, "In my opinion they did."

Mr. Pricket interrupted, "Objection, Your Honor, there has been no ruling that anything was breached by the defendants."

Judge Colburn overruled. "Overruled. The witness gave her opinion; not a judgment."

Mr. Simms concluded, "No further questions, Your Honor."

Judge Colburn asked, "Mr. Pricket, do you wish to cross-examine this witness at this time?"

Mr. Pricket said, "Yes, Your Honor."

Mr. Pricket stood up from his chair, walked over to the witness stand, and asked, "Are you being paid by the plaintiff today for your time to testify on her behalf?"

Miss Patson responded, "No, I was subpoenaed."

Mr. Pricket asked, "Why aren't you still representing the plaintiff, Mrs. Star?"

Miss Patson answered, "Because at the time she requested me to continue the suit against the defendants, my plate was too full. I did offer her another attorney from our law firm, but she wanted the choice of picking an attorney as she thought fit."

Mr. Pricket concluded, "No further questions, Your Honor."

Neither attorney reserved the option of questioning Miss Patson again, so the judge thanked her and excused her so she could return to her office.

Mr. Simms then called his next witness, Mr. Jones, an assistant attorney of the U.S. Attorney's office. Before I knew it, Mr. Pricket practically jumped out of his chair objecting to this witness, and then both attorneys were in front of the judge's bench arguing. From what I could make out—and I know the jury could hear some of it as well—Mr. Simms was stating to the judge that this witness would clarify that the U.S. Attorney had no interest in the disputed property. This would clarify the federal judge's ruling that the plea agreement between his office and Mrs. King, and they had relinquished any interest in the property. Of course, the judge sided with Mr. Pricket and would not let Mr. Simms call the witness.

The judge then instructed the jury to disregard anything they heard and explained that the called witness would not be testifying. The judge then called in Mr. Jones and promptly excused him. The next thing I knew I was called to testify next. I was sworn in, and I sat in the "hot box," a nickname because of how I felt whenever I was in the witness chair.

Mr. Simms asked me to state my name and address. I gave it and also stated that I was a veteran of the United States Army.

Before I even uttered another word, the judge became angry with me and said, "Mrs. Star, just answer the question and do not anticipate the next question."

I looked at him bewildered because normally he was always trying to speed things up. So I simply replied, "Yes, Your Honor."

Mr. Simms then asked, "Tell us a little bit about you and a little bit about what has happened to cause us to be here today."

I again stated I was a veteran and proceeded to tell the long tale starting in 1991 when Bea purchased the Daisy house. I told the tale of 1999 and all the involvement of Bea and the credit card fraud that Frank created. I told them everything. Before I had a chance to get past what Bea, Frank, and my mother and Big Pete did, the judge again became hostile and told me just to answer the question, which was exactly what I was trying to do. I became angry with the judge, and I said in a professional, but stern tone, "Your Honor, I just took an oath to tell the truth, the whole truth, and nothing but the truth and you are not allowing me to do that."

Before the judge responded, Mr. Simms stood up from his chair and said, "Your Honor, Mrs. Star was answering the question and it will take a bit of time to completely answer it."

The judge then directed his anger toward Mr. Simms authoritatively stated, "Then, Mr. Simms, you need to form your questions to where she is only answering yes or no or short answers."

Next, the judge looked directly at me, still angry, and asked, "Do you understand, Mrs. Star?"

I answered, "No, Your Honor, I do not understand. This justice system is failing me."

He knew exactly what I meant and that I was referring to him. But he also knew that the jury was watching him and he replied in a softer tone, "Mrs. Star, it will be me who decides whether you are telling the truth or not." Then, he looked at the jury, as I did, and you could tell every one of the jurors were very angry with him. He continued, "Well, in this case it will be the jury as well to determine if you are telling the truth or not. Just answer the questions in short responses."

I thought, *What a nasty, backstabbing, maggot this man is!* He did not deserve to wear that robe.

So for the next hour and a half, I answered Mr. Simms' questions until the tale was completed up to the current trial. I thought I had brought every emotion I could have possibly shown to light. I cried, I became angry, frustrated, and the whole time, I was wishing that this whole thing was over.

Then Mr. Simms finally presented me the letter that the U.S. Attorney had written to my mother and me stating that they had no interest in our family property, and as far as they were concerned, it was either my mother's or mine. Of course, I stated that it was a true copy of the letter. After this acknowledgement, Mr. Simms asked that it be admitted into evidence. Mr. Pricket objected and objected with his reasoning, but this time, the judge had no other choice but to admit it into evidence. Mr. Simms prevailed regarding that battle proving the government had no interest.

After Mr. Simms finished questioning me, he asked the judge to reserve the right to recall me at another time. The judge agreed and asked Mr. Pricket if he would like to cross-examine the witness, and Mr. Pricket answered, "Yes."

Then, Mr. Pricket cross-examined me, asking questions about my mother and Big Pete and their criminal activities. Every time he asked a question regarding their criminal activities, I would simply reply, "I don't know, it's just hearsay on my part and has nothing to do with my family members stealing from me."

After about twenty minutes of the cross-examination, the judge became angry with Mr. Pricket and told him to ask another line of questions because the questions didn't seem to have a connection to the property dispute at hand.

Finally, the attorneys finished questioning me. I looked down at my watch and realized that my testimony had lasted three hours. The judge then called for a one-hour recess. I was happy because I was emotionally drained. The witness stand truly was a medieval hot box, even for the victim.

As Mr. Simms and I were walking out of the courthouse, he put his hand on my back, patted me a couple of times, and said in a serious tone, "Well done, you didn't falter once. I'm glad you let your emotions show because the jury knows you're not this monster that Mr. Pricket tried to make you out to be."

I looked down at the ground, shook my head, let out a sigh, and said, "I'd rather be back on the battlefield being shot at because I either come out of it alive or not. I would know my fate right then and there. This waiting is torture."

Mr. Simms replied with a grim expression, "Belinda, it is better to fight with words than a weapon."

I let out another sigh and said, "Everything that I loved and believed in was just an illusion."

Mr. Simms answered with patience, "Belinda, our justice system has checks and balances, the wheels of justice move, but they move very slowly."

I replied, "I know that, but it isn't designed for a simpleton like myself. Our forefathers originally designed it for just that, from the simpleton to the most noble, from the poorest to the richest. It's not like that anymore."

He went to his car, I supposed, to get something to eat. I went back to the rental car where my mother was waiting for me. I drove a couple of blocks away from the courthouse so she and I could use a bathroom and eat. We stopped at a gas station/mini-mart where I knew they kept the bathrooms clean. I bought us a couple of sandwiches and drinks and drove back to the rear parking lot of the courthouse. I told her all I did was tell the truth, and I was drilled for the entire time. She kept pumping me to tell her more and what I thought, so I simply said, "Mom, I don't know. I wish I could tell you, but I just don't know."

The hour flew, and before I knew it, we were in the courtroom again. Once the judge was settled in, he asked, "Mr. Simms, are you ready to call your next witness?"

Mr. Simms stood up from his chair beside me and answered, "The plaintiff rests."

Then, the judge asked Mr. Pricket, "Are you ready to call your first witness?"

Mr. Pricket answered, "Yes, Your Honor, I call Mrs. May Harp."

After May was sworn in, Mr. Pricket asked her to state her name and address. May answered by giving her name and address.

Mr. Pricket began, "Mrs. Harp, could you tell the court how much of the stuff is stored in the house that you are living in after your father passed away?"

May replied, "The entire basement is packed to the ceiling from corner to corner, and the other two bedrooms were packed to the ceiling. We had to move it and put that in a storage bin. We didn't know who owned what. I feel that we should be paid storage fees since we had to pay for several storage units to move the stuff."

Mr. Pricket continued, "Okay, can you tell us the dimensions of the house?"

May asked, "What do you mean?"

Mr. Pricket asked, "How big or small is the house?"

May responded dumbly, "It's pretty big."

Mr. Pricket rephrased, "Do you mean that it's smaller than your aunt's house or is it larger than your aunt's house?"

May looked confused. "What do you mean? I don't really know. It could be larger."

Mr. Pricket restated, again, "So you were basically living in a small house packed to the ceiling?"

Mr. Simms interrupted, "Objection, Your Honor, he's leading the witness."

Judge Colburn agreed, "Sustained, Mr. Pricket, she has answered your question by saying it was a large house. Move along."

Mr. Pricket resumed his questioning. "Yes, Your Honor. Mrs. Harp, did Mrs. Star talk with you regarding moving the property out of the house?"

May answered, "No."

I looked over at Mr. Simms, whispered in his ear the truth, and stated he would have to put me back on the witness stand. He nodded his head in agreement and wrote down the questions I told him to ask her.

Mr. Pricket asked, "Mrs. Harp, did you conduct an inventory of all the stuff that was located in the house that you now reside in per the request of Mrs. Star's attorney?"

May replied, "Yes, and most of it was not located on the list."

Mr. Pricket asked, "So what you're saying is all the other stuff wasn't listed on the Schedule A and that is why you wrote 'not found' on the Schedule A? And is this your handwriting located on the Schedule A?"

Mr. Pricket handed her the Schedule A after he asked the judge to put it into evidence.

As he handed the document to her, May answered, "Ya, that's my handwriting. Most of the stuff wasn't there; just a couple of pieces."

Mr. Pricket continued asking her trivial questions, about which she mostly lied, and before I knew it, the judge asked Mr. Simms if he wished to cross-examine the witness.

Mr. Simms responded, "Yes, Your Honor, I have just a few questions for this witness."

Judge Colburn assented, "Very well then, proceed, Mr. Simms."

Mr. Simms began, "So, Mrs. Harp, you stated your address was this, but the property in question was located and stored at the Daisy house." He showed the address of the Daisy house to May. Mr. Simms then asked, "Have you moved from your father's rented house?"

May answered, "Yes, we moved out about a year ago."

Mr. Simms asked, "Then why did you tell the court that you still reside at that address and what did you do with Mrs. Star's family property?"

May said, "I didn't tell the court that. Mr. Pricket said I still resided there. I didn't think to correct him. I did say that we moved the stuff into storage units, and it cost me a lot of money. I expect to be reimbursed for it, only if the court says it's her stuff. We didn't know who owned the stuff."

Mr. Simms said, "Okay. Didn't Mrs. Star call you in April or around that time in 2000, asking you why your father would not return her things to her?"

May looked directly at me and I stared her down on the witness stand, she became flustered and stuttered as she answered, "Oh, that's right, I forgot, yes, she did call me."

Mr. Simms: "During this conversation, did you tell Mrs. Star that Bea Mills gave your great-grandmother's ring to you?"

May answered, "I don't remember."

Mr. Simms looked amused. "Oh, so you conveniently don't remember that? Okay, do you remember telling Mrs. Star that she would have to pry it off your dead finger before you give it back to her?"

May became angry and blurted, "It didn't belong to her. It belonged to my father and he gave it to me through Aunt Bea. Besides, she was my grandmother, not great-grandmother. She was Belinda's great-grandmother. I was named after her, not Belinda."

Mr. Simms said, "To set the record straight, Mrs. Harp, Belinda's uncle was also named after her. Did you realize that on the summary, Schedule A, when it stated, 'my great-grandmother's wedding ring,' she was referring to that ring? Where is it now, Mrs. Harp?"

May answered, "I don't know what ring she was talking about, and I don't know where it is."

Mr. Simms asked the judge for the Schedule A that was put into evidence by Mr. Pricket. After the judge passed it to Mr. Simms, he asked May, "Is this not your handwriting, Mrs. Harp? You wrote 'not found.' This indicates to me that you knew exactly what Mrs. Star was talking about."

May became even more agitated and answered, "I don't know. I just don't know."

Mr. Simms went on, "Isn't it a fact, Mrs. Harp, that Mrs. Star called you numerous times after your father passed away trying to convince you to allow her to move her property? Isn't it a fact, Mrs. Harp, that you and your aunt just issued a no trespassing notice on the plaintiff because you know that you and your aunt have no interest in the said property from the ruling of the judge in the lawsuit that Mrs. Star's mother filed against your aunt and your father's estate? You have known that the property never belonged to your father from the warrant in detinue that Mrs. Star filed against your father and aunt. So you have always known that the property in question never belonged to you or your father. You didn't even bother to obtain permission from Belinda Star to move her property from the locations where she had it stored. You file a trespassing notice against the plaintiff and you don't even reside at that location any longer. Please explain that as well. While you're at it, Mrs. Harp, explain the bauble that's located around your neck at this moment. You know that necklace belongs to the plaintiff. Explain how you acquired it."

May was clearly rattled by the questioning. "No, I don't know whose property it is and I don't understand why Belinda can sue, sue, and sue us to death! Why can't she just let it go so we can get on with our lives? This is my necklace. I don't need to tell you where I got it. It's on my neck, not hers!"

I heard several of the women in the jury let out gasps. At that point, there was no question to whom the property belonged. You could just look at May and tell she couldn't afford a $3,000 necklace, which was what she had around her neck. Even the clothes she had on told everyone that they were not her clothes. Her rotten black teeth spoke volumes.

After Mr. Simms finished questioning May, both attorneys reserved the right to recall her.

Mr. Pricket then called Sam Gibbs. I watched him as he got up from the defendant's table to be sworn in. He would only give me short glances as he walked and settled in at the witness stand.

The judge gave the usual instructions to speak loudly and clearly so everyone could hear and understand him.

Mr. Pricket then asked Sam Gibbs to state his name and address. Sam answered his question by giving his name and address.

Mr. Pricket said, "Could you tell the court how and why a conversation with the plaintiff, Belinda Star, came about around February of 2000, regarding her selling all of her family jewelry?"

Sam Gibbs answered, "It was about February of 2000, and Belinda called me up and asked if I wanted to hang out with her. She told me she had a high school buddy that lived in Washington D. C. that would hock her mother's jewelry for her."

I became livid that it took every ounce of strength to keep my facial expression in check. I leaned over to Mr. Simms and again whispered the truth to him with questions he should ask Sam. As Mr. Simms was writing down notes of the correct information I gave him, I could see the anger written all over his face.

After Mr. Pricket finished questioning Sam regarding this conversation that never took place except in Sam's imagination, unfortunately for Sam it was Mr. Simms' turn to question him.

Mr. Simms asked, "Mr. Gibbs, are you sure it was in 2000 that you had this alleged conversation with the plaintiff, Mrs. Star?"

Sam Gibbs responded, "Yes, I'm pretty sure because it was windy and still cold with snow on the ground."

Mr. Simms continued, "Mr. Gibbs, I believe your memory may be off by a year because it was in 1999 that Mrs. Star was here in Virginia cleaning up the mess that her mother, your father, and her great-aunt created.

Sam Gibbs shook his head, "No, no, I'm pretty sure it was 2000."

Mr. Simms went on, "Isn't it true, Mr. Gibbs that you went to see Mrs. Star to borrow $6,000 from her so you could pay your personal taxes?"

Before Sam answered, he was looking straight at me and I gave him the same evil stare I gave to May. He answered with a stutter, "We-well-well," as he looked down toward the ground and looked over at me. I continued giving him the evil eye. "Well, yes, I was having financial trouble and, yes, I did ask her to loan me the money."

Mr. Simms said, "Is it not true that Belinda spoke with your father regarding this matter since she did not have the funds to loan to you, and your own father gave you his gun collection so that you could sell them to pay the IRS?"

Sam responded, "Um, yes, he did."

Mr. Simms asked, "So the guns that your sister May is claiming were her father's. You know that is not true, correct?"

Sam Gibbs answered, "Um, yes, I guess that is true since my father already gave me his collection."

Mr. Simms asked, "In your opinion, Mr. Gibbs, who owns the guns that your sister, May, is talking about?"

Before Sam had a chance to answer, Mr. Pricket objected and the judge sustained.

Mr. Simms continued with his questions. "During one of these alleged conversations, you stated to the plaintiff, Belinda Star, that you were a spy for the union and you were tape recording the management and taking these tapes back to the union. Is that correct?"

Sam answered, "No I didn't say that."

Mr. Simms asked, "Didn't you write the plaintiff, Mrs. Star, a bad check during this time period?"

Sam Gibbs became visibly uncomfortable. "I don't remember."

Mr. Simms concluded, "No further questions, Your Honor."

Sam was excused and both attorneys requested the right to recall him.

Mr. Pricket then called Ed Weird to the stand.

Ed was sworn in, and after he settled in the witness seat, the judge gave the same instructions to him as he had the rest of the witnesses.

Mr. Pricket asked him the same questions to state his name, his address, and his relationship between the defendants and the plaintiff. Ed answered by giving his name, address, and stated that he was an old friend of the family. Again, I became angry and whispered in Mr. Simms' ear.

Mr. Pricket asked, "How and when did you become involved in this issue with the family?"

Ed answered, "Well, I guess it all began when Belinda's mother, Jane King, asked me to help out."

Mr. Pricket asked, "What do you mean 'help out'?"

Ed answered, "Well, I was asked to pay for and supervise the move of the stuff from the Kings' place to Bea and Frank's houses. When we moved it up there, Bea and Frank were surprised and didn't want the stuff stored there."

Mr. Pricket asked, "What do you mean they were surprised?"

Ed answered, "Well, Bea was angry, as well as Frank, and I had to convince them there was no other place to store it. Bea stated that no one had asked her for permission."

Mr. Pricket asked, "Okay, so Belinda Star wasn't party to this move at all, correct?"

Ed answered, "Yes."

Mr. Pricket continued, "Okay. Then what happened?"

Ed answered, "Well, Jane King asked me to keep an eye out for her aunt and uncle for her. Nobody knew who the property belonged to."

Mr. Pricket had no more questions at this time but requested the right to recall if needed.

Mr. Simms just simply stood up from his chair when the judge asked if he had any questions for the witness.

Mr. Simms asked, "Mr. Weird, were you not compensated for the payment of the move?"

Ed responded, "Well, yes, I was given a dining room table that was well worth more than what I paid the movers."

Mr. Simms asked, "Wasn't Belinda Star's little brother present supervising the move?"

Ed answered, "Well, yes, he was."

Mr. Simms continued, "So you were not asked to supervise the move because that responsibility was already bestowed on Belinda's brother by

Belinda's own request. Did you know that? I remind you that you are under oath, Mr. Weird."

Ed answered, "No, I was not aware of that. I guess I assumed I was supervising."

Mr. Simms went on, "In fact, Mr. Weird, you showed up during this move even though you were requested not to be present. Isn't it a fact, Mr. Weird, that you moved some of this property to your own residence?"

Ed answered, "No, that is not true."

Mr. Simms pulled out one of the moving company's receipts and handed it to Ed. He asked, "Is this not one of your addresses for the location and is that not your signature at the bottom stating you received property at that location?"

Ed became irritated. "Well, yes, it is my address and signature. Oh, I forgot, there wasn't enough room to store it at Frank and Bea's place, so I had them deliver it to one of my farms."

Mr. Simms nodded. "Oh, I see. Now explain to the court how and when you met the plaintiff, Belinda Star?"

Ed said, "Um, I don't think I actually met her or her sister, but I did know of them because of the members of the church."

Mr. Simms said, "Oh, I see. What about Frank and his children?"

Ed again appeared irritated by the question, "Um, well, okay, I guess, I didn't really meet them except for John, I think, once, but again I knew of them because of the members of the church."

Mr. Simms went on, "Oh, I see. So in other words you are not really an old friend of the family, correct?"

Ed responded, "Well, I was friends with the Kings."

Mr. Simms restated, "I asked, you were not really an old friend of the family since the people I mentioned are some of the family."

Ed replied, "No, I'm an old friend of the family because I know who most of them are."

Mr. Simms asked, "You stated that Mrs. King asked you to keep an eye out for her aunt and uncle, not to guide them into stealing from her children, correct?"

Ed replied, "I don't understand the question."

Judge Colburn directed, "Move along, Mr. Simms."

Mr. Simms concluded, "No further questions, Your Honor."

Both attorneys reserved the right to recall Ed Weird.

Mr. Pricket then called Bea. Mr. Pricket asked Bea to state her name, address, and her relationship to me. Auntie Bea answered him by giving her name and address, and she told him that she was my great-aunt and godmother. Mr. Pricket then asked her to tell the court in her words what had happened in 1999.

Auntie Bea gave her version, which contained many lies. Then she said, "Well, Belinda took off back to Germany with bags of stolen money because the FBI was hot on her tail."

I couldn't help myself. I started laughing aloud, and I heard the entire jury laughing with me. Mr. Simms started laughing and the judge started beating his gavel, but he was smiling and doing everything in his power to keep from laughing. He said, "Order in the court. Order in the court."

After the laughter settled down, Mr. Simms said he had no questions for the witness. Mr. Pricket stated, "The defense rests, Your Honor."

Mr. Simms requested that I be recalled to the witness stand. The judge reminded me that I was still under oath.

Mr. Simms asked, "Mrs. Star, could you please explain the real reason you had to go back to Germany in 1999?"

I answered, "Yes. I had to go back to Germany because my boss couldn't hold my job for me indefinitely. I'm a damn good accountant, but I had to get back to my life and make more money so I could come back and fight for the return of Auntie Bea's farm. And, no the FBI was not hot on my tail. There was no money. If it weren't for me, Auntie Bea would have been sitting in a jail cell right next to Jane King. My mission was to undo the crimes that had been committed. I still do not understand why my family would rather steal than wait for me. That's all I asked of them, was to wait for me. I gave them one more chance and I turned my cheek for them again because my father and mother asked that of me, so I did it out of love. So here we are after all these years because I trusted the wrong people once again. I will never turn my cheek for them again—never.

"To set the record straight, I was and still am a soldier that fights by the rules of engagement dictated to me; whether it be my commander-in-chief or the rules of this justice system. This courtroom is my battlefield. I carry the shield of truth in one hand to protect me against lies and the sword of justice, which is this jury, to swiftly strike down my offenders."

Mr. Pricket objected and objected, but his response was the loud clapping of the jury, as the judge kept beating his gavel down, calling for, "Order in the court! Order in the court!"

Before I knew it, it was finally over. The judge gave a recess of twenty minutes, and after the recess, the two attorneys would have the opportunity to give closing statements.

Mr. Simms stayed inside and I went outside to smoke a cigarette. It was completely dark, and I looked down at my watch and noticed it was 8:30 p.m. As I smoked my cigarette, I noticed that Mom had the rental car parked in front of the courthouse parking lot. I got into the driver's side of the car and Mom stated she had no other choice because she had to go to the bathroom and was afraid to drive elsewhere. I told her that they still had closing statements and I didn't know how the jury would rule. I just thought that I could not to tell her everything right now because I had a headache from hell and it would not go away.

I walked back into the courtroom and Mr. Simms, Mr. Pricket, and the judge were discussing the language of a form that the jury would need to fill out. It had "award to plaintiff" with a blank line for the "judgment amount," and then the same for the defendants. They continued arguing back and forth until an agreement was made and it was passed with all their notes to the court secretary. She walked back to the offices behind the wall of the judge's bench. A few minutes later, she came back in with the completed form. All three of them looked at it and agreed to the contents. Then the judge called for the jury to return.

Mr. Simms and Mr. Pricket gave their closing statements. Mr. Simms stated that the evidence had been shown as indicted in his opening statements. Mr. Pricket said the same thing in his opening statements as well. Essentially, they both chose to close with the same statements they had opened with.

The jury deliberated. After thirty minutes, the bailiff came back in with a note from the foremen. The judge read it and said to both attorneys that the jury was not happy with the form. So the two attorneys and the judge created another form for the jury. After the secretary prepared it, she handed it with several copies to the bailiff and he went back through the door where the jury was waiting.

Another thirty minutes passed, and I asked Mr. Simms why it was taking so long. Mr. Simms simply said that he didn't know, but he had a bad feeling about it. He felt that a verdict in our favor would have come quickly and easily.

Finally, the bailiff came back in and whispered in the judge's ear. The judge then said, "Finally, the jury has reached a verdict."

After the jury members were seated, the judge asked, "Has the jury reached a verdict?"

The foreman stood up and answered, "Yes, we have, Your Honor."

Then he passed the form to the judge. The judge opened it and read it. Then he passed it back to the bailiff, and in turn, the bailiff gave it the foreman of the jury.

The judge said, "You may read the verdict."

The foreman read aloud, "We, the jury, rule in favor of the plaintiff, Belinda Star . . ." As he read the ruling, which was basically the agreement that was reached between us during the warrant in detinue, I put my hand over my mouth and just started crying. I thought it was over now. I had won another battle. The victory was so sweet I could barely contain myself!

I looked up and over at Mr. Simms and he looked at me with a stunned expression. He absorbed the ruling and said in an almost whisper, with a smile merging on his face, "See, Belinda, our justice system has checks and balances." Then his expression turned toward a proud look. He seemed to have his self-confidence back again.

I simply whispered back to him, "I have a headache from hell!"

He leaned down toward my ear and whispered back, "I have one too. This was the longest case for a dispute over material things."

We both contained our joy as best we could while the judge dismissed the jury and thanked them for their time. As each juror passed us, I smiled at each and every one of them and mouthed the words, "Thank you." Each one of them smiled at me and nodded their heads, acknowledging my thanks.

As Mr. Simms and I gathered his papers and put them into his large briefcase, Mr. Pricket came over and shook Mr. Simms' hand. Both men looked at each other and Mr. Simms responded by simply saying, "Thank you."

Of course, it wasn't over because they did not have a true value of the property, but the jury took care of that for me, stating in the judgment that if all the property was not returned to the plaintiff, the true value of each and every item not returned would be compensated. The judge did stipulate that a future hearing would determine the value of any missing property, but first, the defendants would have the opportunity to return the property.

As Mr. Simms and I walked out of the now empty courthouse, we chatted about our victory, feeling that justice would soon be served. We also both complained of the painful headaches we had. Before we reached the rental car where my poor mother had sat all day, "I'll let her sweat a bit."

Mr. Simms responded with a frown, "Belinda, don't do that to her."

When we reached the car, the windows were both rolled down and Mom was sitting in the front passenger side.

I said, "Oh, Momma, I have bad news."

Mom said, "Oh, no, what happened?"

I started laughing and said, "The bad news is we won, and now we are going to have to move all that stuff to Colorado!"

Mr. Simms busted out with a laugh and then put his hand on his head as he stated, "Oh, my headache."

We both laughed with our aching heads.

Mom got out of the car and hugged both of us. She started asking questions, and Mr. Simms started telling some of what had happened and explained what our next step would be.

He said to my mother, "Well, I need to go home and take care of this headache. Belinda, can fill you in with the rest."

We said our goodnights, and Mom and I got into the rental car to go back to the hotel. I looked down at my watch and it was 11:30 p.m. *Good grief,* I thought, *this is ridiculous!* At least it was finally over.

CHAPTER XLV

I started telling the battle tale when we decided to stop at the corner gas station and burger joint so I could change out of my business suit into a pair of jeans. When we pulled up into the parking lot, we both realized I was parked right beside Auntie Bea's car.

May had the light on inside the car sitting in the back seat looking at papers as I was getting out of our car. She looked up at me with her thin lips in a snarl and I bent forward and started laughing at her. Then I looked back into the window of our rental car and told Mom I would be right back. I went into the bathroom of the fast-food place and changed into my jeans, t-shirt, and sneakers. Then I went to get into line to order some food and drinks, and Ed and May were standing in line in front of me. I looked behind me and Auntie Bea was sitting at one of the tables waiting for them. I never saw May's older daughter. I guessed she must have left with Sam. I didn't realize it until this moment, but I hadn't seen May's daughter at all after the trial.

I walked toward May and Ed and they were talking. I heard Ed tell May, "This was an injustice."

I stated in a loud voice so that everyone around could hear me clearly, "Mr. Weird, it was not an injustice. May, Bea, and the rest of you are nothing but liars and thieves, and justice prevailed."

They both practically ran from me.

Mom was sitting in the car as I returned with my hands full of a bag of clothes that I had changed from, the food, and the sodas. There was May standing outside the passenger window yelling and screaming at my mother, who in turn was yelling right back. The next thing I saw was my mother opening the car door and pushing May to the ground. I instinctively dropped everything in my hands and ran toward the beginning of the catfight.

Auntie Bea and Ed were still inside the fast-food restaurant and there was no one else outside the parking lot, so I grabbed May by her waist and her hair, jerked her straight up into a standing position while my mother was still kicking her, and I yelled at my mother, "Stop it, Momma! Stop it!"

Mom's eyes were filled with hatred, just as mine were, but this was not the place or time for such actions.

May started throwing her hands and arms around in the air trying to get my grip loose from the back of her pants and her hair at the back of her neck, but it was doing her no good because I wasn't finished with her yet. I barked orders at my mother, "Mom, move out of the way!"

Mom quickly moved from the side of the car where the door had closed, and I pushed the rotten snaggle-toothed skeleton into the side of the car. She used her hands to stop the force of the impact; before she knew it, I had her face pushed to one side of the side window, and she had both of her hands trying to push herself off it. I leaned into her back, put my face and mouth close to her ear, and I threatened, "Where's your fighting spirit when you have someone closer to your own age to fight with, or you just get the guts to try to beat up an old lady? I guess you have forgotten that my momma is a tough old bird. The drugs you have been taking seem to have even taken the strength from your body to even take her on."

As she tried to fight me, I pushed her harder into the car and I cut her off before she had a chance to respond. Through clenched teeth, I whispered in her ear, "Listen here, you diseased cunt, you're damn lucky this is a different time and place. As I said earlier today, nasty little people like you always get your comeuppance—always. You ever come near my mother again, and I swear to God, I will kill you."

As I let go of her and she turned to face me, I jerked the bauble from her neck before she had a chance to react, and I stood my ground staring at her as I passed it to my mother. She then lunged toward my mother, and I grabbed her with one arm, and with my other hand grabbed the back of her hair again and pulled. She stopped fighting and yelled, "Belinda, that's mine, give it back!"

I stated, "It is not yours, you diseased cunt. Have you lied so much you don't know the truth anymore? Or is it because of the drugs that have eaten up what little bit of brains you have? Get out of here before I really do hurt you." She stopped arguing and trying to fight me and just looked at me. Then she ran back inside.

I calmly walked back over to where I had dropped my clothes, food, and drinks and picked everything up. Mom had already gotten back into the car. I told her, "Lock the doors. I'm going back inside to get us some more sodas."

Mom simply said, "Okay."

As I was walking back inside, May had already had Auntie Bea and Ed walking outside of the burger joint, but it was already too late. Auntie Bea was ready to scold me, and I said, "Shut up, you old, moldy cunt. I caught her goading Momma. My advice is for you to leave or stay. I don't really give a shit, but you better stay out of my way."

Ed had the nerve to raise his fist at me right in the entrance of the restaurant, and he yelled, "I'm going to kick your ass!"

I yelled back at him, "Bring it on, motherfucker—bring it on! I'll take you down in four seconds!"

I stood there waiting for him to complete his threat, but he looked at me and dropped his fisted arm. I goaded him, "Coward! I can break your neck in a second! At this point I truly don't give a flying fuck!"

He continued to look at me, but before I knew it, the manager of the restaurant was standing there and said, "Take this somewhere else."

They all got in Auntie Bea's car and left. After I was sure they were not returning, I went up to the counter and asked for two more sodas.

Mom and I drove back to the hotel in silence. The only thing Mom said was, "Thank you, Belinda. It was dark and I didn't see she had my necklace on."

I replied, "You're welcome, Momma. I still have that headache from hell."

As I was driving us back, I truly regretted letting my hillbilly, undisciplined, fowl mouth see light again. I had lost my temper, but I knew I could have easily killed May that night.

We got back to the hotel and I slipped back into my jeans after taking a shower, and we went down to the bar in the hotel so that we could have a victory drink. I told my mother about the events of the day and what Ed had said at the restaurant. I felt responsible for May's behavior toward her.

CHAPTER XLVI

Toward the end of June 2006, Hank Harp called me and stated, "I hear you needed me in court."

I replied, "Who is this?"

He said, "Hank Harp. I have some of your belongings hidden for May and Bea. I would like to give it back so I can get out of trouble with you and your momma."

I asked, "How did you get this number?"

Hank answered, "My daughter-in-law looked it up for me."

I said, "Wait a minute; I want my mother and husband to hear this as well."

He said, "Okay."

I covered up the mouthpiece of the phone, and I yelled, "Mom, Thomas, come into the kitchen ASAP! Hank Harp is on the phone! He says he wants to give back our stuff. I don't know if this is some kind of trick!"

They both came running from different parts of the house.

Once they were standing in the kitchen beside me, I stated, "Hank, I'm putting you on the speakerphone so that all of us can talk to you at the same time."

Hank replied, "Okay." I then turned on the speakerphone.

I told him, "This better not be a trap of some kind. If I make arrangements to come get my property and you then refuse to return it, I promise I will sue you too."

Hank laughed and said, "No. This is no joke or trick. I swear I want you to come and get your stuff as soon as you can."

Thomas jumped in and started drilling Hank with questions. Hank answered everything. He said, "Thomas, I swear, I'm telling you the truth and I completely understand your distrust, but I will do everything you ask of me; I swear it. I just want to make things right again between the two families."

Then Mom started peppering him with questions and he answered them to her satisfaction.

We started talking and planning off the top of our heads; Mom and I would go there the next week to recover the property. I wrote down his phone number and stated we would call him back the next day with our travel plans and the exact day we would be there.

As soon as we hung up with Hank, I immediately made arrangements. Because we had no idea what he had, I reserved two large moving trucks and a two-man moving team to move and pack the property into the trucks. I was given the option to downsize a truck if I needed to do so.

I called Mr. Simms and told him what was going on. I told him I was making a generic receipt of what he would return to us. Mr. Simms said that was a good idea.

We arrived in Snobville the following week. We picked up the rental car and went straight to the hotel.

Once we were settled in the hotel, my mother called Hank and told him where we were. She informed him that we would meet him at the location of the storage units the next day. He asked if he could come over now and talk with us. My mother agreed and said that we would meet him down in the small restaurant at the hotel.

We met Hank, his son, Jeff, and Jeff's wife, Patricia. This was the first time I had met Jeff and his wife. In fact, I never even knew they existed. Of course, they already knew my mother.

Then, the entire truth came to light during the long conversation my mother and I had with the three of them. Patricia said, "Well, I went to the courthouse and went through the public records until I found a document with your telephone number on it, Belinda."

During the conversation, Jeff stated, "Patricia and I told Dad and May to give the stuff back to you guys a long time ago."

Hank then joined in and told much of what I believed to be half-truths, "I didn't know what was coming. The next thing I knew I was handcuffed and charged with child abuse by my wife and my daughters. For Pete's sake, I can't even get it up anymore!"

As Hank went on about being in jail and the expensive attorney he had to hire to defend himself, Jeff stated, "I told you, Daddy, not to tell the cops anything until you had an attorney."

Other statements randomly came from Hank. "I've been married to that woman for twenty years. I can't believe my own children would say such lies. I would never do something so nasty. The only thing I did was walk around in my boxers. There was nothing obscene about that. I never laid a hand on May. I never pinned down anyone. They made some things that were totally innocent on my part sound monstrous and ugly."

Then, Patricia made a statement during this period of the conversation. "Jeff and I saw that incident that they were talking about. Hank was sitting in Uncle Frank's old recliner chair and Ginger, his youngest daughter, ran up and jumped on him and his pickle popped out of the slash in his boxers. Everyone started laughing, including May. Of course, old Hank went back in his bedroom and threw on a pair of trousers after that."

Patricia continued talking and told another story. "The other incident happened when Jeff and I were there as well. That's when Jeff hurt his back moving y'all's stuff to the new house that May made Hank buy her. Ginger was jumping up and down on the trampoline and fell off it and her side hit the corner of your dresser that had not been moved into their new house yet. She came running inside crying, and Hank said to Ginger, 'Where's the boo-boo and I'll kiss it and make it feel better.' So Ginger pulled up her shirt where it was bruised right below her left breast, and he kissed the boo-boo and it appeared to me, as being a mother myself, totally innocent. Well, they are charging him with two counts of sexual battery because old Hank here had to open his mouth when they were arresting him trying to clear his name."

Over the next four hours, this ugly story was told. The whole time, my mother and I kept quiet. All we wanted was our stuff back, and as far as I was concerned, old Hank got his comeuppance for stealing and lying ten times fold. I just laughed in my mind.

The next day, Hank met us at the first location where my family's property was hidden. I had him sign the document that I prepared stating that he was giving me the keys, that everything that did not belong to me would stay in the locations, and that he would take repossession of those items if any. I had my mother take a picture of us standing at the first location as he handed me the keys.

Then we opened the first storage unit. Boxes and some furniture were thrown into the unit, including empty boxes. We said nothing.

Then Hank took us to the next location, which was a 30—or 40-footer MILVAN container on wheels. It was rusted and you had to climb up on it to unlock the large doors located at the back of the MILVAN because of the way it was stationed on the large wheels. I climbed up and unlocked it; again, stuff had been thrown into it and it wasn't quite filled to the ceiling. I wanted to cry for my mother and for myself. Again, we said nothing. We got back into the rental and said thank you to Hank. We had to leave so I could get the moving truck. I already called the moving team to meet us at the first location. Hank said he had to go to work anyway, and he would come by after work to see how things were going.

I drove our rental car up the road to where the moving company was located. I completed all the paperwork for renting the truck for us to drive back to Colorado. I drove the truck, and Mom followed me back to the first location of the stored property. I backed the large truck into the position that would be the easiest.

I opened the door once again to the storage unit, and my mother and I started going through it. My mother started crying. My heart broke at the sight. I also felt like crying, but once again, I stifled my emotions. Within an hour, the men we had hired to help us pulled up behind the moving truck. It was an older gentleman with a young man to help him. We began the physically hard labor. We left all the crap that didn't belong to us in the unit. It appeared to me that they were giving us their trash in lieu of our family property. Most of what we did recover had already been destroyed.

Once we were finished there, we proceeded to the next location. Once again, my mother started crying. I backed up the large truck so it almost touched the MILVAN. It made it much easier to move it from one location to the other. After we filled that truck, we decided to get a smaller second truck. We broke for a late lunch. I left the larger truck locked next to this MILVAN container and went back and got another, but smaller truck. Most of the property belonged to other relatives, but we did recover a smaller truckload. There were still at least five more large truckloads missing.

After going through junk for an entire day, we came to the conclusion that our precious belongings had been thrown into these storage units haphazardly. Most of the items were destroyed or badly damaged. One piece of furniture was merely remnants; legs were broken off and never found. Ninety-eight percent of the property that was located in these storage units did not belong to me. It appeared to belong to May and Hank, their children, May's mother, Bea, John, Frank, Sam, and Samantha.

So I turned back over the keys to Hank; the bulk of it was not mine. I only removed what was definitely my property and no one else's.

I recovered a few rugs from the storage units. They were not rolled up and packed the way Thomas and I had left them in Ms. Daisy's house. They had been thrown into storage. It appeared that someone had used them and allowed their animals to defecate on them. These solid wool rugs had been in my family for centuries; they could never be replaced. They had been passed down from one generation to the next. Prior to now, they had always been well-maintained.

The most important items that I was able to recover were my computers and one hard copy of the detailed inventory/property reports with the cost values. Prior to now, I only had the inventories and property reports with no dollar values on them because the military's JPSO did not require dollar figures, just detailed inventories/property reports giving locations. From my understanding, it was intended to provide an indication of weight and space, and they were able to plan our military moves from that. They did not require dollar amounts or values, so I hadn't had the lists with those on them until now.

Another very important recovery we made was the receipts, owner manuals, and appraisals for many of my belongings. Without these, I had no idea of the true value of my personal property. There were still a lot of receipts, owner manuals, and appraisals missing, along with a myriad of personal papers.

There were about two hundred or more empty boxes located in the storage units filled with wrapping paper and nothing else. We took one picture of one box that someone had written "cameras" on, but the word was misspelled. The box was completely empty. We recovered some other empty boxes where the camera lenses should have been packed, but they were empty, as were the camera cases.

During this time in Virginia, Hank kept asking me about my coin collection. He knew its value and wanted it for returning my belongings. I told that he could not have my coin collection. I stated that I did not know how much it was worth, and he could not have it. It should have been in my safe at Bea's house. I asked how he knew about it, and how he knew the value. I asked him to return them to me. He said he had them appraised, and Bea had given them to him, but now May has them. I discovered they had been fighting over some of my coin collection during their divorce. Sadly, I probably would never see them again.

At the end of the day, all we had were two truckloads. One that was the largest you could rent and the second was the smallest truck you could rent. For the most part, it had been a wasted trip. As far I was a concerned, we had recovered nothing of true value. We went back to the hotel, washed up, ate a light supper, and went to bed. I don't think either of us slept well. I heard my mother softly crying several times during the night. At daybreak, we checked out of the hotel and headed home. It was a long, sad trip. I drove the large truck, and my mother followed in the smaller one.

Thomas was home when we arrived two days later. Once I was in his arms, I allowed my emotions to break free. I sobbed for several minutes while he held me. I then pulled myself together and put on my soldier's face. We unloaded the trucks and returned them to the local dealer.

The next morning, I set up my computers. It was then that I discovered that May had tampered with my computers. When I turned the computers on, May's name appeared on the password windows. I guess she did not know with these old PCs, all you had to do was click the "x" and close the window. I discovered that she had erased all the inventory reports and my genealogy from the computer. I immediately called our local computer programmer and he asked to me bring the computer in to look at it. He said there were still "ghosts" in the computers and I might be able to retrieve the lost files. He did not have the technology to do so and gave me a number in New York to contact.

I called the number and was given the runaround. Eventually, I was connected with someone who was able to help me. I explained what had happened, and the tech said she could help me, but they needed my hard drive. I wrote down the mailing address. Of course, it would cost a small fortune and so I was unable to send it.

CHAPTER XLVII

Toward the end of July, the court orders were finally signed, and justice had finally been served. All suspected parties were being held accountable. They had thirty days to return any property in their possession that did not belong to them.

Mr. Pricket fought tooth and nail to prevent me from receiving my property. He actually threatened several of the local sheriff's departments that he would file charges to have me arrested if I stepped foot on any of their properties. Thank God, we prevailed.

On the morning of August 14, 2006, Mom and I met with the deputy sheriff of Greenville at a local fast food restaurant. I had contacted the movers again, and they met us there. The deputy sheriff was initially hostile toward me and treated me as if I were evil for wanting my belongings back. We drove around to the various locations to collect the items. The deputy sheriff was there to enforce the writ but never did. By the end of the day, the deputy sheriff's attitude seemed to change as he became more empathetic toward me, but he was still a lazy piece of shit and didn't really give a damn.

Our first stop was Julie Pane's home. She was Ed's daughter. I had never met her. I saw several toolboxes, various tools, and snow globes around the house and in the sheds that could have been mine, but Julie stated they were hers. She claimed to have had them for several years. Unfortunately, most people have these items in their home, and I did not have proof that these exact items were mine. It would have been up to Julie to tell the truth, but she did not. While we were walking through the living room, I noticed that one wall was lighter in an area than the rest, as if a large piece of furniture had recently been moved. From the shape, it looked as if it could have been a secretary or curio, but I was not sure. I asked her directly if they had moved any furniture or hidden it, and she said no, but she could not look me in the eye when she answered.

Next, we went to May's house. This was the first time I had been there. I decided to start with the two small sheds she had on her property. May and her two daughters yelled and screamed at us, saying there was nothing in there that belonged to me. We started going through the first shed, and I found a carving I had purchased, then my wedding portrait—in fact, almost everything in the shed was mine. I carefully instructed the movers to remove my belongings and put May's belongings neatly back in the shed. In all honesty, she did not deserve the courtesy I was giving her because she had just thrown everything in there, but I did not want any accusations that I had damaged her property.

As I stepped out of the shed for the final time, I saw May bend over to put her cigarette out. An opal necklace that belonged to my mother spilled out from under her shirt. My mother also spotted it and asked her to return it to me. Of course, May refused. She stated that Bea had given it to her. She turned around and stomped back into her house.

While we were going through the other shed, we discovered the four carved wooden pineapples that topped the post of my mother's four-poster bed. That was all we found of her bed. The expression on Ed's face spoke volumes. We knew then that Ed had removed all the antiques and valuable furniture. It was written all over his face. Knowing them, they probably used all of it for a bonfire. My mother found a quilt that my great-aunt Clara had made in the early 1900s. She had passed it on to Ms. Lita, who then gave it to my mother. It was crumpled up on the floor. I could tell that it had just been tossed into the shed, and it had several rips in it. My mother burst into tears when she saw the blood stains on it, which appeared to have been caused by someone's menstrual flow.

In that shed, I found my mother's sewing cabinet. Inside it, we found the embroidered tags that had the names of the fur coat companies and my mother's name on them. I guess May had removed the tags from the family furs. When we went through her house later, she had one fur coat in her closet. When questioned, she said that Bea gave it to her and it was a fake. I also found the rod that went into the expensive wardrobe boxes that Thomas and I bought to store my furs and other special coats. I found two of the hangers with the fur company's name on them. We never found the coats and never found my mother's clothing.

I know that there was no way that May and her children could own these things and this jewelry because their house and trailer had mysteriously burned to the ground in Tennessee. Witnesses stated they came away with nothing but the clothes on their backs. We also found, mixed in with our papers, May and Hank's tax returns. Those forms showed they never listed expensive antiques or fine clothing as lost property from when the house burned down.

Almost everything I found in the sheds that belonged to me either had been damaged or destroyed. Every time I said an item was mine, May and her daughters disputed my claim. Even though I had the receipts and pictures to prove they belonged to me, the deputy sheriff did nothing. After the sheds, we moved on to the house. I walked toward the front porch, and I saw two sculptures that I had made. May started to dispute them, and I said, "Just stop it. My name is engraved in the porcelain because I made these. You have destroyed them. They were not made to be outside."

Then, I entered the house armed with my video camera. May did not object to the camera, but she continued to dispute each item I claimed as mine. Despite my emotional upheaval, I still managed to capture some of what happened in her house. After returning home, I also had stills made from this video tape. On the tape, you hear her disputing all of my jewelry and jewelry boxes, my guns, my furniture, my clothing, my linens, and many other items. She claimed that Uncle Frank had given her my guns. Again, I had to correct her.

"May, you know that is an outright lie. When I stayed with your father in 1999, he gave his entire gun collection to your brother Sam because Sam needed money to pay his taxes. My guns were stored in the upstairs closet at Bea's house, and now they're here in your bedroom."

She stopped arguing about the guns and admitted I was right, but still she refused to return them. She was going to return my grandfather clock, but Ed was there by then and said, "No." I could do nothing more about that.

I saw my jewelry strewn all over her dresser. At first, she admitted that it was mine but quickly changed her story. She claimed that Auntie Bea had given it to her. Then she disputed all the other jewelry I said was mine, but she said it was hers because Auntie Bea gave it to her. I knew this was a bold-faced lie because some of the jewelry May had, Bea did not know existed. I had them hidden in my mother's clothing. Not only had I hidden smaller jewelry boxes in my mother's clothing at Ms. Daisy's house, but I had a witness to her theft. Jeff Harp said he watched her take my jewelry boxes out of the boxes in my mother's clothing. The diamond rings, cocktail rings, and costume jewelry that belonged to my mother, and my diamond earrings and bracelets all had been stored in my safes at Bea's house. May had one of my dressers in her bedroom, but of course, she claimed it was hers and refused to return it.

I opened one of the top drawers and found a jeweler's box that held two of my cocktail rings and one of my wedding bands. May started yelling that it was hers, and Bea had given it to her. I quickly shut the drawer because she had a dildo with a used condom on it. I did not want to embarrass the deputy sheriff, so I said nothing. It was a waste of my breath to dispute it verbally because the deputy sheriff was refusing to do his job. To me he was just wasted space.

May allowed us to take the other chest of drawers, and when we returned to Colorado, I discovered a 1925 dime in one of the drawers. It still had the glue on the back of it. It appeared to me that it had fallen out of the folder from my coin collection, which had been stored in a safe at Bea's house.

I took all my jewelry out of my jewelry boxes so I could video tape the collection. While I was doing that, I discovered a drug pipe. I informed May I could not be around illegal substances. I had security clearance, and I did not want anything illegal seeping in my system. The deputy sheriff clarified my ignorance and said that I would not get it in my system just by touching the pipe.

May's oldest daughter interrupted, "Mom has not smoked out of that pipe in ages; for God's sake, Belinda, it doesn't even have a screen in it."

Then the youngest daughter, Ginger, said, "That's right Mom has not smoked out of that pipe in a long time."

Appalled at their knowledge of their mother's drug use, I asked, "How do you know about such things?"

"That's enough," May said to her daughters.

The deputy sheriff witnessed the entire conversation, and he took the pipe from May without a word.

May had several of my old video cameras located in her closet, but at that point, I was unable to prove it. We had recovered some negatives from the sheds that May had failed to destroy, but I didn't realize that we had proof of ownership. I was only able to prove a fraction of what I found belonged to me. Even that didn't matter anyway because the deputy sheriff wasn't going to make them return anything they disputed.

From our frequent military moves, I had learned to take pictures of your belongings. It was something I had practiced for the previous eighteen years. The only problem was that all my pictures were in storage, and now May had them. I believed some of the clothing she had in her closet was my mother's, but I could not prove one way or another because May had not returned my pictures. I did locate my husband's university jacket in her closet. She threw it in my face and said, "Take it!" I guess because Thomas's name was written inside the jacket, she couldn't dispute it.

After I finished in May's room, we went to her oldest daughter's bedroom. The oldest daughter had already started pulling out jewelry. The first thing she threw in my face was a pair of small diamond earrings still in the jeweler's box and my grandmother's faux pearl necklace. By this time, she was yelling and screaming that she had purchased them with her own money, which I knew was a lie because she had dropped out of high school. The local gossip was that she had a job at a pizza joint but had only been there a few months. Even during her own testimony during her parents' divorce hearing, she had stated that her income went to her mother to help pay bills. There was no way she could afford or even obtain credit to purchase a $3,000 pair of earrings. Thanks to Hank, I had the receipts and appraisals. That was the only reason I knew the exact value.

By now, my hands were shaking because I was so angry, and I had no way of releasing my anger but through crying. I went out to the front porch to regain control. I guess they were not satisfied with the emotional turmoil they had already caused because the oldest daughter followed me out on the porch and flaunted my grandmother's faux pearl necklace in my face again. She said to me, "It's no big deal. They're just fakes, Belinda."

"I know that, but they are special to me because they belonged to someone I loved very much, who is no longer with us on this earth. I miss her very much, but that's something you will never understand because what is happening to me has not happened to you," I responded.

After a few minutes, I went back into May's bedroom. In the middle of her bathroom, which I had previously checked, was a large lockbox. I went over and as I started to open it, May yelled, "Not yours! Nothin' in there's yours!"

I opened it and discovered my small jewelry cedar box that I had stored at Bea's house. This box had been a high school graduation gift to my mother. She, in turn, gave it to me on the day I graduated high school. Before I could touch it, May snatched up the jewelry box and refused to return it, stating Bea had given it to her. She would not even hand it to me so that I could look inside to see if some of my coins were in it. Jeff had told me that she had stored her drugs in it for safekeeping, so I knew why she was so possessive of it. Then, out of thin air, she pulled out my black beads. Again, she claimed that Bea had given them to her. I just shook my head in disgust.

I looked inside the lockbox and saw a few coins from my coin collection, including a set of 1941 birth year coins in a plastic container. My mother was born in 1941 and these coins had been given to her as a birthday present. There were also a few half and whole dollar coins that belonged to my grandmother's collection. I pulled out my video camera and taped them. Before I had a chance to set the camera down and pull out the coins, May slammed the lid on the lockbox closed. At this point, I was becoming infuriated.

Every bone in my body was shaking from rage. I could barely control it. If the deputy sheriff had not been there, I would have easily snapped the necks of May, her two daughters, and Ed. I hated and loathed these people so badly that I wanted to kill them all. I was disgusted with our justice system.

We finally completed our search of May's property. I saw the deputy sheriff give me a sympathetic look. His attitude toward me had changed since earlier in the morning, but he still did nothing.

When the deputy sheriff and I were outside talking with my mother after coming out of the pigsty that May called home, and we were both breathing in fresh air again, I released my anger and said to the deputy sheriff, "Why didn't you arrest her?"

He became angry and yelled at me, "I'm doing my job, and I have to send it to the lab first before I can do anything."

I yelled right back at him, "I don't know who I'm more hurt by, my relatives or a brother in arms. You have treated me like a piece of garbage the majority of this day. You have not made them return one damn thing—even when I have the receipt of ownership!"

He yelled, "You'll have to go back to court to straighten that out!"

My mother yelled at both of us as the argument started to intensify, "Both of you—that's enough!" To this day, I did not understand why he did not arrest May.

I was drained emotionally by the time we arrived at John Gibbs' in-laws' house. I had not met the Pricks before in my life. John's wife was there and met us outside the door. She showed her true colors and started carrying on like a fool. She was actually making threats to the deputy sheriff and made sure that everyone within hearing range knew that she was a state police dispatcher. In reality, she was a telephone operator for the state police.

She loudly stated, "I will make a complaint if you allow Belinda's mother in here. I am cooperating under protest and I want to make that perfectly clear."

The deputy sheriff calmly stated that he understood. I heard Mr. Prick tell the deputy sheriff that he could not believe I had gotten this far, and the deputy sheriff replied, "I know."

I did not even try to claim anything because there was no way of proving it was actually mine. They could have easily had the same things I had. All I knew was that not all of my property was returned to me. Visiting the Pricks' house was a waste of everyone's time.

The deputy sheriff then took me to Bea's house. Bea hobbled outside her house yelling that my mother wasn't allowed in, and she was also yelling for Jeff and Patricia to get off her property. The deputy sheriff informed her that they were staying. I was so shocked to see my vehicles stripped of all their parts, and the driver's side of the Cadillac was dented, as if it had been kicked. The body of the pickup truck had numerous rust holes, broken windows, and parts had been removed. The deputy sheriff said we could take them because we had the titles. I called my attorney, and he said to leave them alone because Bea had stripped the vehicles of their parts. It would cost more to repair them than to replace them, so I left them.

Back in 2004, May and Bea tried to transfer the car titles into their names fraudulently, but the clerk had discovered it and called our attorney. At that time, Mr. Simms told her that his client would like her vehicles back, but obviously, that never happened.

Bea told me that I could not go into the sheds, so we went into her house. Bea refused to open her safe. The jewelry organizers and jewelry storage boxes that should have been in the safes were located in Bea's bedroom on top of my jewelry chest that she refused to return. The organizers were full of jewelry from my direct lineage, which had been stored in my safes. I opened these small organizers, but they were empty. There was another one of my organizers sitting on my bed in her guest room. The bed even had my linens on it!

239

In her bedroom was my sculpted flower basket, but she did not even deny that it was mine. She said I might get it back when she was dead, but she doubted it. She had some of my jewelry located in my jewelry chest that she was using and refused to return it. She had jewelry from my safe sitting on her dressers.

She had stolen my grandmother's and my mother's perfume collections. They were sitting on her dresser along with the mirrored vanity tray that belonged to my grandmother. These items had been stored at the Daisy house. She had my mother's muumuus in her utility room. which I had bought in Hawaii when I was stationed there. I was in total shock! I could not believe this. I realized then why Bea's junky property had been in the storage units that Hank had shown to us. She had to move out her property to make room for ours! She had stolen my property, but had tried to give me hers. Bea was using my coffee table and my good chairs, all of which were pieces that Ms. Lita had left to my mother, who had given them to me. She had boxes and boxes of my property sitting in her utility room that she would not give back.

She had my blanket chests and wardrobes, my secretary desk, and many of my pictures that belonged to me and were originally stored at the Daisy house. She even had some of my spider plants!

Bea returned two safes to me. The first safe was empty; the only things left were a few legal documents, and she also returned one armoire chest of drawers. She put some of my family jewelry in the armoire, trying to pass it off as a jewelry chest, and filled it with parts of jewelry that were located and stored in other jewelry chests. I even found some pieces that I supposed they did not realize were real, and put them in the armoire. I recognized these items from the safe, but it was just a few of the pieces. Some of the jewelry was broken and there were cigarette ashes in the one jewelry chest that she did return.

She returned our dogs' ashes after she had promised me in 1999 that she would take good care of them until I returned to the States. As she was giving me the boxes of ashes, she said to me, "Do you know I wanted to just throw these dog ashes away?"

I just stood there and looked at her in disbelief. She had conned me into keeping my things there so that she could steal from me again. Everything she had said to me in 1999 had been a lie. I looked down at the dog ashes and shook my head. I could not believe she had removed the names from the boxes of what was left of our beloved family dogs. Now we did not know who was who. I just swallowed my pain.

I asked Bea where my guns were. She thought she was being clever, I guess, because her response was, "I have never owned any guns in my life."

I knew she had given them to May because I had just come from May's house, where May had claimed that they were her father's guns. I stated, "I did not ask you if you owned any guns. I asked where my guns are—the ones that I had stored in your upstairs closet."

She ignored my statement. She started yelling that we needed to leave right away.

Sadly, I turned and walked out of her house. It hurt so badly that someone I had loved so deeply and trusted had used my love and trust to steal from me. I couldn't believe she could continue to stab my bleeding heart continuously with no remorse. Was this really my lineage?

My mother and I spent a sad night at the hotel. We spoke very little. There was nothing to say. We both knew how the other felt, and neither wanted to start crying.

The following morning, the deputy sheriff of Pineville County met me at Shelia Weird's house. Shelia was Ed's daughter. The deputy sheriff waddled out of her house with a hostile and derogatory attitude toward me. He immediately started telling me who I could and could not allow in the house with me. He told me that I could not photograph or video tape anything in the house. As a result, I was unable to prove what they disputed by putting receipts that I had alongside pictures of the same item.

He demanded to see my personal property summery. As he paged through it, he mocked what I had written there. I felt a tear slip down the side of my cheek. It hurt so deeply to have a brother in uniform treat me with such low regard when I was the victim of a sad, sad crime. It was even more painful that he did not believe me. I softly told him, "I have been robbed and had fraud committed against me not only by my own family but by people I never had met before in my life. These people have stolen everything I owned and everything that meant something to me."

He looked at me and, in a softer tone, told me that he was sorry. He understood and he didn't mean it that way, he was just trying to lighten the atmosphere.

We entered the house, and he stood in Shelia Weird's kitchen going through my summary report. He asked if they had each item on the list, and each time they stated they did not have it. By the time he got to the kitchen items, I was already looking at my microwave that she had hanging above her stove. It was an older model and didn't match her other appliances, so I was certain it was mine. When he asked about the microwave, she again said that she didn't have it. I didn't bother to say anything. What good would it have done to show a picture of the same microwave?

I did, however, dispute one of the vanities that they had in their house. I even showed him a picture that I had taken years before, but it did not do me any good. They produced a picture as well, but their picture was in the same room and the same place with no dates. I also found my curio/hutch located in Shelia's house, but when I showed the deputy sheriff a picture of it, he still would not make them return it because they disputed it.

They told the deputy sheriff that they had some of my property stored in their chicken coop and they wanted it removed so they could have it cleaned out at my expense. It was mostly Christmas decorations, but only one-fourth of my family's collection. Porcelain figurines that hung on a tree were collecting mildew. Shelia told the deputy sheriff that Hank had been moving and needed a place to put my property, so they did a favor for Hank and stored it for him.

Shelia disputed the dog mailbox, bird feeders, and post that were a set. She said they were hers. We turned the mailbox around and my mother's last name was still on it. We looked at her and I asked, "Are you still disputing this?" Her face turned red and she walked out of the nasty chicken coop without responding.

I was so upset that I sat down and let the movers continue helping my mother sort through things to be sure it was our property and not someone else's junk. I walked back to my rental car parked to retrieve my cigarettes and our drinks.

Ed stopped me as I was returning to the chicken coop and he said, "Belinda, this is becoming less profitable for me. I was just trying to help."

I could not believe this creep. "Help? Help who? The only thing you did was *help yourself* to my family heirlooms. I don't know what you are, except for a thief and liar. I had put a bandage on this mess until I was able to return home and finish it, but instead another crook—you—came out of the woodwork and unleashed the evil from my family . . . ."

Before I could continue, the deputy sheriff got out of his car. I think he knew I was getting ready to beat the shit out of Ed. I walked back to the chicken coop to help my mother and the moving team get the stuff packed and put into the moving truck.

Now that everyone had figured out that all they had to do was dispute anything in their possession, Ed called the deputy sheriff in Snobville and told him we could come to his house next. I had to call the deputy sheriff in Snobville because it took us longer at Shelia's house than we had expected. I asked if we could reschedule for the following day with John, but he said that John would not be home. Instead, we would go to Samantha's house, which we did.

My mother's cement tables and benches were sitting in Samantha's front yard. As soon as I mentioned that they were mine, Samantha disputed it, and said they belonged to her live-in boyfriend. My mother discovered one of her small refrigerators in a spare room in Samantha's trailer. Again, Samantha disputed it and said it belonged to her boyfriend. In these cases, she could have been telling the truth, but it was doubtful. It would have been quite a coincidence.

I felt relieved because this deputy sheriff treated me with compassion and understanding that I deserved as the victim; the other deputy had treated me as I were the villain. I appreciated too that he was stern when speaking to Samantha and the others, but of course, he did nothing regarding the disputed items. So, even though his attitude was better, the outcome remained the same.

The deputy sheriff and I then went to Ed's house. Ed had Confederate bills and Japanese's yin notes sitting on his steps on top of his mail. It appeared to me as if he took my old money that was stored in my safes from the day before and dropped them on his steps with the prior day's mail. I asked him to return it, but he said it was not mine. He claimed that it belonged to his mother who had passed away. I later discovered that his mother had passed away a decade earlier.

I looked outside on his deck where some of our family patio furniture was, but of course, he disputed it. His garage was packed full of garden things and boxes of miscellaneous plant pots and cleaning supplies scattered throughout. I did not say anything. I then had my mother go through the house because Ed was begging her to come in. I told my mother about our family's old currency on his steps. One of the first things my mother looked at was the steps, but Ed had removed them from her sight.

She went through the garage and she discovered one box of marble floor cleaner. It was the same brand that she bought in bulk, but he disputed it, saying it was not ours. Then he said he did not know where he had purchased it. The man didn't have marble tiling anywhere in his house, so he finally let my mother take it for me. One of my birdbaths, or at least part of it, was in his yard. We had recovered the little boy part from his daughter's house the day before. He disputed it like all the rest. Mom found our family windmill. She just stood there and I looked up and could not believe my eyes. Ed Weird could not figure out what we were looking at and he said, "Oh, Big Pete gave it to me."

My mother sadly responded, "And Pete is dead."

Next, we went to Sam Gibbs' house with another deputy sheriff in Poca County. I felt so relieved again because the deputy sheriff treated us with respect and understanding. Sam was not there but his wife was. I allowed my mother to go inside instead of me because I was emotionally drained at this point. She went through the house and discovered a handmade puzzle box that had been made by her father-in-law. When he passed away, he left it to my mother who in turn gave it to me. Sam had never met this man before in his life. My mother had always stored it with our Christmas boxes and displayed it at Christmas in remembrance of this great man. Sam's wife disputed it but allowed my mother to take a picture of it.

We were standing by my rental car with the deputy sheriff and Mrs. Gibbs came out and said, "I'm not disputing this, here you go."

"Thank you, and please tell Sam to return the rest of my family's property and to come clean regarding the guns that May has," I replied.

Mrs. Gibbs said, "I wasn't married to Sam when this all happened, but I will tell him to tell the truth." She had a scarf around her head to cover up where she had lost all her hair to chemotherapy. I felt sympathy for her until the deputy sheriff told us that she had tried to use her illness to avoid our visit. It was a well-known fact that she was a thief as well.

John and his wife would not cooperate. They refused to let us go through their home to recover my property. They kept making excuses. So the deputy sheriff called them and told them if they were not there, he was going to get their apartment manager to let him in because we needed to return to Colorado. We met the deputy sheriff at their apartment, which I had never seen before. John's wife carried on like a fool about allowing my mother to double check behind me.

I found video tapes and asked John, "Are these my family video tapes?"

He made comments that he had a video camera in those days and he had been videotaping my grandparents too. If they were not mine, how did he know what I was talking about? He said he would make copies for me. Of course, I never saw them.

My fishbone mesh dagger was in its stand sitting on his bookcase. The handle had been broken off. When I said something about it, he said that Bea had given it to him. I looked up and on the other bookcase was a ceramic St. Nick that I had made. I said, "John, that is my St. Nick figurine; please return it to me."

He said, "No, it's not yours, it's mine. I bought it. I love Christmas, Belinda, you know that."

I said, "John, it's impossible that you bought it because I made it."

"No, you didn't," he replied

I said, "Yes, I did; take it down please and you will see my name is engraved in the ceramic."

He pulled it down, looked at the bottom of the figurine, and said, "Your name is not on it."

"John, please let me look at it." He passed the figurine to me and the deputy sheriff was standing beside me when I turned it upside down and my name was engraved in the bisque with the year when I made it. The deputy sheriff looked at it and then looked at John.

John said, "Just take it."

I noticed he was wearing my grandfather's ring on his finger. I decided that was not even worth mentioning.

Each of the homes had been a complete disarray of filth. Most had smelled of animal urine, but this apartment smelled worse than the rest.

Deputy Patrick instructed me that if I wanted my mother to take a second look he would allow her to come in. I agreed. I had not gone through their closets, but my mother did and discovered one of our local university blankets that she had bought. Of course, they denied it.

After going through all the houses, Deputy Patrick asked, "Is this a family trait? Living in your own filth?"

I said, "No, this is the trash we are related to, and the Weirds are strangers to us. They are no relation."

Deputy Patrick said, "I'm so sorry, but I guess we all have some trash in our families."

We hit the road with the largest moving truck that you could rent. Sadly, it only had about four to five feet of recovered property in it and most of what we had retrieved was damaged or destroyed.

My mother rode in the passenger seat this time because we only needed one truck. As we turned onto the interstate to head back to Colorado, I thought, *What a waste of time and money.*

CHAPTER XLVIII

Because my relatives did not return all the property, I was going to have
To present new testimony and evidence. Jeff Harp, Hank's son produced a
sworn affidavit for the court to prove that May, Bea, and the other parties
involved had disobeyed the court's order. Our goal was to convince the
judge to hold them in contempt of court.

In my opinion, Jeff was only cooperating to seek vengeance against
my relatives for what they had done to his father, but at that point, I did
not care what his motivation was. I gladly took help from wherever I
could get it.

Mr. Simms e-mailed me a copy of what Jeff had prepared for my
approval, since he had not requested a hearing yet. If we did get a hearing,
I would not be present. It is still sad that Jeff and his wife gave excuses as
to why they could not physically be there to testify in person before we
even had a hearing date.

The sworn affidavit Mr. Simms sent to me read as follows:

> I, Jeff Harp, allege and declare as follows:
>
> If called as a witness, I could testify competently and
> with personal knowledge to the matters set forth herein.
>
> My father is Hank Harp ("my father") and my
> stepmother is May Harp ("my stepmother"), collectively
> "my parents."
>
> Prior to March of 2001, my parents' home and all of
> their belongings were destroyed by fire. On or about April of
> 2001, my parents moved into the house formerly occupied
> by Frank Gibbs, who had then passed away. Frank's house
> (known as the "Daisy house") was fully furnished with
> household items that belonged to Belinda Star and/or her
> mother Jane King.

On or about June 2005, I helped my parents move from the Daisy house to their new home at 666 Evil Road, Greenville, VA 66699. At that time, my father and I moved the property belonging to Belinda Star to the house at 666 Evil Road and to storage units located in Greenville. Prior to that time, my stepmother had gone through Ms. Star's property, which had been stored in boxes in the basement of the Daisy house, and we removed many items. During the time we were moving the property from the Daisy house to 666 Evil Road and into storage, my stepmother asked me to stop so that she could look again through the boxes to see if she wanted anything else. I then saw her remove several jewelry boxes containing jewelry, which were packed inside a box wrapped in clothes.

I was aware of the litigation on between Ms. Star, my parents, and my Aunt Bea for the last few years. After the recent trial in 2006, my stepmother told me that whatever items had been listed that Belinda Star could not find, she wouldn't be held responsible for. She also stated that even though she had the wedding ring listed on her own finger, the only way she would part with it was if Belinda Star herself pried it off her dead body. At that time, my stepmother also told me that she needed to return to the storage units so that she could remove anything that remained of value before Belinda Star was given access to the items.

I have had the opportunity to review a summary titled "Schedule A" of personal property belonging to Belinda Star. I am familiar with many of the titles on the summary list. I am aware that the summary represents thousands of items, most of which I'm very familiar with.

I understand that my stepmother testified at the trial that a large number of the items on the summary could not be found. A copy of the list showing what my stepmother testified could not be found is attached to this declaration as Exhibit "A."

Because I helped my parents move and have been in their residences (both the Daisy house and 666 Evil Road) numerous times, I have personal knowledge that the following numbered items from the attached list—which my stepmother represented as not found—have been in my parents possession since the time they first occupied the Daisy house after Frank's death.

Currently, my parents are divorcing, and it is my understanding that my father has been denied access the marital residence at 666 Evil Road. Recently, my father provided Belinda Star access to the storage units. Attached to this declaration as Exhibit "B" is a true and correct copy of a receipt signed by my father whereby he allowed Belinda Star to retrieve some of her property and acknowledged that the remainder of Ms. Star's property, which had been stored at the Daisy house, was either at the marital residence (666 Evil Road) or at Aunt Bea's house.

I declare under penalty of perjury that the foregoing is true and correct.

Mr. Simms filed the affidavit with the court and requested a hearing regarding this newfound evidence. Mr. Simms was granted a hearing regarding it. The judge considered it but nothing was done when we proved that they did not intend to return *all* the property. My heart was completely broken from this expensive long battle and I was realizing that our justice system was broken.

CHAPTER XLIX

The attorneys continued to battle for several months after my mother and I had returned to Colorado. Because I had only recovered a few family heirlooms and Thomas's jacket, the fight dragged on. Even though I had won the major battle, nothing was accomplished. I did not receive any of the valuable items that I was trying to get back. After a few months, during a conversation with Mr. Simms, we decided it was time to stop. My nasty relatives were playing evil games and refusing to return my valued possessions. Because they refused to return my possessions, I would now try to retrieve the monetary value of the stolen items.

We had finished reconstructing the receipts, appraisals, and even pictures of the items that were stolen and never returned. It was very apparent that the deputy sheriffs had not performed their jobs during the entire situation.

I hired an appraiser to help with the next step. It cost seven thousand dollars for the licensed appraiser to go through the thousands of pages of inventory and match them with some form of ownership and authenticity. As I reviewed my finances, depression covered me like a heavy, suffocating blanket. My accounts were almost depleted. My retirement savings had been spent, and the war had not yet been won.

Once the appraiser had finished and provided the results, Mr. Simms and I spoke via telephone to amend the dollar amount. We had to have everything ready prior to a hearing that I would not be attending.

At the hearing, the judge denied the amendment, even though we had everything needed to prove it. The judge said, "This is my final ruling on this matter. First of all, it took you too long to get the information ready, and secondly, it would be prejudicial to the defendants."

Mr. Simms called me as soon as the hearing was finished. "Belinda, I have bad news."

I gasped and asked, "What now?"

He replied, "This judge doesn't follow the law; he just shoots from the hip with no law to substantiate his ruling. That crooked judge violated your constitutional right to make an amendment. He turned us down again, Belinda, and the only thing I can do is file an appeal."

I answered, "What good would that do us? If you do that, he will just deny the internal appeal because it was his ruling. I have run out of money. I can't even afford the second part of the trial. Can we seek an evidentiary hearing and make them prove they own the things they refused to return? You know now we can prove all these items belong to me without a doubt."

Mr. Simms sighed and said, "I don't think that will work with this judge, but I still want to do some research regarding an internal appeal. That shouldn't cost that much."

I groaned, "Okay, but every time you say it will not cost 'that much,' it's always a fortune to me."

We set a date for the evidentiary hearing: January 10, 2008. When I told Thomas, he angrily replied, "What is the price for honor and duty, Belinda? Enough! Our justice system has failed us. We have put ourselves in harm's way for what, Belinda? For what? We are not the only family that doesn't have any morals or values any longer. We fought and spilled blood, sweat, and tears for this nation that should represent unity, freedom, and a higher plain of values, but instead we have a nation filled with greedy, selfish, spoiled families, just like yours, without any morals or values. How many of our friends died in our own arms give freedom to other lands and to protect our own way of life? Remember, Belinda, you have sacrificed our complete financial future over this. I have believed in this cause for too long; you have won the battles, but you have lost the war. You have done your duty at the expense of your financial future and mine. Let it go, Belinda! Just let it go! If nothing is accomplished from this hearing, you have lost the war to see that justice is served fully.

"Remember, as an American warrior yourself, you know that it takes money to have a military force. It costs money to fight and to win the war, but in our case, we do not have the funds to continue. Let's recoup our losses and save up again so we can take up this fight in the future, if our fate allows it. Then we will have money in our pockets, and we can again hold our heads up high. If that never happens, at least we know we fought valiantly here and now, as we always have. We stood up against evil and tyranny, but sometimes—or should I say, most of the time—the bad guys win no matter how hard we try to fight.

"Wake up, Belinda; our nation is not perfect as we both believed it to be in our youths. Our nation, along with our justice system, lost its way a long, long time ago. Our justice system is no longer about right and wrong. It has turned into a profit-making empire. It not only feeds off the villains, but it also feeds off the victims. We have lost freedoms, yet the people in this nation don't see that. We have lost the knowledge that peace and freedom is not a right—they have been fought for. Sometimes you have to fight so the next generation weeps for the blood that was spilled on their behalf. Our nation should be learning from its mistakes, not feeding off of them."

Tears filled my eyes as I reached over to my husband. She Wolf's eyes and fangs once again reflected in my face, and I held my head up high as I touched my husband's hands. I said in a sad, but strong tone, "We don't know the meaning of defeat because we've never surrendered to anyone or anything. Our bodies are covered with battle scars of the great warriors we once were, but you are right, my husband, every war is won at a high price. This will be my last battle in the courtroom. Win or lose—it's over for now, but I will not surrender, never. I will only retreat and regroup. If it takes me the rest of my life, and even if I never have the funds to finish this battle, I swear I will find another way to fight this tainted blood that has wronged me."

Thomas leaned over, hugged me, and kissed me on my lips. "That's fair enough."

The following day, November 11, 2007—Veteran's Day of all days—Thomas and I received a phone call from Sam Gibbs and his wife.

Sam's wife was the first one to speak. I was glad she introduced herself because I would have had no idea who she was. Then she said that Sam was listening on the other handset. Sam jumped in, "Hi, Belinda."

I responded to Sam's voice, "Hang on, Sam. I want Thomas and Mom to hear this conversation as well."

I covered the mouthpiece and yelled for Mom and Thomas to come. They quickly headed into the kitchen.

"Okay, they're here. Wait a second and I'll turn on our speakerphone."

Sam and his wife chattered nervously, updating us on their lives as if nothing had happened between us. The acted as if the lawsuit never took place, or as if everything had been resolved. I finally jumped in and asked, "Why are you calling? What do you want from us?"

Sam's wife answered, "Well, we figured that since everything was resolved between Sam's family and you guys, we wanted you to help us on a battle with Janet."

"What battle with Janet?"

Sam's wife answered, "Well, you know that Frank left half of the hollow to his four kids undivided, but Janet, being the widow of Jane's brother, owns the other half, and it is still undivided. Belinda, your mother's name is on the title as well. Janet will not pay to have it divided, and Sam has an Australian buyer who has offered us a lot of money for the entire hollow so he can develop it. We need Jane and the two of you to pay for the legal fight. Of course, once the land is bought, we will be able to reimburse you with interest."

I tried to control my anger. "First of all, Aunt Janet did not wrong us in any form that I'm aware of. Second, you guys did not return all of my family property. The fight between us is not over and never will be until you either return all the property or pay for it since apparently you have destroyed or sold most of it."

Sam angrily retorted, "Belinda, we didn't have anything to do with it. That was between Aunt Bea, Ed, and my sister, May. John, Samantha, and I had nothing to do with it!"

I was becoming increasingly more angry as I spoke. "Bullshit, Sam! My mother found a handmade puzzle box, made by her father-in-law whom you never met, in your house. What about the weapons in May's house that she claims her father gave to her? Bullshit, Sam—you know damn well that you took your father's collection when he was alive. You easily could have helped me get my property back. Now, you have the nerve to call us to do something for you to someone who has done nothing to us? I don't think so."

"Okay. Okay. You're right about Bea being a liar and I believe you. I'm sure Ed had a big part to play in this as well. I admit I lied in court, so forgive me and help me," Sam said.

Then Sam's wife started crying on the phone. "We have nothing for you to take. We are in debt and are about to lose everything. I wasn't even married to Sam when all this started. I have no clue who owns what! Keep taking us to court because we have nothing, no money, or anything for you to strip from us."

"Strip?" I asked incredulously, "How dare you! You and your husband along with the rest of these people stripped us, and you did nothing about it—nothing! Which to me makes you just as guilty by going along with them. If you do anything to harm even one hair on my aunt's head, I swear to God I will take what little bit of funds I have left and help her fight you to completely bankrupt you. You will never see one penny off my family's land. Do you understand?"

Sam yelled, "I swear to God, Belinda, if you do anything to mess up this deal I've got going, you will never—and I mean never—see the rest of your stuff again!"

I could not believe it. They were trying to blackmail Thomas and me to pay attorney fees to do something to my Aunt Janet. I couldn't believe they were trying to force her into selling her portion of the Gibbs homestead! We already knew May and Sam Gibbs had fraudulently probated Frank's estate, and from my understanding, the court would be dealing with them in that regard. Although I knew nothing was likely to be done about any of it.

Thomas lightly pushed me away from the speakerphone. He had been drinking whiskey, and Sam and Thomas started arguing very loudly. Thomas yelled at Sam, "You better return the rest of our stuff! If you hurt one hair on Ms. Janet's head, I will bury you down under the court steps. In other words, we would legally hurt you again with our justice system!"

Of course, Thomas was bluffing because we did not have the funds to continue the war, but we didn't call Thomas "Bear" for nothing in the Army. His grizzly bark, on many occasions, had She Wolf's hairs standing up on the back of my neck. I had backed down on several occasions, not just because he was right most of the time, but because the Bear was stronger and more powerful than the wolf. Of course, the wolf was smarter and more cunning. After all, the wolf hunted and fought mostly in packs.

Thomas stormed out of the kitchen and I was left on the phone with Sam's wife. She was crying even harder than before and tried to say that Thomas had threatened to kill her husband.

I said, "Come on, he did not say that, but I will tell you one thing—Aunt Janet has done us no wrong and we will protect her from you people at all costs."

Sam's wife asked, "What can I do to get your help?"

I answered in a softer tone, "Return our property."

Mom was so upset that she was also crying. She pushed me away from the phone so that she could speak to Sam's wife. She voiced her hurt about her own beloved family stealing from her and her children. She tried to explain to Sam and his wife that they burned their bridges, and Mom didn't think the family could mend from their deeds.

Sam yelled at my mother and stated, "Well, get a job, Jane."

I yelled, "Shut your stupid, drug-induced redneck, because my mother has a job! Why don't you return our things, get a job, and buy your own!"

My mother said, "Just shut up! Both of you! This has gotten us nowhere. I'm hanging the phone up now. If you decide to return the rest of our things, you have Belinda's number. If you decide not return the stuff, then we will see you in court again."

Mom pushed the button on the speakerphone to turn it off. She was crying and I could tell she had been deeply hurt. I hugged her. Thomas came back up the stairs, still angry, and the two of us hugged with my mother in the middle. It was the end of part of my family forever. The saga of She Wolf's legend was now gone for good. There was now only hatred, no unity.

Mom immediately called Aunt Janet. Aunt Janet said that Sam Gibbs had threatened her and her son Jim. Sam had told her that my mother and I were going to "take them down." Aunt Janet said she could not fight against all four of Uncle Frank's kids. She didn't know what to do, and she went to our law firm, but they could not help her because I was their client.

After we finished speaking with Aunt Janet, I called my attorney. He went ahead and advised me to advise Aunt Janet, so we could help her that way. I was instructed by Mr. Simms to report the fraud to the courthouse, which I promptly did. Of course, I already knew that our justice system wouldn't do anything. Mr. Simms also informed me that I could have recorded that conversation because they were planning to commit criminal activity. It was still okay because all three of us were on the telephone at the same time with Sam and his wife. I had thought it was illegal to record someone without their permission. According to my attorney, it was only valid when they were talking about committing a crime.

CHAPTER L

Now that I was almost out of funds, I was resigning myself to calling the war a stalemate. I decided that the time had come to fill my father, his wife, Christina, Theresa, and Joan in on the past several years. Since my stay at Uncle Frank's when Christina was unwilling to support me, I had not told her much of what was happening. The time had now come to share my sorrow with my family. I wrote a very long e-mail telling them what had happened and what I was expecting to happen. All I asked was that they took a few minutes of their time to read my story. I told them that I did not expect any response.

To my pleasant surprise, I received many emails in response saying that I had their support and sympathy. I was feeling good about my family until a few days later when I received another email from Christina.

She wrote that after thinking about the situation, she had concluded that she did not support me and never had. She said that she did not want me writing to her about it ever again. Once again, she was acting as if I were a monster. I guess I had made a grave mistake by trying to open my heart and share my feelings with her. Obviously, she considered Auntie Bea, May, Sam, John, Samantha, even Ed, and his family to be her family—not me. This seemed to be the norm for her. We were truly like oil and water, but I was still grateful that my other two baby sisters supported me and believed what I was doing was noble.

I respected Christina's wishes and did not mention it again. Then, one morning not much later, when I opened my email, there was a message from Christina. She had written that she thought we should talk.

As we communicated via e-mail, we argued and tried to explain our sides to one another. Little did I know, Christina was betraying me once again by forwarding my e-mails to others. Those emails were intended for her eyes only, and they were full of very personal emotions. She sent them to everyone in our family, my other two sisters, my father and his wife, and God knows who else.

I don't know how long this was going on before Teresa sent me a copy of one of the emails. She wanted me to know that our sister was betraying me. Teresa wanted me to know that I had her total support, as well as Joan's support. She did not know about the other people who had received the emails, but she wanted to make sure I knew I was not alone.

I mulled over the situation and discussed it with Thomas. I was so hurt that my sister had once again stabbed me in the back. I decided to play Christina's wicked little game. The next email she sent to me, I sent my response to the rest of the family. I wanted to make sure that they were hearing both sides of the story.

Did you ever stop to think that it was Bea and Frank who refused to return the property? Did you ever stop to think that Hank was in Tennessee when this all began? Did you ever stop to think that I had already won the case with Bea and Frank's estate, and that they—not Hank Harp—breached that contract? After all, a jury trial upheld it. Did you ever stop to think that maybe you could have been more involved and then you would have known that it was Bea and Frank—encouraged by Ed—who were the underlying force behind this mess? No? Then just maybe it is time for you to look at just where and how it all began. Please bear in mind, I am not blaming you for anything, but I do want you to think about things a little more carefully before making determinations.

I know perfectly well that Hank is not a hero, and he was not the one who returned the few things that he had. His attorney and his son and daughter-in-law convinced him to return what he had because he was already in enough legal trouble. I know perfectly well that he became part this conspiracy too, but you do not seem to know the entire story. Perhaps you have been lied to about a lot.

If you had the history that May and Hank had before they returned, after Frank died, don't you think that you would say anything to get out of it?

Hank does not wear our mother's clothing or the jewelry that belonged to our mother, grandmother, great-grandmother, great-great-grandmother, and Mom-mom. It is Bea, May, and the two girls who do that. Hank may have moved the furniture and other household items, and he may have helped sell some of the stuff, but it was Bea, May, and Frank's other children that reaped the benefits. Not one of them stepped forward and said, 'Come and get your stuff.' How do you explain Ed's involvement? Did Hank rule him too?

I don't believe Hank was involved in what happened to Ginger. The school reported this. Hank drove a truck. He was on the road more than he was home. May was the responsible parent. I do not know what went on in those households, but I have seen evidence that suggests that May was just as much to blame as Hank. Hank didn't take May's mother's money. It was Ginger and the other daughter who beat her up and took whatever they wanted from her. Hank was on the road and May was working the late shift at a local store. Think about it. You also lived with these people—how do you explain that they have made no effort to 'do the right thing'? How do you explain the refusal to return property that Bea, May, Sam, Samantha, John, and Ed displayed when I went to retrieve it? Remember May had already kicked Hank out and he was in jail—so why continue to do this?

Hank did not have the money to fight it and took the plea. He did not rape any of his children; he ran around in his underwear and kissed a booboo on the younger daughter's belly. Why? Because she was jumping on a trampoline when they were stealing Thomas' and my things and fell off and hurt her side so he kissed the booboo. This was witnessed by May's family, not mine. He was not charged for rape or anything of that nature; he was charged for two counts of aggravated sexual battery and one count of indecent liberties with child by custodian. That is what that means. To continue the story, May came up with that idea because his son was charged with the same thing regarding his wife's child, not May and Hank's children. Then the person who fondled the child was charged for the same crime eight years later and confessed, but Hank's son did not have the money to have the charges removed from his records. People every day are charged for crimes they did not commit. So before you start acting as if you know a truth based off a partial lie, put out a little effort and money and look up the details for yourself. Discover the truth for yourself instead of relying on others for information for a change. As far as I am concerned, Hank is a liar and a thief and he is where he belongs no matter what he was charged with.

So I believe that the true issue is the continued refusal to return the property that I have seen in their homes, not the abuse. Hank hasn't been an issue for a long time now.

Of course, our argument continued regarding everything that had happened over the past few years. The argument still raged up to when I was packing our SUV full of boxes that contained evidence, documents, and legal material. It was going to be a long drive since my mother and I would be driving cross-country this time instead of flying.

CHAPTER LI

I prepared to leave at 3:30 a.m. with my sleepy mother in tow. I gave my husband a kiss goodbye as he helped me load our SUV. As he squeezed the last suitcase into the back of our SUV, he said with a sad smile upon his face, "One way or the other, it is finished after this trip."

I simply nodded my head in agreement with him.

He then said, "Be safe, She Wolf, and remember you may have to leave her spirit there."

I responded once again with sadness, "I may retreat, but I will never leave She Wolf's spirit behind. She is a part of me, and she always has been."

He nodded in agreement and gave me a passionate kiss goodbye.

I drove all day and all night until we reached our destination, Snobville. About twenty-six hours after we left Colorado, I checked us into the same hotel where we had stayed on previous trips. My mother was exhausted because during the 1,500-mile trip, I had stopped only for brief bathroom breaks and to fill the gas tank. We arrived earlier than I had expected, so we had time to catch up on sleep and relax.

We met with Mr. Simms the following morning. For five hours, we went over the incredible amount of evidence. He appeared overwhelmed with all the documentation that I had gathered.

He said, "I can't believe this. We started out with no evidence and now we are flooded with it. Belinda, we have only two hours and I just want to use a few examples."

I asked, "What about the video tape and the still shots we had an expert make from it?"

He said, "We shouldn't need it, and we don't have time for it."

I was shocked! Out of the thousands of documents I had brought for evidence, Mr. Simms decided to use only twenty items. I agreed because I trusted my attorney, who I viewed as my paid warrior.

Mom and I decided to go around to the junk and antique stores to see if they had sold any more of our stuff. We discovered a new antique shop that had not been there the last time we were in Greenville.

As we looked around, I spotted two unique ivory hand-carved bracelets along with a jade and sterling silver bracelet that were unique and very rare to find. I gasped. My mother walked and looked inside the glass display cabinet and put her hand over her mouth and her eyes welled up with tears. She immediately asked the store associate, who was standing close by, if she could see the ivory bracelets. The price was $250. At first, we were going to buy them because we knew they belonged to my grandmother and her mother before her, but we decided to call Mr. Simms first to tell us how we should handle the situation. First, Mom decided to ask to speak to the manager of the store.

An older woman walked out of the office area and asked if she could help us. Then my mother asked the manager if she knew the history of the bracelets. The manager answered, "I know that they were made around 1880 or early 1900s. I know that they are hand carved and hard to come by, but my price is not negotiable if that is what you are seeking."

My mother answered, "Oh, I know they are worth much more than that since they belonged to my mother. Please tell us how you acquired them. They were stolen from me."

The woman became flustered and began to tell the story. "Well, a gentleman came in here; I guess it was 1999, the latter part of that year. I don't know if you know who the notorious Pete King is, but anyway, he said he was Pete King's attorney, and Mr. King had given him a lot of jewelry to sell to pay for his attorney fees."

"Was the attorney's name Ed Weird?" I asked.

The manager, who we discovered during this conversation was not only the manager but also the owner of the store as well, answered, "No."

Then my mother asked her, "Was he Rick Cart?"

The owner/manager answered, "Yes! That was the name."

My mother and I looked at each other in total shock. Then all of sudden, the owner of the store became angry and started yelling at us. "Get out of my store now! You are not getting anything for nothing. I know who you are now, Jane King! You both came in here pretending to be somebody else! Get out of my store now! I normally have sympathy for someone that has been robbed, but you, Jane King, I have no sympathy for you whatsoever! You're not getting anything for nothing from me."

Mom started to cry. "I was willing to pay for them right now. Please sell them back to me."

As the owner was taking the bracelets and putting them into the side pocket of her pants, she said, "No. I will not sell them back to you. I will take them home and hang onto them for myself."

I lost my temper once again and yelled at the storeowner, "Shame on you, you nasty little thief! You knew you had stolen property in here and God only knows how many more victims you have stolen from by fencing stolen property! You know damn well no attorney comes around hocking other people's property. Why else would it be displayed in your shop now, after all these years? You thought it was safe to sell it because time had passed by. As soon as I walk out this door, I'm calling the cops on you!"

She yelled back at me, "Get out of my shop, now!"

We walked out and called Mr. Simms. He instructed us to call the police immediately and he was on his way after we gave him directions.

I told Mom to stay in the car. I walked right back into the store and said to the owner, "My attorney is on the way along with the police. I have been instructed to inform you that you are in possession of stolen property."

I didn't even give the woman a chance to respond. I simply walked back out the shop's door and got into my SUV. She stood inside the glass doors of her shop looking at us as we watched her and waited.

Within 15 minutes, both the county sheriff and Mr. Simms pulled up beside us. Mom and I got out of my SUV and met both men at the front of her glass doors as she watched us from inside. We pointed at the cement furniture that she had around her shop with our receipts and pictures of it around my mother's old house. We pulled out pictures and appraisals of all the jewelry that we located in her store. There was no doubt whatsoever she had more things that we were trying to recover. There was no doubt this was not just coincidence. We told both men the story she had told.

Mr. Simms and the sheriff walked into the store, and she moved away from the doors as they walked in. I saw the fear in her eyes and I just glared at her as they talked to her.

She made the mistake of telling us too much before she realized that my mother was the wife of the crook.

Of course, the sheriff didn't retrieve the stolen property. Instead, we were given the same old song and dance that she was going to provide an inventory of what she bought from Rick Cart, but she also said that both of you had a booth at her old location. I simply retorted, "We are not claiming what we sold, just the things she stole. There is nothing in her shop of what I sold or what my mother sold; just the things that were stolen."

Then the sheriff stated, "I don't even know for sure if this would be in our county since she just moved here from Snobville."

Mr. Simms became angry and said to the sheriff, "It's quite obvious this is my client's property that has been stolen. She was awarded all of this and here it is in this shop."

Of course, they talked longer and debated.

I was very exasperated at the entire ordeal. Of course, nothing was done; we never recovered the property that was in her possession. What a messed-up judicial system our country has.

CHAPTER LII

The ringing phone woke me up. It was the wake-up call that I had requested. My mother and I got up and prepared for another day in court. We were both exasperated from the lack of protection from the law over the past few years. The previous day was just another prime example of how, with the blessing of our justice system, the crooks get away with everything and seem to have more rights than the victims have.

Before I left home, Thomas said that our nation had lost its morals and values because the justice system protected the crooks instead of the victims. It appeared to me that society as a whole had lost all common sense regarding right and wrong. The whole system had turned upside down. What used to be wrong was now right, and what used to be right—like belief and trust in God—was now wrong. I felt like vomiting as I was dressing for court.

Deep in my heart, I knew I would lose this last battle for justice because this time I would not have my peers, "the people," to protect me. I had no jury, just a judge, who had proven himself unfit. All I could do was give one last good valiant fight, as I know She Wolf would have done if she were in my shoes.

Once again, we hid my mother in the SUV, which I parked behind the courthouse. I wore the same business suit that I had worn since my first day in this court battle. Before I knew it, Mr. Simms and I were standing as the judge entered the courtroom.

I looked around the courtroom. The only people who showed up were Ed, his older daughter, his younger daughter's husband, John and his wife, and his wife's parents—that was it. Sam, May, Samantha, and even Auntie Bea were not there. *How strange*, I thought. I wondered what they were up to this time.

Before court started, I heard John's father-in-law speaking to a county prosecutor. "I need to talk to you about this woman, Mrs. Star; she keeps suing us repeatedly. Is there any way I can have criminal charges brought against her?"

The prosecutor looked at Mr. Simms and me, because we were looking directly at him, and the prosecutor said to him, "If you're not careful, sir, you could be facing criminal charges yourself. My advice to you is to work it out with Mrs. Star." Then the prosecutor walked away from the elderly man.

I took a small measure of comfort from those words. Apparently, I had most of the legal community on my side after the years I had spent fighting this, but it was apparent that the judge who controlled my case would never admit that he could be wrong. He was still doing everything in his power to prevent me from prevailing triumphantly.

The judge immediately excused everyone because they were all on the witness roster, with the exception of Ed's son-in-law. For some reason, his name was not mentioned. The thought floated through my mind that Ed had brought him along so he would have eyes and ears in the courtroom. I really wished that I had eyes in the back of my head so I could have seen if he was taking notes.

The judge looked over the courtroom, looked at the papers in front of him, and said, "Why are the rest of these people on this lawsuit? It appears to me that the court did not have authority to issue these writs to them."

Mr. Simms answered the judge, "Your Honor, May Harp, Samantha Gibbs, John Gibbs, and Sam Gibbs are the estate of Frank Gibbs. The two co-executors fraudulently probated Frank's estate, and the evidence presented today will show the court that they divided the stolen property amongst themselves. As for Ed and his children, it will be proven that they stole much of the property as well, along with John Gibbs' in-laws."

The judge said, "Well, I will listen since I've given the plaintiff a chance and then I will make my ruling on this matter."

Mr. Simms simply answered, "Yes, Your Honor."

I was the first witness. We tried to review the evidence in order to prove the property was mine, where it was located, and who had it in their possession. The judge kept throwing it out repeatedly.

Mr. Simms finally gave up, and Mr. Pricket had his turn. Once again, instead of fighting the current case, he brought up the crimes that my mother and her husband had committed. Once again, I had to repeatedly state, "They have nothing to do with my family members and these strangers stealing from me."

Mr. Pricket called his first witness, Ed Weird, to the stand. During the cross examination, Mr. Simms asked him if he sold any of the property in question or had taken any of it. Ed gave an evil laugh and kept repeating, "I didn't sell it, and I didn't take it." He laughed each time he said it. Mr. Pricket went through the rest of the witnesses, who predictably all denied any connection with my missing property.

The judge ordered a recess so he could make a decision. The judge didn't even give us the two hours he promised. The judge had us recess so he could deliberate, and only five minutes later, we were called back into the courtroom. I believe he only did that for appearance and for him to go to the bathroom.

The judge had reached his decision. He ruled, "First, the writs that were issued to all of these other people are dismissed because they were not part of the original lawsuit. The Court did not have authority to issue these writs in the first place. My advice to the plaintiff is to seek remedies elsewhere regarding these other parties. The second issue is I believe the deputy sheriffs, the plaintiff, and the defendants did everything in their power to uphold the writ. The third and final issue is the evidence brought forth by Mr. Weird. It is believed by this court—and there is no evidence on the contrary—that the writ was upheld and all the property that was awarded to the plaintiff was returned . . . ." As he kept running his stupid mouth, I gasped. He looked up at me and then said, "My rulings are founded from the evidence presented and the plaintiff could not corroborate . . . ."

I cut the nasty prick down and said in a loud voice, "Then let us play the videotape, Your Honor . . ."

Mr. Simms grabbed my arm and gave me a stern look. That nasty little maggot of a judge could not even look me in the eye when he was calling me a liar. Then, that creep of a judge said, "I'm sorry, Mrs. Star, but that's my ruling. If your attorney had presented better evidence regarding this matter . . . I'm not calling you a liar in any form."

I said loudly, "Then what do you call this after you allow my violators to get away with highway robbery and not hold them accountable?"

The judge became very angry, but he still could not look me in the eye said, "Young lady, if you cannot contain your tongue, I will hold you in contempt. Do you understand?"

Since he widely swung open the door, I answered him by saying, "No, I do not understand. What are you doing now, Your Honor, but another violation of my constitutional right called, freedom of speech?"

By then I did not realize it, but we had a large audience in the courtroom and people started talking loudly and angrily. The judge slammed his gavel down several times and yelled to the courtroom, "Order in the court! Order in the court!" Then he looked directly at me with his beady little black eyes and said, "Mrs. Star, my advice to you is to stop while you're ahead. Mr. Simms, I advise you to control your client."

Mr. Simms immediately grabbed my forearm with a stern grip, bent down, and whispered in my ear, "Belinda, he holds the power. We have none. Just be quiet!"

I glared at the judge as if he were a nasty little fly that needed to be swatted down. I wanted to take that black robe of his and hang him from the ceiling with it, but I minded my tongue as he continued with his nonsense ruling. It was over! I had lost the war!

During the ruling, Mom had moved the SUV to the front of the courthouse. She got out of the SUV to meet Mr. Simms and me. Mr. Simms told the sad tale and how very close I came to being thrown in jail for my sharp tongue. As we were huddled in the parking lot, Ed drove by with his window down.

I looked at him and yelled, "You better sleep with one eye open!"

That stupid piece of shit actually stopped his car, backed up, and said, with a smirk on his face, "What? I didn't hear you."

"Fuck off, maggot, and you better sleep with one eye open from now on. Get out of my sight."

I started walking toward the driver's side of his car. The coward put up his window and sped away. I just laughed. I turned my attention back to Mr. Simms and my mother.

Mr. Simms was angry. "You know he can press charges against you for that?"

I said, "That figures, since freedom of speech is out the door in our country, and our justice system is filled with spineless jerk-offs."

My mother yelled at me, "Belinda!"

Mr. Simms said with a sigh, "I'm sorry, Belinda. I warned you this could be the outcome."

I simply said, "Whatever. Thank you for your time."

Mom and I returned to the hotel, checked out, and hit the road back to Colorado. Neither of us had an appetite. It was a quiet ride for the first several hours. We were both deep in our thoughts and too angry to speak.

Not many families had such a rich history of personal property in their possession, but then not many daughters had thieves as mothers and relatives—or do they? This outcome hurt to no end. It's about an object that triggers memories and the stories that are passed down from generation to generation. I don't know . . . .

The one and only great possession that belonged to my three sisters and me was the shield, the sword, the armor that our ancestor "She Wolf," a Spartan princess warrior, had worn during battles a long, long time ago. Had the legacy and legend of "She Wolf" died because I so foolishly trusted my relatives? Had I lost her armor because of their greed? She fought for and battled for "her God, country, and family."

In the months that followed my final battle in court, our country would be hit by high gas prices, remain at war overseas, and the economy would become bankrupted. How coincidental that my country as a nation had been hit as hard as I had been. On the television and in the newspapers, I heard the majority of my fellow Americans yelling for the government to *give everything* to them. They wanted the government to take away from those that had more and give to those that wanted the American dream handed to them. We were at the end of our democracy, our republic, and my fellow countrymen had lost their way completely. They had lost the true meaning of democracy. The land of the free was fading into the sands of history as so many other great societies had before us.

I did not know what the future would bring. Would my great nation continue down this path of destruction by taking more of our freedoms that our forefathers bled and died for? Or would we, as a nation, find our higher morals and values once again? Would we once again work together as a nation/family? Our nation was comprised of family units and if our family units were broken down and destroyed by greed, then what would happen to our nation? I thought, *United we stand; divided we fall.*

I used to trust my family, and I used to believe they loved me, until I experienced deceit and betrayal by those closest to me. I tried to help my loved ones, and as I was doing so, they stabbed me in the back. This was the saga of my life. I used to think that family was there to support you and provide a safety net, but fate had a way of revealing the cold, twisted truth.

My nation had forsaken me because I now knew the truth of our society and what we had become; my grandparents' and great-grandparents' fears had revealed themselves to me. All I knew was this fight for justice was not over. I had no other choice but to retreat, but it was not over, not yet.

My mind drifted back to a train ride from a long, long time ago. It almost seemed like a different dream—the beginning of my deadly journey called life. That had been the last time I truly thought of the legend and legacy of the spirit of She Wolf that courses through my veins.

AUTHOR'S NOTES

This story is a work of fiction. Much of the information contained herein is created from the author's imagination, such as the ghost agency, the recording of a soldier, and other aspects. The author is fully aware that factual inaccuracies exist in this text, but it is meant to be a work of fiction.

Any theories and/or opinions are solely the author's and are just that, nothing more.

By writing this story, the author intends to entertain the reader and give food for thought.

ABOUT THE AUTHOR

Linda D. Coker was born and raised in the surrounding valley of the Appalachian Mountains of Virginia and currently resides in the beautiful state of Colorado.

She is an honorably discharged veteran of the United States Army and has a degree in business management.

Linda was one of the first women recruited after the Women's Army Corps (WAC) was disassembled and integrated into the Army. After Linda married another soldier, it became harder for the two of them to stay stationed together; she gave up her military career so she could be by his side. She still played an active role throughout her husband's military career by volunteering her time to support the spouses and family members of her husband's fellow soldiers during many hardship deployments.

Linda was blessed during her travels with her husband, and she had the opportunity to work with many major contractors that support the troops. With these opportunities, she was still able to be part of the Army in the background and support her husband and his units in some capacity.

After her husband retired, Linda nearly died from the stress of her job; she took a three-year break from daily working and started writing stories. She considers herself to be a pretty good storyteller.